Dead Broke Hearts— Copyright © 2016 by Shay Lawless

ISBN-10: 1-940087-17-1
ISBN-13: 978-1-940087-17-7

I0566291

21 Crows Dusk to Dawn
Publishing, 21 Crows, LLC

Cover Images:

Andrey Kiselev
Nejron
Flas100—Algirdas Urbonavicius
Geraktv -TETYANA KULIKOVA

SHAY LAWLESS

Chapter 1

Standing in my t-shirt and panties in the parking lot of the Bel-Air All-Nighter Motel and Diner watching him ride away

He left at a quarter past four in the morning. I didn't hear him slip off the old bed with grinding box springs. I didn't wake up when he walked across the shabby brown carpet in his stocking feet with his boots in one hand and a guitar slung over his shoulder. When he quietly pulled the door shut to the room, I must have been deep in sleep.

It was the sound of his Harley starting up five feet from the paint-peeling red door of the Bel-Air All-Nighter Motel and Diner forcing me to open my eyes.

"Chase?" I blink twice, rub a bit of crusty sleep from my eyes. They are sky blue, my eyes. Chase always tells me they are as big as fists and bluer than blue. I turn slightly, to the side of the bed where he had been sleeping. My hand pats on nothing but cool, crumpled sheets. "What the hell?" I whisper, bewildered. Where's he going? Hell, I don't even know what state we're in. He always guns the engine twice and hard. My eyes open up when the sound bangs off the outside brick walls of the shabby, off-the-highway two-story motel with paint-peeling railings and an in ground pool that's as green and slimy as a Florida pond in August.

I catch a little bit of light dripping out of the two inch span between bathroom door and banged-up frame. I see the raggedy olive green shower curtain with rips along the seams and I catch the shadow of my backpack slouching next to the doorframe.

I push myself up with bent elbow. It isn't fast. It's

kind of a roll to the side and a fling of my legs over the edge. I'm nine months into a belly full of baby. When I push myself to my feet and waggle walk to the door like a fat turkey two days past due for Thanksgiving slaughter, I make it to the smudged window, push the curtains away. I lean on the sill dappled with dried-out flies, my bony arms like tiny twigs compared to the fat ball between my legs and my usually-tiny size 32A boobs that are now topping out in the least as a mega 34C.

"Chase!" He's straddling the bike, doesn't even look back. I release the curtain, rush to the door, and grapple for the grimy knob. When I swing it open, the grind of his tires deafens my ears while he peels out between the two faded white parking spot lines. His head turns slightly, then straightens toward the horizon.

I rush outside, oblivious to the sprinkles of rain tapping my cheeks. I'm standing on the broken concrete sidewalk in the oozy almost-morning darkness in an oversized big men's t-shirt and my underpants. I'm sure it's not a pretty sight for those who opened their doors to me screaming out his name and dancing barefoot and way-too-pregnant across the damp, gritty pebbles of the asphalt parking lot like I could tackle him and drag him back.

I stop there, toss my hands to my head and look up to the sky. The scent of bacon slips into my nostrils and threatens my desire to think irrationally. I'd rather chase him farther down the old highway. However, I think I'm so hungry I'd chew the rims off the first of three of the long line of truck tires lined up in front of the diner.

"Shit," I curse, turn around in a circle while the sound of the engine fades away into the night.

"Ma'am, I think he's gone."

I swing my head around. All's I can see is a handful of shadows shifting from truck to diner. Cowboys? They are wearing frigging cowboy hats. Who the hell wears cowboy hats anymore?

"Go to hell. He'll be back." Right? He left to go get gas or something? I'm usually not this grumpy. I backtrack, wish I could take my mean words back. But my back hurts, my feet ache and Chase had this strange, wild look to his eyes while he was watching TV tonight. Then I stop. "Where—are we?"

"Bel-Air."

"Bel-Air. Bel-Air—where?" I chew on the name, shake my head. Never heard of it. There's a soft and sweet southern twang melting in the air even if the voice is deep. "Like—California? Oklahoma?"

"Tennessee."

"Holy hell, I'm in Tennessee?"

The waitress who is serving me at the Bel-Air All-Nighter Diner seems to think Chase isn't coming back. She catches me holding the little Polaroid picture of my brown-eyed, brown-haired mama in my hand.

"Who's that, sweetie?"

"My mama," I answer quickly, stuffing the picture back into my backpack. I'd watched her look from me to the picture and back again. "I know she doesn't look like me. You don't have to point it out. Everybody always says it right off the bat," I tell her softly. "I'm skinny, blonde and have blue eyes. She's chubby, dark hair, and brown eyes." I know it's a nervous thing, bringing out that picture and staring at it like I can get real-life advice from a printed version of the real thing. I haven't seen her in way over twenty years. Still, she's the only mama I really know. I wonder where she is right now, dead or alive or maybe thinking of me while she's sipping strawberry daiquiris on a white beach in Fort Walton Beach, Florida.

"No, I don't know. You just got pretty heart-shaped lips like the girls that sell lipstick on the commercials. She don't. That's all I see. You want to use my phone to call her?" The waitress's name's not Esther Price as the name tag on her drab red-brown uniform implies. She looks about fourteen, although I'd guess she's closer to twenty-two or three. She's chubby and has dimples on her cheeks, pretty brown eyes and a mop of red hair she's got in a messy bun on top of her head. And she's bedecked in the tail-end of a black eye still yellow and green under a thick coat of foundation.

"I don't know where she is."

She keeps staring at my fingers that can't stop drumming out a beat on the counter. I tell her it's a nervous thing. I suppose it is for the most part. I always feel like I've got a thousand songs playing out in my head. It is especially applicable when I'm nervous, scared, or I'm on an emotional high or low. I don't have to hint at where I stand on that ladder right now while I look down at the only thing I own, my backpack, near my old brown boots stuck on my feet.

"Are you okay, honey?" she asks me when I don't answer. "You're not hyperactive, are you? Or high on meth? That's not good for the baby. They come out goofy when you do drugs like that."

"No."

"Oh, good. You know, you're so tiny." She has actually told me that three times. "Did I tell you that's not my real name," she tells me poking at the name tag while she leans over and slaps a glass of milk in front of me. Yes, she had mentioned it twice. "If I put my real name on here, I get creeps looking me up online and following me home. The creeps aren't from here. They're from out of town. We ain't had any murders here in Bel-Air. None. Nada."

"We wouldn't want that, would we?" I ask her and she looks at me a bit warily so I point to the milk. I'm a smartass today. "I didn't order milk."

"That's okay, honey, it's on the house. You're not a serial killer or anything, are you?" She taps my back with the nubby end of her pencil and winks. I'm sitting at the front counter on a red, ripped faux leather bar stool listening to my belly growl and letting my boots bang against the counter wall. I know she's working her eyes down my clothes and stopping at my old, brown boots. They are three sizes too big and one has a red bandana tied around the ankle. But the boots and the bandana were my daddy's and I wear them when I'm upset.

"No."

I'm hungry and haven't eaten but a bag of barbecue potato chips in the last twenty-four hours. "Okay, then I'm Gin," she goes on. "It's short for Ginger like the spice and not the kind of gin you drink to get drunk on at the Crazy Filly in town. Well, you don't drink. You're how many months in? I'd say ten. Ha ha. You're really skinny for somebody who's pregnant. Like a stick. You look like a stick with a watermelon on it. I heard you got dumped out in the parking lot. Too bad for you."

I don't ask why she's divulging this information to me, how she knows I got dumped, or even why she keeps coming by to make small talk. I feel enough out of place here. Everybody's all baseball caps and cowboy hats, blue jeans and old t-shirts. Me, I'm wearing a black tank-top, cut off sweatpants and old, brown boots. I got a colored tattoo on my right arm and seven piercings on my face alone—one on my eyebrow, one on my lip, one on my nose and the rest on my ears.

The restaurant isn't that big. It looks like any

highway restaurant with tables and booths and a counter with bar stools for folks who are dining alone or in a hurry. It has windows all around it and the kind of curtains that don't close so I'm sure me running out in my t-shirt and black granny panties across the parking lot while Chase's motorcycle sped off is now engraved in all the minds of the crowd inside. I nod. I've got a handful of one dollar bills and my backpack. She plops a plate down in front of me.

"I just ordered toast," I tell her, poking my finger at the three pancakes settled there. "I don't have that much cash." I feel like I'm going to cry. There's also two eggs, four slices of bacon and grits. Grits. I love grits. And there's even a little side of shredded cheese to dribble on them. Of course, I'm so hungry, I'd thought about dumping the sugar shaker into my backpack for lunch later.

"Baby girl, we get lots of people come through here," she tells me in almost a whisper while she leans into me. "We get the sweetest good ol' boys with hope in their duffel bags going to Nashville to make it big. We get little girls coming home from New York with their hearts in their suitcases because life ain't what they thought it was outside their daddy's white picket fences. I've seen some sad things come through here at all hours of the day and night. But watching him take off like that and you standing there screaming his name, it broke my little heart."

"Kind of like a sad movie?" I sigh a bit sarcastically.

"I just don't understand why you're not bawling your eyes out. Is that a northern thing?" she asks.

"A northern thing?"

"Well, you ain't from around here."

I'm thinking she means because I'm not crying. Then she waggles a hand in front of me. "This. All of it." Oh, I guess she means my left ear that's pierced from top to bottom. Or maybe the piercing above my eyebrow? I've got my white-blonde hair braided tight to my head and the rest stuffed into two tight little balls on top. There's a couple swatches that are cotton candy pink. My cherry red lipstick? No—she points to my right arm and just below the top of my tank top. I've got a tattoo from wrist to nearly my shoulder, it's green and pink with blue spirals and twists and ends in a unicorn right before my bony shoulder blade. "We don't do that here. You eat now before it gets cold."

So I eat with everybody staring at me and leaning in for a whisper. I suppose I'll be the talk of Bel-Air for at least the next two weeks. I've got nothing better to do than either sit here all day or start walking to somewhere—maybe, I figured, I'd head to Nashville where Chase was planning on stopping for a bit. I'm just about finished and sipping on a glass of water when a barrel-chested man comes strolling into the restaurant. I see him look to the left and then to the right. Just a few seconds later, a flannel-shirted man sitting at a booth points a finger my way.

"Oh, shit," I whisper. My tummy jerks right, then left. He looks small town and cocky like an over-zealous cop ready to drive a homeless man twenty miles south of town and far enough away to make him good and gone. He's big and wearing a suit and tie. He's got that funky politician look—too thick colored-blonde hair, big jowls, and beady eyes. He comes over, settles himself down next to me and folds his beefy arms across his chest.

"Bo Littleton's my name." He extends a hand. I hesitate, shake it warily. "Back in the day, we used to just get a Bel-Air police cruiser and take tramps away that came in along the railway. We'd drop them off outside town. Gone," he tells me. "Now our attorneys tell us that's stuff for a lawsuit. So here's the thing. They say you been hanging out here most of the morning. I've got a good idea that something's going on. It's a small town, but we ain't fools. If you're thinking about pulling some scam on us, we're going to figure it out. Now, girl, tell me the truth and I'll let you leave. Is that you and your boy who's been stealing horses around here and outside Nashville?"

"No, sir."

"Well, it's time to move on. Or I will take you down to the jail and we'll process you as a horse thief. We got good, upstanding people here." He looks down at the tattoos on my arm. "Get and go. I'm not opposed to arresting you for loitering if I need to. The next town's Denton. It's just up the road."

"Okay," I say. He stands up and towers over me. I get the hint, stand up too and leave. On my way out, though, I stop in at the front desk of the motel and stare an old lady behind the counter. She's bent and craning her neck up at me. I think she's only four feet tall.

"What you want?"

"I think my boyfriend pawned off my guitar to pay for our room last night," I have to stand on my tippy-toes to rest my elbows on the counter and peer down at her. I can't get too close because my belly stops me. She's got peach lipstick on and a thick sweater. It's early spring, but it isn't that cool out.

"That man you checked in with paid cash here. Might have pawned it off in town."

"Where in town?" I ask. "It's my life, all I got. My mama gave it to me." She doesn't seem to care.

"Is she dead?"

"Huh?" I ask.

"Your mama. Is she dead?"

"Oh, no. I mean, I guess I'm kind of dead to her—"

"Well, you shouldn't have been hanging around with

the likes of that man," she tells me. "I bet two to one that's what your mama would say. Why don't you give her a call, see if she can come get you?"

"I don't know where she is."

She tells me the town of Denton is just a few miles south. I get the awful feeling she's trying to nicely shoo me away so she doesn't get stuck with the homeless woman begging for a room tonight. What can I do? I snatch up my backpack and slip out the door and head toward town.

It's eight at night when the storm hits. I saw the dark clouds stalking me long before I felt the first aching pang just below my belly button. I shake off the pain as just too much walking. I'd gone up one road, then another and never saw the town. The hills aren't huge like mountains here. But they are big enough to suck the wind from my lungs going up one, then down the valley to the next. Now I'm down to an old asphalt and gravel road and I'm keeling over realizing I'm going to have this baby all by myself in the middle of a dark patch of backwoods Tennessee unless I crossed a state line somewhere. I can't see any houses and no cars have passed me in two hours. While I blink past the sprinkles of rain that are fast turning to a downpour, the only twinkling light I can see on a distant hillside looks far, far away. I want to turn around. I figure, I'm not going to make it back to town.

I suppose, in retrospect, there had been ten or twelve roads I passed and could have turned down. Each would have led me to a different fate. Miller Hollow. Fox-Dinsdale Road. Possum Hollow South. But Bel-Air Hollow was the destiny I chose. I followed the lights, managed to crawl across two worn wooden fences and one with barbed wire. It was too late when I realized what a hollow implies—it ends. Because the last little set of hills form a cup, somewhat, at the bottom of one larger hill. And it stops.

The light, it was nothing more than a barn, a stupid barn enveloped by hills coming together. But when I go up to the open door, there's two men inside. It is a long line of wooden stalls up one side and down the other. One of the men is wearing a ball cap and he looks a bit scraggly with a bit of brown-red beard and navy blue pants and shirt. He looks in his thirties. He has a horse tied up to a post and he's wheedling something out of the horse's hoof. The other is older, kind of keels to the left as he walks when he sees my shadow creep into the light of the barn. Lightning flashes behind me. A crack of thunder blasts through the wide valley that the old barn is tucked within. It slams hard into the raggedy hills beyond and disappears into the deep valley between. I see him squint against the sudden light, then tip his head to the side when I step in.

"I think I'm going to have my baby." It's all I can say before a sharp and deep pain rips through my insides. It hurts so badly, I fall to my knees. "I don't know what to do."

It's like the baby in my belly realizes that I'm somewhere out of the rain even if it is with two strangers in a dark and dusty barn reeking of horse pee and old leather saddles. It's time to come even if it is on a dirt-ridden, worn wooden floor with dust sifting through the air. I feel the rain pelting my back, feel the wind blowing my hair toward my face while I lean on my hands and grunt against the agony. The two men just stare at me for two blinks. "Please help me," I grunt.

I see the older man turn to the other. He's gray hair and blue eyes, lots of wrinkles and an old jacket. He reminds me of an old sea captain fresh from a journey and angry at life. "Holy crap, Jack, go up to the big house. Get a squad out here. And Boone, give a holler for Boone!"

I think I remember every second of having the baby straight down to the number of times the thunder cracked holy hell above our heads. Thirty-two times. I know the old man's name is Dutch Cates. He made a bed for me out of hay bales tucked in the corner and dusty, woolen saddle blankets. Then he held my hand while the horses in the stalls ate hay and whinnied once in a while. He told me I was going to be alright and then went into great detail a story about a baseball game he went to in Cincinnati last year and how two of his horses had girth sores right now.

"Baby girl," he whispers to me softly, pushing past his churlish tone. "You've got to hold off until Boone gets here, alright? He's done this before. You understand?"

I try to do the little breaths I read about online and I nod while he tugs a raggedy red bandana from a hook on the wall and swipes it across my forehead. I tell him okay and he tells me the same thing about Boone coming for what seems like an eternity and each time, I promise him I'll wait. Because Boone, whoever he is, must be a doctor because Dutch says he knows everything there is about birthing a baby.

About halfway through his account of the second inning of the ball game and right at a big blast of wind, I can hear the screeching sound of a truck pulling in outside the barn, then the slam of a truck door.

"Where is she?" I hear the voice. Jack waves a hand toward me.

"Well, that's no horse, Dutch."

I can see the man. He's wearing a cowboy hat and boots and stops just short of me. He looks all cowboy-dressed-to-go-out to some small, hick town dance. I can smell aftershave. He's got on a nice t-shirt and new blue jeans. He's squinting and shaking his head. "Jack called.

Said one of the mares was—"

"No, it's that girl from the diner. She must have followed us home."

"I didn't follow you home. You're Boone?" I interrupt the conversation and look back and forth between Dutch and the man standing there. I push up on my elbow and I feel this urge to push. It's dark in the barn except for the yellow bulb lights above the stalls. "I got lost looking for my guitar. And that Bo dude told me I had to leave or he'd put me in jail." I know it's time even if these dumbasses don't and want to have a conversation about horses.

"Yeah, that's me. I'm Boone."

"You've done this before?"

"Yeah, a hundred times. It—" he pauses, scratches his head and looks over at Dutch. I can see a flash of baby blue eyes beneath the hat. There's a finger-long scar from the corner of his right eye down to his cheek. I notice it. I don't care. I just want to have this baby. "Never you mind, the squad will be here before I've got to do anything—"

"Okay, good, because I can't stop now."

I suppose Dutch had no clue the baby's head was crowning. Boone, he leans over and I about die right then because I'm figuring he is an old guy or something, and at least a doctor. He's young, buff and pretty, really twenty-something young. He's got what my dad used to call *lazy hardscrabble* on his cheeks, that rough dark beard stubble guys get when they don't shave first thing in the morning. But his is expensive salon rugged, not lumberjack. He's doing this patting thing on his legs with his hands like I've seen drummers do when they've got a beat in their head. I get it. I've been known to strum a song or two that's playing in my head. It soothes me a bit.

Then he gets this sudden blank look to his face like

he realizes I'm really having this baby right now on the old blankets and the hay and beneath a bunch of old yellow bug light bulbs barely lighting up the barn. He reaches up, takes off his hat and stops halfway with it at his chest like he's getting ready to sing the *Star Spangled Banner*. But I'm just seeing his blue eyes. His eyes are this weird color of white-blue and they are like two big marbles against his black hair.

"Oh, shit, you're serious?" he says and I must have looked scared because he swipes away the alarm on his face and gives me a big smile. "I'm just kidding. You're going to be fine. What's your name?"

"Skeeter. Everybody calls me Skeeter."

"Hey, Skeeter, what did the pirate say on his eightieth birthday?" I'm grunting and shaking my head. "No, look at me, little girl. Tell me what you think he said."

"I don't know. It hurts."

"He say aye, matey, get it? Like I'm eighty."

I didn't get it. But Boone, he smiles at me. "You're going to be alright, okay. I'm better at birthing babies than making jokes."

"Well, that's good," I say. And I felt safe and alright looking at those blue eyes. Safe and not-alone and alright. "That's good."

CHAPTER 2

FEELING LIKE A STRAY CAT LEFT ON SOME OLD, CREEPY DUDE'S DOORSTEP

My daughter came into this world kicking, screaming and twenty-eight minutes before the Bel-Air South Fire Department truck barreled down the old muddy lane leading to Dutch Cates's farm. She was bundled in an old orange towel and shoved into my chest when, eleven minutes later, two police cars and two more fire trucks from surrounding counties came tearing down the road.

It seems there was a bit of a miscommunication. Cell phone service reception isn't great on this side of the rolling hills. The dispatch misunderstood the farmhand's broken words—*There's a girl having a baby in the horse barn and Boone's trying to get it out* as: *There's a fire in the barn and Boone's putting it out.* Such, she requested backup for a barn burning down.

I was shuffled off to the Bel-Air Community Hospital when the ambulance arrived forty minutes later. Johnny Crabtree, who drives the ambulance, forgot he was on call tonight. He was two counties over playing poker with his buddies. When I finally got to the hospital, I laid there the rest of the night in the darkness and most of the way into the day while they tried to figure out what to do with us.

"You got nobody to call—Skeeter—Schwartz? Is that your real name? That's what you put on the billing stuff." It seems preposterous to Janie, my nurse, that nobody wants us. "They said you didn't have any IDs." But she is cute with bleach-blonde hair and big brown eyes. I'm sure in this town, she is the hot pick of the decade. She keeps talking about me at her desk with the other nurses like I can't hear her. *Poor thing ain't got nobody and no flowers, you see that? She ain't said a word since she got here. A broke heart, that's what it is. She acts like she don't want that baby, hasn't even asked to see it. You know she's the one that got dumped at the motel off the highway, right—? My uncle was there. He said she was standing in the parking lot in her underpants just sobbing—*

She is wrong about the sobbing. It was more a frustrated yowl. However the nurse is right about my baby. I haven't asked to see her. They asked me what I am going to name her. I draw a blank. Baby? I want her, but I don't want her. When they plopped her on my chest, I realized up until that point, I hadn't even thought much about what I was going to do after she was born. I figured I'd give her up for adoption or—I don't know. Is that bad to say? It sounds so cold. But Chase, he didn't give me many options so I felt like I had to distance myself from the situation. Yet, the thought that I might want to adopt her out hasn't seemed to cross their minds.

I just know the moment I found out about her was the moment Chase started pushing me away. He kept asking me what I was going to do with a baby riding on a motorcycle from town to town singing gigs. Where was *that thing* going to stay while we sang in the bars? Because that was our life, singing. Now, I guess I'm thinking that little girl laying in the plastic bed in the newborn room has taken that away from me. I don't know what to do with her. I am just sad and lonely and hurt. Maybe, the nurse is right. I've got a heart that's broke.

It doesn't help I am sharing a hospital room with another woman by the name of Amanda Wells who's just had a baby. Mine's teeny and scrawny and screams like holy hell. Hers is plump and quiet and coos softly. Half the town has marched past my bed to get to Amanda's sunny side by

the window. They all give me these sad eyes and whispers—
that's the girl who got dumped off the highway. Amanda
has so many flowers and teddy bears, they are overflowing
off the heater vent and dripping on to the floor.

"Baby," the nurse asks me. "You want to use the
phone to call somebody?"

I was afraid to tell her I didn't have anybody. It has
just been me and Chase for the last two years. I figure they
are gonna ship me off to some homeless shelter. So I poke
Chase's number into the phone at the front desk while they
all stare at me. I listen to his cell phone ring. Then I hear a
sleepy woman's voice on the other end. Crud. Brooke
Canter. My heart lurches. She's twenty-four and her daddy
owns three high end bars outside New Orleans and in Baton
Rouge. She's all four-hundred dollar dresses and fine hotels
to my old jean shorts and highway motels.

I hang the phone up. Then I tell them I've got a ride.
I'm thinking they are just going to wiggle their fingers and
let me go out of there. I guess it doesn't work like that. The
hospital staff has to wheel outgoing patients down to where
a foyer leads to a parking lot. Then, they wait with you for
your ride to stop at the doors. And so, I wait and wait while
Janie takes the time to catch up on her social networks and
texting and conversing with her mama about what they're
going to do after church on Sunday.

"Uh oh." Janie peers upward over the phone, over
my head, and to the parking lot. "It's Mayor Littleton," she
whispers guardedly. "Let's take you for a little walk."

It's like the place goes on shutdown mode all of a
sudden. I can see the girls at the counter go rigid. I see the
security guards with their striped shirts stand up straight
like Pixie Sticks still full of sugar. "Did I do something
wrong?" I ask Janie softly.

"He don't like strangers," Janie says.

It was nearly an hour of me fidgeting in the wheelchair in a bleak, vacant break room while the baby screamed holy hell before I see the old man that met me at the barn last night coming through the door. It is probably seven in the evening and I'm sore and tired and cranky.

"I called my boyfriend, Cody, and he got ahold of Dutch," Janie says to me, hardly looking up from her cell phone. "Dutch told Cody he'd come get you until your family could get to town."

"No, I did not tell Cody that." Dutch is just standing there with arms akimbo and an angry-impatient stare. Every time the baby hits a long *na-na-yaaa* screech, he cringes and looks like he's going to snarl. His raggedy cowboy hat's in his hands and he's turning it around and around. "You called your cop-boyfriend and he come knocking at my door in full uniform and said she was my responsibility like I put that baby in her belly and I didn't. It ain't my fault she ended up in my barn last night like some stray cat. She needs to call that good-for-nothing boyfriend of hers and tell him to come get her. What the hell, Janie?" He grumbles. "I don't got the time or the money to deal with—all this."

"Well, Bo Littleton was sniffing around for her. Do you want him to get ahold of her?" She waits for him to answer. He doesn't which shows me he probably would rather have Bo get me than take me home with him. "Everybody knows you take in all kinds of old horses and strays, Dutch," Janie tells him, then leans into him slightly. "Some of them aren't so legal, isn't that right? So I hear." She's a bit forward, but I notice her eyes get a little scared look when he starts growling at her.

"Are you blackmailing me, girl?"

"Dutch, she doesn't have any place to go. She's right up your alley."

I think they argue back and forth between each other for a good five minutes. Janie finally just pushes my wheelchair toward him and then starts to walk off. Dutch follows and his voice is getting louder and louder so everybody is turning to look at him. When they are almost to the front desk, I wiggle my way out of the wheelchair with the baby clasped in my arms, snatch up my backpack in my free hand, and sling it over my shoulder. Then I just push the heavy metal doors open and walk outside.

It's still raining. I shove the baby to my chest. I'm a body full of pain right then and I know I'm walking like a seal. It isn't ten minutes later that an old beat up truck pulls up beside me. The window is down and I can see the grumpy old guy jabbing a finger at me.

"You're a pain in my ass, you know that right?" he snarls at me and adjusts the hat on his head angrily. He's a big, old man. He's tall, slightly bent, gray-haired and thick-jowled. He reminds me of an old bulldog whose bone just got dragged off by a bigger, younger pup. "Get in the truck. You can stay at my house. You got three days to figure something out."

"Go away."

"I'm only going to tell you twice, then I'm outta here. You can't walk to wherever your boyfriend disappeared to and I don't want no police knocking on my door again. Get in the truck or you're on your own." The madder he gets, the more his southern Tennessee accent deepens. It's almost like Dutch started walking in southern Ohio two minutes ago and with each step heading south toward Alabama now, his drawl thickens. His *can't* sounds like *caint* and *on your own* becomes *yorn*.

I keep walking and he drives away cursing up a storm of words. It's not five minutes passing when I realize he went around the block and is sidling up beside me again.

"Get in. You two are going to catch your death in this rain," he narrows his eyes at me, then drops them to the little bundle of blankets. I know he's right. "You ain't crazy, are you? Because you're acting like you are."

"Leave me alone. Quit stalking me. I'm going to call the cops."

"With what? You don't got no phone. The hospital, they are calling the cops as we speak to come get you. You either come with me or they're gonna take you to some homeless shelter or the preacher's house or if Bo Littleton gets ahold of you, you might end up in a gully on the side of the highway in northern Alabama. And the preacher, he'll make you take all that junk off your face and wear a dress. Do you understand me?"

I stop, throw back my head. I make a big deal of rolling my eyes and standing there to the count of ten. Then I sigh as loud as I can, grab on to the knob, and tug the door open.

"There will be no drugs, no stealing."

"What the hell?" I gripe, sliding into the ripped seat. "Are you just going to assume that I'm trouble because of how I'm dressed?"

"Yeah, pretty much."

"You sound like my daddy."

"Maybe if you woulda listened to him—" he stops there, must see my wary gaze. Dutch shakes off whatever he is about to say with a wiggle of his head. "Never mind."

CHAPTER 3
| GOT THE LEAVING MY BABY BLUES

Dutch lives in a huge old farmhouse a stone's throw from the barn where I had my baby. It is almost gray because it needs painting and it is tucked into big old maple trees. The inside has old brown shag carpet in the living room and shabby linoleum floors in the kitchen and bathroom. He lives there all alone except for more cats than I can count inside and out, and six or seven coon dogs running around.

"Don't make yourself at home. You're leaving in three days," he tells me. "Dang, my life would be easier if this was the old days," he grumbles. "I could trade you off for a horse." He points to the stairway and my eyes follow until the dark sucks away the upstairs. "If old Bo Littleton finds out I took you in, I'll have hell to pay. There's a room straight up the stairway. Sheets and stuff are in the closets. There's a bathroom up there. Stay out of my way. Try—try to keep that *thing* from crying all the time. It gets on my nerves."

I make that *thing* a bed out of one of the drawers I pull out of an old white dresser and some soft baby blue blankets in the bedroom at the top of the stairway. The room is cozy and covered in drab daisy wallpaper and there is a twin bed shoved into the corner. Old, dusty pictures of spring flowers line the walls and there's a brown rag carpet over the wood floor.

I wiggle-walk the chest up next to the bed, pushing it with my toes. There's a double window and I open it, let the warm spring breeze sweep in. It smells like fresh mowed grass, horse manure, and more rain.

It reminds me of home and makes my tummy ache a bit just above my belly button. I sit on the bed and fall back, stare at the ceiling and trying to rub the homesick away with my fingers. I pat out a beat with my thumbs on my belly and my fingers knotted. *Thump-thump. Thumpety-thump-thump.* I feel a little letdown that my beats aren't making music in my head and such, melding into song words. My piano teacher used to tell me I had a gift with music. I'm scared that maybe having a baby has taken that gift away from me. I listen to the evening crickets outside, wait for their rhythm to stroke my creativity. Nothing. I want to go home. I can't. I want my mama to coo over the baby and my daddy to walk around all proud about her. I want Chase to come riding back on his motorcycle and tell me it was all a mistake, he didn't mean to leave me standing in the rain all alone at the motel. It was just a momentary lapse of judgment. Then we'll kiss and ride off into the sunset on his Harley just like some new twist to an old western movie. I sigh, realize the baby wasn't in that picture. I suppose right then, I wanted a lot of things. But the one thing I didn't want was the baby.

Or maybe she just didn't want me. It doesn't seem like it. She stops crying for a minute. I roll over in the bed, dribble my fingers over her tiny face. She's got white-blonde hair like me and she looks bald, it's so light. I stare at her. She stares at me. I know she'd be better off with anybody else but me. I think something's wrong with me because I don't feel this undying, maternal love like I saw on my mama's face when she looked at me. I want my mama right then even if she hasn't been but an old photograph I've got stuffed into my backpack since I was five or six.

I suppose it is strange I dig into my backpack and look for support in the very picture of the woman who abandoned me when I was little. The white edges are smudged and crumpled. The image of the smiling woman in a red dress and red lipstick inside the border is fading. She's standing against a brick wall, holding up a peace sign with her right hand and hugging a white bundle that is me when I was a baby in the cleft of her left arm. Leaning into her legs and holding on tight is my bigger brother, Will. She doesn't look much like me. She's got thick, short, sandy brown hair. Mine's fine and long, but twisted in two tiny balls on my head. She's chubby. I'm as skinny as a sapling trying to grow on a rocky hillside.

I fall asleep staring at her and knowing the best thing for my own baby is leaving her. I'm dead broke, homeless, and the one thing I ever wanted to do was sing and I just don't feel like it anymore. At three o'clock in the morning, I wake up. The baby's sleeping. I snatch up my backpack with my entire life in it and slip quietly down the stairway.

The front door squeaks when I stumble out to the front porch. I stop at the steps, sit down for a minute. I can hear the baby crying upstairs because of the stupid door. It is loud and like a sparrow *yank, yank, yanking.* After I work myself up to it, it's as easy as counting to three, walking out to the gravel-mud driveway and blinking past the sprinkles hitting my face to the old Bel-Air Hollow Road at the end. I pause halfway. I don't know what's stopping me. Maybe the ache in my chest. Crud. I take two steps back to the croak of frogs in the puddles. I let my head roll around my neck and take another six steps. I see the white mailbox that's bashed-in on one side and looks like some teenagers took a bat to it. I'm thinking once I pass that, I'm home free. I'll just—but I stop there, thinking that maybe ol' Dutch will probably bundle up the baby, dig a whole and dump her inside to shut her up.

So I do this stupid dance back and forth between the house and mailbox six times. The seventh time, I stop and get ready to just all-out run past the end of the driveway. But I don't make it. The baby's cries stop. I imagine Dutch pushing a palm over her little lips to stifle the sound.

"Shit!" I hiss-yell that curse, grimace, and kick the wooden pole to the stupid mailbox with my boot three times. I can't hear her crying anymore. I can't do it.

I'm whisper-cussing all the way to the front door, a little desperate to stop Dutch from killing her. I slip off my boots when I slink back inside. To my utter horror, when I look to my left, I can make out a little lamp light on next to the couch in the living room. I blink. Lounging on the couch, is the man who delivered my baby. Boone, wasn't that his name? He's shirtless. He's got short buzzed hair up to his ears and longer hair on top that's askew. He's holding her against his chest, patting her back with one hand and she's completely quiet and staring up blankly at him.

"You know, the fifth time you made it to the mailbox, I thought, man, she's going to do it. She's flying the coop. She's really going to break whatever barrier it is between the driveway and the road and set herself free." He stifles a yawn with his hand over the baby's head. He has a way of dipping his chin toward his right shoulder. I can't tell if it's because he can't see out of the right eye that has the scar beneath, or he's just sizing me up. Either way, I can even see from here, his eyes are bloodshot from being sloshed. "Then you did that little funny jumping thing with your hands at your sides and turned around. I told her—" he pauses and puts a big hand over her head and gently rolls it around the crown. "—what's her name?"

"Huh?" I'm kind of dumbed by the idea he is here and I didn't know it. But now, I hear his gentle leg drumming—*tap, tap-tap, tap.* "I mean, she doesn't have one."

"I get it. Like a stray cat you don't want to keep. You

name it and that's the point you know you're too attached to leave it, right?" *Tap, tap-tap, tap.*

"I don't know." He annoys me. He thinks he knows what I am thinking. He doesn't.

"Well, I told her mommy was having a crazy moment and she'd come back. And you did. I told Dutch you've got postpartum depression. My mom used to call it the baby blues. But Dutch said whatever it is, he's never seen anything like it. He tried to trade you to me for a horse—"

"Are you serious? You can't do that."

"It doesn't matter. I told him he'd have to give *me* a hundred horses for the likes of you. You're a tall order."

"No, I'm short."

"No, a tall order is something that's a pain in the ass to work with, you know, like a six year old stallion that hasn't been broke or gelded."

"Are you a doctor?" I interrupt and now his tapping is starting to get on my nerves. "Can't you stop that tapping?"

"No, I mean, yes." It stops.

"Shouldn't you be at some hospital somewhere irritating patients?"

"I'm not a doctor."

"You delivered my baby."

"Because I didn't have a choice. Dutch called me because I'd delivered calves and lambs and horses." *Tap, tap-tap, tap.*

"No shit," I hiss in realization. I rub my temples with my fingers.

"Yeah, we did okay, right?" He snickers a laugh. "You survived."

"Do you live here?"

"Naw, Dutch picked me up from the Crazy Filly. I got a little drunk. They didn't want me to drive. He saves my butt. My mom and my sister freak out when I come home drunk."

I don't ask him why he's twenty-something and still living at home and kowtowing to his mom and his sister. I also consider the fact he's probably still drunk and holding my baby and he's doing a better job at it than me sober. Instead, I come up beside the couch and feel my chest ache.

"I changed her diaper and she likes this," he tells me. He's got her wrapped tightly in the little pink baby blanket they gave me at the hospital. She's shoved up to his chin and he's rubbing her back between his obsessive tapping.

"She likes you," I grumble. "In fact, she appears to like you better than she likes me."

"Yeah, I've done this before. She must sense your fear." He thinks he is funny and laughs. "You're quiet. Like a mouse. Is your voice always that hoarse? Or do you have a cold?"

"Yes. I mean, yes it is hoarse. No, I'm not sick. Nice people say it is smoky. Mean people tell me I sound like a boy. Screw off. You can have her. I don't need—"

"I didn't say it sounded like a boy. It's just deep like the kind of grumbly nicker my horse makes when he hears my boots walking toward the barn door." He shakes his head, sighs. "You're going to dump her like your boyfriend dumped you? I'm assuming you both come from a long line of throwaway relationships." He looks mad, then. Enough so, he doesn't seem to care to dip his head like he's trying to hide that scar. "You don't deserve her. There's a million other people out there that could give her a better home, you know that, right? But you got this perfect little thing with perfect chubby cheeks and perfect chubby legs and you are ready to walk out the door, give her to any stranger walking by—"

"They said she was scrawny at the hospital."

"And they are idiots there. She just needs a few days of mama's milk and she'll be pudgy as a newborn calf in the spring. But what do you care?" He sniffs sarcastically. I'm staring at him while he just goes off on me about abandoning a baby and how he could call the cops and I'd go to jail. "I should do it right now." He doesn't lift his voice, but his words are caustic and they are like daggers to my heart. "Look at these chubby, beautiful fists and her lips, they are heart-shaped just like yours."

I finally hold up a hand. "Boone, is that your name?"

"Yeah."

"Okay, Boone, I got nothing," I spit back. I know my voice is soft and a little shaky. It's already naturally hoarse and raspy-sounding like a boy. It doesn't help I think I'm scared of all these people. "I got nobody. I've got no family. I don't even have a house or a car or a job. Everything I had was wrapped up with that guy who drove off on that motorcycle except what you're holding there." I scoot in, poke a finger at the cleft of his bare arm where the baby is settled. "You think this baby is better off with a mama who lives by the seat of her pants every day of her life? You don't know what it's like to be one step away from panhandling for a hamburger because you are six months pregnant and starving to death. I could tell by your big, brand new truck and your expensive, high-end jeans you have no clue what that kind of life is like. Feast or famine, that's what my life is from one day to the next. I live from town to town, job to job. I can't feed myself half the time, much less a kid. My jobs are in dive bars and diners, on street corners and stages. Should I drag my kid into that? Hell, I don't—I don't even know how to do—that!" I point at him, the way he's holding her and she's not squalling a storm of tears.

"Well, I don't know about all that—stuff," he says matter-of-factly. "I just know a baby needs her mama. And if you can figure out how to survive like you just said, you can figure out how to take care of her." He pats the couch next to him. Even from here, I can smell the beer on his breath. "Sit down, you're making me dizzy staring up at you."

I hesitate, then sit down beside Boone. It is awkward sitting next to a strange man without a shirt. He's somewhere between slim and buff and well-muscled. He's the type ladies in the old romance westerns I like to watch called strapping. He's not my type. But I'm thinking in other circumstances, I might like to take my bundled baby's place and sink into the warmth between his arms. I blink. Having a baby is making me weird, I'm thinking. I turn slightly and lean against the couch so I'm as far away from him as possible. *Tap, tap-tap, tap.*

"Oh, my God! You can't stop the tapping?"

"I'll try. When I'm drunk, it's hard. I have to constantly focus." He licks his lips, looks toward the ceiling. "First, you got to give her a name—I don't even know what *your* name is."

"Skeeter."

"Really? I thought that was just—" he starts to ask me with a shift of his eyes like he's going to roll them. "Did you make that up or—never mind." He stops, rubs a hand across his head. It doesn't erase the condescending gaze he's giving me. "Okay, *Skeeter,*" he says it with a funny twist of the words. "I don't know why I didn't expect anything less."

I narrow my eyes. "What does that mean?" Is he

being mean to me?

"Nothing," he sighs. The baby is squirming and even I know she's going to start bawling in a second. I can see her lips start to mean-pucker. "Forget it. You're like in a motorcycle gang or something, right?" He nods to my tattoos, jabs a thumb toward my eyebrow piercing. "How about Scout or Billy or—"

"A motorcycle gang?" I cut in. "Are you from the 1980s? Do they even have those anymore? No, I'm not from a motorcycle gang." I hold up my arm. "I'm wearing a unicorn, asshole, not a picture of Jesus."

Now he's giving me this snarky, wide-eyed gaze like he's going to say something, but he's holding back.

"What?"

"Why would a biker wear Jesus and not a unicorn?"

"I don't know. I'm not one. Are you mean-drunk or are you crappy like this all the time?"

He ignores me. "How about Alexandra," he sniffs. "It means brave, someone who defends. She's going to need something strong to fend off her mama's razor sharp little teeth."

And the only thing I can think of to retort is: "I don't like you. You're mean." It sounds like a four year-old sniveling at her big brother. But I've got the sniffles and I know I'm going to cry. I'm not sure why. It is just there, bubbling up from my chest. I notice he is patting her a little harder now with his free hand, rocking her softly. It's like the dude can sense she's getting upset. I'm staring at him and I can see his face getting red like he wants to yell at me.

"Okay, listen, I feel sorry for you," he says softly. The baby is grunting when he just thrusts her at me. "I get it. You don't have anything. I'm trying to help. But I know your type. You whine and complain about being poor and how everybody craps on you. But you won't make yourself any better. You're just fine with sitting around and just spending the rest of your life being stuck in that rut."

"You don't know me worth squat," I growl. I don't have a choice but to take her. And when she realizes she's out of the comfy warm pocket that knows everything there is to making her happy, she starts to do that screaming thing that sounds like a cat with a stepped-on tail. I watch him start to rise. Then I think he realizes I'm about ready to burst into tears because he gives the ceiling a hard glare, then bites down hard on his upper lip and sits back down.

"She's hungry, Skeeter." He grabs a little throw blanket and tosses it over my shoulder. "Have at it."

"What?" I blink. "I do—baby bottles and formula."

"And that's your problem. Just feed her."

"No, I'm not good at this. The bottles are better."

"No, bottles are not better. They are just easier at first. You don't bond as well with a bottle." He shakes his head. "Listen, I'm not a doctor. But I've raised a lot of pigs. If a stupid old sow can figure out how to feed a baby, you can too. It makes the piglets healthier."

"Are you comparing me to a—dumb pig?"

"Pigs aren't that dumb. And yeah, kind of." He starts to get up again. I can't even be angry while the baby's howling. I'm just scared. The nurse at the hospital said it's just getting them to latch on. I just know that the moment she does, I'm not going to be able to walk away.

I'm staring up at Boone. I know my eyes are already as big as fists normally. Now they have to be big, blue freaking out, scared basketballs. "Well, don't leave me." *Argh*, my voice is way past a whine.

This time, he's the one throwing back his head, rubbing the dark hair on his head. "Alright, scaredy cat." He shrugs and snatches up another blanket and flops himself on the couch next to me. "You realize you're afraid of a five pound baby."

He's right. So I just keep my mouth shut.

"How can you tell if a snake is a baby snake?" he asks me.

"I don't know. How would I know that and why? Is there one in here?"

"No, goofy, it has a rattle."

"That would make it a rattlesnake, wouldn't it?" I retort. He rolls his eyes.

"I thought it was a funny joke." He tells a couple dozen more stupid jokes while I bumble through ten excruciatingly long minutes of knowing I can't possibly be doing it right because the baby's blubbering under my shirt. Then there's silence except for the soft sound of suckling.

"Yay." Boone says that like a flat-lined joke and tosses one hand up in the air. "I knew you could do it." It's quiet for a few while I feel the tickle of my milk coming in and the wonderful, but painful feel of the baby suckling.

"How do you know what Alexandra means?" I ask him.

"It's my mom's name."

"Okay, I'll call her Lexie for short."

Boone doesn't answer. I think he's fallen to sleep. So I practice rubbing her back like he was doing. He's not asleep. His hand comes up and snatches on mine and he swipes my hand across her back like I'm rubbing a brush over a horse's winter coat.

"Wake me up when you're done. I'll show you how to burp her."

He knows an awful lot about babies for a cowboy

who hangs out at bars. I tell him that and end with: "I think I can handle the burping, smartass."

"You got to kiss the top of her head, too, and look her in the eyes." I look up, think he's kidding. He's smiling, but not like I'm the butt end of his joke. I don't smile back.

CHAPTER 4
SKELETONS IN THE CUPBOARD AND MEAN GIRLS

This place has skeletons in every cupboard, I think. Those skeletons being secrets I just can't figure out. And it has mean girls. Those aren't such a mystery, just difficult to avoid.

First, there's one secret here—there are three rooms upstairs at Dutch's house. There is a stairway that leads to the attic that stops at a door. The only room that isn't locked is the one I am staying in directly at the top of the stairs. Dutch makes it a point each night to trudge up the second floor stairway and walk to each room to my right and left and wiggle the door to make sure each is still locked. Then, he goes to the attic room up another set of steps that hang over the doorway of my room. He is gone for about an hour. I can hear his footsteps above me while he walks around up there. It scares me that he's got dead bodies rotting inside, girls like me he has taken in with the help of the townspeople who use wayfaring girls as sort of a sacrifice to protect their own children. Maybe he feeds them, fattens them up, and then murders them in their sleep. Maybe I'm next.

Who am I to judge, though? I've got my own skeletons. The third day I was here, I was standing at the bottom of the stairway and peering up to the second floor when Dutch comes out of the attic, locks the door and stares back down at me. It is right then he reminds me of the past I don't like digging up. Because my secrets are starting to pop up like they always do, following me from town to town like a scary clown in a horror movie slinking two soft steps behind his next victim. I just wish I could crumple up those worn out memories in the same way I ball up the pieces of paper with the words to songs I never finish and toss them in the trash.

"You got something you need to tell me, baby girl?" he's asked me that day in a really soft voice.

"No, sir," I answered.

"Let me tell you something, Skeeter. I was down at the hardware store yesterday. Pickle Beatty said there was a couple suits looking for a young lady about your age." He waits like he thinks I'm going to answer, then Dutch leans his elbows on the banister that runs along the upstairs. "You'd tell me if you been in trouble, wouldn't you? Because I don't need no trouble from the mayor's office or the police."

"Yes, sir."

"I thought so. I told Pickle that too."

"He didn't tell them where I was, did he?"

"No, sweetie. He figured the girl in the picture they showed him didn't look nothing like you. She had on a fancy red dress and was leaning against a Ferrari." Dutch nods his head toward the kitchen. "A couple do-gooders from the church got word of you havin' that baby in my barn. They brought over some diapers and a rockin' chair so you can rock her. Holly Young, she's the kindergarten teacher in town. She brought over a bag of clothes from her little girl and a swing. She says they get colicky and it rocks them to sleep, makes them stop crying. And the preacher from Holy Unity, he stopped by with little blankets."

I rubbed my hands together, stared at the mound of bags and boxes of diapers a minute in the silence following. Then I looked back up the stairs and to the tired eyes watching me closely. "It's not me. I've never dressed like that and I prefer Lamborghinis," I try to kid. He doesn't laugh. "Do you want me to leave, Dutch?"

"No. Since we haven't found a place for you to go, you can stay three more days. But you got to keep a low profile. This town's kind of funny about strangers."

"You mean that mayor who was ready to escort me out of town at the diner? He was at the hospital, too."

"Yeah, stay away from him."

And then there are the MEAN GIRLS. I capitalize those two words to stress the magnitude of the situation here in Bel-Air. It appears there are two classes of people here. There are the rich farmers whose families have been here for at least two hundred years. They've been through the clearing of the land, then the Civil War, and then the rebuilding again. That's a nutshell image of them because they'll be the first to give an excruciating long lecture on exactly how difficult it has been for them and how they survived and now, deserve to reap the profits because they are historically and genetically better than the rest. These people have a bit of a chip on their shoulder for those in the second class—everybody else. That includes the small family farmers, the folks who live in the little white houses in and around town, and those in the subdivision about a mile from the cemetery. And me, the homeless girl.

THE MEAN GIRLS are three twenty-somethings whose daddy's own the biggest farms here. I'm kind of a closet sappy, romance movie buff. I like to watch them on the women's channels in the middle of the night, especially the westerns where the girl and the guy go riding off into the sunset. I almost feel refreshed getting a good cry and then a happy ending. But all of those movies seem to have a posse of mean girls, the kind that like to pick on the heroine in every story. Bel-Air's got them too. Meeting them is like turning on the TV and watching the scene get set for a show down for good versus evil. They are the evil.

I got to meet three of those girls three and a half weeks after I got to Bel-Air. The three days Dutch told me I could stay with him got wheedled out to three and a half weeks. At least once a week he got mad at me for something stupid like leaving a towel on the bathroom floor or Lexie waking him up at night. He's so surly. I'd pack my things into my little backpack and hug Lexie to my chest and we'd start down the stairs with him growling and yelling at me, and me waggling my head at him while I mouthed out what he was saying.

"You ain't well enough to get anywhere yet, girl," Dutch would grumble. "Get your stuff back up there." Then on that three and a half week point, Dutch tells me my room and board isn't free anymore.

He informs me of this while I watch him ride one of the horses around in circles in a wooden pen next to the barn. For an old guy, he's quite graceful on a horse and I like watching him work with the gray mare. There's sawdust on the ground and he keeps kicking it up into my face while I stand there with my backpack over my shoulder and just about ready to tell him I'm leaving for the last time. He made me mad again. I was minding my own business sitting on the bed shoving the last of the hospital diapers in my backpack getting ready to leave. I've got my hair bundled up in two little balls on the back of my head. He tells me I look like a mouse when he stands just outside the door of the bedroom and peers inside. I made the bed, cleaned up what little we have. It is five-thirty in the morning. I already made him and Jack breakfast—five pieces of bacon, three eggs, toast, and grits. And coffee. The two drank almost a whole pot.

"You do talk, don't you? You're not mute? Because you ain't said more than a handful of words to me since you been here."

I shake my head back and forth.

"You ain't going anywhere right this minute. I sent Jack to the store to get more diapers. I'm not letting them go to waste."

I look up, tug on my lip. Lexie is laying on the bed all swaddled like Boone showed me. She is tiny and making suckling sounds with her lips. She stares at me. I stare at her. She blinks. I blink. I smile and wish she'd smile back. She doesn't yet. She looks more like me than Chase, I think.

"You got a voice, girl?"

I tug my head away. He kind of scares me. I've stayed hidden in the upstairs almost the entire month to avoid him and his attic ramblings.

"So answer me. All's *it* gots is the pajamas they gave you at the hospital and a few hand-me-downs that are too big. Little girls need dresses. Pink ones and the likes. So we're going to get some. And some shoes for you." He points down to the old brown boots I'm wearing. "Them things is ugly."

"They're my daddy's boots."

"I don't care. They are still ugly." He shrugs. "You're going to cook like you did this morning. In a couple days, you can clean the stalls to earn some money to pay me back for her clothes and staying here, you understand?" When I don't answer, he reaches out and knocks on the top of my head. "You hear me?"

"Ow," I say. "Yes. I'm better at playing the guitar."

"Well, you ain't got no guitar, do you?"

"No." He's right. I don't.

"So, until you got a guitar you're hired cooking and cleaning stalls."

"Are you really going to trade me for a horse?"

"What?" Dutch looks at me with a scrunched-up face. "Who told you that?"

"Boone. I heard you say it too."

"I'd get arrested if I did that." Dutch rolls his eyes, shakes his head like an old bull. "This ain't the nineteenth century. But I suppose if it was, I'd do it for a donkey."

I have a job, then, and a place to stay even if it is with an axe murderer who is going to, eventually, sell me to the highest bidder. It isn't a half hour later, he tells me to get into the truck. He's taking me to the Goodwill in town to pick out some clothes because there's nothing but muck boots, cowboy hats, and jeans that are way too big for my scrawny butt at the big agriculture retail store in Denton three towns south. Otherwise, we have to go to a mall in Nashville to pick up something. He laughs when he says the last part and adds: "Because I sold two horses this week and got some cash, but that ain't happening."

Goodwill doesn't have my clothes. I can tell right off that it's full of the same thing the Denton Farmer Supply has, only way too used and big for me. I'm beginning to think they don't make people my size in southern Tennessee. Even the kids' pants are big on me.

I walk to the front of the store to tell Dutch this news at the exact moment I see three girls dressed in sporty leggings and knee-length tunics digging out black garbage bags of clothes from the open trunk of a cute little red convertible next to Dutch's truck. I'm holding Lexie in the cleft of my arm and she's pooped her diaper and it stinks.

Two of the girls are curly bleach blondes with dark roots, and perfect tiny and upturned noses. The third and what appears to be their leader who is carrying the car keys, is perfect-ironed black hair and puffy lips. They've got matching pink lipstick and pink fingernails.

"Does this place double as a plastic surgeon's office?" I kid. Dutch's eyes get wide and he shushes me with a forefinger. I thought it was funny. So does the Goodwill lady working at the register because she stifles a snicker. She's got brown hair piled on her head in a messy bun.

"Don't be like that, Skeeter."

"I know. I should use them as an example." I roll my eyes. "Girly girl and shit. Speaking of shit. I'm going out to change the baby's diaper."

"Honey, did you try the slim boys' pants?" The Goodwill lady says those words while the girls come marching in the door in single file. Her name tag says: RITA MAYS. She's chewing on the pink eraser of a pencil before she pokes it toward the back of the store. "You're probably a size 10-12, slim girls. You could probably hem them up."

Dutch turns to me, I'm shaking my head. "No. No way."

"It's not like you're that picky," he tells me, eyeing me up and down and then scooting to the entranceway to open the door for the girls. He nods toward them like my tastes should match their elitist, catalog-ordered fashion. I've got ripped jeans cut to the knee and a little cami.

"Over my dead body," I say softly. They flow on through without even a thank you to Dutch who has that silly smile old men get when pretty girls walk by. They are chatting it up and stop just short of the cash register.

"We cleaned our closets," the first blonde announces. She looks around the room as if waiting for applause from the three old ladies digging deep into the winter sweaters. They don't look up.

"Hi, there, Goodwill worker," another one says while she drops her bag on the counter. "Can you take these for the poor? Adriana's mama wanted us to drop them off.

There's probably a thousand dollar's worth of winter pants and shirts in these. Her mama says it's time to go shopping and she doesn't have a single place left in her closet to put new clothes. And it is a walk-in closet."

I assume the dark-haired girl is Adriana. She's cool and chewing on a piece of gum, twirling a pink key fob around her manicured-nailed fingers. She stops long enough to drop her eyes to me. I see her slowly take in my arm with the tattoo. She rolls her eyes immediately after.

"You're the little homeless girl who had a baby in the barn, aren't you?" she asks me. Her voice is soft like velvet. "I can tell it's you they were talking about at church. You're like in a gang or something. I hope your gangsta boyfriend isn't coming back to rob the town or something."

The two girls with her make a lazy hide of their giggles behind their hands.

"Gangsta," one repeats. She wrinkles her nose, lets her eyes make a lazy swing toward Dutch and then, to Lexie like she can't figure out which one is stinking. "Oh, something stinks like poo." I realize right then the two blondes are twins. I can't tell one from the other. They don't seem to care that Dutch is standing there listening to them and just might realize she is implying he's dirtied an adult diaper. The matching blonde waves a hand in front of her and shivers.

"Can we hurry this up, Goodwill person?" she asks RITA MAYS. I'm getting the feeling they feel like they can say anything they want to anyone they want because their daddies or their husbands have lots of money.

"I'm going to the truck," I mumble to Dutch. He nods, turns to follow. That's when I see the microphone sitting half in and half out the dingy, thick curtains at the front window. It looks like it was tossed there, leaning precariously to the left of two fold-up chairs and a bunch of green, lazily-folded draperies on top.

I'm drawn to it, make a twisty pivot of my feet that forces Dutch to stop behind me.

"Walk," he grunts with a knuckle to my spine when he almost bangs into my back. I reach down, touch the old microphone with my finger.

"That's junk leftover from the church yard sale," RITA MAYS tells us. "They're putting in new curtains and the preacher says there ain't nobody to play the piano so there ain't no choir, so why have three microphones cruddying up the back room?"

"How much is it?" I ask, rolling my finger along the smooth silver surface. It even has the stand attached. It's a vintage cardioid microphone from the 1950s or '60s. It's the type of microphone used in places with bad sound feedback. It doesn't suck in the background noise and throw it back out at the audience. It's perfect for crummy old bars and churches, places with poor acoustics. It cuts out the crud in the background and focuses on what's in front of it, especially when a voice is hoarse and deep like mine. My boyfriend used to tell me it made my voice sound like a sultry July New Orleans night.

"What do you need a stupid microphone for?" Dutch grumbles. "You ain't got a penny to your name and—I don't see you singing in any church choir."

"It's three bucks plus tax," RITA MAYS tells me. "The draperies are fourteen bucks a piece and the foldup chairs are ten for both."

"Three bucks?" I know my eyes are wide. Everybody's kind of doing their own thing but me and Dutch. I turn and look at him with wide eyes and I see there's no way he's going to buy it for me. Ug. I want it so bad. I'm thinking I could plug it into the outlet in the barn and sing my heart out.

But Adriana interrupts my eye-plead, waves her hand at Dutch. "I have four more bags I need carried in to the store. You can do that, right?"

I don't turn. I know he will be her five-minute servant and he won't buy me something he thinks is a waste of money better spent on clothes and food. I push through the door and walk to the truck, change Lexie's poopy diaper at the passenger side with the door open. I watch them come out, following Dutch into and out of the store twice like they have to monitor his carrying in of the bags. On the last time, I hear one of the girls whisper loud enough for me to hear. *That is the ugliest bald-headed baby I have ever seen in my life.*

I grit my teeth and let them flow back into the store. Then I take Lexie's dirty diaper and I slowly make my way to the back of the truck so I am even with the trunk of her car. Then I take the dirty diaper and toss it deep into the trunk of the little convertible and close the lid with a soft bang.

When Dutch comes out, he gives me a funny stare. Still, he's holding the microphone and stand in his hands and he flops it in the back of the truck. My heart is making a jiggy-jag of excitement while I crane my neck to watch him scoot around the truck and get in.

"Oh, thank you, thank you—"

"Stop it now, girl. Don't get all happy about it. You owe me three dollars and twenty-five cents."

"Now, I just need a guitar and I'm back on my feet." I grin and I see him watching me while I sit back quietly in my seat, trying not to keep looking at the microphone back there in the rearview mirror. I swear he gets a little smile on his face like he thinks he just bought me a new car on Christmas day. I kind of feel like he did. Of course, he probably wouldn't have bought me the microphone if he knew I tossed the dirty diaper into the trunk of Adriana's car.

He is quiet heading to Bel-Air Feed and Supply to get grains for the twenty or so horses he's got. When we get there, he tells me to stay in the truck while he goes to pay. His order is all ready. So we pull inside the long mill and four big boys haul out the feed sacks and toss them in the back of the truck.

"Who are you?" One with red hair and a lollipop stuck between his lips stops just short of the passenger side window and looks at me and Lexie. He's got a big smile on his face. "You the old guy's daughter?"

Another man comes by and hits him hard on the shoulder. "Shut up, man," he whispers at him loudly with wide eyes. He gives him a little jerk away from the window. Then he looks at me, turns pale, and exclaims: "Jesus Christ!"

What does that mean? It's like he sees a ghost. I just hunker back in the seat and fiddle with Lexie's blanket. I watch them from the big rearview mirror on the passenger side door all kind of meld together in a little pack while they are loading like they are whispering something to each other. It is discomfiting. Then Dutch comes growling up on the driver's side. He yells at them to all mind their own business and get the damn truck loaded. Then he adds: "Unless one of you hillbillies is interested in looking at the little filly in there's teeth, get an idea of her worth to trade me for a dead broke horse—" He pokes his finger at me on the other side of the windshield while I slide down in the seat trying to disappear in the shadows. "—or at least a nag

DEAD BROKE HEARTS ♥ 43

not dead enough I can actually get money out of in a sale, quit your talk. I'm losing money on this one." Then he stops poking toward the window and digs out his phone and I see him nodding his head like someone's telling him a secret.

"Come on. We got to go." He slides in the driver's side door two minutes later and shakes his head.

"Did you just offer to trade me for a horse?"

"Um, don't worry, nobody made a bid. Not surprised. Those boys are idiots," he grunts gruffly and waves his phone at me. "You know, that boy's going to be the death of me."

I just look at him. I figure it's none of my business who that boy is even though I look around behind the truck and see a woman in a little office cubby leaning out and staring hard as ice at us. She's cupping a palm to her lips and leaning into a tall man dressed in a suit and black cowboy hat.

CHAPTER 5
DRIVING A DRUNK BOONE HOME AND ALMOST WRECKING INTO MARY GREEN'S GRAVE IN BEL-AIR CEMETERY

Dutch drives right through the middle of town and then pops out the other side. He plays this old Bluegrass music really low. It seems to appease Lexie who doesn't like the car seat Jack borrowed from his niece and dropped off this morning. Downtown Bel-Air is one Main Street with a bunch of old-fashioned-looking brick buildings and right in the center, a big old stone courthouse. There's a church on each of the corners leading in and going out. I think the town must have been a lot bigger at one time. Some of the buildings look vacant, but most have signs out front—Justice Pharmacy, Bel-Air Flowers and Gifts, and Reynold's Real Estate.

It is about a mile out of town that the road veers a little upward. I see the town cemetery sitting on a little hill ahead. There's also two police cars with lights flashing and a big truck.

"Crap on a stick," Dutch says. He has such a thick drawl, I have to wade through his words at first to figure out what he is saying. He kicks his foot on the gas and makes a fast peel up the gravel lane running right up the middle. The truck is skidding back and forth. There are new graves and old ones lined up across one hillside and down another. I can hear the feed in the back bouncing up and down in hard crashes at every rut on the road and there is white dust enveloping the hill behind us. I'm worried about my mic getting crushed back there.

My eyes veer from him to what looks like a scuffle between two police officers and a man on the ground in the middle of two lines of headstones. A chubby cop with pasty-pale face is laying an elbow into the fallen man's back. A thinner one is grabbing him around the neck.

Dutch jams on his brakes just short of the first police car and jumps out fast. "Bobby, Bobby, easy on the boy!" he's hollering loudly at a skinny cop grappling with a pair of handcuffs and settling on the back of the man on the ground. The cop's young, maybe in his late twenties. His black hair has a comb over that's flopping in his eyes. I can see a pair of glasses laying askew on the ground by his knee. I'm assuming these are Officer Bobby's because he's got white circles around his eyes like a raccoon where the sunshine can't usually get through the glass rims and make his skin tan like the rest of his face. I get out of the truck and I walk over and pick up the glasses before they get broken. I gently wipe the lenses clean with my shirt.

It's Boone he's holding down. I can see his curly hair and his face while he struggles and cusses. His cowboy hat is toppled to one side and covered in grass clippings. His arms are behind his back and he is grimacing against the pain. I catch the scent of beer and my eyes veer upward to two broken beer bottles and brown glass settled on a newer headstone. Then my eyes go downward to Boone. There's a dribble of blood on his lip and his nose is bleeding. My heart makes a quick jerk. Dutch's hands are up in the air and the chubbier of the two police officers is screaming at him to back off. I can see the one called Bobby tickling his gun with his free hand. The cops are yelling at Dutch and he's yelling at them. Boone is big and the two men on top of him are having a difficult time holding him down.

"Stop it, you're hurting him."

I had come out of the truck slowly and walked across

the damp grass. I didn't realize none of them seemed to even notice me step up and pick up the glasses. They're too busy fighting down Boone who is bucking and jerking like a green broke pony. They are screaming at him to quit fighting. I stop just short of the officer called Bobby who is sitting on his rear with Boone in a headlock. I see him look up to my soft words. He blinks at me and Boone bucks a bit, looks up and I catch his eyes.

"Hey—Skeeter," he grunts casually.

"Hey, Boone," I return with the same flat tone.

The police officer yells at me to get back. I take a step back. Then I get down on my knees because Boone is crunching down on his teeth so hard I can hear them through the cops grunting and grappling him.

"Can you please stop?" I look Boone in the eyes. "You're scaring me."

He just stops and tips his head at me like *what the hell?*

"Can you please let him go?" I ask the cop who is still wiggling the handcuffs.

"No, miss," he growls. "He's going down to the station. He's drunk and disorderly. He's—"

"He's not disorderly now," I tell him. Then I look at Boone. "You're not going to be disorderly anymore, right?"

"I'll beat the shit out of these idiots," he tells me. "I'm minding my own business up here—"

"You were shooting a case of beer off a headstone, Boone!" Officer Bobby retorts. He isn't relaxing his arms and for a skinny man, he is quite strong. Dutch's shadow nearly covers them both and I look up to see him taking in Bobby with wary, narrowed eyes. "I'm not letting him go so he takes off in his truck and kills somebody. He's drunk. He swung at me—"

"Bobby, you know what week this is," Dutch reminds him. "You got to give the boy a break. You got to give me a break. I need out of here."

"Yeah, asswipe, you've—" Boone starts in and his voice is high-pitched like he's making fun of Dutch. I give Boone the meanest eyes I can conjure up and wait for him to finish. He clamps his lips shut and growls.

"What the hell, Skeeter?" he gruffs and spits out some grass in his mouth. "Are you on their side?"

"You are drunk." I shrug. "You won't stop fighting them even when I ask you nicely to stop fighting them. You knocked off Officer Bobby's glasses and almost broke them. Whose side would you choose?"

"Not theirs."

"If they get up, will you stop fighting?" I ask him. "Please. For me."

"Yeah, whatever."

"Will you let him up, please?" I look at the skinny cop and he is wary. I wiggle his glasses at him like I'm wiggling a meat bone at a snarling beagle. I can tell he thinks it's some kind of trap. I'm scared to death Boone is going to jump up and start waling on one of the cops while Bobby nods to the chubby cop. They both shift while I'm staring with eyes dead-set on Boone's glassy gaze at me.

"Please, please, please—"

"What are you doing?" Boone snaps at me. I don't realize I'm tilting my head downward and praying hard to God that Boone doesn't act like an ass and turn on me.

"I don't know, praying you aren't going to be an ass about this."

"Can you pray for that?" Boone mumbles. I don't answer and the cops stand up and Boone rises with a drunk waver. I walk over so I'm right in front of him and try to touch his wrist like it might tame him, keep him from biting at the cops. He grumbles and pushes my hand away. "Go away, Skeeter."

Dutch picks up Boone's hat and I don't move. I'm figuring Boone's not going to step around me and hit the cops who are standing with arms crossed to my left.

"Boone," the chubby cop says. "We got calls from ten different folks about you up here shooting. You've got to stop. Old Missus Richey, she called about seventy times."

"I'm not leaving yet," Boone grouses. He won't look at Dutch who is pale and a bit tired-looking.

"You ain't driving. We'll have your truck towed."

"I'll stay with him and drive him home," I suggest. "Problem solved."

I don't think anybody agreed with me except Boone who I believe just thought I'd walk off into the sunset after they left. When I hand Bobby his glasses he thanks me with a smile while he fixes his hair with a flip of his hand. He pulls me aside, tells me his sister heard about Lexie being born in a barn and she had a folding playpen I could keep. He coaches baseball and there's a couple moms who were talking about dropping some baby stuff off at the station for him to bring to me. He also told me Dutch thought it would be nice if he took me on a date. He kind of laughs and rolls his eyes. Then he shrugs and says we could go out for coffee or something to make the old guy happy. I'd nodded, didn't think much more about it except to make a mental note to growl at Dutch for trying to fix me up.

Dutch makes Boone give me his shotgun and his truck keys which I'm dangling in one hand and holding Lexie in the other. Then he'd shoved the car seat into Boone's truck and gotten a couple plastic grocery bags from under the seat of his truck and cleaned up the glass on the headstones.

"You need to forgive and forget," Dutch mutters before he leaves. "Sitting up here taking out your grief ain't going to fix nothing, boy, and it ain't going to bring her back, you get that? She's gone and it hurts me to come here. I don't want to do it."

Boone deadpan stares at Dutch until the older man just turns and shakes his head at me.

"Don't let him drive," he advises me with a wag of his wrinkled finger. "Don't let him shoot nothing, you hear me? And don't think using this as an excuse to getting out of finding another pair of shoes for those feet is going to work. Them boots is ugly."

I watch Boone look down at my boots. He doesn't say anything until Dutch's truck grunts and grinds back down the hill.

"Go for a walk. Leave me alone, alright?" Boone swipes the grass from his hair and shoves his hat on. He swaggers off toward the headstone. He kicks at one of the ten empty beer bottles laying in the grass and almost falls on his rear. I watch him go and plop down on the ground and hold Lexie in my lap. I think about Chase because it is all I ever do. I think about my guitar and I wonder where it is right now. I miss my guitar more than I miss Chase. Since I was ten, it has been my best friend. I don't know if I even feel like playing it anymore. Like the songs always wandering around my head, the incredible urge I always felt to play and write and sing have faded away like steam off a pot of tepid water.

I don't know how long I sit there in the grass before I get up and walk over to Boone. I can see him hunkering down against a random gravestone facing the one he was shooting the bottles off of with his arms hooked around his knees. He's over drunk-mean and I think he's at drunk-sad because Boone's hand comes up and he's pinching his temples.

He's got swagger like my oldest brother, Matthew. And he's got it coming and going. It's the way he walks, his strut, and the way he throws his head back. Like my oldest brother, too, he's all tough-acting on the outside, stoic and maybe a bit haughty. On the inside, he was always trying to catch the flies on the windows and release them outside before someone took a flyswatter to them.

"Go away, Skeeter."

I sit down anyway like I used to do with Matthew when he was in a bad mood. Boone uses the F-word and tells me to get away again. I start to reach my hand out to push on his shoulder and he looks up and gives me holy hell with wet, mean eyes. "I swear to God, I'll—" he stops and shakes his head. So I reach up and count to five and hope he isn't swearing to God he'll hit me. Matthew never did. He just put up with me. Then I rest my hand on his shoulder.

I stare at the headstone with dried rivulets of beer draining down its front. It's a pretty marble stone about knee-high. It says: Charlene Martinez. That's all. He doesn't push my hand away so I leave it there and give him a pat once in a while. Then after about five minutes, I get a little closer and push up next to him like I'd do after I'd warmed Matthew up a bit. It's like taming a wild kitten. I don't know if he's going to scratch me or not so I got to do it in little steps. I get twenty minutes of Boone putting up with me pressed up to his side. Each time I try to peer up at his face, he tells me I'm going a little too far. "I'm here forever. Or as long as you need me," I tell him. Then Lexie gets fussy and starts making her grumpy hungry whimpers.

"I'm not sure which one of you is more annoying,"

Boone finally says. He reaches out, gives me a little push so I scoot away. He's looking at me a bit sheepishly. He's got red eyes and is probably a bit more sober. I just get up and sit down under a tree and nurse Lexie a little farther away.

It looks like it's going to rain again. I feel a breeze sweeping up from the valley below. I put Lexie in her car seat in the middle so she can sleep. I sit on the hood of the truck and stare up at the sky. Boone finally comes over and wiggles his hand in front of me. "Give me the keys, I'll take you back to Dutch's."

"No." I shake my head and push myself to my feet. "I told them you wouldn't drive."

"Oh, come on, I'm not that drunk, really." He rolls his eyes and doesn't think I see him stagger right then.

"Yeah, I don't think so." I hop down from the hood and he lurches forward.

"Nobody drives my truck but me."

I honestly think he thought he could snatch them out of my hand. I snap my wrist back and realize he isn't kidding. The next thing I know, he's chasing me around the truck and, in other circumstances, I could outrun a drunk idiot. But I'm still sore from having a baby and there's no way I can stay on one side of the truck while he wheedle-sneaks around the other trying to catch me.

"Don't do it."

He recognizes my trick even before I jump into the driver's side seat just as he rounds the trunk. I've got just enough time to lock the doors.

"I did it, butthead," I call back, flip him my middle finger. He's cupping his hand at the window. He is like the body-double of Matthew, all threatening and like a big bully. The black clouds are bunching up on the horizon and I sit back in the seat and try to figure out where to stick the key into the ignition.

"What are you doing?"

"I'm driving the truck back to Dutch's."

"Not without me."

I don't tell him that I don't know how to drive. "Then you have to ride," I tell him. "And you have to be nice to me."

"Christ almighty!" He twists his head around, bangs his fist on the hood of the truck. "Dammit, Skeeter! This isn't funny. I'm not drunk anymore. It's getting ready to storm."

"I'll let you in if you promise to let me drive you home and you promise to be nice to me."

"I promise."

It's against my better judgement, but I flick the little bar that unlocks the door. As soon as I do, he opens the door wide and I see him reaching his hand into the driver's side to jerk me out. "Just so you know, you are the only person in the world right now I trust after getting dumped in a dirty motel by the only person I have ever loved. If you break your promise I will lose all faith in mankind."

"You're kidding me, right?" Boone stops, lets his hand drop from my elbow. I'm leaning away from him toward Lexie's car seat and I shake my head back and forth.

"No."

I turn the key and the engine starts. But I hold it too long and it makes a screaming grind like I'm killing the engine.

"Cripes, what are you doing? You're going to kill her."

"Driving." My words guilted Boone into reluctantly sitting in the passenger seat of his truck. He's got these amazing eyes with thick, black lashes. The retinas are blue, but like the color of a sunset sky with little orange flecks. When he's freaking out, they turn a deeper sapphire and almost the color of dark blue jeans. I recognize this now as occurring when he was gently helping Lexie come into this world. He looked up at me and I had my focus dead set on him for confirmation I wasn't going to die. He's wearing the freaking out blue-jean color now while I shove the truck into drive and hit the gas.

Chase always told me I know enough about driving a car to be dangerous. He's right. The truck shoots forward and I miss Mary Greene's tombstone by maybe three inches. "Oops, that was close." While Boone is holy-shitting with his face nearly slapping the windshield, I kick it into reverse and we speed about thirty miles an hour backward and skid to a halt sideways between two mausoleums.

"Hang on, don't freak out. I can do this. I rode a bike once," I tell him calmly with a wave of my hand. "Put your seatbelt on."

"You're kidding me, right?" He asks me while I hit the gas and zoom forward sixty feet. I shove my foot on the brakes and skid sideways in the gravel. Click. His seatbelt is on and he's holding on to the handle of the door like he's on a roller coaster ride at an amusement park. "You better be playing with my head, Skeeter, this isn't funny." His hat's sideways on his head when I gun the engine and take off in a beeline toward the gates.

"I think I can do this," I say more to myself than Boone while I shoot sideways.

"You—think?" Boone huffs loudly right before the back tires fishtail twenty feet and straighten out only moments before I careen through the cemetery gates and get spit out on the Main Street. There's a dip between the gravel road of the cemetery where it connects with the black asphalt of the main road. I hit it so hard, the front end flies up a foot into the air before I jerk the steering wheel to the right.

"Oh, yeah!" I start to exclaim right before I see the semi-truck barreling straight toward us.

"Wrong side! You're on the wrong side of the—!"

I'm not really good with the steering wheel. There is a certain precision and patience involved with not turning it too far to the left or right. I can't seem to get that down, never have. I'm just not very patient. I suppose, however, when there's a thousand ton truck barreling raw fuel in a tank behind it from Texas straight at me and close enough to make out the type of tire it uses, there's a certain learning curve involved. I gun the engine, slip to the left and I think I hear Boone screech like a cat with its tail stepped upon. I'm not sure. It might have been the semi-truck brakes squealing or the tires of Boone's trucks screaming while they rode the guardrail on the wrong side of the road.

I finally straighten it out and my heart is racing faster than the ninety-four miles an hour I was going before I take my right foot gingerly off the accelerator.

"Holy hell, that was cool!" I'm screaming and Boone's hard-staring at me like he's riding with a crazy woman. It's difficult steering and braking and accelerating all at once. Then, I realize I am perfectly placed between the yellow lines and I just want to tell Chase to shove it up his ass because, by God, I'm driving and he said I'd never be able to do it.

"Skeeter, you realize you're driving like you're in England, right?"

"Huh?"

"You've got to be on the right side of the road," Boone tells me as calm as a lake on a dry, windless day.

"You're on the left side. It's the wrong side."

"Oh." I hear the *tap, tap-tap, tap* of his fingers on his leg. He's nervous. So I end it in a *pat-pat* on the steering wheel and a jam of my foot on the brakes with a beep of the horn. I see him pause right before he automatically makes the *tap, tap-tap, tap* again. I wait him out, hit the brakes gently then tap the horn. "We got a beat, dude," I say. I look over at Boone, just flash a quick grin at him. I'm expecting him to just lay me flat with angry words. I'm thinking he's going to grab the steering wheel and make me pull over. But he's just laughing. I mean, the boy is laughing so hard, he's holding his belly and he's keeled over in his seat.

"What?" I ask, trying to slip over to the right side of the road without overcompensating and hitting the guardrail.

"You're frigging crazy, you know that, right?" he tells me, trying to catch his breath. "You've never driven anything in your life, have you?"

I just roll my eyes. "A bike. I told you I rode a bike. Well, it was a tricycle when I was two or three."

"And I'm afraid to tell you this, but you're going the wrong direction to Dutch's."

CHAPTER 6
I'M OUT OF HIS COMFORT ZONE. IMAGINE THAT.

I know Dutch is standing outside my door tonight in the darkness and while I am laying in the bed. It is a long time past midnight. I fell to sleep at eleven-thirty and although it seems only seconds ago, I feel like I have fallen into a deep sleep. I'm woozy and muddled. Lexie is pressed against my side, her soft breaths tell me she has been asleep for a while. I know she nurses for at least a half hour after I fall to sleep and she breaks away from my breast and suckles air for the next two hours. So I'm guessing it is maybe one or two in the morning.

It is almost like I sense him there. I awaken slowly and peer out of my eyes and into the murky darkness of the hallway outside my bedroom, feigning sleep. I see his shadow darker than the hall through the slits of my almost-closed eyes. I hear his breaths, low and even. I try to keep my own deep and easy. It is difficult because I don't know why he's there. Is he going to slide into bed next to me, touch me? Is he going to slip into the room with a knife and slit my throat?

Maybe neither. Maybe both. I want to think it is the former. It isn't the first time he's stood outside my door watching me sleep. At least a couple times a week, I awaken to him there. The house is quiet except for a box fan in the kitchen downstairs to pull in the cool air of night. Upstairs, it is only the sounds of crickets outside and maybe a truck or two going past the house once in a while.

I count the seconds. I think of five or six things I will do if he slips into bed beside me, tries to touch me with his hands in those little warm, secret places I don't want him to touch. Maybe he didn't do it last time. Maybe he will this time. It makes me quiver and a dribble of sweat forms at the nape of my already-hot neck. *Click-click.* Then, even before I grasp the shadow has eased into the darkness surrounding it, he is gone somewhere outside. I wonder if he isn't a vampire who wants to kill me in my sleep. Instead, out of kindness, he goes into his fields and takes a cow instead.

"Where do you go at night, Dutch?" I finally ask him the next morning at the breakfast table. I'm in a hurry. I want to go out and play with the microphone that I dragged out and stuck inside the double stall Dutch uses as a tack room. I wince a little, thinking he might use the butter knife in his hand to murder me for finding out some secret. He stops with it in mid-swipe over his toast. The butter sits there on the tip with little flecks of toast grit. I wonder if they'll find those little bits of butter and toast in my chest cavity when the coroner does an autopsy after my death. Then they'll know it was Dutch who killed me dead. God, maybe that's what he's preparing to do all along, steal Lexie!

"It's none of your business," Dutch tells me. He also tells me it's none of my business who Charlene Martinez is too. I like his kitchen. It has white wallpaper with little red cherries and red and white gingham curtains on the two windows. He also sighs and shakes his head. He tells me it'd be better if I heard it from him instead of the ugly stuff I'd hear about her in town.

"She was my little girl, Skeeter," he says a bit too softly while I set his plate down in front of him. He looks down at my feet. He bought me a couple pairs of jean shorts, two t-shirts, and a pair of cowboy boots at the hardware store. I got on the t-shirt and jean shorts. However, I'm still wearing my daddy's boots. He doesn't say anything about it. "She was a good little girl, just liked to hang around the wrong people. You get what I'm saying?"

"The wrong people like Boone?"

"Naw, Boone, he's alright. But I work for his daddy and right now, that means he's paying for the diapers your little baby is wearing and you want her to have clean ones, right? So that's enough. I'm not saying more. Did you get the stalls cleaned this morning?"

"I got ten of them," I tell him, roll my eyes. "You've got twenty-two horses out there."

"Well, get them done after breakfast." Dutch sighs deeply and rubs his belly. "So did that young Bel-Air police officer ask you anything—?"

"Like ask me out for a date?" I open my eyes wide to show Dutch I disapprove of his matchmaking skills. "You couldn't ask for two more different people, Dutch, and I'm not over Chase yet. So leave it be. I'm not doing it."

Jack is grunting a laugh looking back and forth between Dutch and me. I roll my eyes. Dutch nods his head toward the door. "Get and go. Do your work."

"Okay, if I do, can I ride a horse out in the barn?" I saw a sign out front of his farm when we pulled in the first day. It said: DEAD BROKE HORSES FOR SALE.

"Can you ride?" Dutch asks me. He points to me. "Are all your lady parts okay?"

"Oh, my God!" I feel my face turn ten shades of red. "Dutch! Don't ask me about my lady parts. They are fine."

"What you gonna do with the baby while you ride?"

"Same thing I do when I clean the stalls. I put her in her car seat and drag her around with me. But maybe you could watch her a half hour?"

"You want him to watch a baby?" Jack grunts. I look up at Jack who shows up every morning for my cooked breakfast. He's got a funny smile on his face like they are sharing a joke.

"Double that up, sweetie," he tells me. Then he acts like he can't eat all his breakfast and puts half of it—a scrambled egg, toast, and two pieces of bacon in a plastic container for lunch. I saw him eat it in the barn yesterday like one, big sandwich for a late lunch. So today, I slip a couple chocolate chip cookies in his bag along with a soda pop. I don't think Dutch pays him much to work with him. Jack's the one who works on all the horse's hooves and keeps them in horse shoes.

"So, can I ride one of the horses?" I ask him.

He laughs. "You ever ridden a horse before?"

"Yes." I open my mouth to press the issue, but I hear the front screen door opening. I watch Dutch cringe even before it slams hard against the frame. "Speak of the devil," Dutch says in a soft, gravelly voice.

"And he will appear," I finish for him just as Boone comes walking through the open doorway to the kitchen. He's wearing coffee-colored chaps and boots. They swish when he walks. Dutch chuckles.

"You look like a real cowboy, boy."

"I am a real cowboy, old man," Boone grunts. "But I'll be more than happy to quit being my dad's grunt cowboy because he doesn't trust anybody else to do the job. I'm sick of running to every God-forsaken town and picking cattle out of the woods and the fields because the rancher's too stingy to pay his boys to catch and corral them for the sale. I went out three times this week. Two times last week."

Dutch picks up his fork and starts to shove it into his eggs. "What you want for breakfast, boy? She's cooking."

"No. I'm afraid she'll poison it," he says matter-of-factly while he grabs a kitchen chair, swings it around and straddles it. "I already got poison ivy from clearing the back pasture fences yesterday." He holds up his arm and points to a couple of tiny red bumps on his elbow. He's got a bulge of muscle I am trying not to stare at. "I scratched at it all night." Holy hell, he looks like a picture from a cowboy magazine. His butt is like perfect sticking out of the chaps. He's got on a tight t-shirt and baby blue tight, torn jeans. They aren't the cheap kind of clothes from the mall, but the high end kind you have to order. *Yeah, Dutch, my lady parts are just fine*, I think. *At least, they are working now.* He takes off his hat, plops it down by his elbow.

"You got any good horses in?" Dutch asks Boone while he lets his fork trudge through a bowl of grits at his elbow. I'm half listening, half dozing. Lexie doesn't sleep at all at night.

"I got a few, why?"

"I'll trade you four for the girl."

I blink, look over at the two. They look serious. I squeeze my eyes together, try to see who smiles first. Neither even breaks a grin.

"I thought it was three the last time we bartered over her," Boone mutters. "In fact, I figured you'd be giving me horses to take her. She's scrawny and surly."

"That was before I knew she'd cook. That's worth at least one horse."

"I don't know. I'd think it was more like a pony. The eggs look mushy. She's three feet tall, half a regular girl."

"Hey," I grunt. "You're kidding, right?"

They all break out in laughter. Boone reaches out and knuckles me on the nose like I'm six years-old. "Yeah, half-pint, you're only worth an old donkey." Half-pint? What the hell? I cross my eyes, stick my tongue out at him.

"Why—" Boone leans forward. "Do you have a ring on your tongue?"

"Yeah, see?" I stick my tongue out again and waggle

it back and forth making a grunty *wa wa wa* exposing the little gold ball. "I got my tongue pierced, my eyebrow pierced, my nose pierced and one other part pierced, in a location that I won't discuss, that I took out right before I had the baby but will put back in soon," I tell him pointing to each piercing but the last. "Cool, huh?"

"No, not really," he tells me. "You were out of my comfort zone at tongue piercing. I just don't get—all that." He waves a hand at me and Dutch grunts a laugh. Then, Boone drags his gaze away with a scowl before he turns to Dutch. "There's Dog Brier growing everywhere on the hill between our properties, Dutch. I cleared out a bunch this morning. But it's like endless." He's got a fresh haircut and a bit of beard grizzle on his cheeks. "Can you send Jack out to clear the hill behind the barn up top? It just keeps coming back over the hollow from your side to my side." He smells of the good kind of sweat like he's been working outside.

Boone rests his elbows on the table and snatches at a toothpick between his lips. His arms are toned and tanned to a gentle burn. *Chase, frigging who?* I'm thinking right now because he doesn't look like the drunk dude I drove home yesterday or the one sitting with me on the couch. I don't usually like buff boys. They're arrogant and picky and spend more time at the gym and sports bars with other dudes than wanting to hang out with their girl. I always wonder if they're one step away from being fat four months into being married. But when they're toned from working on a farm, it throws a wrench in my thinking. He's throwing a wrench into my thinking. "You stay away from my truck." He jabs a finger at me, then turns to Dutch. "She's my baby. I don't want her hurt."

"Huh?" I sound like an idiot right then while I rip my eyes away.

"Stay away from his truck," Jack repeats through a bite of his toast. "You heard him."

"Dad says he wants as many boys as you can hire to get some cattle from Ben's stock house in Texas," Boone is telling Dutch. "He's taking them straight to Abe's for slaughter."

"So," I interrupt the conversation. "I asked if I could ride a horse. You're good if I take one out?"

"Sweetie," Dutch sighs, turns his attention partially to me. "If your lady parts are good to go, you can ride a horse."

"Oh, my God, Dutch," I groan, feel my face turn beet red again. "My lady parts are fine. Even the doctor says so. It is not to be discussed by anybody but me from now on."

"I wouldn't trust her with a horse, Dutch." Boone shakes his head, seems oblivious to the embarrassing part of the conversation. "She told me she could drive a truck. She about killed me."

"I never told anybody I could drive," I retorted.

"Like you know'd how to drive a truck?" He laughs heartily and then Jack laughs along. "Because Boone, he said you don't got no license and you about killed him bringing him over here. How can you be as old as you are and not drive?"

"I don't know," I say with a sigh. "I ran away from home a day after my fifteenth birthday. Nobody ever bothered to show me."

They all three snap their eyes to me. I think I could have jumped off the roof right then and gotten the same shocked gazes.

"Where'd you come from, Skeeter?" Dutch sighs. "You ever call your daddy just to let him know you're alive?"

"That's enough," I spit back his own words he told

me when I asked him a question. "I'm not saying more."

There's a dark-haired girl in Boone's truck when I walk past to the barn. She's got earplugs in and she's got her head bent listening to music, I suppose. She looks a little too young to be his girlfriend; I'd say she's about thirteen or fourteen. She looks up when I pass and I see her eyes follow me. I'm lugging Lexie's car seat carrier in one hand and the microphone stand in the other. The car seat bangs off my leg each step and it weighs a ton. The girl in the truck's got the same dumbfounded, wide-eyed expression the guy in the feed store had the day I drove with Dutch to town.

I leave the microphone in the tack stall and find the horse Dutch told me to use. He's a gelding about thirty years-old, I'm guessing. When I saddle him up, he falls asleep. I settle Lexie outside Dutch's riding arena and take him around for a half hour.

"He gave you Old Blue to ride?"

I look up and acknowledge Boone with a nod. "I suppose his name should be *Almost Dead* Blue," I retort.

"That's funny. I've got to say, I'm surprised you've been on a horse."

"And why's that, Boone?" I ask a little flatly. I know his answer even before he says it.

"You know," he waves a hand at me, doing that dipping thing with his head. "All this."

I tug the horse around, pull him up beside him.

"No, I don't know, Boone," I tell him snidely. "What is it about me that doesn't fit in with your idea of what cowgirl is?"

"It's more like what *normal* is. Where do you want me to start?"

I get it now. He's a prick when he's not drunk or

sitting next to Dutch. I'm guessing he has a whole bunch of rich friends he hangs out with at the gym and a sports bar in Nashville. He's got a drop-dead gorgeous girlfriend and daddy's money lining his pocket. I know his type. And I know his scathing remark is coming.

"Your hair. You keep it tied up in two thingies in the back and you've got pink stuff on it. I don't know any girls that do that here. You've got a silver band on your eyebrow and lip and a tattoo on your arm. A tongue ring. It's gross."

"That's not what my last boyfriend used to say." I take out my tongue and wiggle it with a spicy waggle of my shoulders. "He used to beg me—"

"Again, that's gross. Don't want to hear what you and your old beau used to do. Where was I? You wear bright red lipstick and I don't even know where to start with your clothes. You drum out all your words with your fingers on the table like your life's some kind of song. You're just out of place. You don't fit into the picture."

Ouch. Well, that pretty much sums up how I feel about myself every dark night I spend staring at the ceiling and wondering why I turned out like this.

"Go away," I tell him. My voice is hoarse because my feelings are hurt. He sounds like my daddy. And my brothers. And Chase. It makes me want my guitar so badly, my heart almost aches. I don't even have that anymore to strum out a few notes, come up with a song, and erase the hurt away.

"Your loss." He pushes away from the fence and he stops and looks down at Lexie. "I just think you'd be prettier if you didn't look like—that." Then, he snaps his gaze up to me. "Can I hold her?"

"Have at it," I tell him. "You can watch her while I put the horse away." I don't feel like riding anymore. I take the horse into the barn, unsaddle him and put him back in his stall. When I come out, Boone's rocking Lexie back and forth in one arm and tickling her with his fingers. It's almost comical because he's so big and she's so little.

He doesn't even look up which makes me wonder if he is not in love with my baby. It's like he just can't take his eyes off her. "She's so pretty." He points to her, gives her belly a little tickle, and smiles at her with big teeth. I step up in front of him. "Oh, she just smiled at me," he exclaims. "Holy shit! When did she start that?"

"You're kidding me, right?" I almost groan the words, looking from him to her and then back to him again. I did catch the faint grand finale of her first grin. And it isn't like the bored one she gets right after she eats or poops. "You didn't get her first smile, did you? Damn, Boone." I narrow my eyes at him and then at her. "That's just wrong." I'd been bending over backwards trying to get a real smile since I read online she was just about ready for that tiny milestone.

"No, maybe it wasn't," he backtracks really quickly. But he only looks toward me a second before he turns his gaze to Lexie again. And what the heck? He's smiling at her because she's burst into another toothless grin at him.

They flirt it up ten minutes before I hear the impatient honk-honk-h*ooonk* of a truck.

"That'd be for me," Boone sighs. "She refuses to get out of the truck. They're a lot easier at this age." He gives Lexie a little kiss on the forehead that's cute as hell, then stuffs her back into my arms.

"Daddy! Would you come on? I'm sick of sitting in the—"

I try not to appear surprised when the girl from the truck comes stomping around the side of the barn and stops short of the far side of the arena. *Daddy?* Her lips are pursed, her eyes teenager angry. She is staring straight at Boone. When her eyes veer to the right, she sees me and her mouth just stays open like she's going to say something and she stops cold. She giggles. "Oh." Then just as quickly as she appeared out of nowhere, she just darts off back into the shadows toward the truck.

"What was that?" Boone seems genuinely uncertain. He turns to me like I've got an answer. "That was just weird even for her."

"Ha, you got my kid's first smile. I got your kid's first crazy," I pipe up. He just stares at me curiously.

"I should go."

Chapter 7
Picking up a guy at the crazy filly and getting drunk-kissed at a stop sign

Dutch drives to Texas on a Friday morning to pick up the cattle. It's a two day trip. He's got fifteen men and three women he hires to drive big semi-trucks down south and bring them back to Tennessee. They start showing up at three in the morning, slamming truck doors, banging boots, and making laughter and chatter noise downstairs. It wakes up me and Lexie. When I make my way downstairs, Dutch points to the kitchen and tells me to make them all breakfast.

He seems surprised I can cook for twenty. He doesn't say anything contrary, just watches me above his reading glasses while he's sipping his coffee and bouncing Lexie over his shoulder. I'm slapping scrambled eggs on every plate and bowl he's got in the cupboard, cooking the bacon without burning a single slice (except for Jack's because he likes it overdone and extra crispy). I've got sausage and biscuits. And grits, I think I make two gallons. I like it with shredded cheese piled on top.

"Clean this up. Muck the barns. Feed my cats, my dogs, and my horses. If anybody calls to buy a horse, tell them I'll be back on Sunday." He stops, rolls his eyes. "And no dragging out that damn mic and singing until you get the chores done." I roll my eyes. "Yeah, you don't think I know that's what you been doing most of every day? Everybody in this county can hear you screaming in that barn."

I've yet to see more than a handful of people buy a horse here or even knock on the door. But I've heard Dutch at the fence telling folks he doesn't have any horses. When they point out the little sign he has out front, he walks out and takes it down for a couple days like maybe they just weren't the right kind of folks to sell a good, broke horse to. All the horses in the barn look like they've been ridden hard, then dropped at Dutch's back step.

Still, I nod. He slides on his work hat. It's the cowboy hat with grungy brown along the front where he's worked it back and forth on his head with dirty hands so long it's stained.

"How'd you feed them all in thirty minutes?"

"I had thirteen brothers. No sisters."

"Um," he sniffs a laugh and starts out the door before he hesitates, turns. "Oh, yeah, there's a list on the counter to keep you busy and out of trouble. Make sure it's done before I get back."

The list has eighteen chores on it including cleaning the cat pans and sweeping the floor. I grimace at the thought, but I do as I'm told. It's how I was raised. However, of the countless things he has told me to do, the one thing Dutch doesn't tell me to do is take over babysitting his neighbor's son who is stupid-drunk at the Crazy Filly Tavern across town.

I get the call at eleven-fifteen. It is Tiffany Crider, one of the bartenders at the bar. She asks for Dutch and tells me Rod Elkhart and one of his friends are three seconds from murdering Boone Martinez over Rod's girlfriend flirting it up with Boone. She tells me Rod is like a Sasquatch, big and mean and he just got out of jail. He's drunk and started looking for a fight the second he got into the bar. They had Boone in a back room trying to sober him up long enough for Dutch to get there.

Since Dutch isn't here, I bundle up Lexie and we take Dutch's truck. I drive real slow and only accidently slide through one stoplight in town.

The Crazy Filly is packed full on Friday nights. I load my back pockets with the little pink stun gun Chase bought me for Christmas and a lime green bottle of Toxic Twelve Bear Deterrent I used to spray off dogs that chased us on his motorcycle. It's dark and crowded and smells like old beer and stale cigarettes. I'm carrying Lexie on my shoulder and I'm getting those same odd stares I seem to get in this stupid town.

"I'm Skeeter," I tell the girl at the bar. She is rubbing a wet rag on the wooden counter and stops mid-swipe, seems to latch on to my face far too long. "I'm here to pick up Boone."

"Ha ha, did Dutch send you in here as a joke?" Tiffany is bleach-blonde, thin and pretty. She eyes me up and down. "You're kidding me, right?"

"No."

"Just you?"

"Yes."

"Where's your backup?" Tiffany is looking over my shoulder. "What do you weigh, a hundred pounds? Boone's drunk as hell and ready to fight, baby. There's no way you're dragging him out of here by yourself." She shakes her head. "He broke a half a rack of beer glasses. You going to pay for that? Because he isn't leaving until it's paid."

I grit my teeth and dig out the fifty bucks Dutch gave me for emergencies. "I got fifty bucks."

She holds out her hand, shakes her head. "I guess that'll do."

"Where is he?" I ask impatiently. I was hoping to stockpile the fifty bucks to add to the ten I got last week so I can try to find my guitar. Obviously, it isn't in the cards for me to sing ever again.

Lexie is four minutes from screeching because she likes the soothing grind of the truck and doesn't like it when it stops. I feel her body stiffening and she's making sneezy pre-cry sounds and squirming like a caterpillar caught in somebody's hand. Tiffany has a big bouncer named Paul escort me back through a dark hallway. He's joined by two other buff boys with what I call fake muscles. They're the kind you get from working out on exercise equipment and not by actually working a job like putting up a fence or digging a hole.

"Boone, he's in a time out," Paul tells me. "Just like my four year-old. Me and my wife, we set the kid on the bottom step at home when he's bad. We've got a special room for Boone for his time outs. You sure you're up for this? He's meaner than snot tonight."

Paul wiggles the door knob, bangs it with a fist. "Boone, you got company. You going to be a good boy?"

It is completely silent for a full thirty seconds. Then I hear the longest line of cusswords I've ever heard in my life. My face turns beet red while I look up at Paul. "I think he needs another hour or so," Paul says.

"I don't have time for that," I grump. Then I lean into the door. "Boone Martinez, I swear to God if my baby's first word is any of those you just mentioned loud enough for her to hear, I will personally beat you with a Louisville Slugger while you're asleep."

There is a long, drawn out silence on the other side of the door. I have to lean hard because there is a live band and the music is blaring so loudly, the walls are shaking.

"Skeeter? Is that you?"

"Yes."

"What—what are you doing here?"

"I'm picking you up because Tiffany called and said

you were stupid-drunk. Dutch went to pick up cows and he couldn't come. Can you please not fight and walk out to the truck with me? I've got Lexie and she's getting fussy."

"Okay."

I look up to Paul and the two other men behind him. They are looking guardedly right to left at each other and I can see they are suspicious.

"Can you please open the door?" I ask. Paul nods to the other bouncers and they look like they're getting ready to make a lunge on Boone when he comes out the door if they need to do it. Paul turns the knob, gingerly opens the door.

Cripes. Boone is just standing in the center of what appears to be a maintenance closet. There's a mop bucket in one corner and cleaning supplies on a raggedy gray, metal shelf. He looks beat to heck. He's got blood on his face and blood on his white shirt. His right eye is red-blue like he got full-out punched. He's wiping away the last remains of a bloody nose. I look him in the eyes and ask him if he's good to go. When Boone nods slowly, Paul leads us through the kitchen and out the back doors.

I should have asked the bouncers to walk us through the parking lot. I had to park far back on the old gravel. It's dark and there's people partying at their trucks. Boone is completely silent walking just a few steps behind me. I slow my steps so he comes up beside me.

"It wasn't me this time. I didn't see it coming—" he starts to say. I'm just turning my head to see him in the oozy darkness between the parking lot lights. Boone sees the shadow shift in front of us two seconds before I snap my head in the direction his suddenly startled eyes are staring.

"Boone, dude, you really didn't think you'd get out of there with the last punch, did you?"

It must be Rod Elkhart. Yeah, Tiffany is right. He's a Sasquatch. He's not really tall, but he's beefy and has wild-looking black hair stuffed up under a grungy-looking ball cap. And he's got these wild eyes that are showing whites. He's got a buddy with him that's like two times smaller and keeps rocking back and forth on his high top tennis shoes. The smaller guy's got his hands stuffed into his pockets and he's creepy-smiling me up and down.

"Who's this pretty little thing? I haven't had supper yet. I'm ready for an appetizer."

"Rod, bugger off. I'm leaving." Boone's got his hands out. "Leave her alone. You made your point."

"Yeah, that ain't gonna happen." Rod just gets this grin on his face. Then he turns to me. "I'm gonna beat up ol' Boone here, then I'm gonna have a picnic with you." He takes one step forward and brings back his arm. I mean, it happens like one-two-three and I think he would have waled on Boone bad if he wasn't drunk as or drunker than the man he was getting ready to beat. Being drunk, however, is only one of several disadvantages Rod Elkhart has this Friday night and on the exact second he leans over and wobbles a bit while his fist falters two steps behind Boone's step backwards. I close my eyes for just a moment, say a short prayer—*Dear God, please make this guy more stupid than me and drunker than Boone. And let the toe of my boot be like a well-spent arrow to a dead deer's heart.*

The second disadvantage is the toe of my daddy's boots careening between his legs and crunching hard on his scrotum. It is followed by the free hand I'm not juggling Lexie, grappling with the Toxic Twelve Bear Deterrent. In a flick of my wrist, I spray down Rod's face while he free falls backward like the tomcat that was clawing the front porch screen plunged hard to the floor after Dutch sprayed him with his green garden hose. I have to turn slightly as not to spray myself and my baby. However, after having taken on rottweilers, German shepherds, and an occasional yapping shih tzu going down country roads on Chase's Harley and being pursued by dogs has made me quite quick and adept at positioning the nozzle at just the right place to completely and precisely cover a one foot by one foot area without spraying myself. In fact, hitting Rod and his sidekick between chin and forehead is comparatively simple because I'm not moving sixty miles an hour and they aren't jumping up at me on all fours.

Rod hits the ground screaming and yowling with one hand grappling his crotch and the other trying to swipe away the spray that is dribbling like firewater in his eyes and mouth. The other guy is running circles until he smacks head-on into the rearview mirror of a big Chevy truck.

"Okay, about that picnic," I start to say to Rod who is beginning to rise. "I think I just rained on it, asshole." I think it's funny, but Boone is still standing in the exact place he was when I tugged out the bear spray, just staring dumbly at me.

I wheedle my other hand around and snatch out my tiny stun gun. I turn it on with a flick of my thumb, then I shove the end right into Ron's soft underbelly. He's screaming *damn you!* while Boone grabs my wrist and jerks me toward Dutch's truck.

"Ow, slow down," I hold out my hand, then stuff the bear spray back into my pocket. I look up, Boone's like blinking fast at me. "What's wrong?"

"Did you pray back there like two seconds before you waled on him with that spray?"

"Yeah, I prayed to God my foot made it to that dude's crotch."

"*Can*—you pray for *that*?"

"I suppose," I say. "I mean, I did. And my foot met its mark, right? Get in the truck."

"Oh, dear God, no." Boone stops short of the truck, turns his eyes toward me. "You're driving again."

"Uh huh," I tell him. "Yep, I am."

I take him to Dutch's. I realize, in retrospect, this has been an every Friday occurrence since I came here. Surely Dutch remembered. I'm not sure why he didn't mention it. The entire way back to the house, Boone is doubled over laughing. Then he goes from slap-happy to miserably blue. I stop at a stop sign in town and turn to ask him how long I'm supposed to wait there before I go again. Chase usually just slid on through. Boone's got the drunk-sleepy stare going on with a funny lop-sided grin right at me.

"Hello?" I ask him. "Did you hear me?" All of a sudden, he's shoved up against Lexie's car seat and looking over it and down at me.

"Just so you know, I'm going to kiss you."

"Oh, no, no, no—" I hold up a hand to feign him away. There's no way I want to kiss a guy who is drunk, much less one that's been kissing on other girls at a bar.

"Oh, yeah, yeah, yeah," he returns gruffly. I think he just thinks I'm being coy because he reaches over, snatches the back of my head and drags me toward him. I don't think in his drunk state that he realizes how short I really am and when he pulls me toward him and partially over the car seat, the toe of my boot comes off the brake and just as he lands a too-wet drunk kiss somewhere between the bottom of my nose and my upper lip, the truck lurches forward and there's a loud crunch on the front bumper.

"Shit, dude!" I hear a dog barking outside my open window and watch a light go on in a house to our right. I've completely taken out the stop sign. "What the hell are you thinking?"

"It was good, right?"

I glare at him while he wiggles his eyebrows. "I think I felt your tongue ring." He makes a face. "That was *different*."

"You wouldn't be saying that if it wasn't your tongue," I grouse at him. He's such an idiot.

"Huh?"

"I don't use it for French kissing, dumbass. It's made to rub the pecker. Good God, you didn't realize that's what my boyfriend was begging me for every night?"

"Every night? Oh. Really?"

"Oh, I'm going to so remind you of this tomorrow, Boone Martinez," I tell him while I jerk the truck into reverse and hear something underneath grind over the stop sign I just rolled over.

He seems to forget the drunk kiss. From the moment I pass through the front door, he follows me like a lost pup. He stuffs his hands into his pockets and I can hear his boots treading two steps behind me into the living room to put the truck keys in the drawer where Dutch hides them from me. Upstairs, he's like my shadow, looking out the window while I nurse Lexie and put her into the little drawer by my bed.

"That's her—crib?"

"Yeah, until I can afford one," I look up, tell him softly while he wavers at the window. "I'm saving up money from working for Dutch. He doesn't pay much. Not that I mind. Jack's been going to yard sales. He hasn't found any safe ones yet. He found a baby monitor, though. I can go all the way to the end of the first pasture and still hear her cry when she wakes up." I pick up the monitor, wiggle it with my hand. "You need to go to bed, Boone."

"You want to watch TV or something?"

"You wouldn't like what I like to watch. It's old sappy movies. The kind where they ride off into the sunset at the end. You know, happy ever after endings," I tell him. "I'm going to go ride one of the horse's around the riding arena while I can," I whisper. "It's too hard when Lexie's awake. Dutch put up a light for me so I can see."

"Where's your home, Skeeter?"

"Here for now. I don't know tomorrow—"

"No, where'd you come from?"

"Ohio, actually." I look up and smile. Boone is studying me hard, then turns away.

"You ever thought about going home?"

"I can't," I force a laugh. "You know, because of all this." I wave a hand in front of me like he did. I know I have a sour-sad expression. Boone is mimicking it.

"Is that how you know how to fight? Because home was so bad?" He asks me while I trod down the stairway toward the front door. "I mean, I get it. My dad's a real shit sometimes. We don't get along. We don't agree on anything."

"It wasn't bad like you think," I tell him, wiggling the baby monitor in my fingers. "I just had a strict daddy and thirteen brothers and I was right smack dab in the middle. If I didn't fight a little, I'd never eat." I pause at the door hoping he doesn't follow. He's stopped at the base of the stairway. He doesn't laugh, just looks sad. "That was a joke," I add. "The fighting for food. I just had to cook it all because I was the girl. Slave labor. Goodnight."

CHAPTER 8
LOSING A CONTEST IN A DARK BARN AIN'T SO BAD

Old Blue nickers when I come out to his stall and wake him up. He doesn't seem to care that it is midnight when I ride him. I suppose the peppermint treats in my pocket help to coerce his old butt out of the stall. I don't even bother to saddle him. I just ride him bareback around and around the arena. It's not as emotionally relaxing as strumming my guitar or standing on a bale of hay and singing with my new microphone, but it will do.

"Hey, you mind if I ride with you?"

"Are you going to try to drunk-kiss me again?" I ask Boone while he climbs up on the fence and sits there with his arms leaning on his knees. He turns, eyes the tack stall. He must be able to see inside, because he pokes his finger toward my microphone.

"Is that the old mic from Holy Unity Church? Did you steal it?"

"No, Dutch got it for me at Goodwill."

"You gonna sing in the choir or something?"

"No." I pass him and he doesn't say anything. When I pass him again, I pull up close, wiggle my toes at Old Blue's sides to get him to scoot up next to the fence. I stop there and Boone looks at me like he's not sure. "Hop on, Boone. Because if you thought you were going to saddle up a horse and ride it yourself, you're not. You're drunk. I might be able to get away with putting a dent in Dutch's truck. But if one of his horse's gets hurt, he'll never forgive me."

Boone doesn't hesitate. He throws a leg over and slips in behind me. The horse wiggles a moment at the new weight, then heaves a sigh and relaxes. I guess when I used to ride like this with my little brothers, we didn't sit so close. Then again, I guess we did. I just didn't think about it. But sitting there with Boone's warm body up tight against my back and his hands resting lazily on my hips just reminds me of not being with Chase when the lights went out at night, me on my side and his chest pressed to my back and his arms wrapped around my shoulders spooning me.

"You still miss him?" Boone asks me. "The guy that left you."

"Yeah, I'd be lying if I said I didn't. You still miss her?"

"Her?" He touches that scar beneath his eye when he says that. I am getting a good idea the girl left more than emotional scars with Boone.

"The girl—Charlene. The one you were shooting bottles off her grave."

"Yeah. Everybody looks at me like I'm crazy for missing her. I should let her go."

"Why? How'd she die?"

"Nobody's told you?"

"No." I crane my neck, peer upwards at him. "All's I know is that Dutch said she was his little girl and he looked like the last place he wanted to be that day I drove you home was that cemetery. And you were out there shooting beer bottles off her grave."

"I don't know." Boone shrugs. "Ask Dutch."

"No, I want to hear it from you."

"I don't feel like it, Skeeter." He reaches around, slips his hands on the reins and whoas the horse. "I'm starting to get sober. It's time for me to go." I can feel him shift to slide off.

"So do you still love her or are you just angry at her for leaving you?" I ask him quickly.

He offers up a long sigh while I catch his hand. "What do you mean?"

"Well, I'm starting to realize that at one point, I might have loved Chase. If you would have asked me three weeks ago, I would have told you he broke my heart worse than Dutch's old, mellow horses are broke to ride. It was more that he took care of me, I guess, like a husband. But the longer I'm away from him, the more I'm realizing I'm missing my guitar more than I'm missing him."

Boone is quiet for a moment, then he laughs softly. "That sounds like a sad country song. Why do you miss your guitar?"

"Yeah, it was kind of the only thing I had left of my family," I sigh. "Well, except my daddy's boots." I huff a laugh, point to my right boot. "My mama gave the guitar to me when I was five against my dad's wishes. There was a fight over it. She left. So, I guess it brought my mama and me together, then tore us apart." I shrug it off. "Whatever. It's just the day Chase left me in the parking lot, he pawned it off for the motel room."

Boone doesn't get off the horse, gives him a gentle nudge with his boots. He's quiet for the longest time while we ride around and around the arena. I feel his arms wrap around my waist and I lean back against him. His chest is warm against my back.

"So, I'll let you feel me up if you tell me something about yourself," I tease him. But before I can laugh like it's a joke, Boone blurts out: "My name's Boone Luis Martinez. I live at 4452 Bel-Air Hollow Lane. Bel-Air—"

And dang it if his hand doesn't slip up from the reins and right up under my shirt. I yelp. He laughs. "Holy shit, you're fast," I grunt and catch his hand with my elbow right as it gets to my bra. I'm really surprised, didn't expect he'd really do it.

"Aw, c'mon, Skeeter," he mewls. "I did exactly what you said. I told you something about me."

"Okay, that's a start, but you didn't let me finish." I sneak in, use my free hand to push his hand down three inches. "It's a game. I'm the teacher. You're the student. I'll ask the question. If you answer it properly, you'll get rewarded."

"And if I don't?"

"I'll spank you."

He doesn't say anything. Then Boone starts laughing again.

"What?"

"You understand that spanking's not a bad thing, right?"

I look up, give him a long and drawn-out eye roll. He's got this funny cockeyed grin on his lips.

"Why's your face red, Skeeter? Did I already screw up your game rules? Maybe you're not ready for this—"

"The doctor said I was just fine—" I say, waggling my head snottily. He did. But, I think I'm going to die right then when I spout that out like a pup who yaps impulsively when she sees a meaty bone all by itself and then realizes there are other pups around that will steal it. I grasp up to this point, I'm teasing and he's not. I see him latch on to my words like my rival pup sneaking in and snatching at that meaty bone as if my intention was to share it.

"Okay, then, how about I'll tell you something about me. You tell me something about you. Whoever tells the most, wins. And winner takes all." He laughs, returns my eye roll. He's right, I can feel my cheeks burning. Then he loses the expression, nibbles on his lip. "Don't make me do this."

"Do what? Open up a bit?"

"Yeah."

"Okay," I answer, shrugging it off. "I'm too tired to play anyway. It's late."

I'm the one who brings my leg up over the horse's neck and slides off. "Hop off," I tell Boone. "So I can put him away." I *am* too tired. I think for just a second, I just wanted to prove to myself I wasn't worth getting dumped in the middle of nowhere even if it was just a stupid one night stand.

"Don't be mad." Boone slips off the horse, lands both feet on the ground. He adjusts his hat. "I just don't like to talk about stuff."

I tug the horse and turn, snatch up the baby monitor. Then I walk toward the barn door.

"So what's your story, huh?" he spits out resentfully three steps behind me when I swing open the door to the stall and give Old Blue a little push to go inside. "It's not like you aren't hiding stuff, *Skeeter*. I don't even know your real name. I know two private detectives were asking questions in town about you. What's up with that?" When I don't answer, he sniffs a laugh. "Yeah, see, you're a hypocrite. It's okay for you to hide stuff. It isn't okay for me—"

I turn on my boots. "You're right." I bob my head up and down, lock the stall door. "You're right, Boone. Just drop it."

"So that's it. You're just walking away."

I throw my arms out to my sides. "Yes. We both don't want to get to know each other. Fine. It's not worth getting hurt. I get that. The heart can only get banged up—"

"Baby, my heart is dead broke. There isn't anything

left there to fix, if that's what you're trying to do." Boone snickers a haughty, sarcastic laugh while he steps in front of me. Great, here comes the mean, after drunk and before hangover kind of drunk. "Ask every girl that I dated and tried to fix me. And there's been a lot. They'll all tell you the same thing. I'm dead inside."

"Cool, well you keep being dead inside." I turn, bring my hand out on his chest and push my way past him. Then I stop two steps away. I point a finger at him, wink, and click my tongue. "It looks good on you with all the black and blue and whatever cowboy-hat thing you're trying to put on to hide those scars inside and out. I'm sure those fat-assed, big -titty, fake cowgirls shaking it across the crappy floor at the bar don't see right through you like I do. Because I just don't get the wearing the hat and driving the big truck without really being the cowboy," I tell him, feeling chafed. "Besides, I could give a rat's ass about fixing you. I'm not that needy. I just thought it'd be fun. But if I ever get to the point I've got to stoop low enough to *use* something broken because I can't get the thing that's in one piece, I'll keep you in mind. Maybe." I look up to the ceiling and the yellow lights, rub my chin reflectively. "Naw, I won't."

I flick off the lights, leave him in the dark. I know what he's thinking while I walk past the fence. I'm a big joke. I'm the girl whose boyfriend doesn't even care enough about her to even drop her off at a homeless shelter. Well, screw him. I don't need a guy around.

"I was a sophomore in high school when she got pregnant. She was a senior getting ready to go to college. I was fifteen. We got married, tried to play house but it was hard." Boone is standing at the barn door when I stop with my back to him. And yeah, he tapped that scar when he said it. "Charlene. She was always going home because we'd get into fights about stupid stuff like her not being able to go to college. That's where she was when she had the baby, pissed off and her dreams broken. A week later, she dropped Cheyenne off at my house and said she just needed to get out, get away with her friends. It wasn't her friends. It was a twenty-five year-old guy she'd been seeing. They got into a wreck. She died. End of story. Chey's with me."

I can't see him well when I turn. The arena lights don't shine out into the front of the barn. I don't know quite what to say so I don't.

"That's it. Say something. You could have pulled up an old Bel-Air Tribune and gotten the same information."

"Damn, some guys will do anything for a handful of titty," I say.

"You're nuts," he says dully. He is making his way across the ten steps to the fence where I'm standing. I think he's going to pass me, my head is already turning as if I'm going to follow his shadow all the way to the house. Instead, he stops, turns so he's facing me.

"I loved her. Now I hate her," he says it so softly the gentle wind almost takes his words away. I guess I never expected him to reach out his arm and roll it across my cheek before he slips it behind my head and pulls me close. He kisses me. It is soft and sweet and gentle. It's wet and tastes like beer and it makes my tummy whip and snap and jerk even while he leans back a bit.

I'm thinking holy hell, I can't breathe because I'm holding my breath. "She made me feel used, worthless." He kisses me again, this time long and hard. He's so tall, he has to bend at the knees to kiss me. His hand is cupping my face, his eyes looking down sleepily at me. "I don't think Chey's my daughter. I think she's his," he tells me, kissing me on my cheeks. I feel his hand slipping underneath my t-shirt, his fingers tickling along my sides and making me want to giggle. I don't. "I don't care, Skeeter. It just worries me Chey will know the truth and think I don't love her."

I'm scared. I realize it when he slips his fingers past my bra. It's not a pretty lacy one, but a plain tan and ugly one from the dollar store in Denton. And my underpants, I don't even want to go there. Same store. Kid's aisle because they came in sets of five and they were cheaper. I think they have little kittens on them. "Charlene left me with her mess. I think Dutch figured that out a few years ago when Chey started looking more like the other guy. Dutch really doesn't have anything to do with her. I think he feels guilty because he knows the truth." He pulls his hand from my t-shirt. I think he's probably realized his mistake, he's backing out. Not so. He snatches the bottom of my t-shirt and tugs it over my head. Then, he slips his hand behind my back, wiggles his fingers like a magician and presto! My bra unsnaps. He shit-eating-grins like he's a frigging four year old that just figured out how to climb to the cupboard and sneak out the cookies. "Pretty good, huh?"

"Yeah, I—"

"Hush, I'm not done. I'm willing to risk it all. I'm going for broke." He doesn't fumble around. His fingers are playing on my breasts, caressing the nipple. Gentle. Just enough to make it hard. "I don't like thinking all women are like her." Boone kisses me again. He slips his hand down my side, let's his forefinger catch on the waist of my shorts. Then he slides it around slowly until he gets to the button in front. "But I do think that." He flicks the button between finger and thumb, lets his forefinger run down, tugging the zipper open with it. "I think you're like that—"

"We aren't—all like that."

"Like her? Maybe. Maybe not," he tells me while he slides my shorts down. I feel them slither down my thighs along with the warmth of his palm. "I haven't been proven wrong yet. You leave. You use. I take and take until there's nothing left to take. So I go up to the cemetery and I shoot beer bottles off her headstone. Because she was drinking the night they wrecked. He was drinking the night they wrecked. You know how I know they were drunk?" He turns slightly to expose his right eye, the scar beneath. "Because he almost killed me because of it. So I go to the bars to forget I used to be able to see out of both eyes. Now, it's only one. It helps me forget I was going to a college far away from my dad in California and I couldn't. I ended up going to a stupid community college two towns over so my parents could help me raise her." I feel him tug on my panties. I'm wondering if he's waiting for me to stop him. But he's tasting my neck, tickling it with his tongue. His breaths are warm. I reach up my hand and gently push on his own so he tugs them down, feel them tickle to my knees. "I pick up girls and some, I let them give me blowjobs in the backs of their cars. I'm bored with it." I snap my eyes open, look up at him. My hand freezes. His hand does not. It slides along my arm, tickling to the cleft of my elbow. "Like you. Like now. Maybe. Maybe not."

I see him reading my eyes. I know he can't. It's too dark. What's wrong with me? I don't want him to stop. His harsh words are so contradictory to the gentle way his hands are opening me. That place just below my belly button is burning, begging me to pretend he's not saying those words. *Just do it. It'll feel so good.* I know I twitch when his hand pauses just between my thighs. I'm scared it's going to hurt. But oh-my-God, I'm about to burst. My breaths are in puffs, his cool fingers to my warm flesh. Crap, I'm shaking. I feel Boone lean forward so his hand rests on the fence for support, while his other lifts me up on to him. I let him. "So who wins this game, me or you, Skeeter? Me? Because if it's winner takes all, I'm doing it right now." It's the first time he's paused long enough for me to actually play the game, to dole out some personal proof that I'm broken too. And, I can't.

So, "You win," I say. "Please be gentle. I'm scared."

"Okay." And he kisses my head, then lets me slide down, slowly, gingerly to the warm place between my thighs while he rocks me back and forth. "Tell me if you need to—"

"No, don't stop." I groan when I feel it. I've never done that before. He's saying *Skeeter, oh-shit, Skeeter,* really softly in my ear. It tickles and I get the added bonus of chills right then. But him saying my name like Chase used to say it makes me a little queasy. So I sigh: "It's Waylon, Boone," I correct him so softly I'm not sure if he can hear. But when I look up, he's looking intently in my eyes.

"What—what did you say?"

"Waylon," I whisper. "That's my name."

CHAPTER 9
DALLAS DUNNE SHOWS UP IN BEL-AIR

It's a thing to go to Sunday morning breakfast at the Bel-Air All-Nighter Motel and Diner. Dutch has to get there by seven in the morning the day he comes home. He says if he doesn't get there before seven-fifteen, the early service Bel-Air Holy Unity Church people get there before him and he and his buddies can't get a seat.

When he got home late last night, I know he saw the keys sitting differently in the drawer. He hesitated with his eyes on them, but he didn't ask me if I'd used his truck. "There's a dent on the bumper. It's coming out of your pay," he tells me. What pay? I think. I don't say anything. "You're going down and getting a temporary driver's license Monday. I'm going to teach you how to drive." He also doesn't say anything about the sock Boone left crumpled on the bathroom floor on Friday. It's the one he couldn't find after we went inside. I don't think we said two words to each other. We just awkwardly laid down and he kept looking at me funny like he was seeing me in a whole new light. Every now and then, he'd do the *tap, tap-tap, tap* on my foot. He finally said he was sorry so many times, I kicked him. "Stop."

"I know, I'm trying."

"No, it's not the tapping. Quit apologizing. I'm friends with a guy who drums. He does it all the time too. It's—soothing." He hesitates and holds off for maybe ten minutes. Then he starts tapping on my foot again. I asked him if he wanted to stay the night. He said no. Then we fell asleep on the opposite ends of the couch watching an old movie, feet touching, not talking. Sadly, it is good enough to cover the bases Chase used to cover.

He's gone in the morning and I don't hear from him all Saturday. I don't know if he walked or somebody picked him up. Lexie woke me up at three and I tiptoed upstairs and laid down with her in my bed. Now, I'm torn with wondering if I made a huge mistake and if I can just sweep it under the rug. At least, for the moment, I'm hoping Dutch wants to leave before the Holy Unity Church crowd hits its climax. That's where the Martinez's go to church and I know they must come here too.

However, I think Dutch knows every cowboy and every farmer in a hundred mile radius. It's talk, talk, talk today about the cattle drive. And all of them in different shifts want to hear the story of how I ended up in the middle of nowhere at Dutch's house and how Boone Martinez delivered a baby in the middle of a big storm in Dutch's old barn. I think most of them believe it was some miracle act of God. I think I tell it twenty times and they all nod when I tell them I had to wait until he was there and then, he didn't have a choice. But he did it with a big smile. Then Dutch always waves a hand and offers me up to the highest bidder. They all chuckle. I'm not sure if it makes me feel worthless, or if I simply like the attention while each of them eyes me with a funny gaze like maybe he'll take Dutch up on the invitation.

They fill the diner from four in the morning until nine. It's like a meet and greet for ball caps and cowboy hats and they trade old stories from years ago. Dutch says it's *their* time. I asked him if he means that's the *sinners'* time because none of them are going to church. He told me just because they don't go to church doesn't mean they sin. He's got a point. But after eleven, the late service church-goers start to pour in depending upon how long Preacher Irving's sermon is and how many sins his congregation wants to repent. Their sins have been washed away. Dutch and his cowboys' failings have not.

I suppose, by all rights then, I go in with all the sinners. It isn't like I jaw it up with any of them, though. They talk cattle and horses and trucks. I sit at the barstool and small talk with Gin whose nametag changes weekly. This week, she is Rudina Walke. "It's supposed to be Walker on the nametag, but there wasn't enough room," Gin sighs when she walks past with the coffee. "I mean, I'm guessing that. The only Rudina I know is Rudina Walker and she's like eighty. She must have worked here thirty years ago." She pauses when I just blink at her. "You're the quietest person I know. You ever talk, hon?"

I nod my head.

"You want to hear the latest talk around town?"

"Sure," I say and sip my too-hot coffee. I couldn't imagine I haven't already heard it. I know just about everything there is to know about Gin. She's got three kids and they rent a mobile home about two miles from Dutch. She's tells me she's got a boyfriend that drives trucks and is gone most of the time, but I saw Jack's truck in her driveway when Dutch and I passed by last week. I think the last boyfriend's gone and Jack's his replacement. I don't say anything, though. She showed me a little gold necklace she said her boyfriend got her. I'm thinking a gold necklace from Jack is better than a black eye from the last guy.

"Dan Beatty, they call him Pickle, who owns the hardware store got caught by his wife's niece getting a blowjob in the back of Kathy Winton's Ford. They were parked up behind Hanover's Grocery Store and Katelyn, who is the niece, saw the truck. She thought she'd go up and ask Kathy what Sunday school lessons they were going to teach the fourth graders this week because they both teach that class at Holy Unity Church. She pushed her hands up to the window and boy, did she get an eyeful."

I giggle. It seems to encourage her urge to chatter and she holds up a forefinger. "Give me a minute, I've got more," she says and whisks off to the back of the diner to give refills of coffee to the boys in the back. "And something that has to do with you." I rock Lexie's car seat with my foot and yawn into the cup of my hand.

"Me?" I ask her back. I guess it isn't a shocker. I'd hoped something newer and juicier had happened to outshine me getting dumped at the motel last month. I get the feeling it must be getting close to time for the early service folks to come in because I see a couple dozen suits starting to slide into the diner, lingering at the doorway waiting for a seat. Nobody seems to notice but me. I think it's a control thing, like two packs of wolves vying over the carcass of a deer. The farmer/rancher crowd lingers just a little longer to draw out their time, show they are dominant. The early churchy folks start eyeing the tables, vying for a seat if anybody gets up.

Gin swoops in again, leans her elbows on the counter. "Did you hear the sirens last night?"

"Nope."

"Oh, I've got some juicy stuff then," she says to me, slants hard toward me. "Don't look, but Harlan Martinez just came in the door." She has to reach out and snatch my chin just as my head turns toward the front of the diner. "I said *don't look*. He lives right over the hill from Dutch. You had to hear the sirens. But, whatever. His kid, he was the one that got Dutch's girl pregnant when he was like fifteen. And she got killed in a car wreck. You know that one, right?"

"A little bit. I know about the wreck and stuff."

"Okay, let me fill you in on the dirty." Gin sighs and rolls her eyes like I'm amiss at not knowing the dirt on everybody in town. "The Martinez's are like millionaires.

They got more money than they can count. Dirty money, I presume. Harlan's dad and Harlan were from Mexico and sneaked across the border. They worked for some cattle companies in Texas, then started their own. They had some kind of a falling out with the town they were in and sold everything, moved here. In high school, Harlan's boy, Boone, he got Charlene Cates pregnant. She had the baby and then all of a sudden, she gets in a car wreck and the Martinez's, they end up with the baby. Strange, huh? Some people say she was murdered. I don't think it is coincidence that she suddenly up and dies." Gin takes a breath. "Everybody thinks old Harlan hired somebody to kill her— but what's worse is that Bo Littleton's got it out for Harlan. His son Marcus, he's the one who was in the car with Charlene when she got killed that night. Marcus was her English teacher and like ten years older than her and died too. But nobody ever talks about him. Bo wouldn't even let them put a stone on his grave." She pauses and peers over my shoulder. "The other night Bill Peters with the fire department got called over to the Martinez's house because they said there were gunshots. When they got there, Harlan Martinez and Boone were fighting in a knock down drag out fight with Bo Littleton. Mayor Littleton was screaming he was going to get them kicked out of town one way or the other. There wasn't no way a bunch of Mexicans were going to take over his town—" Suddenly Gin stands up straight. She's got on a wide-eyed gaze and a forced-shock smile.

"What can I do for you, Mister Martinez?"

"A seat, please. We've been waiting over twenty minutes." I roll my head around and try not to stare at the man whose shadow is encompassing both Gin and me. I also try to stifle a grin. Gin's cheeks are like two red balls of embarrassed. He's a big man like almost seven feet tall, not too fat and not too thin just like his boy. His accent is barely audible, but his words are slow as if each one is carefully thought out and he is making a concerted effort to utilize a mix of southern Tennessee and Texas tone of voice.

He's got the churchy suit and tie, but while the other suits coming through the door are retail store, his are tailor made. His looks almost match his son's with their dark hair. However, Harlan's eyes are brown. I'm guessing they have the same holier-than-thou attitude. While I blink at him for a moment, taking in a dark bruise on his cheek. He looks me up and down with a pursed-lip gaze like he's just checked out a dead skunk on the side of the road. My eyes veer a little to the left of the man and I see Boone. Then, I see the girl who was dropping off the clothes at Goodwill— um, Adriana. I cringe. I should have recognized the similarities between the two. The queen mean girl must be Boone's sister.

I'm thinking right then that the pressure is off of me for having the latest, greatest scandal in Bel-Air, Tennessee. Because when Gin swoops in after seating the Martinez's and grabs a tray from the kitchen, she says: "Did you see his bruise? Now, you know I'm not lying. His son, he's got a black eye." I was wrong, though, about the bearing the burden of the latest gossip—

I watch her leave and catch a glower from Dutch who is sitting with his group of old guys. He even shakes his head like he knows I'm getting the newest gossip. But it's time to leave anyway. The rest of the church crowd is coming in. Dutch snatches up his guest check, pats the shoulder of the guy he's sitting beside, and stands. It's my cue to leave, too. And I didn't get to hear the newest chatter about me Gin promised.

I drag Lexie's car seat up with me, careful not to work my gaze around the restaurant and make eye contact with Boone. She's sound asleep still. I let it bang my legs while I stand by Dutch in the line to pay our bill. I suppose I've become something of a fixture in the community now. Nobody in Dutch's circle raises a brow at me. However, just as I'm thinking I'm not the center of attention anymore, I feel a gentle knuckle-poke to my right shoulder. I'm thinking somebody needs around me, so I shift a little to the left and start to look up.

"Hey, I used to know a girl that looked just like you a long time ago."

The voice, it sounds so familiar. It is deep and smooth like the sound of a train rolling steady down the tracks. I remember the deep Alabama twang and I haven't seen the face attached to it in almost a year. I see Dutch sweep his careful eyes over my shoulder and I turn, look up and take in the man hovering over me. He's grinning too-white teeth, a face full of freckles, and navy blue eyes. His hair's covered by a dark cowboy hat that's probably only to hide his identity. But I know underneath, it's a deep auburn and cut short. In blue jeans and a button up, he looks like he just stepped off an album cover for a country music band.

"Dallas Dunne." I look him up and down, feign rolling my eyes. I'd already let Lexie's car seat rest on the floor. My palms are over my lips in complete surprise and, I have to admit, elation. I have to let my fingers drop to finish. "I thought red-haired country boys weren't in fashion anymore."

"And this heavy metal, grungy shit is? What the hell, girl?" He waggles a finger at my face, then just snatches me up and gives me a bear hug regardless that he almost knocks the ball caps off three men sitting to our left. "I mean, what's going on with all that?"

When he sets me down, the line for the cash register has turned to take us both in like two pieces of fresh gossip meat. In fact, the entire restaurant is sinking their teeth into us.

"It's the new look of country, boy," I sass back. "Didn't they tell you that at the last meeting of the Ruin the Crap out of a Good Guitar by Playing Country Music meeting? Oh, they didn't invite the good boy of country again, I guess," I tease him, then let my smile drop. "What are you doing here in the middle of boondocks Tennessee?"

"No, no." He shakes his head. "That's my question, Skeeter. What are you doing here?"

CHAPTER 10
THE CLOSEST THING TO A COWGIRL YOU GOT TONIGHT

I can see it in your eyes, that faraway stare.
I'm not the one you're looking for,
still I'm the only one here.
It's like they've all paired off in this ol' bar
And I'm not trying to be impolite,
But I'm the closest thing to a cowgirl you got tonight.

Dutch gives me a long gaze when I tell him I'm going to hang out with Dallas for a while. I don't know if he recognizes him or not. I've heard Dutch sing along with Dallas's songs on the radio. I've never seen him buy an album so maybe he hasn't seen his picture on the cover and doesn't know the guy who is leaning against the red truck rolling his eyes at me is the same guy with whom he sings along between bouts of static. Maybe he doesn't care.

Dutch wiggles his keys, looks at Dallas across the parking lot and his huge cherry-red truck. Then, Dutch nods his head up and down so lazily, it is difficult to tell if he is actually acknowledging me or getting ready to spit out the tobacco he's got between cheek and gum.

"Yeah," he says, spitting out a long line of tobacco on the parking lot between his truck and Jack's. "You be back to feed by five."

I'm not back by five. I'm sitting in Dallas's motel room and he's picking his guitar and I'm listening to him hum a song while I lay on my belly on one of the two queen-size beds in the room. I've got one hand lounging over the side, rocking Lexie back and forth so she goes to sleep.

"I hate you, you know. You tick me off." That's what I tell him. He just snickers a laugh. "It's not working. You can't make me want to sing anymore."

It was noon when we got there. He turned on the TV and we sat at the miniature table with two wooden chairs. "So the story is that you just decided to quit, ran off. I think most folks think you OD'd and got put in a rehab in Texas, Waylon." He's got burnt-coffee fuzz on his cheeks already and it's only mid-afternoon. "Chase, he was at the music festival in Alabama you all go to every year and he's got some girl with him that can't sing shit. He can't play the guitar. So together, they are like those goofy boy bands that can't sing unless they've got a recording studio manipulating their off-key voices. And she's screwing up your songs. He's telling everybody you're gone, calling you a bitch because you left him high and dry. What's up? That doesn't sound like you."

"Dallas, we left from California, did the circuit." I look him in the eyes. "Show after show, we'd done maybe twenty-two or twenty-three from Washington State to Florida. They were all small venues, bars and stuff. All of a sudden about six months ago, he buys a brand new bike and says we're going to ride it instead of going with his buddies who take care of the equipment and the sound and all that stuff that's way over my head. He's spending money right and left, eating sushi and hitting the bars every night while I sit in the hotels alone, you know? You know me. I'm just along for the ride. Chase, he does everything. I write the songs. I sing them. He handles the money and getting us gigs. My belly was full of Lexie, here." I smile down at her. She smiles back. "I'd been wearing these long coats to cover up so nobody knows I'm pregnant. But you know how I sing."

"Yeah, Skeeter's modus operandi, the way you operate. Half naked and screaming."

"I take offense to that," I say with a roll of my eyes. "Still, some jerk makes a comment after we're done playing about me singing what I sing and looking like a pickle with a grape tied on. It really got to Chase because he thinks I got to look all cute and wearing t-shirt and panties up on stage."

"Imagine what it did to you," Dallas says softly. "Some people are idiots. And I'm not just talking about the rude dude. I'm talking about Chase."

"Three weeks later, I'm standing in the parking lot in my t-shirt and panties watching him drive away. I've got nothing but my backpack. Chase, he pawned off my guitar for the room."

"My God, Skeeter," he whistles softly between his teeth. "Your guitar with all your songs written on it? What happened then?"

I nod. I tell him about Dutch and all his cowboy buddies taking me in like I was a part of their family. I tell him about having Lexie in the barn and Dutch griping about everything, but he's going to teach me how to drive.

"You remember, I told you country folk are good folk," Dallas tells me softly when I'm done. "Back when we first met, you rolled your eyes, told me I was just saying that to make a buck on my music."

"Oh, my gosh, do you need to rub that in on me?" I stick out my tongue. "The old guy's always trying to trade me off for a horse. He thinks it's funny. He did it at the hardware store the other day and twice to old dudes at the diner. They all think it's funny and offer an old donkey for me every time." I scratch my head. "Then he says something like he'll even trade me for a donkey with three legs because I do nothing but go out in the barn and scream into an old microphone. I keep thinking I'm going to wake up one morning with some old, toothless geezer standing at the end of my bed with a white wedding dress in one hand and a donkey in the other."

"Are you serious?"

"Naw, Dutch is joking. I think. He says they used to do that on this side of the hill when his grandpa settled here. It was a tradition. It started because there weren't that many women and lots of men in the coal mines and putting in the railroad. Whoever had the most horses was the richest guy. He got the girl."

"I'd have to bring in a thousand for Jenna," he sighs. "Glad that wasn't the tradition when I met her. I had an old beat up truck and was living in a trailer off the highway." He rubs his chin, kicks me with the toe of his boot. "I didn't have a pot to piss in."

"I've been to your house now and you got four of them. Don't know why. I peed in them all to test them and they all worked the same."

Dallas snickers. "You're funny." He rubs his face. "Did you really?"

"Yep."

"Hmmm. Folks have been saying on the social networks they can't identify with me anymore, can you believe that?"

"Honestly?" I turn to look at him, size him up and down with his expensive jeans and designer shirt and boots. "Look at you and look at the boys in the diner, Dallas. You stuck out like a sore thumb and almost worse than me. People get dirty every day working crappy jobs. They like to drive home, forget about it and sing your songs. But they like to feel like what you're singing is good and true, right?"

"What do you mean?"

"That you got dirty too and that's how you got the inspiration for that song. You get the crap they have to do like—" I shrug. "—like worrying about what you're going to do with the kids because you can't afford a sitter. Dealing with a shitty boss. Or cleaning barns or working in the mines. That you have to work a twelve hour day, then go home to a house where the roof leaks, but in the end, it's going to work out."

"So you got any new songs that fit that bill?" he asks me then. I realize he isn't quite getting my message, but I let it go. "Because I'm looking. You know Anise Wells? She's kind of in style right now. She wants to wear me around her neck a bit and sing with me. But I've got nothing new in the last year."

"Anise. Bleach blonde and ditzy, right? Oh, that's every country girl I know," I tease him. I stare at him, size him up and down.

"Yeah, you look pretty bleach blonde and country right now."

"Touché," I grunt. "Dallas, I haven't really felt like writing anything down since—" I let it linger there. "You know, Chase took off. I've been taking care of a baby, mucking out poop from horse stalls, cooking breakfasts for cowboys. You know, living that life your fans live."

"So—there's your inspiration, right? And now you've got a taste of country, you ever thought of mixing it up a bit and singing something different than—"

"Don't say it. It's blasphemy." I bite my lip so I don't laugh. We've got this thing. He says heavy metal sounds worse than fingernails running down a wooden wall. I tell him country sounds like a bunch of hound dogs yowling. "It is blasphemy. I would not turn my back on all those people who listened to me sing."

"Little girl, they think you're dead right now, already flipped them off for not being there. Your old asshole boyfriend's replaced you." He kicks his feet up on the table, leans back in his chair looking all smug and like he's closing a sweet deal on a brand new horse.

"It's been less than two months, Dallas," I retort. "Nobody even knows I'm gone."

"You think?" He leans forward, tugs his phone from his back pocket and fiddles with it for a few seconds. "You know Brooke Canter?" He asks me. Yeah, I do. The sleepy voice that answered the phone when I called after Chase drove off into the sunset.

Dallas turns the phone toward me. "If you don't, maybe this will ring a bell." There's a video playing. I blink. I can barely hear it. I don't need to. It's my song. One of them I wrote. It's not me singing it. It is Brooke Canter. I can see Chase is strumming his guitar next to her just like he used to play next to me. "This was four months ago. Maybe you didn't know about it. But he must have left some nights to go get cigarettes or something because you weren't at the performance."

She's trying hard to hit the notes, trying hard to look like me. I blanche, feel sick to my stomach. I shove the phone away. "Four months ago," I whisper, try not to sound surprised that I'm realizing those late night meetings with the sound crew or the show managers wasn't really happening at all. "Yeah, well, screw it," I huff. "I don't feel like playing anymore anyways. Maybe I'll go to college, get a degree. Maybe I'll be an engineer or something."

"Suit yourself." He lays his phone down on the table between us, taps his finger on his knee. Then Dallas gets up and walks over to his guitar case and opens it up. He comes back over to the chair and sits down, starts strumming out a few old country songs and he hums along. That's when I go lay down on the bed rocking Lexie to sleep and telling him he's a crap for thinking he can coerce me into singing.

Sadly, it's working. "I got another guitar in my truck. You're welcome to borrow it." Ten minutes later, I'm glowering at him and plucking along with him.

"You're so cute when you're angry," he tells me.

"I'm going to tell your wife you're flirting with me."

"She knows better. I like girls all sweet and soft-spoken and wearing pretty, lacy dresses."

"And still, country music's favorite good guy cowboy is sitting here with heavy metal's biggest badass in a skanky old Bel-Air motel room. Oh—" I sigh, realizing he isn't as stupid as I thought when it comes to what his fans are looking for in his music. "This is how you're getting dirty for your fans, huh?"

"Well, mixing it up a bit."

"I should think it is a putdown and call you a dick. Instead, remind me to ask your wife how she keeps such a hottie around for so long."

"I can tell you that," he says. I'm thinking he's going to tell me it's because she's so sweet and kind and wears those stupid almost-to-the-knee dresses. Instead, he just chucks me on the chin like a grandpa does to a four year old. "Just be yourself, whatever it is."

"Yeah, ask me how that's working for me so far."

He just grins at me. He's so damn cute I don't wonder why his wife is still hot on him after ten years. "I tried to chase you down once before, you remember that?" I nod. I do. I dig out some of the songs I've been working on that I've kept in a notebook in my backpack.

"This is called: *Closest Thing to A Cowboy I got Tonight*." He just stares at me while I sing the third one, tips his head to the side. It is one that usually has a quicker beat. I slow it down, soften it out.

"What?" I stop, cross my eyes at him. "You know I disgrace it by slowing the beat."

"Yeah, I like that one. You think we could sing it together?"

CHAPTER 11
I CAN'T——WHAT THE HELL DOES THAT MEAN?

Dutch is mad at me. I didn't get home this morning until seven. He's got three of his buddies lined up waiting for breakfast. I think Dutch believes his kitchen is a fast food restaurant and I'm the free cook. Dallas and I played our music until four in the morning and I fell to sleep with my head on the table. We'd stopped long enough to wait for the cops to leave. Somebody complained about the noise we were making. We were trying to play guitar and jump from one bed to the other. I don't know why. We were tired. I suggested we do it to wake up because the coffee at the front desk of the motel was thick as black tar. Dallas tripped and hit the headboard, broke the hasp where it was affixed to the frame. The headboard flipped up, banged across the wall.

Dallas just smiled at Officer Bobby Moretti and said: *We're so sorry, sir. We'll turn the TV down.* Officer Moretti had stood with his mouth slack for a good fifty seconds, then he whispered: *You're—you're Dallas—Dallas Dunne, ain't you?* One autographed Bel-Air Motel napkin later, we were good to go again. However, I fell to sleep waiting for Dallas to go to the restroom. When I woke up three hours later, he was taking a shower. I don't think he slept a wink.

Dutch stares at me coming in the door to the sound of Dallas's red truck spitting gravel out of the driveway, watches me with wary eyes.

"When you don't feed the horses, they don't get fed," he tells me. "When you don't clean the stalls, they don't get cleaned. I don't ask much of you, Skeeter, and I expect you'll do what I say to continue living here."

I nod.

"I'm sorry." He doesn't say anything about me being gone all night. Instead, he tells me he'll hold Lexie for me while I take a shower, cook breakfast and clean the barn.

So I'm cleaning the barn by eight in old jean shorts and a black tank top. I let the horses out to the pasture, shovel out the manure, and take it by wheelbarrow loads to add to the huge mounds Jack will level with the tractor at the end of the week. I think about my guitar. I try not to conjure up the memory. I suppose it just reminds me that Chase would do such a mean thing and sell the only thing I cherish. I haven't even called the pawn shop in town. I think my heart's more dead broke than Boone Martinez's. It doesn't matter. I've only got sixteen dollars to my name and Lexie needs more diapers.

I'm on my third dump of manure out back when another truck pulls into the drive. I figure it is Boone hiding out from his dad and hanging out with Dutch. Then his shadow covers the light I use to see the backs of the stalls and streaming through the open barn doors. I look up in mid-shovel and pause, take in Boone standing there. He's leaning against the frame with hands in his pockets staring at me.

"So—I guess your name is Waylon—Waylon Ryder," he tells me. I stare at him, nod my head. I hate when people find out who I am. They treat me differently.

"How'd you find out?"

"Well, that day Chey came with me and sat in the truck, when I got back in, she was freaking out. *Daddy, that's the singer, Waylon Ryder,* she kept telling me. *She's with the band Deadly Aftermath. They're really big.* I haven't seen her this excited about something since she got an electric car when she was four. She's kind of in this hating me phase. I asked her who Waylon Ryder was and she pulled up a million videos to show me. I just laughed at her, said you just looked like her. Lots of people probably looked like her." He leans his back against the frame of the stall and rubs it up and down to scratch between his shoulder blades. "Then when Dallas Dunne shows up at the Bel-Air All-Nighter Motel and Diner and he's like all buddy-buddy, Tim from the feed store is beside himself telling everybody he thought that was you getting feed with Dutch. He's a big fan, likes the hard rock stuff."

"Oh." I push the shovel through the manure, bring up a big load and dump it in the wheelbarrow.

"He left?"

"Yeah, Dallas went back to pay for a bed we broke. Dallas beat the crap out of the headboard. You know, with his head." I smile, pat the top of my head. "Bang, bang, it was broke. I told him he about killed me banging me so hard, he had to pay for it. He said it was me doing all the bouncing."

Boone's hard-staring me. "So you're leaving, I guess."

I start to lean the shovel against the wall while I shift the wheelbarrow. He takes two steps toward me and wiggles his fingers at it. I hand the shovel to him and it seems just automatic, Boone digs it into the dirty wood chips and starts to scoop them up.

"Leaving?"

"With him," Boone says. "You know, moving on."

"Yeah, probably," I lie. I don't know why. I guess I want to see his reaction. "We're like this—" I hold up my forefinger and middle finger and cross them. "Close. He's just got it going, you know. Truck. Money. Bang-bang."

"Yeah, he does," Boone says. "I'm not a girl and I can even see that." He's digging hard with the shovel and I scoot up on the boards of the wall, climb them and sit on the top to watch. "I like his music." He is silent, goes about the task of cleaning the stall and then moves the wheelbarrow to the one next door. I straddle the boards, watch him dig into that one. He's like a tractor, clearing the manure. About the fourth stall and me climbing across the back of the barn to follow him, he stops long enough to take off his shirt, toss it across the door and he looks up at me. Then he plops his cowboy hat on top. Holy hell, when I see him do that, I almost forget my first name.

"So this is how it works with people like you and Dallas? You just come in like a storm, use everybody and walk away? I mean, surely you've got money coming out of your ass. You don't need some rich guy to come sweep you off your feet."

"Huh? Oh." I stand up, wobble a bit on the boards while I balance there. Then I make a big deal out of looking at my butt. "No money coming out."

Boone sniffs a laugh. It isn't a very convincing kind of laugh as if he likes my sense of humor. He tosses the shovel into the wheelbarrow. Then he snatches up the handles and rolls it to the last stall.

"I am what you see, Boone," I tell him, working my way around the fence. I'm holding on to the top boards and scooting my feet on the bottom. "Did you just come over to tell me things I already know or—"

"I stopped in on my way to town. I'm dropping off new curtains Mom ordered for Holy Unity Church. They're in big boxes. I just wanted to say—"

"Okay. You've had your say. Go to church."

"I opened up to you. You didn't tell me anything about you."

"I gave you something in return. That was the game, wasn't it?"

Oh, that makes him mad. He snatches the shovel and

digs hard. I turn to the sound of footsteps crunching in the gravel outside the barn. Dutch comes in right after in a spray of dust.

"Hey, I forgot to give this to you yesterday morning." He's still got Lexie over his shoulder and a white plastic bag dangling from his forearm. I think he's going to give me this. He doesn't. Instead, he wiggles something in his hand. "That little waitress said the cleaning girls found this. They didn't want to toss it." Lexie's chewing on her fist and snuggled in tightly to his neck. Lexie's favorite things go in this order: One, Boone. Two, Dutch holding her while he reads the paper and yells at the dogs. Three, her swing. Four, her mama. Right now, she's in heaven with everything but her swing in the room. She coos, looks lovingly up at Dutch. Dutch doesn't seem to notice the adoration in my daughter's eyes looking up at him. He holds out a brown paper bag, gives Boone a funny stare before he looks at me sitting on the fence. "I hope you're paying him to do your job."

I give him a big smile, take the bag. Boone looks up with a bit of infuriation and realization like it is just sinking in that he mucked the whole barn for me. "It's fairy magic. I'm a fairy, put a spell on him."

"Well, no more fairy spells for you, girl. It's your job. You do it."

Then Boone drops the look quickly, feigns like he meant to do it while he plops the shovel on top of the wheelbarrow. I'm thinking it's probably some of my sheet music. I'd written down the musical notes for Dallas's two songs I was working on.

"Listen, we need to talk," Dutch says to me while I hold the bag. "Boone, can you give us a minute?"

Boone nods. He gives me one last expressionless

gaze, then swaggers out of the stall. "Skeeter's getting in trouble," he says softly in a sing-song voice. He swipes an elbow over his forehead. I'm not thinking about his words at first, just the way the sweat's glistening off his perfect abs. His butt. I'm frigging staring at his butt and Dutch clears his throat. My face turns red. Still—I'm stuck on the way his hair's sticking up on the top of his head. His eyes, rich blue with those thick lashes. Then he gives me a snotty roll of his eyes.

"Grow up," I tell his back. I see him grabbing his shirt and hat before Dutch leans his free hand on the top of the stall door.

"You grow up, Skeeter," Boone mutters rigidly. "Quit looking at my butt."

"What? You wish I was looking—"

Dutch holds out his hand, shakes his head. "People are talking, Skeeter," he says. "I understand everybody's got their demons. But you can't go jumping into bed with every man that comes along. Even if he's famous and stuff. It's a small town, baby girl. They see what you do. They talk. They point a finger at me."

"Just because I go to a motel room with a guy doesn't mean I sleep with him." Okay, I know it sounds stupid when it comes out of my mouth. I'm embarrassed so I wiggle the brown paper bag, think I'll show Dutch just what we were doing in that room. I unclasp it where someone had rolled the top closed and push past the crinkly brown paper to a piece of paper at the bottom. I tug it out, hold it up about chest high. It isn't a music sheet. It's just a little piece of note paper from one of the free notepads the motel leaves in their rooms with *Bel-Air All-Nighter Motel and Diner—Tell Your Friends About Us!*

It's crumpled like it had been tossed into the

garbage, then reopened again. I read it. It says: *Skeeter* at the top and then right underneath: *I can't.* And it's in Chase's scrawled writing. *I can't.* I feel sick right then. *I can't* what? I'm thinking. I can't love you anymore? I can't be with you? I can't raise a kid? I can't stand to look at you? *I can't.* There's a thousand endings I could add to that sentence, but I know the answer. I've heard it before.

"Skeeter, you okay? You look like you just saw a ghost." He says this and makes an awkward shift of his arm so the white plastic bag dangling there slides down. "Here, I got you something." It's like he's trying to fix whatever is going wrong in my head by handing me the bag.

"Huh?" I look up from the paper and stuff it back into the paper sack. I reach out, take the plastic bag he's giving me. Inside, I can see some material. I extend my hand into the bag and tug it out.

"A dress?" I ask him. I mean, it is black and really pretty like the ones Dallas's wife wears, all girly-girl and sexy. "What's it for?"

"It probably shows a little more than I would suggest, honey. Jack asked Gin to pick something out of one of her catalogs that would fit you for your date with Bobby. There's some sandals in there too."

"I don't think he really asked me out, Dutch. He's just not my type. Bobby was trying to be nice—"

"And nice might be good for you instead of—"

"Yeah, yeah, being a whore—?"

"That's not what I said," Dutch grunts. "You just need to be a little more—"

"A little more *what*?" I don't know what went pop in me, but something did. It's like that stupid note opened up the box in my chest and made all those little demons of my past jump out. "A little prettier? A little less stupid? A little more blonde than the cotton candy pink in my hair? You want me to stop wearing makeup or take off my piercings? Maybe I should grow two inches. Oh, sorry, can't do that. More what, Dutch? Because I am what I am, dammit! I tried to be everything everybody else wants me to be and this is what I end up with. I know I'm not good enough. I get it! I don't make the damn grade with you. I didn't expect I ever would because I'm obviously not worth keeping because everybody else has left me or dumped me or made me leave! But I didn't want you in the first place. And it seemed easy because you didn't want me just like everybody else. I hate you!"

It makes Lexie cry, my screaming. I grab her out of Dutch's arms and feel my own hot tears streaming down my cheeks when I toss the bag with the dress on the floor. "I hate you," I tell him. "You were stupid taking me in, you understand that? Stupid. I could have told you I wasn't worth it. I should have. It would have saved me from this—"

CHAPTER 12
CHASED DOWN IN A CORNFIELD

My mama was married temporarily to an evangelical preacher when she had me. Back then, it was just me and her and my big brother, Will. She'd always whisper to me we lived in a big mansion on top of a hill in West Elkton, Texas for the first three years of my life. It wasn't far from San Antonio. It had walls and electric fence around the property like a big prison. It was before we moved a few times around Texas and twice in South Dakota. After that, we had a handful of moves around North Dakota, lived in three places in Indiana and four in Michigan. Sixteen temporary daddies later, we settled in Ohio.

At least my travels stopped in Ohio. Well, me and Caleb, my younger brother. Mama had Caleb somewhere between Texas and Indiana. But mama wasn't safe there. One day, she just took Will and was gone. She left me and Caleb when I was six and he was a one year-old on a sunny day in June just like today. Before she disappeared, she showed me the places we'd lived. She put little dots on the map she hid in her bible, all sixteen of them. She didn't show me the point on the map where the mansion was because she missed it so badly. She told me to never, never go near there.

"Your daddy, he was a big time preacher, sweetie," she told me. "He had thousands of people show up to listen to him speak the gospel of the Lord. He'd talk about the bible for hours, start in the morning and he didn't stop until way after dark. And he could sing. Lord, child, his voice was like the angels. He was good to his people. But he wasn't a good man to me. And I was afraid he would be a bad man to you. We're safe here. I just know we are. He can't find us."

She just vanished. Ten years later, my temporary daddy in Ohio told me I had to leave too. So I'm no stranger to being rejected. I'm no stranger to not having a home.

"Hey, where you going, Skeeter?" It's Boone who is rolling the window down to his truck and driving real slow beside me on the highway. "Don't leave. Dutch, he didn't mean to be so gruff about it." I don't answer him, just push Lexie into my left arm. "It's just a small town. Folks, they talk, you know?" She's getting heavy on nothing but her mama's milk. And that's all she wants. Right now, she has decided to start bawling for some of it.

"Well, let them talk. I'm moving to the next town so I'll be old news before you know it. Then old Dutch won't have to worry about me embarrassing him."

Boone is almost blocked by the girl who came with him the other day. She's got big blue eyes and dark brown hair. She's skinny like me, but has freckles all over her face. She's staring at me with expressionless lips, turns her head toward her daddy when he speaks.

"Well, get in. I'll give you a ride there."

"It's far away, Boone. Please leave me alone."

"No," he says loudly. His fingers are *tap, tap-tap, tapping* the steering wheel. "I'm going to follow you all the way—now, crap, don't do that."

I stop, wait for his bumper to pass me and then I cut across the road to a big field. It has little shoots popping up and I start down the line toward the four lane highway. I can see him craning his neck in the rearview to see me. Then when I come into his vision again, he jams on the brakes. Then, Boone puts the truck in park, rolls down the driver's side window and starts yelling at me.

"Skeeter, for God's sakes, you can't hitch a ride with a baby! Just come home."

"I am going home."

"You've got a home?"

"No."

I've got my back to him. I hear the truck door slam when he gets out. His legs are too long and although I start running, he catches up with me. I feel his hand on my arm and I almost trip on a nubby, tan stalk of last year's corn.

"Stop, dammit! You're going to fall and hurt that baby." He pulls me around so I'm facing him. I know my face is red. That's the problem with having fair skin. My nose and eyes turn a solid shade of beet red at even the slightest inclination of a tear.

"What was on that little piece of paper, Skeeter?" he asks me softly. His fingers are just barely resting on my forearm like he knows he can snatch on to my wrist if he needs to stop me from running again. "Did somebody say something mean to you?"

"No. It was nothing."

"You want me to wrestle you down, take the backpack and dig it out? Because I will. I don't care if my daughter thinks we're crazy. I'm going to do it." He takes a step forward and extends his free hand toward my backpack. "It isn't any of your business. I just want to go home."

"Home. I thought you didn't have a home."

"I don't."

"I don't understand, Skeeter. I want to and you won't let me. Are you going back to Dallas Dunne's? Is that where you're heading?"

"No," I grunt.

"Let me take you home."

"It's not that easy, Boone," I say quietly. "It's complicated. It's like seven hours away and—"

I don't know how he talked me into it. When I slide into the leather seat next to his daughter, she just stares at me with wide eyes. Boone tells her to slide into the back seat and she does, slowly without taking her eyes from me. The truck smells new. I suppose it is new. It is also loaded.

"We're going on a road trip," Boone tells the back of her head. "Cheyenne, I'm stopping at the church to drop off the new curtains for your grandma. I'm going to drop you off at home—"

"I don't want to go home," she whines at him, swings her head back around to face him and scoots up against the back of the driver's seat. "Daddy, please. Papaw is having that stupid dinner tonight. Olivia's back again and her mom and dad are coming. I don't want to be there with all those old people."

"Oh, I'm daddy now and not *the big bully that's ruining my life*?" He asks her, shifting the truck into gear. "Because when you were screaming at me earlier, I was everything but daddy. You don't have any clothes. It's going to be straight up and straight back, no stopping every five minutes for snacks or a hotel room." I see him reach around behind her to the seats in the back of the truck. He pulls something over her head and I see it's an old brown and banged-up guitar case. My guitar case.

"Oh," I huff over Cheyenne's head, blinking at the guitar and then at Boone. I'm stunned. I'm speechless.

"Yeah, Merry Christmas and Happy Easter and Happy Birthday for the next ten years. You maxed my credit card with this one." Boone holds it out to me. I take it and I swear, my hands are shaking and there are tears in my eyes. "The guy at the pawn shop sold it to some dude at the flea market. He found out it belonged to Waylon Ryder because of the songs you've got written all over it. He saw a picture of it online. It was going for five-thousand dollars and forty-two cents on some auction site. Just be glad it was the first day. I told him it was stolen and I was calling the cops or it could have cost me my truck."

I'm trying to juggle the guitar and Lexie and tears are spilling down my cheeks. It almost takes up half the front seat when I flick the little latches to open it. It's mine. It has the names and dates of the songs I've written on the front in black indelible marker. I know my eyes are puffing up and my lips are puffing up. I've got those little hiccups even before I start sobbing like a big baby.

"Thanks, Boone." I want to give him a peck on the cheek. I'm thinking maybe it might be inappropriate in front of his kid.

He's got that scared look guys get when girls cry like he's trying desperately to find a shut-off valve that isn't on the surface of whatever pipe is leaking. He's adjusting his hat and blinking and trying to soft-smile it away.

"I can't," I tell him while I sniff and close the guitar case.

"You *can't* what?"

"That's what the little note said. It was something Chase started to write and stopped and tossed in the trash." I tell him with three sobbing huffs. "I got to figure out why nobody *can*—put up with me long enough to keep me. That's why I'm going—home."

I'm waiting for him to waggle his hand toward me like he does and say *because of all that.* He doesn't. Maybe he'd be right. It is *all that.* I just got to know. So I figure, I'm starting with my last daddy and I'm going to work my way back. I don't tell Boone that because I know if I say it, it will sound stupid.

"Skeeter, I'm not sure if that's a good idea."

"Well, Dutch wants me to go out on a date with that

cop, Bobby. I don't want to do that either. He thinks he can put a Band-Aid on me and fix me by patching me up with another man, a nice man. He bought me a stupid dress. I—"

"Come on. We'll go for a ride. You don't have to do anything you don't want to do." Boone leans back in the seat. I know he's looking in the rearview mirror at his daughter and trying to figure out how to talk me out of this crazy and just go back to Dutch's. "They're just stupid. I can answer it for you. Your Chase dude, he was just an idiot. He didn't want a kid. I can tell you most guys aren't like that—" He tosses a hand in the air. "Put your seatbelt on. We're going."

We stop off at Holy Unity Church. Boone backs up to the rear door. It's a big white church with a little house next door where Chey says the preacher lives. He's got a son and her eyes twinkle when she ogles the house like she's looking to see if he's there. I follow Boone in while he unloads the boxes, drag two little ones myself. Then, I see an old piano sitting in the dark storeroom. It looks sad and lonely while I push open the fallboard to expose the keys. I poke a couple, listening to Boone slide a box past me along the grit-dusty floor.

"You play piano?"

"Yeah, I sneaked lessons from a Mennonite lady down the street where I grew up," I tell him. He doesn't ask why I had to sneak music lessons. "My daddy didn't allow music in the house," I divulge anyway. "He was really religious. I heard her playing one afternoon and followed the sound."

"Um." Boone mutters and walks back through to grab another load. "Give me five more minutes. We'll be out of here."

I watch his shadow fade and tug out the piano bench, wipe the dust off with my palm. Then I sit down. It makes me homesick for so many hours I sat on Missus Becker's piano bench while she patiently worked my tiny fingers over the keys, day in and day out. I let my fingers start to play the keys, feeling the coolness against my warm, guitar-calloused fingertips. The music is sweet to my ears, the scent of old building mixed with the way the music echoes off the walls reminds me of Missus Becker. She always smelled like rose talcum powder and mints. She was a widow and alone and had gone to a Mennonite college and learned music, herself. I always wondered if daddy knew all the time at her house was spent with music lessons. I think he just thought I needed a mama figure. If so, he never said.

But she taught me all the hymns and then—Mozart, Bach, Beethoven and any classical music she could afford at the little bible bookstore in Berlin. After I went home at night and slipped into bed, I would play the music with my fingers in the air over and over while it played in my head.

"Holy cow." Boone's voice stops me. "Is that something from the movies or just a hymn?"

Maybe ten minutes had passed while I played. I get caught up in it, don't know how long he was there. He'd stopped just inside the door with a helper which I assume is the preacher's son. They both are staring inside when I pull my fingers from the keys.

"Well, it could be from a movie and I know most of the hymns," I laugh, slipping from the seat and gently closing the fallboard "But that's Beethoven. Moonlight Sonata. Piano Sonata No. 14."

"You should come play on Sundays. We don't have anybody to play the music on the piano," the boy says. "The choir here sucks when we have one."

I laugh and Boone nods in agreement. "Thanks, but I don't think most church folks would welcome me here." It's true. My daddy's church folks said there was no room in church for people like me. It hurts. So I don't usually come close to churches.

I slip out between the two and wait in the truck with Chey whose eyes are stuck hard on the boy each time he comes and grabs up a load.

"So you like the boy?"

"No," Chey giggles when she snaps back around in her seat. Then she shrugs. "Maybe. Kinda."

CHAPTER 13
DADDY'S HAND-ME-DOWN BOOTS AND MAMA'S MYSTERIOUS JEWELRY BOX

"Stop here."

Abram Miller's farm is settled deep in Holmes County, Ohio. His sons run a dairy farm and he's also a building contractor. His fields are huge and roaming between solid hills thick with oaks and maples. The gravel road leading to the house is about six miles off the highway.

Abram also has a huge cornfield not far from the big white house he shares with a few of his sons and where I grew up. That's where everybody is while Boone careens down the road in a spray of gravel and dust. He looks at me strangely, tips his head. I know he took in the hats and clothing—plain baby blue shirts and dark trousers for the men working the horses down the rows of freshly turned dirt and blue dresses for the two girls hauling out stones and tossing them outside the field. It is like he never conceived my daddy's farm would be Amish.

Boone stops and puts on the brakes. It takes me five minutes to work up the guts to get out of the truck. I walk around, lean on the front and fold my arms across my chest. I can see my family's eyes peer up at me. They all then turn to the biggest of the men, a tall gangly man with wrinkles and tan hat.

I see him shake his head at them declining any reunion. It is worse than getting a boot in my belly. I've cried enough. I'm done. I just stand there and watch them while Boone rests his arm on the door and pats out a beat with his fingers. I guess I know the answer to my question

anyway. I'm different than they are. My family is all
packaged up in uniform shirts and pants, dresses and hats.
There is no variation, only conformity. It was always the
bitter ending to every fight leaving me running up to my
room—my quiet, quiet room.

I must stand there for an hour and watch them. I sit
by the road, I sit on the bumper. I go to the back of the truck
and sit there for another twenty minutes. Neither Boone nor
his daughter tell me to hurry. Once in a while, I hear their
low voices talking back and forth.

It is nearly two hours into sitting there, I wiggle off
one boot and then the other. I pick them up, walk them over
to the side of the road and jump the small ditch there. Then
I plop them down on the edge of the field. I'm barefoot and
the sharp bits of gravel the county throws out from their
trucks in the winter to keep the roads less slick and runs
into the grass in spring, hurts the bottoms of my feet.

I jump back over and go to the back truck window. I
peer at Chey holding Lexie. I reach in, wiggle my fingers to
take her. "You can go if you want."

"You're staying—here?" Boone stutters. "This is your
family, right? They don't act like—"

"Yes, they were my family. No, I can't stay. They
won't let me because the church won't allow it. I told you it's
complicated. I'm not allowed to come back. Ever."

"What's with leaving your boots?"

"It's a thing. I used to walk around in my daddy's
barn boots when I was little." I scratch a mosquito bite on
my arm. "Then it became kind of a family joke. When
daddy's boots got too worn, he'd give them to me. I'd find
them outside my room. I guess it was kind of an *I love you*.
He's a quiet man, doesn't say stuff like that much."

"Okay, I get it. But he obviously doesn't want—he
obviously wants to keep to himself. I'm not leaving you. Are

you crazy? Girl, you don't even have any shoes now. Where would you go?"

"I don't know. Dutch doesn't want me. I'm going to try to find where my mama went. Maybe she wants me."

"She's not here?"

"No, Boone," I say softly. "She left me here when I was like six."

He starts to open his mouth to say something. I can guess he wants to point out that if she left me and hasn't come back in twenty years, the odds were slim she still wanted me. He doesn't say anything, though. I see Chey's head shoot up over my shoulder and then see Boone's uneasy gaze settle behind me.

"Gracie."

Caleb. I turn. He's standing across the creek, my biggest and gruffest brother. He's a few years younger than me, but three times larger. I faintly remember Mama holding him when he was a baby. He's got on his straw hat, his blue shirt and a vest. He's got a beard now and long hair. It must be his wife working beside him who looks up warily from beneath her bonnet, then turns away. He's always been cool to me, but my biggest protector. He's not one of Abram's birth kids like me. Mama had him before we moved there. I push away from the truck and turn.

"Before you say it, Gracie, it was your choice." Gracie. Ah, yes, that was my name here. His voice is loud and he's not speaking Pennsylvanian Dutch like we always spoke at home. I'm not used to hearing him talk to me like this even when I've done this in the past. It adds a wall between us that I've never felt before.

"Caleb," I start, my accent thick. "Wie geht es dir? How are you?" He shakes his head, holds a hand out.

"Ganz gut. I'm doing good. I know what you're

thinking. But you're English now so I'm talking to you English. What do you want?"

"I wanted to see you— and everyone," I say, rubbing my arms nervously. "I wanted to know you're alright. I wanted you to know I was alright." He is looking over my head toward the truck. I turn. Boone is eyeing us cautiously. I can hear Lexie cooing inside.

"So you see us. We see you. You need to leave. If someone drives by, the bishop will hear you were visiting and Daed will be lectured. You know that."

I want to jump the creek again, give him a big hug. I used to ride on his shoulders when we went swimming in the little creek behind the house. I want to sneak into his room in my bare feet on the bare wood floors and cuddle up next to him in bed. "Ik mis je, I miss you."

"Again, it was your choice."

"Will you tell everybody I love them?" I ask. He doesn't answer. I know what he would say—if I loved them, I would be like them and I would never leave. "Can you ask Daed where Mama and Will went after she left here? And I need to know her whole name."

"Don't dig up old bones. Mama abandoned you and she abandoned me." I think it always burned Caleb that Mama took our oldest brother, Will, who was two years older than me with her when she left us with Abram.

My dad, he calls out Caleb's name and Caleb sighs. "I have to go. You have to go."

My heart aches standing there. I feel tiny. I feel alone. I imagine myself in a little white bonnet with three kids at my waist and a husband by my side. "Is that Annie that Daed's driving?" I ask of my old pony on the plow. She still shakes her head up and down to shoo away the flies.

"Yeah."

I turn. It is slow, I know that because I can see Caleb walking to my daddy and saying something to him. My eyes are on the ground when I walk back up to the truck. "I'm done." I force a smile. I hear a holler behind me. It is Caleb. He is telling me to wait a moment. One of the little boys is running toward the house. When he returns, he hands a feed sack to Caleb.

I'm standing with my back to Boone's truck when Caleb steps over the ditch. I meet him between road and truck. He extends his arm, hands me the bag. "This was Mama's," he says. "Daed said to give it to you." I look up over his shoulder toward my daddy. He isn't looking at me at all, but patting the boy's shoulder who brought him the bag. "He said to tell you about six months ago, two men came into his barn and had a picture of you. When they were there, he didn't think it was you. He just shook his head. Gracie," he sighs, looks over his shoulder. "I know Daed told me that the same kind of men dropped by the town when our mama first came here. She was running from something. She always said she had a husband that was a preacher that beat her. Right before she left, they came again. I'd leave well enough alone if I was you."

"Did he tell you her name?"

Caleb looks up at the sky, does this part-nod thing and then bobs his head up and down. "She said her name was Hannah Schwartz." But his head tips to the side and he shakes it back and forth. "I'll tell you this, though. Daed always thought she'd pulled the name from the sign outside town. You know, the one Abe Schwartz put up to sell his furniture. Gracie, that's all I know. Maybe that's not her name at all."

"So, let me drop you someplace closer to town," Boone tells me out the window five minutes later. "I'm starving. We can get something to eat." I'd nodded, climbed into the truck. I know he's not going to let me get out. I really don't want to go. Cheyenne, she's looking hard at me when I reach out to get Lexie from her from the back seat.

I open the bag with my free hand while I feed her. Boone keeps turning his head, curious what's in the bag. I'm smiling. I know he can see it.

"Boots?" he smiles back.

"Yeah," I dig them out, hug them to my chest.

"So you grew up there, huh? That's your daddy?" Cheyenne asks softly from behind me.

"He's not my real daddy," I tell her, turn slightly. "My mama moved a lot. I guess she got tired of lugging me around. She left me with him and thirteen brothers when I was six. He's the only daddy I know, but I had like sixteen."

"What?" Boone asks. I'm ignoring him. The bag is still heavy. I reach down, see a wooden box about half the size of a shoebox. When I dig it out, I see it has little gold-plated corners and latches and a little key tied with a ribbon on the front.

"Oh, what is it?" It's the first time I hear Cheyenne sound excited while she leans over the seat of the truck and blinks down at the box in my hand. "It looks like a treasure box." I flip the latch, open it wide while Boone peers over at it. The interior is covered in a silky red fabric and hand painted with silver flowers. Inside, I see some rings, a cross, some feathers and some coins, a little leather bag and some folded envelopes. There's more deep down, like one of the drawers in Dutch's kitchen that has been collecting stuff for ten years. "This was my mama's," I say softly more to myself than the two staring at me. "I remember playing with it."

"Can I ask you something?" Boone says and I look up at him. He doesn't wait for my answer. "What are you searching for, Skeeter?"

Chapter 14
He's Got a Frigging Girlfriend

I never answered Boone. Because I don't know the answer. I suppose that's one of Chase's *I can'ts* from the note he started at the Bel-Air All-Nighter Motel. I've always wondered where my mama went after she left me at Abram Miller's. I wondered if my real daddy finally caught up to her and killed her like she feared. Or maybe she didn't want me—I don't know. But in every town Chase and I stopped along our way, I'd look for her. It wasn't just online or in the phone books. I would look out in the crowds of faces staring at me at our performances and think maybe she was out there. I'd pass a lady on the street looking like her and my head would turn, beg for her to turn and say she was my mama and she still wanted me.

There's an old restaurant off the highway. Everybody stares at Boone with his cowboy hat. He takes it off and sets it on the seat of a chair self-consciously. I tell him that now he knows how I feel walking around Bel-Air in my daddy's old boots, tattoos, and pierced brow. He just grins a little and tells me he feels like he's on Mars with me.

I plop the jewelry box down on the table and Chey's looking at it with hungry eyes. I push it over toward her and we both delve in, poking through the little treasures and jewelry. I'm keeping a stiff upper lip. My heart hurts. I miss them so badly already I could scream.

"Chey, leave the box alone. Let Skeeter look. It's hers," Boone scolds gently. Chey starts to back off and I shake my head.

"I don't care. Give me the envelopes, you can play with the rest." I push the box toward her so I can situate Lexie. There's a couple still staring our way. They are younger, maybe in their twenties. Boone reaches out and takes the baby from me, shoves her on his chest. He smiles down at her and she smiles up at him. Did I just hear her giggle?

"She just giggled at me."

"Dammit." I growl at him. "Why are you getting all the firsts?" I take the envelopes and stuff them into my backpack. I want to look at these alone.

"I did get to see her first."

"Oh, gross," Cheyenne mutters, but she is digging deep into the box and pulls out a little Celtic ring with crosses all over it. "Cool."

"You better not get her first steps," I say it and then realize too late what I just said. Boone hears it.

"So you're not leaving?"

"I am," I reply. "I want to find my mama. I don't know what else to do. Chase has every bit of whatever money we've made. It's probably spent by now. He's good at buying stuff. I've got nothing. Everything's in his name."

"What if I helped you and you stuck around?" Boone offers. "You're going to kill that old man if you leave."

I look up. "You're kidding me, right? The same old guy who about lost it the other day when I left my underpants on the bathroom floor? He tried to trade me off for a mule to a guy working the register at the gas station."

"No. I'm not kidding. That's just his way." Boone isn't looking at me. He's holding Lexie in front of him and trying to get her to giggle again. I look away.

"Dad, stop, please, everybody's staring." Chey is pushing the ring on her finger and holding it up before she glares hard at Boone. It's cute as hell, him playing with her. I recognize that even if his daughter does not. There isn't a woman in that entire place not eating him up with her eyes.

Lexie giggles really loudly. Boone is like a proud daddy and laughs just as loud.

"I'm torn here," I admit. The men in the restaurant are glaring at the women staring at Boone. "You are causing a scene." Now I understand why Rod Elkhart wants to kick his butt out of the Crazy Filly. He takes all the girl attention away from the men. But Boone's shy about my remark when he glances up. I think it's his scar making him self-conscious. I really believe he thinks that's why people stare at him with dumb looks instead of the real reason—he's so damn pretty with that black hair and cowboy hat.

"I'll stop if you let me take you back to Dutch's," he bargains without looking up from Lexie.

"Why? Because you love my baby *maybe* as much as I do?"

"Yeah, pretty much." He looks up and smiles at me. I'm sad and it makes me feel better. "How about if you come back with us, me and Chey will help you find your mama. Dutch has called me ten times asking if I found you."

Chey looks up almost like she's surprised, her eyes steady on Boone like she's waiting on a punch line to a joke that she knows isn't going to be funny. "It'd be fun, right, Chey?" Boone goes on.

She looks at me like she thinks I'm crazy if I say I will. "Will you?" Chey asks bashfully, her cheeks pink.

"Yeah, alright."

Boone gets up to pay. I take the jewelry box and close it up, stuff it in my backpack. I start to get up. Then I see a girl rise, the one that kept staring at me earlier.

"Are you Waylon Ryder? From Deadly Aftermath?"

I want to tell her that I'm not anymore. Technically, the band doesn't exist without Chase. I just can't. "Yeah."

"I've got all your CDs. I just got your new one. It's in

the car. Will you sign it?"

"My new one?" I say it aloud, then notice she's giving me a funny smile. "Yeah, yeah of course."

"I knew he was making a live CD," I'm telling Boone after I sign the plastic cover and sit down quietly in the truck. I'm on the front of the cover singing at a concert in Maine. I barely remember the performance. It was before I started showing with Lexie. "I didn't know it was done. I mean, he's gone all the time. There's always cameras rolling at the shows."

"That's so cool," Chey says almost so quietly, I can barely hear it.

"It'd be even cooler if I got any money from it." I sniff a laugh. "I've never gotten a dollar of the sales. Just clothes, room and board and food. Of course, maybe that's all we've sold. Chase says everything's expensive."

"Why do you let him run everything?" Boone asks. "Don't you have a manager?"

"Yeah, his uncle."

"Oh. I'm going to teach you how to drive a truck," Boone announces when he takes off down the road. "Do you know how to use a debit card or—do you even own a phone?" I ignore him. I tug out the envelopes in my backpack. I'm tired. It's late.

"Skeeter, did you hear me?" he asks me.

"No, Boone, I don't own a phone."

"Well, you must have one. I hear one coming from your backpack. It sounds like it's on vibrate."

He's right. In fact, I'd heard that buzzing sound earlier, couldn't quite place where it was coming from. I dig around the backpack, tug out a cell phone and hold it up.

"Oh, my God," I grunt, shake my head. I recognize the background picture. Dallas took a picture of me jumping on the bed in mid-air. It took ten tries to get it right. "This is Dallas's phone. He must have lost it. We were tossing stuff all over the place after we broke the bed looking for the screw—"

"How'd you break a bed?" Chey asks.

"Don't answer that, please." Boone glares sideways at me.

"Why not?"

"She's thirteen."

"I jumped on beds when I was thirteen." I roll my eyes. "Obviously, I still do." I turn to Chey. "You know who Dallas Dunne is?"

"Yeah. He sings country music. Daddy likes him." She points a thumb at Boone. "He's always getting awards."

"Don't go any farther, Skeeter." Boone is shaking his head.

I ignore him. "Boone, you're an idiot."

"I'm so glad you found your voice."

"Well, let me use it," I say and turn so I can see Chey. "Me and Dallas, we were hanging out and knocking some songs off each other. I got tired and he went down and sneaked some sugar from the front desk where they give out free coffee. I had like ten sugar shots and got all hyper and started jumping on one bed and he started jumping on the other. Then we decided to trade sides and the first time, it was okay. The second, he went toward the wall so he didn't kick me and he hit his head on the headboard." I hold up the phone and show her the background picture of me in mid-air. "See?"

Boone grabs the phone and almost skids off the road. I see him looking at the picture before he peers at me. "So the boom-boom headboard story you told me—"

"Really?" I ask him. "Dallas is married and happily so for like a million years." The phone keeps asking for a password. I try a few, then settle on 1-2-3-4. Sure enough, it's his security code. It isn't ten seconds later, the phone rings again.

"Hey," I say.

"Who is this?" a woman's voice asks me on the other end. It is Dallas's wife, Jenna. She is so beautiful with long dark hair and big, brown doe eyes. She used to be on a cop show. She was the pretty coroner with a quick tongue.

"This is Rosemarie Delray, your husband's beautiful Italian lover. We were meeting in the darkness of night in a black alley of Rome and while making love—"

Boone's eyes are getting wider and wider and he turns slightly to look at me.

"Good God," Jenna says. "Waylon is that you?"

I know Boone can hear her voice and he shakes his head, rolls his eyes.

"How'd you know?" I'm a bit distraught that my acting isn't as good as I thought. I can hear sizzling in the background of the phone. She must be cooking bacon.

"Dallas is too lazy for a lover, much less leaving the country. And you don't have an Italian accent. It sounds— like one of those singing chipmunks with a Kentucky accent."

"Oh. That would be me."

"What are you doing with his phone?"

"I found it in my bag. We ran into each other at a diner in this little town in Tennessee. I swear it was random."

"Just like his phone showing up in your bag."

"Yeah." I hear Jenna talking to someone and she sighs. It is Dallas's deep voice I hear in the background. "He says to keep the phone. He wants to keep in touch. He bought another on the way home. "Baby, are you alright?" Jenna asks me. "He says Chase dumped you there. I knew he was a rotten egg. You had a baby? I didn't even know you were pregnant. You should have come home with us."

"Chase wanted me to hide it."

"You're better off without him. Hey, sweetie, can I call you back? I'm getting supper on the table."

"Yeah, Jenna. Love you guys."

"Love you, too."

We stop three hours later in a nice hotel in a town just inside Kentucky. I can't tell if Boone is just sick of me playing my guitar in the backseat or he's tired. The entire time, Chey is craning her neck and talking up a storm about whatever thirteen year-olds talk about. She's taking pictures and when we stop at a rest stop, she has some lady take a cell phone picture of us all together making faces. She's funny and silly and makes me laugh. I'm dying to look at the envelopes when we stop, but Chey asks me to show her a few notes on my guitar. She's so anxious when she asks me, I can't tell her no. So we sit for two hours and I show her how to play some notes and I sing along.

"Oh. Wait, wait, wait." Then it hits me. That old craving to write out a song. I mean, the one that keeps me up for days, obsessed with getting the notes and the words on paper, what is churning in my head.

We're sitting there together while Boone is laying back on a bed in his stocking feet and jeans watching TV and watching us. I scrabble through the hotel drawers for some note paper and pen and write down the notes I'm having Chey play. I keep telling her to do it again kind of dancing around with the song on my mind while I fumble with the words, jot down the notes. *Sitting in a hotel room. It's half past four. I keep waiting, waiting, waiting for you to come back, open the door. The knock comes. It ain't you. I've got the leavin' me baby blues. Then when the dust settles and you can't be found. I realize this whole time, I'm glad you never turned around. Keep going. Get along. Them blues, they're gone.*

Boone tells me six times, Chey needs to go to bed. She whines at Boone, I beg for ten more minutes until two in the morning and I see her trying not to look at her fingers. She has little blood blisters from strumming the same notes over and over and they have to be sore.

"Run them under some cool water," I tell her. "I'm so sorry." I figure Boone's going to be mad at me even after I get a little ice and wrap it in a towel when she lays down on the bed. Lexie's asleep on the bed next to her with a pillow fort around her. He'd left three times to talk to his parents. By his rigid stance, I think they might be angry at him. Then when Chey lays down with the TV on low, Boone jabs a thumb towards the door. "We need to talk."

"I'm sorry—" I say it three times even before he sits down beside me on the curb outside the room. I'd left a minute before him, called Dallas and got him out of bed. I tell him I think I have a song coming, it'd hit me like a tornado tonight. He laughs sleepily, tells me to sing it to him on voicemail tomorrow morning.

"I know, Boone, I get—intense, obsessed—I wasn't thinking about the blisters. My fingers," I hold my hand up. "They're so calloused from playing, I forgot."

"Skeeter, this is the first time she's talked to someone over fourteen in the last three years, much less me," he says. "She's going through some rough stuff, like you, without her mama around. At the last rest stop, she cornered me at the restroom and was begging me to stop for the night so she could ask you to show her how to play the guitar."

"So you're not going to yell at me?"

Okay, surprise. He leans to the left pushes a hand to my chin and draws my head toward him. Then while I'm trying to figure out what the end play is to this game, he bends toward me and kisses me gently on the lips. It's two little pecks, then a long kiss. He takes my breath away, I'll admit it. I'm lost in that kiss. Even when he pauses, I'm blinking up at him with a stupid expression on my face.

"You're beautiful, Skeeter," he says in a whisper.

"I thought you didn't like *all this,*" I tease him, doing that old hand waggle in front of me.

"I never said I didn't like *all this.*" He leans in again, kisses each of my cheeks. "I said it was different. I like—different." He reaches up, wiggles one of my buns on top of my head. "You okay about your family today?"

"Yes and no." I'm honest. "I want it all, you know? I want to be with them and still be able to be who I am—me. I can't. Life should be so easy."

"Yeah, you're right," he agrees. "Skeeter, I want to help you find whatever you're looking for—if it's your mama or where you've been, or something you don't even know yet, whatever."

"How far do you want to go with this, Boone?" I ask him. I suppose it's right out of the blue for him. Not so, for me. About an hour and a half ago, Boone left the room. I know he was calling somebody. I assumed it was his parents. Now, I'm not so sure. Because Chey turned to me when the door closed and said: "I think my dad likes you. I just haven't seen him like anyone, not even his girlfriend. She's back again." Oh, that must be who Olivia is who was coming for supper at the Martinez's. *Again*? What does that mean?

"What do you mean?" Boone asks me now.

"You and me," I say. "I, um, I'm not one of those girls who does the one night stand thing. Maybe my different clothes or the *uniqueness* confuses you. What I look like on the outside, the wild girl image I portray with my music does not fall over to my relationships. I don't sleep around with boys who have girlfriends or wives. I wasn't raised that way." I roll my eyes because he's giving me a blank stare. "Let me spell it out for you. I didn't know you had a girlfriend."

"Oh, yeah, that." He pulls away, rests his elbows on his knees and tugs at his lips.

"Oh, yeah, *that*."

CHAPTER 15
DUTCH MAKES ME GO ON A DATE WITH A COP

Dutch tells me I'm late for my appointment to get my temporary license to drive. He doesn't say anything about our fight yesterday and how I screamed I hated him. He doesn't seem surprised I'm sitting nervously on the bed in the room waiting to see if he's going to come inside and jab a thumb toward the front door, tell me to get out.

I can tell he's mad standing there in his stocking feet with little holes on each big toe. If he's in his stocking feet, he's been wearing his old rubber barn boots and he's kicked them off at the back door. And that means he's been cleaning the stalls which is my job.

He catches me closing the little jewelry box. I had noticed a little piece of paper sticking on top. It's one of the little note papers from the hotel last night. It has Boone written on the top and a short note: *If you need me. If you want to figure out who you are—* and his phone number.

I see Dutch glance at the box. There were three folded envelopes in Mama's jewelry box and two of them stick out when I shut it. I push them in with my thumb. I was just finishing looking at them for the third time. The first envelope has WAYNE PELOSI– Louisville written on the front. It has ten, plain blank bank checks inside. The address is to a P.O. Box in Louisville, Kentucky. The second envelope has BUD MOONEY–Nashville. It, too, has checks inside. There are four of them with an address of 1010 Copperfield Drive, Nashville, Tennessee. And the third, it has a folded napkin from the DayLight Lounge. On it, is written: Stevie C. There's an area code and a phone number, but the last four digits are rubbed out.

"Did you find what you were looking for?" That's what he asks me next. I look up at him. I suppose that's the big question now. His eyes are worried. It kind of scares me. Maybe hurt. It's like he cares about me. I want to think it's time to run. I know he thinks I'm broken. Poor old guy probably thinks he can fix me too.

"No." I shrug my shoulders. "I mean, I don't know."

He starts to turn to go. Then he wheels around again. "Skeeter, maybe you don't need to look no more. Maybe— maybe here's the place you're looking for." He smiles a little. "Anyway, Bobby called. I told him to call before he came. I didn't want to make a decision for you about the date with him. I just told him you had to leave for a bit, weren't sure if you'd be back on time. I'll watch the little one. Maybe it'd just be nice for you to take a little break from her."

He's being so kind. I know he doesn't have hardly a cent to his name. I can see the stupid dress bag sitting by the bed. "I'll go. That's fine. The dress is—" I swallow hard. "It was really nice of you to buy it for me."

So where do you take a date in backwoods Bel-Air, Tennessee on a Friday night? Obviously, Bobby and I have different ideas of what options are available. He shows up at the front door in nice jeans, a button-up shirt, and hiking boots. I'm standing at the bottom of the steps in a little black slip dress that's off the shoulder and cut straight up to mid-thigh. I've exchanged my daddy's boots for gray stiletto heels. I let my hair down so it falls past my shoulders and halfway to my back, something I seldom do. I don pink lipstick instead of cherry red.

Bobby just stands there with wide eyes staring at me. Dutch comes out with his newspaper in one hand and his coffee in the other and nearly creams Bobby coming around the corner. Dutch's coffee splatters to the floor.

"Um." That's what Bobby says and I turn to Dutch and ask him to interpret what he's said because I'm about to turn around with a sob and run back up the stairs.

"Where'd Skeeter go?" Dutch is just staring at me like he just ate his first piece of pickle. "Wasn't she just here in those weird boots?" He blinks then, makes this funny shake of his head and gives a dumb stare at Bobby. "Bobby, are you going to take the girl on a date or stand there and look like an idiot 'cause she's so cute?" Dutch finally seems to shake off the stupids too when he leans over, raps his newspaper on the top of Bobby's head. I'm getting the feeling Dutch paid Bobby to do this because Bobby nods his head up and down. "Bring her back by eleven."

"I'm not fourteen, Dutch, I can stay out as long as I want."

I find out when we get to the car that Bobby had done some research on me on his own. I mean, not the kind that would warrant a creep button on his shirt, but the kind that comes from the social networks and magazines. Because he found out on one I had listed hiking as my favorite recreation on some silly fan club website. I giggle and his face turns beet red.

"I do like to hike," I tell him while he opens the door for me. "I mean, I can go back in and change and we can—"

"No, no." He holds up a hand and shakes his head while I sit down inside his truck. It's big and he has to grab my elbow to push me into the seat. "There's just not much to do here. Nashville's just an hour away. We can find a nice restaurant there."

I know a good restaurant called The Find. It's dark and comfortable with tables around a small stage. Some nights they have bands. Other times, it's just chef-made food. It isn't too big or too small. I sang there a couple times with Chase. I know the owner and I give her a call because it's hard to get reservations unless you call weeks in advance. Her name's Gina Craig and she sets us up with a nice table. The servers are a bit carried away with their desire to make everything perfect. One keeps over-smiling and stuffing napkins at me and another has brought out a third round of ginger ales.

I'm sipping one of those ginger ales and Bobby's got a beer. "So Dutch told me you're kind of looking for home—for your mom." He reaches into his pocket, pulls out a little pad of paper. "While I was looking up Waylon Ryder's favorite things—" He grins at me sheepishly. "I found a few things that might be clues of some sort. You interested?"

"I guess, sure." I must be looking at him cautiously while the server overindulges us in another round of water. "Dutch really doesn't know that much about me, though."

"Yeah, you're right. Because I don't think he would have let you drive Boone home that day in the cemetery if he'd known you didn't have a driver's license."

"How'd you find out?" I cringe.

"Because Boone's father asked me to run a background check on you."

"He—he can do that?" And why?

"No, but right after I told him that at the front desk and he left, Nannette Lowry who was standing with me and who works at the license bureau said she knew there wasn't much on you because you didn't even have a birth certificate to apply for your driver's license." He stops long enough to point at the back of the restaurant. "Imagine my surprise."

"I'm sorry."

"If you promise me you won't drive Dutch's truck again downtown like I saw you doing the other day—"

"That wasn't me," I lie playfully. I went to pick up diapers. I figured if I did it fast, nobody'd know.

"Well, yeah, it was you. I saw you try to duck down which is another thing you need to stop doing while you're driving. You almost creamed Missus Gibson walking her wiener dog."

"Okay."

"I'll take you out driving a couple times and help you get your license this week. From what I saw, barring the Gibson lawn job, you did fine." He stops, points behind me. "You realize they are taking videos of us with their cell phones." He nods to the right and the kitchen staff staring out the doors. I nod, wave him away so he goes on. "Yeah, I texted Boone and asked him what kind of stuff you liked. He told me about visiting your family and figured I might be able to do some research because, well, I'm kind of into genealogy—you know, looking up family heritage stuff. I know, I'm a boring guy. But there's not much to do by yourself in Bel-Air on weeknights. That is, until you came along. You've kind of stirred things up a bit."

He smiles then. He's got a sweet, lop-sided grin and an overbite. "I'm not good at dating, Skeeter—or is it Waylon? Which do you like?"

"Skeeter's fine, Bobby. And honestly, I'm having fun." I reach out and poke his hand.

"You're just saying that. I'm such a geek."

"You realize most guys can't shift gears like you did when you saw me all dressed up. I mean, who would have thought Dutch would get Gin at the diner help him buy a dress, right? If you looked me up online, my usual attire is—well, pretty much as little as possible or cut up jeans and a tank top." But I find him strangely intrigued when I mention Gin's name. It passes quickly.

"You're really like—gorgeous," he tells me. "You blew me away when I came in the door. I felt like an idiot. I couldn't talk. I wasn't expecting—this." He waves a hand at me. "Not that I would have minded you either way. You're cute—aw, crud." He is wiping away the embarrassment from his cheeks and I'm shaking my head trying to stop him. "But—um, Boone told me a little about you. I thought maybe it would be good conversation. All the stuff they say online for guys to talk to girls, it tells them to have the girls talk about themselves. But Dutch says you're really quiet and so I didn't want to make it awkward for you—oh, Skeeter, I took notes." He gives me a guilty gaze and reaches into his breast pocket and pulls out a tiny notepad. "I don't date much. Obviously. I've got a bunch of questions I can ask you, but my mind is completely blank."

Okay, I'm usually the awkward one. We are in the far reaches of the restaurant, tucked into a corner. The band is playing in the bar area. It's set up so they are sitting around in chairs and people can come and go, listen to them play or they can sit at the tables and eat. I can see them across the room. They are young, all men. The Find is really good about giving bands a try before the larger venues come in at eight or nine. I find Bobby refreshing. Still, I've got an ear for music and I can't help but tune the band in, hear the guitar player hitting the notes like a professional. I don't recognize him. I just know there are a million others like him out there looking to get a break. And he's good, maybe a big notch better than the rest.

"You okay? You want to call Dutch and check on Lexie?" Bobby asks me. "You look kind of worried or something."

I reach out and wiggle my fingers. "No, she's fine," I

say. "I was listening to the music. Give me the notebook."

I say that with confidence only because I'd gone to the bathroom twice and called Dutch already. I just didn't want to tell Bobby that. He sighs and gives up the notebook. I wiggle it open, squint at the handwriting. "It says here: what is your favorite color?" I read it aloud and nibble on my lip. "I like baby blue. But that's today. Tomorrow, it's probably going to be different. Colors match my mood. I'll be black tomorrow if I have to clean Dutch's stalls and that old mare tries to kick me again. It puts me in a bad mood when she does that. I feel like she's the popular horse and I want to be a part of their herd."

Bobby laughs and holds up a hand. "And blue? Why blue tonight."

"Being with you, Bobby, is kind of putting me in a baby blue happy place even though I'm worried about Lexie," I tell him. "I'm having fun. Blue's fun, right?" I offer. "What's your favorite color?"

"Black. Like your dress."

"You're flirting with me," I tease him just as the server slips by again and asks if everything is alright. I'm absently watching the band play across the room. Bobby nods and shoos the waitress away with his hand.

"I am." Bobby laughs and we small talk for twenty minutes before the food gets to the table. By then, Bobby's telling me about the information he'd dug up about my mama. "I looked up a two year span of the time you said you and your mama moved to Holmes County in Ohio. Boone said it was when you were about three. He said her name was Hannah Schwartz and the man who raised you said the name might not really be her real name. Well, he might be right. There really was a Hannah Schwartz from Adams County, Ohio. Now, Hannah's a common name. And so is

Schwartz. However, the one from Adams County died about six months before you and your mama moved there. I found a short two-sentence newspaper article referencing it. She died during childbirth and she was twenty-six. So let's assume your mama was doing her homework. She may have very well found a woman of her same age to emulate her next move."

"I don't know what good that's going to do me," I say with uncertainty. "I still don't have a name."

"But maybe she left you a clue with her age. If you know where she came from before, you might be able to find a woman who came up missing who is twenty-six with a child."

"I'm trying to find out where she is now, not before," I sigh. "Bobby, I appreciate your help, but I don't know how going backward is going to help."

"Maybe someone in her past can tell you where she would go. Maybe she's contacted them or maybe they know her secrets."

Her secrets. I chew on that for a second. It isn't long before I see a shadow by my elbow. I'm thinking it is the waitress coming back again. It isn't. It is Gina Craig, a thin and surly fortyish woman who could easily be Dutch's female doppelganger.

"Is everything to your liking?" she asks me. She's wearing a white chef's tunic. She chit chats for about two minutes, then closes her eyes and pushes a hand on my wrist. "Waylon, I don't want to ask this. But Harley Mason would like to know if you want to sing. We read about the band break up. About the other stuff—" she pauses and I turn my eyes to Bobby before she quickly goes on. "I wasn't sure if it was true. You know he's in town in two days with— um, what's her name?"

"Brooke Canter. No, I didn't know that. I don't care," I lie flatly. "But whatever rumors you heard—the drugs or whatever. They aren't true. I had a baby."

"Oh." Gail looks surprised, then congratulates me and Bobby. I don't have time to tell her the baby's not his before she looks up toward the band. "Listen, Harley's dying to have you come up and sit with them before they're done for the night." She looks at her watch on her wrist. "And that's in ten minutes."

"Who's playing the main performance tonight?" I ask her.

"It's Bare Roots. You want to wait and sing with them? Maybe you can't on your contract."

"I'm not under contract right now. I don't mind. I like to play." I turn to Bobby, toss out a hand. "You mind a song or two?"

"No, it'd be cool."

It was cool even if I was in a black dress, didn't have Chase standing beside me, and I didn't have my guitar. I borrowed one from the band and maybe it wasn't the perfect match, but they did my background like they knew my songs by heart. I just sat on a little barstool in the middle of them and strummed out a few notes, then started singing. I look out and smile at Bobby a couple times and he's singing along like he knows my songs. I sang four or five songs, then Harley Mason introduces himself three times and shakes my hand hard. He gives me his card. I'm thinking the way he played, I should be the one shaking and begging for a picture with him and not the other way around.

CHAPTER 16
GETTING CALLED TRAILER TRASH IN THE BATHROOM OF THE CRAZY FILLY

"The night is still early," Bobby tells me on our way home and just outside Bel-Air. "We're going past the Crazy Filly. I know it probably wasn't as relaxing as just getting a supper for you in Nashville. Maybe I can buy you another ginger ale without having to sing for it. They're too poor to pay a live band there. Or—or maybe you need to get back home?"

I laugh. We did get a free meal out of The Find. "Best date ever, huh?" I laugh at him. "Especially when your date can sing your way out of a two-hundred buck meal. I should have dragged you up there to sing along."

"I would have to pay them to let me be up there with you, Skeeter," he divulges. "I used to sing in the choir at Holy Unity when they had an organist. The director was always waving his hand at me to quiet down I'm so off-key."

"You know," I'm ready to call Dutch again. It will be the twenty-fourth time, I kid you not. "You've been really nice about me worrying over Lexie, I'll get a drink."

I suppose I know everything about Bobby Moretti. He likes kids and he's got twelve nieces and nephews and coaches their soccer and baseball teams. He wants a big family someday. He likes the Civil War reenactments they do down at Bel-Air Village Park commemorating a battle that happened outside town. He dresses up like a Rebel soldier and shoots blanks at the Yankees at a full run. He has a cat name Mikey and he grew up on a chicken farm between here and Denton. What I don't know until we sit down, is that he has an ulterior motive to taking me to the

Crazy Filly Tavern. Her name is Gin—

"You're kidding me, right?" We are sitting on barstools at the bar being stared down by everyone there. Two minutes after we entered the doors, Bobby leans over and nudges me with this sappy grin. "Hey, look, there's Gin Bean." I do follow his gaze. And yes, the girl who works at the diner is plopping beers down on the tables here.

"Her last name is Bean? Like it is Gin Bean?" I thought by the size, this building must have once been somebody's big, old pole barn for their cattle. Bobby says that no, it isn't. It was an old slaughter house until the 1960s. The owner gutted the building, put in a bunch of tables and chairs and called it a bar. It's evolved since then, but has kept its local look. There's bull heads on the walls and stalls where some of the tables are tucked inside.

"Yeah. Kind of like the whiskey," he says. "Cute, huh?"

It is dark and packed. There's three pool tables, a strange smell coming from the wall that harbors the restrooms, and an actual dance floor where a group of line dancers are kicking up wood chips on the floor. Where else are you going to go in Bel-Air on a Friday night?

I turn back to Bobby. He's got that silly grin looking over at her. I see a man in a dirty, red baseball cap sitting two stools down turn quickly away like he's staring hard at us. Okay, I suppose going to a bar with the local small town cop might not make you the most popular person there. I suppose he's given everybody there at least one speeding ticket and a few arrests for DUIs.

"You ever watch those old western movies, Moretti," I hear a voice behind us. I recognize it even over the jukebox blasting out some 1980s rock. It's Jack's voice. "Where the local sheriff walks into the bar and everybody dives under the tables waiting some kind of shootout?" He's got a beer bottle in his hand and he takes a swig, chuckles. Bobby looks at him hard. Maybe he's like me. I'm not sure if Jack's kidding or not.

Bobby twists a bit on his stool, gives me a sideways glance. Then he shakes his head, looks behind Jack to a second man holding a beer and looking toward the jukebox.

"Hey Boone, I thought you got kicked out of here last time for good."

"Huh?" He turns and it's like just then he focuses on Bobby and then his eyes make a lazy sway to me. "Hey, Bobby. No, my sister and Livie are babysitting me tonight." He holds up his beer. "One beer. Yahoo," he says dully.

"Going out with Livie again, huh?" Bobby starts to say. "So she's done with college or just back in town?" Then Boone blinks and keels slightly forward, tips his head like he's just seeing me there for the first time. "Jesus Christ, no way. Skeeter? That's not Skeeter, is it?" He's blank-faced, then laughing like I just told the funniest joke he's ever heard. "You're—on a date?"

"How about we get out of here." Bobby leans in, gives me an impatient nod toward Boone. He looks like he's going to rise, leans forward. I see him reach out for my elbow to help me off the seat.

"No, no," Boone holds out a hand. He's suddenly sober but still staring at me hard. "I wasn't laughing because—I don't know. Listen, I'll go back to where I was sitting. Don't leave on my account."

So we decide to stay a few more minutes and we make awkward talk about the things first dates usually talk about. I laugh at all his stupid jokes and he looks attentive while I try to give him a verbal guitar lesson that sounds stupid and looks stupid while I play a plastic fork.

"They've got a slow dance. I assume you dance." Bobby wags a thumb to the dance floor. "How about one before we go."

So if I can't make a first date anymore awkward, I lie and tell him I dance. I don't. Well, I don't slow dance. Slow dancing just didn't come up for the big ten years of my life living with the Millers in Holmes County. I mean, it doesn't look that hard. I can see other people doing it. But when we get up there, we end up laughing more than dancing because I confess I'd never slow danced before growing with thirteen Amish brothers. "I can, however, kick the crap out of your shins if I need to," I tell Bobby while I finally figure out to put one hand on his shoulder and another on his waist. "And I can run fast."

We go from two slow songs to a couple that are faster even though we're still in slow-dance mode. The entire time, I know Bobby's looking over my shoulder and watching Gin slip through the patrons to wait on the tables. And why am I suddenly jerking my gaze away when Boone peers our direction?

"Does she see you?" I ask him finally.

"Huh?" His face looks stunned like a rabbit who just ran head first into a wolf.

"Gin." I nod right when she looks up and she waves at us.

"Yeah, she doesn't like cops. She says we're judgmental bastards. I arrested Jack a couple times for drunk driving and you know, hitting her."

"She doesn't know you."

"And she never will, I'm thinking." Bobby leans in and smiles. "She looks at me like I'm a spider on a wall. I'm sorry for this even coming up—"

"For discussing your crush while on a date with another girl?" I giggle because it is kind of funny. "Have you asked her out?"

"Are you nuts?"

"Are you asking that as a police officer, a date, or because you are a squirrel?"

He rolls his eyes at my stupid joke. "See?" I say. "You couldn't say anything more stupid than that on a date. Ask her out."

"I must be a catch," Bobby smiles down at me. He's got sweet eyes and the disposition of a well-fed pup. I have no clue why he's a cop. He's too open and level-headed. "I'm on a date and my date is fixing me up with somebody."

"Dude, I'm not fixing you up. You can't take your eyes off her."

"Like Boone can't keep his eyes off you?"

"Huh?" I say it and he rolls his eyes. "He's just a friend."

"Well, tell that to his girlfriend," Bobby leans in, nods toward the pool tables. Boone is holding a pool stick and I can see a dark-haired woman across from him tossing her hands out to her sides. "And there was a huge hesitation when I called him to ask about you for the date. I mean, a long silence." Her chest is rising and falling from the huffing breaths she's taking like she's laying hard into him.

"She's really pretty," I mutter. I don't realize I'm pressing my lips together when I say it until Bobby chuckles softly.

"And smart." I peer over his shoulder at the girl. She's got deep black hair and elf-life features. She's long-legged, big-boobed, and has damn-near-perfect features and obviously, a fiery temper.

"Olivia DiFranco just graduated from Southeastern Tennessee University as a veterinarian," Bobby discloses. "Harlan Martinez paid for her degree so she'd come back and work on his million dollar horses. He's assuming his son's going to marry her and keep the services in the family. She kind of comes and goes when she pleases. It's probably a good match. He doesn't seem to care if she's there or not."

"With that in mind, I am going to the girl's room, then I am ready for you to take me home."

He lets me drive his truck back to Dutch's and spends a good half hour showing me the right way to back into the driveway like it's a parking spot. Then Bobby walks me to the front door and kisses me awkwardly under the little porch light. He tells me he had a great time while Dutch peeks out the front window curtain.

I tell him I had fun, too. I don't, however, tell him while I stood in the short line inside the bathroom doors, Olivia DiFranco and Adriana Martinez slipped in behind me three or four girls back.

"So *that* is the trailer trash," Olivia had sniffed a laugh and stared hard at me before I turned my attention to a wooden bathroom stall door. "You thought I'd be worried about that ugly thing?"

"God, no. Just saying."

"Okay, because if he's hitting that slut on the sly, I'm thinking I could catch something bad."

It doesn't really hit me until a half hour later after I tuck Lexie into her bed and go out to check on the horses. Everything really hits me dump-truck-style. Those mean words. And I'm moving on. But where? The sound of the radio Dutch keeps in the barn has an old sad, country song. The soft beat leaves a melancholy twist in my chest and is like a fist punching into my belly. It's not just Boone's girlfriend's comments, performing, or Chase or my daddy. Or knowing I'm taking that step I need to take to find my mama. I suppose while I rest my elbows on one of the stall doors and kick at the dirt with the muddy toe of a boot, I'm really nothing all by myself and that's why I'm feeling alone and like I've got to find something that maybe never existed at all. Because I can't imagine leaving Lexie. What could I have done so wrong that my mama left me? It's almost horrifying figuring that out beneath the murky lights of the barn in my dress and Dutch's old mucking boots. I don't know who I am so I can even dig my way out. Not even the thought of dragging out the microphone and singing appeals to me.

"Skeeter?"

I turn my head to Boone's voice on the other side of the barn. I didn't even hear his truck pull into the drive over the boombox music and the low nickering greeting of the horses.

"I'm on the other side," I say softly in return and just as he walks around the corner.

"Yeah, I should have just followed the nickers," Boone laughs softly while he rounds the corner. "Dutch said you went out to make sure the horses were all tucked in for the night."

"Yep, what'd you need?"

"Dunno, just got tired of the bar." Boone shrugs. "I had Tiffany drop me off on her way home." He narrows his eyes, looks at me hard. "She asked to find out if you wanted to play there on Fridays or Saturdays. She knows it's a long shot, but figured, what the hell. She thought she might be able to talk the owner into it. I told her I'd tell you."

"I don't have a band, Boone."

"Yeah, I know. She said the same thing. I'm just relaying the question. Regardless, Chey really wants to take you up on that offer of guitar lessons. I'll pay you."

He comes up beside me, leans his elbows on the door

like I'm doing. "I told her I would. Just bring her by."

"Tomorrow?"

"Whenever. You know I'm either cleaning stalls, riding the horses, or cooking for Dutch and his buddies." We're both staring into the empty stall.

"What made you decide to—?"

"Go out with Bobby Moretti?" I interrupt.

"No, um, he's a nice guy. You need nice." Boone lets out a breath when I look up. He waves a hand toward me. "Yeah, I knew that was coming. But—dressed like that."

"It was a dinner date. It's dinner date clothes."

"Oh."

"You don't like it?" I roll my eyes, smile up at him. "All of this? Damn, boy, what do you like? Straight cowgirl? Because your girl tonight was wearing heels taller than me. She's about as cowgirl—"

"She does the horse shows, Skeeter, on the weekends. Her dad owns that big ranch in Texas Dutch picked up the cattle from—"

"So she's a three-horse kind of girl?" I ask blandly.

"What?"

"Dutch is always trying to sell me off for a donkey. I would say if your girl's that good, she's worth three good mares at least, right?"

"I suppose, yeah. She's about as cowgirl as I know. I mean, you're beautiful. It's just not—you. Not being beautiful, I mean. Hell, you'd look good in—a pair of muck boots and a feed bag."

"Look down," I say and point to Dutch's boots on my feet. They come to my knobby knees. I wiggle forward so he can see them in the oozy light.

"Well, you ain't cowgirl," he says in a sing-song voice.

"But you're the one I want tonight." Then he laughs. "That sounds like the songs they were playing on the jukebox at the bar."

"I ain't cowgirl?" I eye him a bit peeved. "Just so you know, you can sit a boy on a horse and plop a cowboy hat on his head and boots on his feet, but it don't make him a cowboy."

He twists his head like he doesn't understand, maybe thinks the joke's on him. "That's what my brother used to say when we'd go to the fair and watch those kids whose mamas and daddies plopped them on old, trained horses once a year to pass by the judges who didn't know shit. They wanted to be cowboy. They were just a bunch of town kids. Kind of like you and your girl."

"What do you know about being cowboy?" He sniffs a haughty laugh.

"You're kidding me, right? I was raised on a farm, dumbass. While your stupid girlfriend was primping her hair in her daddy's five-hundred thousand dollar RV in the parking lot of whatever show she was going to for the weekend, I was out working the fields and getting kicked by ponies teaching them to drive. While she was having the same trainer work the kinks out of the horse her daddy leased for her that was already trained and already worked to the bone, I was out saddling my own four year-old mare and riding her to school. Hell, I can beat your sorry ass in a race with any horse in this barn wearing a frigging dress, makeup and muck boots."

"So, let's see it."

CHAPTER 17

BOONE'S GOT A THING ABOUT MY TONGUE RING

At one in the morning, I'm lying flat on my back on the dusty ground of Dutch's little riding arena. I can hear Boone laughing so hard, he can't catch his breath. He was sitting on the fence, but he must have jumped off. I can hear the last raggedy edges of his chuckles and the sound of his boots on the soft dirt. One second I am on the horse making a perfect angle around an old orange barrel and the next, I'm making a wild twisty-spin in the air.

"Is that why your Amish daddy called you Grace?" he says with a funny twist of his lips. He thinks it's funny and I know he's not drunk, but he's really acting like it. He bursts out in another round of laughter at his stupid joke and extends a hand, lifting me up.

"Eat shit. I would have beat your time by a mile."

"Naw, you didn't." He wiggles the watch he has in his hand. "I timed you."

"You can't even see the big hand in this light, Boone Martinez," I grumble. "I'm not an idiot."

"Yeah, I know. I counted in my head. You okay?"

"You count slower when it's me." I push him with my hands and smile. "And I'm fine." I see him reach out and he starts slapping my back to get the dirt off. It's a little too hard and aimed a little too much at my butt.

"Stop!"

"What?"

"Trying to touch my butt. You've got a girlfriend."

"Yeah, you're right. But you're damn sexy in boots and a dress, you know that, right? And I'm starting to get a thing about that tongue ring." He scoots forward and acts like he's making a teasing snatch for my arm. I pat him away. I give him a shove with both my hands and face him.

"Stop it. That sounds like a stupid, R-rated country song and I'm not that girl."

"Whoa, whoa—" He's taken a step forward feigning my shoves and I step back. "Not what girl?"

"Do not whoa me, cowboy," I growl, holding out my hands to stop him. "Do not think you can put spurs on and you can ride me, get it? I'm not the girl sitting around the trailer park waiting for some woman's boyfriend or husband to lay down fifty bucks a blowjob on the bedside table like your girlfriend and your bitch sister implied tonight in the bathroom. I'm thinking it's the other way around. But I'll give you ten bucks for the try."

"Well, okay." That's what he says. He takes another step forward. I match it, take one back. I'm mad as hell and I swear, my hair is standing on end. "Ten bucks. You can use a verbal IOU if you want. What do you want me to do?"

He's caught me off-guard and I'm just standing there staring at him with a lazy gape of my lips. "Wh—What?"

"I'll be your whore. Ten bucks gets whatever your little heart desires," he tells me softly and with a deadpan face. He's only two steps away and he slips forward one step while I slide my feet back. I know the barn wall has to be somewhere close. I can sense it. I don't want to turn to see it, though. "Whatever you want, whenever you want it. I'd be an idiot to say no. I'm not sure how to do this, but if I do it wrong, let me know. I'll fix it." He reaches a hand out like he's going to snatch my fingers. My eyes are big when I pull my hand back. "I mean, a girl like you doesn't need to pay a guy, but maybe you do it just to keep idiots from sticking around when you just—need someone to do those things and walk away. Well, I'm not sure if I can walk away,

Skeeter, so you might have to kick me out the door. I'm here and not there with her. Isn't that a huge hint about how I feel? And then I might come back here like I've been doing over and over, if not physically in my head night and day, twenty-four seven. Because I don't know how to stop thinking about you, wanting to be with you." He takes one step just stops there, holds out his hands. He must know I'm going to hit the wall this time with my back. And I do. "So what do I do? I want to be with you."

"Boone, I can't—" I want to run. Whatever is happening happened way too fast. He's in front of me, the wall's behind. My mind is battling it out, one side screaming to take his offer because maybe, he thinks I'm cute. The other's yowling he's the kind of guy that knows exactly what to say to a lonely, ugly girl to get a quick screw. My hands are up like I can push him away and his hands come out in front of him and I pat them down.

"Okay, then I'll wing it." He takes one step forward and he's so close I can feel the heat from his body against my chest.

"Boone, I know you think I sleep with a lot of guys—"

"I don't care." He leans over and cups my jaw, tugs my chin upward. My eyes shut involuntarily. I don't tell him to stop when he kisses me his two pecks then lays in with a heart-pounding kiss.

"I don't—sleep with a lot of guys."

"Okay, baby, whatever you want me to hear."

"So maybe you need to stop."

"Yeah, okay," he tells me and works his way up the slant of my neck. He stops just below my earlobe and tickles it with the tip of his tongue. Dammit, I take in a healthy, excited breath. "Yeah, that's what I want to hear. You like it Waylon? Tell me what you want me to do."

His right hand swoops in, rushes down along the side of my dress until his fingers stop just at the hem six inches from my knee. "I can dance better than him, you know that right?" My hand absently lights on the sleeve of his arm.

"Him?" I don't want to look up. I know he's talking about Bobby. I focus on my hand laying there and the feel of his fingers working around my skin.

"You know who I'm talking about," he whispers. They patter on the outside of my thigh, cool and gentle, then slowly slip around to the soft skin of my inner thigh. I feel him press in with his body. I feel captive, restrained. Would it sound bad if I said it was making my heart beat harder in a good way? He's maybe three inches from my panties, just lingering there.

"Boone," I whisper-hiss. I feel him stop.

I snap my gaze upward, see him blink. His eyes are barely open staring down at me. I see a little smile creep up on the corner of his lips.

"What?" I feel his fingers slip up to the elastic of my panties tickling there, feel his body pushing me up against the wall. "Tell me you want me to stop. I will." He reaches his free hand around, slides it between the wall and my rear and tugs me harder against him and up an inch or two. He's almost holding me there. I'm on tippy-toes feeling his heart beat, knowing he feels mine.

"What I'm trying to tell you is I can't just sleep with you and you walk away or come back whenever we—we just want sex."

"I don't know what that means," he whispers. And he's smiling like I'm joking or playing a game. Maybe he is. I feel his fingers part the cleft between my legs. They are cool to my warmth and I try not to make a wispy moan while he barely fingers me, makes me want to grab his hands and make them delve deeper. Who is in control here? Him or me? Then he makes a hasty unlatch of his belt.

"Holy shit, Boone. It means—hell, I don't know."

"Whatever, I'll do whatever you want." He slips his finger out, releases his grip, gives my shoulder a little push downward.

"Shit, don't stop—" I groan deeply. I'm two seconds from feeling that blast of an orgasm and I know he knows that.

"Yeah, I will. But, Skeeter, do me a favor first," he says pressing me downward still. He's holding my chin up, looking me in the eyes. "Baby, do that thing you talked about with the tongue ring. Please."

And suddenly, I'm the one wriggling downward with my bare knees to the cool wood floor and he's pushing himself into my lips. He's cursing and groaning and telling me that's all he can think about, that ring since I told him, while I ease in and out, grasping him with my hands and rubbing my tongue from one end to the other. I suppose if there's one thing other than leaving that Chase ever taught me, it was how to give a good blowjob.

Boone suddenly jerks me upward by my arm. He's got this wild look to his eyes when he wriggles up my dress and tugs me upward. "Wrap your legs around me. Damn, please hurry." He's got me pressed to the wall so hard I can hardly breathe. Boone's got one hand to the wall, the other slips behind me again, makes a quick spread of my legs, while he grunts softly, lifts me up. It doesn't matter. I think I'm holding my breath the moment we come together in perfect harmony, his lower body gently rocking back and forth.

He slowly releases me. I stand up straight, tug down my dress. It is quiet except for a few horse nickers and the staticky sound of an old country song softly playing from the boombox on an old table at the front of the barn.

"So this is where you leave," I whisper. "Ride off into the sunset, cowboy." His hat had dropped to the ground and Boone picks it up and rubs the dust from the brim.

"I am tired," he says. "You don't have to be so mean."

"I didn't want to do it—"

"You didn't want to do it? You're kidding me, right? Not once did you tell me to stop."

"And you're the one that implied I wasn't cowgirl enough for you. Why bother? Why aren't you doing this with your stupid girlfriend if she's all cowgirl and shit?"

"She's staying at my dad's."

"You're kidding me, right?" I know my eyes are wide because he's being so open. "You mean you just can't crawl into bed with her at your dad's because—well, that's not proper?"

"Well, she is—staying there and dad wouldn't allow it." Boone stuffs his hands in his pockets and gives me a half -cocked grin.

"Get out." I yell-whisper.

"Does that mean I can't bring Chey by tomorrow for guitar lessons?"

"GET OUT!"

CHAPTER 18
ASKING FOR A JOB AT THE CRAZY FILLY

"Hey, I need some extra cash," I say to a guy they call Oaky in a little dark room inside the Crazy Filly. It's a Tuesday evening right around five o'clock and the only time I could get Dutch to watch Lexie for the two hour span between feedings. I said I was going out to find a job waiting tables at a restaurant in Denton. "I was wondering if I can play my guitar a couple nights a week here." It smells like stale cigar smoke and vanilla scented fragrance oil wall plug-in. I feel awkward, like a little kid. It's been a long time since I asked to sing at places. After I met Chase, he always did this for me. I suppose, Red did it before him.

Oaky's big and burly enough I can't see the office chair he's sitting in. He's smoking a cigarette and scrubbing a hand through a mop of gray hair on top of his head. He's got a long beard that stops just short of the top of his red-flannel shirt.

"We don't do heavy metal here, baby," he tells me. "The folks that come here, they like classic '80s rock and country. We can get that on the jukebox without paying a band. Then, I get a kickback in quarters."

"Okay." I say that, feeling a little relieved and a lot rejected. That old feeling before I met Chase comes barreling back at me like it had a hundred times while I leave through the dark hallway. I think before I was eighteen, I'd gotten rejected by at least thirty bars even playing on Tuesdays to two drunks and a jukebox playing in the background. Then, like now, I figure I can wait tables at a bar.

Tiffany's sitting on a bar stool behind the counter and talking to a customer when I walk up and put my guitar down. "Well?" she asks, looking up over the man's ball cap that says US VETERAN on it.

"He said I did the wrong music," I tell her. "You think you can talk him into letting me wait tables or something?"

She chuckles like I'm joking, then tips her head to the side. "Waylon Ryder waiting tables at this old bar?" she asks me and sighs. "Why don't you go up there and play me and Fred here a couple songs. Let Oaky get a hear of you."

"He won't be mad?"

"Not if we don't have to pay you. Do something old first."

"Okay."

There's eight people in the bar including Fred and Tiffany. It's dark except for a few places the dingy curtains on the few windows at the top of the walls let the summer evening light creep in. I set up the old microphone, the kind that sits on a base. I work my guitar over my shoulder. Fred at the bar counter asks me what I'm going to sing and says he likes some classic rock song from the 1960s.

"Okay," I say. "I know that one. I used to have a few gigs at birthday parties, weddings, backyard barbecues—" I start my guitar and hum a few notes so I know I'm singing the right song. "I'm like an old jukebox," I tell the old guy. "That's what my ex-boyfriend used to tell me. He said I can't find my way out of a plastic bucket, but I can hear a song and play it on the first try."

So I must sing to Fred's liking. He's tapping a finger on the counter and he's got a soft smile to his lips and a shine to his eyes. They start throwing songs at me like it's a game, 1980s rock, 1970s country music—in retrospect, I've sung them all at one time or another working my way to get to my dream. I'm thinking it's funny right then that I never thought about how much I liked these old bars and the quirky people in them. On a few, I show them a beat with my hands and have them bang out the drum part to get me started.

I keep watching the clock. I told Dutch I'd be gone two hours and while I squint up along the wall, I'm realizing it has been a long time before that little hand has changed. And I also notice that more than a few people have come in like it's the end of a factory shift because they're dressed in the bright yellow Denton Valley Automotive t-shirts and ordering food and beer. I suppose it's the Tuesday busy time because they've got a couple waitresses now taking orders and giving me funny stares. Still, Oaky hasn't come out of his office to kick me out yet.

"Hey, anybody got the time?" I finally stop long enough to ask.

"It's eight," somebody calls out and I about drop my guitar trying to get down off the stage. Dutch is going to kill me. I'm sure Lexie is screaming holy hell for supper. I slap Dutch's phone number on a piece of paper in front of Tiffany and tell her if Oaky wants to hire me, call me. And if Dutch asks who it is, he's from Schutte's Homestyle Diner in Denton.

"That's alright. He just phoned me up here. He says you can play on Friday and Saturday nights for three weeks to see if it works, one hour starting at nine and he pays you seventy-five bucks a night plus whatever tips you want to take. Bring your own tip jar."

Chapter 19
The secret about the room behind the locked door

When I was eleven, there was a Mennonite widow living just down the road from Abram Miller's farm. She had been teaching me how to play piano and guitar since I was five or so. For six years, I had walked over there every day but Sunday while the man who raised me and his sons worked in the fields.

I knew Abram was aware I went to her house. I knew musical instruments were forbidden in his home so I hid the fact I was learning to play them at Missus Becker's home. I also knew he went for a walk each evening toward her place and didn't return for about an hour at a time. It always scared me he was going to stop by her house while she was working in the garden and ask how my day was and if I was being a good girl during my visits. And she would tell him about my music lessons. So there was a point that I asked Abram if I could walk with him thinking I could waylay any questions so he didn't know the truth. But he told me that in the evening, it was his time to be alone, talk to God, and think things over about the day.

Of course, I didn't listen. I followed him one evening. Sure enough, he made a quick twist along her little stone walkway and knocked on her door. He went inside and I crept up to the window and listened to see if my secret was being exposed for his ears to hear. There were little mewling noises like they were petting one of Missus Becker's beagles and curiously, I peeked up into the window. Instead of beagles, I got an eyeful of Abram Miller's bare rear on the couch and Missus Becker untying her long hair and letting it dangle off the armrest. I was stunned.

I should have learned my lesson. The image was burned into my eyes for years to come. However, it didn't stop me from standing on the threshold of knowing too much and wishing to God, I could take three steps back and let fate take me a different direction fifteen years later.

There's a little table by the front door. In it, Dutch keeps all the truck keys and barn keys and house keys. After he goes up to the rooms upstairs and checks the doorknobs to make sure the locks are secured, he takes one of the keys from the drawer and visits the attic room. When he returns, he quietly places the door key into the drawer. Then he walks out to the front porch and stares off into the trees and raggedy hills beyond. After ten minutes, he comes back inside and snatches up his keys. He gives me a holler, tells me if I'm going to the diner for coffee and a doughnut, I'd better get my butt downstairs. And I always do.

However, today is different. I feign a sneeze and drag my favorite blanket down the stairs with me and Lexie. My hair's all tangled and down my back. I grab a hair scrunchie from my wrist and tie it all up on the top of my head. "I got a cold," I lie to him. "I'm watching TV, feeding Lexie, and going back to sleep."

He nods and leaves. I listen for the truck tires to spray gravel from driveway to main road. When it does, I know I've got one hour and fifteen minutes to snatch up that key, make my way upstairs and find out what the hell he's hiding in that room.

"Be good." I tell Lexie while I shove her car seat up so she is facing the TV. She stares at it and I snatch the key out of the drawer, bound upstairs to the attic room.

The key slides right into the lock and the door opens with a sucking sound. I catch a whiff of old stuffy room. It's like stale perfume and old, old spoiled milk and—

I blink. The room is white and pretty. There's a twin-size bed with a frilly pale comforter, lazy curtains and fuzzy carpets on the wooden floor. I'm taking it all in. That's when I see an old glass sitting on a baby blue bed stand. It is crusty like the milk poured into it was left there for a good ten years. "Oh," I whisper. "Ten years."

It's Charlene's room. I guess I conjured up worse like she'd be laying like a skeleton there. Instead, of a carcass, there's a brown cardboard box. It's just like she must have left it that night. I can see a folded napkin by her glass. It is stained from a cookie long decayed. There's a TV set and a pink landline phone. And there's a little note hanging by an oversized safety pin to a lacy lampshade on the bedstand. Daddy, please don't be mad. I'm telling Boone the truth tonight. It's never going to work—I'll come home after everything cools down.

I feel the blood run from my face. It's like I've taken a step back in time and I can see this horrible thing about to occur, but I can't stop it. I step back. I just want out of there. I can hear Lexie starting to cry downstairs. I bump the bed. The box tips to one side and spills over the edge.

"Shit." I feel my heart beating. I'm creeped out and freaked out and my heart is racing. I wheel around, make fast tracks to the pile of papers and knick-knacks and photographs that have toppled to the floor. While I'm tossing them into the box, I am hoping Dutch didn't have them in some order. It is a jumbled mess. I backtrack, take the stuff out and try to put it back in one piece at a time so it appears in some sort of order.

That's when I find it. The image of me peeking in Missus Becker's window lurches into my mind like a drunk hippo. I feel my hands reach for the paper. I see POLICE REPORT on the top. I regress fifteen years and feel my little fingers on that windowsill, feel my feet working to tippy toes. And while I stare at the paper, I know I am looking at the equivalent of seeing Abram Miller's bare bottom grinding up and down again on top of my music teacher. But it isn't Abram Miller, it is Dutch Cates and Bo Littleton and Harlon Martinez's dirty little secrets I am staring at.

"Why didn't you leave well enough alone, Skeeter?" That's all Dutch says behind me while he hard-gazes me and shakes his head.

I jolt. Every fiber in my body jerks to attention when I hear Dutch's voice behind me. I was so intrigued with the words settled on the paper in front of me, I completely blocked everything else out.

"I'm sorry. I'm sorry. I'm sorry," I tell him jumping up and feeling like the blood drained from my body. He's got a donut box in one hand, a to-go Styrofoam cup of coffee in the other, and a betrayed glaze to his eyes.

"That one was never filed formally. You'll forget you even saw it." He wiggles the donut box. "I was worried about you, didn't want to stick around the diner if you was sick. I brought you a donut and coffee."

I shove the paper into the box, make a messy stab at grabbing the rest up and pouring it into the cardboard box. "I didn't see anything, Dutch." But I did. I did see it.

Chapter 20
A dumbass in the driveway & Mama's dark past catching up to me

"Why's dumbass sitting in my driveway again today?" Dutch is grumping two days later. He hasn't mentioned anything about me sneaking into the attic room. He simply locked it up and returned the keys to the same place by the front door. For an entire evening, he gave me a mournful gaze leaving me feeling horribly guilty. Then, it's almost forgotten except my residual shame.

"What?" I ask. "What dumbass? I see seven of them in this kitchen. Which one is it?" I'm dropping scrambled eggs on a stranger's plate in Dutch's kitchen. He's one of six men sitting at the table waiting for breakfast. A couple of them chuckle at my teasing. Dutch does not. I'm beginning to wonder if Dutch didn't go downtown and pick up stray homeless men and bring them back here just to be served a free home-cooked meal. He told me they are from Community Halfway House. He brings them out here to earn a little bit of money and help him in the fields.

"What dumbass?" Dutch grunts a reply. "You know who I'm talking about. The one who sat out there like a kicked pup when you screamed at him yesterday to go away."

"Well, it worked didn't it?" I ask.

"Don't make him mad, girl, you hear me? I don't need the Martinez's down my throat. I've already got Littleton creeping around every time I drive out of the town. Just sit inside when he's out there until he goes away. I told him he needed to stay away for a while. He understands. Harlan Martinez stood on my front porch last evening, telling me he'd shut down my farm, my business if his boy got into any trouble with you. He doesn't want any stink going around town and making the Littletons mad. You understand who the Littletons are, right?"

I hold out my hands to my sides unsure. "Just more stupid political puppets?" I suggest while Dutch squats down next to Lexie laying on her belly on a comforter on the floor. He tickles her cheek with his fingers. He smiles softly. She smiles back and reaches out her arm precariously. "I'm not the one who keeps showing up at the Martinez's house, Dutch. I am staying away. And that boy he talks about is full grown with a thirteen year-old daughter. Surely, he's old enough to make decisions for himself. And why would the Martinez's be afraid of the stupid mayor?"

"Bo's not just some mayor. Half the town belongs to him including the land they've got the new high school on. It ain't that easy," Dutch mutters. "He owns it. He's got the ability to shut it down. Bo, he—" Dutch sighs. "Bo's a bigot and a bully. If you haven't heard, it was his son in that car with my baby girl the night she died. Bo hasn't forgiven nobody and especially Boone Martinez."

"Well, the whole thing wasn't Boone's fault, was it?"

Dutch sighs. "Baby, it don't matter who they point the finger at. It was just stupid kid stuff."

"Oh."

"Everybody knows that. Harlan, he's had Boone on a tight leash until you got here. He has to. Every time Boone moves, Bo sends the cops out to arrest him for something."

"Can't they do something to stop him? How does that work?" I roll my eyes. I can see the men looking back and forth between me and Dutch, taking in our conversation. Dutch sees it too.

"No, Bo Littleton owns Big Bo Oil and Gas and ninety

percent of the underground rights to pull natural gas out of the ground here." Dutch swipes a napkin over his lips. I turn to flip the bacon on the stove, listen to him talk with my back to him. "We're right on the Chattanooga Shale Field that runs from Kentucky, through part of Tennessee and into Alabama. We're right smack dab in the middle. If that don't mean anything to you, it means Bo Littleton can come in and tear up my property anytime he wants, drill it for natural gas. It's called fracking. When they're done, my farm might as well be dead because it pollutes the water and poisons the ground."

"He'd do that?"

"I'm going to take you for a drive this afternoon," Dutch tells me sharply, nods his head toward the door. "Then you can answer that."

I don't know how long Boone sat out there in his truck. He never came inside. When we left to get my learner's permit, Dutch takes me across the county and past this huge, vacant lot. There's a well tower there and a cute little farm with overgrown grass. He has me roll down my window and I wriggle my nose.

"It stinks."

"Yeah, well, it does more than stink." Dutch pulls off the side of the road, points across the tree line to a bare swatch of graveled land. "That's Carl Walters's old place. Well, it was. He got the property from his daddy who got it from his daddy and so on all the way back before the Civil War. Carl worked down at the city offices for fourteen years. He was the treasurer. One day, he said Bo walked in and Carl made an offhand joke about the taxes going up for everybody since Bo'd become mayor. Three weeks later, the trucks start driving right on to Carl's property. He tried fighting it, ended up with a second drilling rig coming in.

He was living here for a year, but the nosebleeds for his three boys were so bad, they had to move out. His wife had headaches and ended up in the hospital twice. The stuff in the air peeled the paint off their cars."

"So your point is, stay away from Boone Martinez or this is your place next."

"I can't tell you what to do. I just know I don't want to get on the bad side of the Littleton's. I don't want to cause trouble for Harlan Martinez. Baby girl, my farm's my life." He points to a tall white sign near the drilling rig. It says PRIVATE PROPERTY. NO TRESPASSING. BIG BO OIL/GAS— BEAUREGARD B. LITTLETON, OWNER.

"But I think you are telling me that." I roll my window back up. "It doesn't matter. He's got a girlfriend. And I don't think she'd take too kindly to us hanging out."

"Do you do drugs, Skeeter?"

It's right out of the blue and I blink, look up at Dutch sitting next to me in the truck.

"Why do you ask that?"

He gives me a big sigh. "I just had a bit of money in a coffee can under the sink. It's gone." He taps his fingers on the steering wheel. I look up through the windshield at the sky while we sit in front of Carl Walters's old property.

"Well, why didn't you ask me if I was a thief?" My heart sinks. "I don't do drugs. I don't even do weed. And I don't steal. Why would I? I haven't asked you for a cent. I would have asked you for it before I took it." I feel like crying. I don't know. I hate having fingers pointed at me. "How much was it? I'll go get a job and come up with it. I didn't take anything from you."

"It was almost three-thousand dollars, Skeeter." He sighs, leans over and tugs something from under his seat. I watch him pull it out, hold it up over Lexie's car seat between us.

"Dutch, why do you have that much under the sink? I mean, who does that anymore?" I huff while I absently take a folded magazine from his fingers. "Why don't you deposit it in the bank?" I turn my attention from him to the magazine, lay it down on my lap and open it up by pressing it down with my fingers.

"You had the little jewelry box. And you had your guitar case. I saw it, sweetie, what am I to think?"

"I don't know. But you don't think I stole your money because I didn't. My daddy gave me the box. It was my mama's. Boone said he used his credit card to buy my guitar back. Ask him, he'll tell you the truth."

"Your daddy? You went home?"

"Yeah, Dutch," I say. "I went home. But it isn't home anymore. It's too late for me to go—home. He doesn't want me. I don't want to talk about it." I figure right now in Dutch's eyes, I'm not worth a donkey in trade.

"Oh."

I sigh, let my eyes fall lazily to the magazine at my fingertips. "Oh, no—"

"The cover," Dutch says softly. "Then go to page three." He takes off in the truck. I already know. It's Countdown Celebrity Magazine, one of the dirtiest gossip tabloids on the market. It's hard to look at the picture on the cover. Me at fifteen, mostly naked and singing on stage. WAYLON RYDER RIDES AWAY INTO THE SUNSET, that's the storyline. Then, I turn to page 16. I scan it. It reads like an obituary with quotes from Chase telling everybody I OD'd and went crazy. There's a picture at the bottom with his new singer and they call her Chase's new sidekick, Brooke Canter. They are smiling and waving for the camera on stage. It just makes me sick to my stomach.

There's pictures of me being loaded in an ambulance back when I was seventeen. There's some of me last year on stage. That's why the owner of The Find asked me about the drugs.

"Where'd you get this?"

"Harlan Martinez slapped it on my front porch banister. He said he knew you were trouble when he saw you at the diner the other day."

"I suppose you're not going to believe me when I tell you I didn't do anything more than weed and beer. It was a long time ago. I was so naïve. The hospital picture was when I got drunk and fell off the stage. I was young, dumb, and—I don't know." I swallow hard. "Dutch, you don't know me worth crap. So it's hard to ask that you trust me that I wouldn't do anything like that, steal for drugs. And no, I don't do drugs. That part of my life when I was fifteen and stupid and naïve will haunt me forever. I can't shake it. I got caught up with the wrong crowd. I got out. I know Chase wasn't a dream catch, but he took care of me. When I left home, I didn't even know how to turn on a cell phone or—never mind." I sigh, close the magazine. "I guess I'm still naïve. He's the one that dropped me cold turkey in Bel-Air and probably called the magazine to make a buck."

"How can you *not* have a birth certificate?" Dutch had shaken his head when we were standing at the little desk in the BMV office.

"I never had one," I say and tug him aside, lean in. "I have a couple fake IDs, but I don't think they'll work here."

"No, they won't work here," he snarls. "What? Were you born in France or something?"

"Kind of. Ohio. I was Amish."

"Well, that explains the dress." Dutch says like he's a

smartass. I roll my eyes and he just shakes his head. We have to go and get a birth certificate and a social security number for me. He grumbles and bitches and then he says he isn't going to do anything until he gets a cup of coffee at the Bel-Air All-Nighter Motel and Diner.

In retrospect, it was going to happen, my mama's past catching up to me. I wish it wasn't. I was a spoonful and a half into a hot fudge sundae. I'm watching Bobby who is sitting at a table in plain clothes and what little hair he's got is all slicked back. He's dressed up with a nice button up flannel and jeans like he's got a date, but he's alone. I don't think he even notices Dutch and I are sitting in the front. I watch him from the corner of my eye sliding his glasses along the bridge of his nose in slow motion. Then, he's acting like he's poking something into his cell phone, but he's looking to his left over the top of his glasses. I follow his gaze. It stops at the counter where Gin is pouring a chubby businessman some coffee.

I'm fascinated and half listening to Dutch growling with another old farmer about something political that makes no sense. There's only a few of us in the diner. It's no wonder when a couple cars pull into the parking lot, we all look up. I'm a little more sluggish. I'm licking off the spoon and I half-glance out the huge windows with the bamboo shades still rolled up to the top of the frame.

In any other circumstance, I wouldn't have noticed the man in the checkered button-up shirt and khaki pants. I could see him making his way out the car doors with two men in black suits and walking along the outside sidewalk rounding three-quarters of the building. They kind of spread out, though. One went toward the right of the building, the other two the left. Khaki Man, he headed toward the front door.

"Sweetie, those are the two men who were looking

for somebody like you yesterday." That's Gin leaning over to my right and telling me this softly while she nods toward the kitchen door. I jump. I didn't see her step up, I was so focused on the men right then. "I know there's been a lady with some gossip magazine running around town asking folks about you too."

Boom. Oh, my God. I remember the man in the khaki pants. Long ago. Long, long ago. I blink, remember Mama's voice—*baby, mama's sorry. We got to go. Your daddy, he found us. He sent the Bogeyman—* The Bogeyman. I remember him. I clearly remember him and I remember the night. He was a man with thick red hair and thick red beard. He wore glasses. I was just maybe four. But I remember blinking up at Mama in the blackness of my cozy bed with princess blankets and princess flounces and a little tent surrounding it. Then, I remember being chased in her car and flopping around in the backseat. Hands. Yeah, I remember him trying to reach his hands into the open car window and trying to get me out—

The next thing I remember is me holding Lexie as hard as I can and smashing my back against the opposite side of the counter while Gin blinks strangely calm down at me. I crawl into the kitchen and I'm shaking so bad, I can hardly stand.

Sweat is beading down my forehead. I don't think I've ever been so scared. Run. That's all I can think of to do while I find myself standing smack dab in the middle of the kitchen staring at Trevor Howard who works in the restaurant and who is flopping a hamburger on the grill and staring up at me with curious eyes.

"Trevor, right? You're Trevor?" I ask him breathlessly. He nods like he's trying to figure out why this woman is standing in the middle of the kitchen holding a baby. "Yeah, I need someplace—okay, I need to hide."

Chapter 21
Someplace safe

"I'll go, Dutch, I don't want you to get hurt."

"You ain't going nowhere." Dutch swings his head like a horse with a fly on its muzzle. "You know, you spend so much time walking out that door, then coming back in if you keep this up, I'm gonna take out my old wood door and put in a swinging one that spanks you in that scrawny butt of yours each time you try to leave."

I pack my little backpack with diapers and the clothes Dutch bought Lexie, a little pink dress with tiny shoes. This time, it isn't me leaving in a temper. Dutch told me to find someplace else to stay. It isn't the money or the magazine or even Harlan Martinez slowing down when he passes us on Bel-Air Hollow Road.

They found me in the little storage room closet Trevor Howard had showed me. He didn't question me. Just pointed me in the direction of the office, then tucked me in among the paper towels, toilet paper, and brooms. When Dutch and Bobby Moretti finally coaxed me out the door twenty minutes later, I was holding a window squeegee as a weapon and shaking like a leaf.

"You know what they're wantin', baby girl?" Dutch is cautious with his words. I know he doesn't believe me when I tell him I don't. "Because I'm asking you to tell me. I know everybody's got their secrets. But if those secrets are going to hurt others, you've got to tell somebody. Ain't that right, Bobby?"

Bobby stands there. His eyes are kind and he smiles at me like I'm a little kid. He scratches his head. "They asked me if I knew a girl in the picture—" He reaches out, extends a sheet of paper at me. "I'm sure they didn't know I was a cop." I take it, turn my attention from him to the paper. "The one man in the suit said he was looking for a girl named Emory. He didn't say anything else, said he couldn't." It has three pictures copied to the front. I squint. They are a little blurry. One is a young woman in a slinky red dress leaning against a nice car. Her hands are clasped together and she's smiling white teeth. I blanch. Strangely, she looks like me straight down to the way her nose arches and her eyes are squinting against the sun. However, she has shoulder-length hair. "It's not me," I say to Bobby while my gaze eases downward to a little girl in a softball uniform. It's the kind of picture they take for sport recreation leagues. She's grinning my grin at maybe eight or ten. The third is probably a kindergarten school picture. It's a little white-haired girl with big, blue eyes smiling hard at the camera. "I mean, it looks like me, but I didn't go to regular school. I—went to the Amish schools until eighth grade. I didn't play ball. I don't know who she is other than she looks like me. But I suppose everybody's got somebody out there that looks like themselves, right?"

"Yeah." Dutch bobs his head up and down, turns to Bobby. "I think they're barking up the wrong tree. What'd they say they wanted with her?"

"They said they couldn't disclose the reason." Bobby puffs out his cheeks. "I don't know, Skeeter. I'm wondering if they didn't see something online. You know there's videos all over the place of you singing two nights ago at the restaurant. And the pictures, they look like this girl on the paper. Maybe they think you are her."

"Okay, my mama said my real daddy was a bad man," I offer. "He was from some town near San Antonio. She called him the Bogeyman. He tried to kill her and I remember running from him. Like I can still picture us sneaking out of the house and Mama had to climb some kind of a fence in the middle of the night and stuff. Maybe's he's trying to find us still." I don't tell them she also taught me how not to cry if I was scared so nobody could find us.

"Where's your mama?" Bobby asks me. "That's the big question still. You sure you have no way to contact her?"

I feel a little sick to my stomach, still feel like I did something bad to make her leave me. "She left me with a man named Abram Miller when I was maybe five. It's the last I saw of her. That's who I call my daddy. He raised me with his boys. He always said he had to guess my age and my birthday because he didn't know anything about me except I belonged to my mama when she came to live with him. Nobody really talked about her after she left. It was like she died. I don't know. Maybe she did."

Bobby and Dutch are gazing at me with distant stares. I try to focus on Dutch. Trust hasn't always come easy for me. Even before Chase. I suppose that's why I choose the company I keep. It's easier to walk away from people who don't really care about me. It's kind of a game, I guess, running away from other people right before they reject me. I've always got the toe of one foot standing in the crack of the door. I've gotten good at seeing it coming. Well, maybe not so much with Dutch. He's an enigma in that way. I see Dutch reaching out to me emotionally broken too, I guess. Because then he pulls away.

"Skeeter," Dutch sighs. "We're going to put you someplace safe, alright? Someplace a little more out of the way until Officer Moretti here can do some investigating."

"I'm going to start looking up all the girls with the name Emory in San Antonio," Bobby tells me. I think he's trying to appease the scared look in my eyes. "It isn't a common name. It's a start. I've got lots of options. Anybody could have seen my truck the other night leaving the restaurant in Nashville. They can look up my picture on the Bel-Air Police Department website—"

I roll my eyes. "I feel safe with you, Dutch."

"Well, you're not," he says softly and looks to Bobby. What the hell does that mean?

CHAPTER 22

HIDING OUT IN BEL-AIR . . . WITH BOONE

There's an old dirt road leading from Dutch's house back behind his cattle fields and stops along the old main county road. Between the two, there's a beat up green, white and blue 1972 motorhome shoved up to an old log cabin that must be two-hundred years-old. It's settled into the hill and almost at the top. There's nothing but trees and forestland for as far as the eyes can see.

"There's no way I'm living here. How the heck could this be safer here than your house?" I'm ogling it listening to Lexie suckle her fist hard while she's tucked into my shoulder. "Dutch, really? I mean, it looks like the setting for a B-rated horror movie."

"There's been carnage here, that's for sure," Jack divulges to me. "Dutch rents it out for hunting in the fall. But there's been plenty of love-making too. I've brought a few girls up here."

"Gross and stop," I hardly note Jack other than a scathing smirk and my hand up and holding his words at bay while I try to plead my case to Dutch. "See? He's probably got those girls buried in the backyard."

"Beggars can't be choosers," Jack drops his laughing gaze and settles on a glare. "You got someplace else to go, princess? I figured with all the horse trading Dutch here does, he'd have sold you off by now."

"Screw off—" I start to retort. I'd walked inside. It was dark and musty and— "Where's the bathroom?" I ask. "Because I can't do an outhouse again."

"It just needs a little fixing. Haven't you ever camped out before?"

"No. I did outhouses for ten years. Not going back."

"It's just for a week or so." Dutch holds out a hand and stops Jack from saying more. "Skeeter, Bobby says he can't find any background information on those three men. The license plates come back to an elderly woman. They are offering cash to anyone who knows something about that girl and you. Bobby went around to some different businesses including Annie Upton's gift shop in town. She got the license plate and it was different than the one Bobby got at the restaurant. Each time those men stop by to ask about you, they are driving a different vehicle. He can't even find anything on an Emory in San Antonio."

But there's more to me moving up here on top of the hill than Dutch is revealing out loud. I can see it in his awkward stance, note it in the way his eyes don't meet mine. I ask Gin when we stop in for breakfast and she just gives me a faraway, dazed look and doesn't answer. "Everybody's got their secrets, honey. Maybe it's that woman asking everybody in town about you." She reached into her pocket, pulled out a business card with: MINDY POTTER, CREATIVE DIRECTOR—Celebrity Lifestyles. TEXT ME WITH YOUR NEWS!

So there's nothing but gossip about me. I feel like this entire town has some deep, dark secret. Then, I do a quick rifle through the internet on a search engine on Dallas's phone. I find myself looking at the image of Dutch in one of those awkward jail pictures. He looks ten years older and fifty pounds lighter. But it's him. There's no explanation and the cell phone service is sparse so I let it go for now and settle into my new home.

The only nice thing to come out of the move is that Dutch buys me a four-hundred dollar truck at Don's Used Cars in town so I can drive back and forth between the house and cabin to clean and feed his horses every day. Then I'm supposed to park it at the cabin and not use it unless I have an adult licensed driver. It's red and banged up and has a crack in the windshield, but he says it's mine. It looks better than the cabin. Because there's holes in the floors, no curtains on the windows, and the front door is locked by a broken latch. All of those things in themselves aren't so bad in comparison to the railroad tracks running right through the front yard before they take a dip down into the valley and disappear into a huge tunnel. At two in the morning, the trains come barreling through loaded with coal and screeching out a horn for the old county road crossing a quarter mile away. Then it echoes like an army of banshees while it screams through the tunnel.

But about the truck. I also use it to sneak out on Friday and Saturday nights to the Crazy Filly. I could probably tell Dutch the truth that I'm working there, but I don't think he'd approve. He's got this thing about saying grace when we sit at the table and although he doesn't go to church, I've seen him read the bible at night before he goes to sleep. I figure just like those rooms at his house, I've got my right to have secrets.

"Cripes almighty!" Every night at two, I awaken and sit straight up, my heart pounding. The train's so loud, I can only see Lexie's wide-open screams in the light of the moon. It looks like nothing is coming out until the train grinds past at a hundred miles an hour and leaves me wide awake with a terrified baby. The night of day four, I try to rock her, but I think she is traumatized. Then I can feel her little forehead pressed to my neck and it's hotter than fire. I try to call Dutch. He doesn't answer. So I've got nobody else but the guy who I'm not supposed to hang around with and the one who put his phone number on the little paper in Mama's jewelry box. So I take it out and unfold it in my fingers while I bounce my screaming baby up and down. Then I sigh and poke in his number.

"Listen, Boone," I know my voice is wispy and trembling when I hear him make a sleepy answer on the other end. "Um, dude, you told me to call you in an emergency. I don't want to bother you, but I can't get Dutch and I'm stuck up in that old cabin on his hill and Lexie feels like she's got a fever, a really bad one. I don't know what to do."

"You're—still here?" he asks almost like he thought I'd left town. "Yeah, yeah. I'll be there."

He hung up on me he was in such a hurry. It was excruciating, but Boone came careening up the gravel road forty-eight minutes later with four bags of baby stuff.

"Everything was closed in town. I had to run to the all-night pharmacy in Denton," he tells me, almost out of breath from running up the muddy path to the cabin. He sets the bags down on the old counter that's covered in some kind of a linoleum and I see him looking around. There are lights in the cabin, but they are dim. They cast little shadows on the old couch that I've tossed quilts and blankets over top to make it homey. I've got candles lit to get rid of the smell of what I think was a dead opossum out on the front porch and whose stench was leaking through the windows. There's six or seven pots and pans and plastic bowls catching the rain dribbling through the roof to keep it from hitting the floor and the little table Dutch covered with a red-checkered dollar store tablecloth.

Boone sees me watching him and snaps his gaze away and forces up a smile. I'm patting Lexie's bottom while she rides my shoulder and he reaches out a hand and touches her bare back.

"Yeah, she's hot. I got a thermometer and some medicine to get her fever down—"

"I'm scared."

"It happens." He shrugs it off as easy as when he birthed Lexie. "Baby's get sick. If her fever doesn't come down, we'll take her to the hospital. It's simple, Skeeter."

It might be simple for him. It isn't for me. It's like everything else. It comes hard to me. Dallas always tells me that when God gave out the gift of music, he gave me an extra dose. But in exchange, he took away a bunch of the common sense usually given in equal amounts to folks.

He's right, I suppose and I tell Boone what Dallas said while he shows me how to give her medicine through the eyedropper. I'm shaking and I know Boone can see this. It's embarrassing and he doesn't say anything while Lexie makes that sighing sobbing sound when she sees him. And, oh my God, she holds her little fist out and reaches for him.

"You're kidding me, right? It's like she knows she's safe now." I roll my eyes. "Boone's here, so Mama's not going to kill her with her stupidity."

"You're funny. You're not stupid, you know that right? How long's she been reaching for stuff?"

I glare up at him when I shove her toward him. "Two seconds ago."

"Oh." Boone makes this fake, haughty smirk and plops down on the couch. I laugh while he settles Lexie on to his chest and rocks her side to side.

"They told me you left."

"Who told you that?"

"My dad." Boone yawns and looks up at me, watches me sit down next to him. "He said Dutch told him you were leaving. It was offhand and just a part of another conversation he was having with Adriana. But Chey heard it. Then she completely lost it. She grabbed the tablecloth and jerked all the food and plates off. Everybody was just staring at her like a bomb had gone off. There was glass flying everywhere. Then she stormed off and hasn't talked to us in two days. I mean, she hasn't spoken to anybody."

"Why?" I ask him. "I mean, I've only been with her a couple times."

"Yeah, well, to a thirteen year-old whose got your CDs sitting in her room, it's like you've been there all along with her. The way she looks at you, it's like she's got a mama crush on you." Boone yawns and reaches out his hand. "Let's hold hands." It was a strange request. Still, I reach out, take his hand in mine. "You're shaking."

"I know. I'm sorry. Can I make it up to her somehow?"

"Actually, she was with me when you were screaming at me to get away, Skeeter." Boone reaches out and ruffles my hair. "Chey was sitting in the truck and crying asking me what I'd done. You were going to give her guitar lessons, remember?"

"I didn't see her," I sigh, feel my heart drop. "She shouldn't have heard all that. What'd you tell her?"

"I liked you and you didn't like me. But I was working on it."

"Don't give me that crap, Boone, I'm—"

"It's not crap. I don't want to be with Livie. She comes. She goes. I know she's just waiting around for a better looking, richer man. Can you tell me if this is weird? My mom and my sister and Livie went to pick out an engagement ring yesterday."

"Is she wearing it?"

"No, it's in a little box on my mom's bureau."

"Are you going to give it to her?" I pull his hand around, twine our fingers together.

He doesn't say anything quickly. Boone kisses the top of Lexie's head. Then he gazes over at me. "I don't want to.

It's not what I want. But I feel like I'm a passenger on a commuter train that isn't stopping, is out of control."

"What do you want, Boone?"

"Three months ago, I was all in for nothing better to do, Skeeter. I mean, Mom says she's a catch, right? Dad says she's beautiful and smart. God, even Adriana loves her. The perfect woman," he says softly. "She is a keeper. And then, along you come like Fourth of July fireworks and blew up that thought process." He brings his hand into the air and wiggles it imitating fireworks. "You and all that—whatever it is that's you. Boom."

Chapter 23

Telling America's Sweethearts to screw off

"Hey, get in the truck. I'm kidnapping you because I need an adult in the vehicle with a license so I can drive. We're going on a road trip." I am standing in the middle of the Martinez's living room. It is huge with four big screen TVs, one in each corner of the room. There are five leather couches, a bar and alpaca rugs all across the floor, that which I am kneeling down and petting and holy shitting at the same time.

"How the heck did you get in here?" Boone is sitting with the remote in one hand and his mouth dropping open. Chey is sitting next to an immense stone fireplace poking a finger into her phone.

"Huh?" The fur is soft and it doesn't look like anybody's ever stepped on it. "Oh, I just walked in. But my truck looks really out of place even though I lied and told your security I was delivering something for Dutch." I hold out my hands to my sides. "Do you really need big steel gates here?" I sigh. "Halfway up the hill I figured I'd have to cross a moat to get to this—castle." It is like a castle, a huge white mansion sitting on top of a hill and surrounded by a basin-like valley. I would guess it has sixteen rooms. "This place is like a fortress. Quit staring at me like idiots and come on!" I'm wagging my hand at them. "The dude outside said he'd watch Lexie for me as long as it was only for two minutes. She's all better, but she fell asleep. I don't want to wake her up."

"There are three rules for riding in my truck," I'm telling Boone and Chey when we hit the highway. I'm a little over the white line and they've got little strips that make the tires go bumpety-bump. Boone's in the front seat and Chey's in the back with Lexie. "It may not look like much, but it's my first vehicle and it is my baby." Both still look like two scared little kittens cornered inside a cardboard box. "Don't play with the duct tape on the window. It's the only thing holding it together." I see them both peer upward at the silver tape framing the rear window. "Don't touch the radio. I can get one station and it took me a half hour to tune it in with the homemade antennae—" I point to the old metal coat hanger stuck into the hole that used to be the real antennae on the hood of the truck. "And three, whoever is in the back has to tell me if there's any other cars in a hundred foot radius. I'm not good at driving in a straight line when somebody passes me. I freak Bobby out because I go toward the other car if somebody's coming."

"Chey, I'm scared." Boone breaks their silence by saying those words in a high-pitched tone. They both laugh out loud and I swerve a bit to the right.

"Don't talk loud," I whine. "It makes me nervous."

"That's five rules, then." Boone nods his head up and down. His eyes are wide and he makes a funny face at Chey.

"I'll make it six, then. No back talking me!" I swerve, give a sly smile. "I'm just kidding. I swerved on purpose."

"See this is why you need an adult in here. Don't do that," Boone returns. "So where are you taking us?"

"Here." I plop Dallas's phone down on the seat along with a map. I poke my finger on the map and he gently takes my hand and works it back to the steering wheel.

"Please keep your hands on the ten o'clock and twelve o'clock position."

"Huh?" I ask. He holds up his hands and places them on a fake steering wheel and I nod. "Oh, yeah, I thought I read that in the driver's book last night."

"Oh, God, please save us all." Boone looks up to the dirty windshield, then back to Chey who is giggling. I turn and laugh at him. He pauses and makes a point of smiling at me. "So really, where are we going?"

We're going to the Music City Amp Up Festival. It's downtown and I tell them that while I drive out on to the highway at thirty miles-per-hour. Cars are flying past me when I finally say a short prayer myself and get up to fifty miles-per-hour. Chase and Brooke are there singing together in the brand new Canter Stage donated by none other than Tyrone Canter, her dad. I'm going to try to get the rest of my things including my clothes, my big bag of music sheets, and my electric guitar. Boone doesn't think it's a good idea. I tell him I don't really care. He can wait in the car if he wants.

"I need my electric guitar," I reveal. "Dutch had a few thousand dollars stolen from his house. I figure maybe I could make some money and pay him back—"

"Dutch had money stolen?" Boone asks me with a furrow of brow.

"Yeah. He thinks it's me buying drugs or something. I didn't take it."

"I don't know what he expects. He's got half of the world's homeless working in his fields."

"Yeah, well, coming from one of the strays he's taken in, me, he doesn't see them like that. And I want to pay him back. Getting my electric guitar is a start. And the guy I played with at the bar in Nashville the other day gave me his card, said he wanted to play with me. Maybe he'd play with me—"

"You played in Nashville? Skeeter, I'm not sure that this guy would want to come out to a dive bar in Bel-Air for a hundred bucks or whatever they can pay you guys."

"Yeah, well, I played at a restaurant and got a free meal out of it so it is what I've got, what I can do." I pause in my thoughts, let his words sink in. "You haven't seen how bad I am at waitressing or parking cars, both which I have tried and failed. I can sing. I can play. You saying I'm not good enough?" I roll my eyes at him. "You sound like Chase, you know that? And that butthead told me I'd never be able to drive because I was such a dingbat. Well, look." I hold out my hands to encompass the steering wheel and Boone's eyes open wide in panic. "I'm driving."

"She is—good enough," I hear Chey giggling from the back seat. "Daddy, stop it."

"Yeah, it's straight in and straight out. I'll find Chase's motorcycle and the band bus and that's it."

That's what I tell them. What they don't know yet is that I also dug out one of the envelopes from my mama's jewelry box. It was the one with BUD MOONEY written on the front. The blank checks inside have an address of 1010 Copperfield Drive, Nashville, Tennessee. That's where we're headed afterward.

And it isn't so straightforward. We get to the festival at three in the afternoon. It's food and beer booths, mostly Tyrone Canter's restaurants and breweries. He's got a country singer setting up on the stage and people milling around. I can see busses parked along the side streets.

"Look." Chey is holding Lexie in her arms and she wiggles one hand out and points to a big billboard hovering over the festival and part of the highway beyond. "Isn't that Chase?"

I look up and it sure is. There's a billboard with Chase and Brooke smiling and looking toward the sunrise with cowboy hats on and written above is: *AMERICA'S NEWEST COUNTRY ROCK SWEETHEARTS—BROOKE CANTER*

AND CHASE MARTIN LIVE ON STAGE JUNE 12 MAIN CANTER STAGE NASHVILLE. Country rock? Chase used to make fun of country music. Behind the two is my old band—red-haired, freckled Red Benson on the drums and blonde-haired, blue eyed Johnny Carol with a guitar. I squint at Brooke's arms and the guitar she's holding. Dammit, that's my guitar!

"Oh, don't look at that." Boone has stopped in front of me and I almost bump into his back. He was eyeing a food booth with these huge grilled steaks splayed out on a grill. It's too late. He turns and I can see him wince. I know he sees my eyes narrowing, sees my jaws churning. "Skeeter." He reaches out and knocks his knuckles on the top of my head. "Look at me." He waits until I veer my head downward. "Let's just go. I'll buy you a new guitar. Whatever you want. I mean, we got the one that had all your songs on it, right? That's the one that really counts."

I feel really sick to my tummy. "But it's my guitar—"

"Maybe it *isn't* the guitar, Skeeter," Boone says as softly as he can over the sounds of the festival. "You know that. I know that." I see his hand come out like he's going to latch on to me. I glare at his fingers wavering there. "Okay, you know, maybe you need to put all this behind you. Move on." I'm looking at him, looking at Chey who is staring hard at me like she's trying to read my expression. "Maybe closure this way isn't the right direction?"

I know he's right. I know he thinks I'm going to explode right this moment. Somewhere inside my brain, I know I should just walk away. But something in my chest says Chase wins if I just turn around, tuck my tail and leave.

"That's my guitar she's holding on the billboard, Boone," I extend my hand, point to Brooke's arm. "She took my guitar. And—and just so you know, he's never ridden a horse. He's a disgrace to wearing that cowboy hat."

"Okay, so let me put it this way. Do you still love him?"

"Not really. I'm kind of at the hate stage right now."

"Do you like me? I mean, more than just hanging out together? Because here's the thing. I'll stick up for you. I'll be there for you if you walk up to that stage and find him there. I just really, really don't want to take a punch at—" he tosses a hand in the air so it is pointing to the sign. "America's sweetheart underneath his billboard and with a thousand people looking on if I don't have to do it. But, Skeeter, I will."

"Are you asking me to choose between you or him?"

"Nope. I know by the look in your eyes, you're not there yet. That's fine."

"And not just because you've got an engagement ring on your mom's bedroom cabinet," I mutter and knuckle him in the arm.

"I do." He wags his head back and forth like a horse stalled too long and wanting to get out to pasture. It's like he's stuck inside that stall himself, wanting to break free but won't.

"Boone, you're right. I'm not sure if I'm there yet." I look up at the sky and away from the billboard. The bitch is singing my songs. She's taken all that I built from scratch and she's taken the place in Chase's heart. She's stolen my band. Now she's taking all that hard work and without paying any dues, she's taking it three steps farther. "You're killing me, boy," I say, bring my head down and meet his eyes. Those beautiful eyes. "Go get your stupid steak on a stick or whatever that is they are cooking over there and we'll get out of here."

I think we had a moment then, me and Boone. When I look down, his eyes are going back and forth between my own like he's not quite grasping that maybe I might not be wherever it is he was talking about, but I'm thinking it could be worth getting there. "I just want you to know I used to sleep with that damn guitar in my arms at night." I grunt while I reach over and take a fussy Lexie from Chey's arms. I did. I use to hug it to my chest and pluck those strings to get to sleep. Boone, he just grins.

We would have made it out of there without an altercation if it wasn't for Boone slopping steak juice all over his t-shirt. Standing in line at the restrooms delayed us twelve minutes. If we would have gotten out of the festival at five-thirty-eight, I would have been home free. However, we were cutting down an alley near the restrooms which is also right where the front stage is planted at five-fifty-two to get to my truck that I had to park in a garage.

Just as we're rounding a corner, this huge band tour bus slides up to the curb. I'm looking down the far side of the street because the bus has blocked the corner where we were going to cross. The crunch of the bus brakes scares Lexie who starts crying. I'm just trying to avoid the traffic. I don't even notice the driver get out to move the cones placed there to keep others from parking in that spot.

But Boone completely stops. Chey is right in step behind him and bumps into his back. He's got this funny twist to his lips, almost a cringe while I turn my head slightly to follow his gaze. *AMERICA'S NEWEST COUNTRY ROCK SWEETHEARTS—BROOKE CANTER AND CHASE MARTIN.* It's an exact duplicate of the billboard painted on the side of the luxury touring bus. There's a motorcycle on a carrier on the back.

"No, no, no," Boone's tossing back his head and reaching for me with his hand like I'm a little kid that's getting ready to run into the street. "Skeeter, please, no." Because the second I turn, I see Chase making his swaggering stride off the steps of the bus. He's got an entourage of roadies hopping out of two busses behind the RV and four buff body guards. Body guards? I was lucky if he got me a ball cap to hide behind when we went to an amusement park.

"Shit." I just say it. It slips out of my mouth and lays there flat while I see Chase snap his head up and in the exact location one of his body guards is pointing toward, which is me. I turn to poor Chey who is blinking innocently at me. I hold out Lexie for her to take. They all stare at me with tipped heads like I'm a coyote stuck in a chicken coop.

I feel my feet stomping across the sidewalk and the hoses and electric lines laid out for the festival. It is dim here because of the high rise buildings and it smells like gas fumes, fresh asphalt and the sweet scent of barbecue cooking. "Hey!" I yell it. "What the hell is up, bud?" I see him swivel on his feet, nod to one of the bodyguards. "You just going to drop me off in the middle of nowhere and never come back, asshole?"

"You need to get her out of here."

But I'm not done. Because I can see Brooke with her perfect hair and long, long legs peering around the door of the RV. She's wearing a little flowered dress and cowboy boots and tugging on her hair. And I'm screaming at Chase and poking a finger in the air. He's smiling and nodding because there's a small crowd. "Now calm down, Waylon," he's saying and pushing his hands out while the bodyguard makes a skip in front of him. "You're going to be fine, just fine. We'll call somebody to get you. Are you drunk again?"

I suppose that's when I lost it. I mean, I literally dive toward him and the bodyguard catches me in midair. I'm kicking and screaming and probably not doing anything to help my case that I'm not a nutcase with an alcohol addiction. Chase, he's laughing and saying the baby I had, it wasn't even his. It is Red Benson that drags me backward and I think he's the one that Boone punches between the eyes. I'm not sure. I hear Chey scream and it must scare Lexie because she's bawling while Red falls back hard on his rear.

"You frigging bitch!" Red's a big guy and about six feet and five inches. I mean, it was Boone who hit him right before the bodyguard grabbed him around the waist and swung him toward the sidewalk. But Red's anger is at me while he rises up and stops dead still with his hand out to hold Boone back.

"Get the hell out of here, Waylon. You're a frigging loser. Go back to whatever meth house you've been living at—go find your stupid baby daddy and—"

"Meth house?" I hiss. "Is that what he's told you? Big frigging liar," I growl. "Asshole dumped me in the middle of nowhere three hours before I had my baby. And yes, it is his. You all can go to hell. That's where you'll be, stealing all the songs I wrote, taking the money from my album."

"It's not yours. Chase wrote those," Brooke calls out from her safe place in the RV. I see her strut out and she's got my guitar in her hands. "Is this what this is all about?" she asks. She's got this really high-pitched, screechy voice. I'm thinking she's going to be nice and bring it over, hand it to me. I am wrong. "Well, I can take care of that." She brings it up in the air and smashes it hard on the cement curb. It isn't once, not twice, but four times until it falls into two separate pieces on the street. I literally jolt with each bang and feel the blood running from my face while I slap my fingers to my lips.

"Skeeter, it's just a guitar," I hear Boone saying that. "Walk away." I see him looking wildly at Chey and Lexie while he's being pushed backward by the security guards. I hear my own whispered words repeat it while I turn my attention to the ground. Then I look up. Chase is on his phone and I know he's calling the cops. I hold out my hands, back up and waggle my head until I can find Boone again. He's tugging Chey back from the crowd that's gathering and waving me over with his free hand. He's locking eyes with me. I can almost guess he thinks if he blinks or looks away, I'm going to start waling on Chase. I want to. I really do. But something just tells me it isn't worth it. Chase isn't worth it.

"Just walk."

Chey keeps looking back at me while we take the busy sidewalk to the truck. I'm trying hard not to sob and to comfort Lexie who is crying too. It isn't in my nature to attack people. I don't know where it came from. People on the street are staring. Boone looks livid while he keeps swiping the blood from his nose with his sleeve. I'm waiting for us to get out of earshot before he lays into me hard for being such an idiot. I know it's coming. I'm feeling the guilt even before we listen to the echo of our feet in the parking garage grind to a halt at my truck.

"I know it wasn't just a guitar. I'm sorry, I shouldn't have said that. I'm—kicking myself for saying that."

I'm fumbling with the keys. I look up and Boone is right next to me at the driver's door and staring down before he turns his attention to a lady stopping near the back of the truck staring at us. She's chic-pretty with a tiny nose, Gucci clothes, heavy makeup and perfect sandy-colored hair. She reminds me of the six o'clock news lady.

"Ma'am," Boone says with a forced smile. "Can you please give her a second? She's upset."

I suppose this was as close to a breaking point I was going to have. I just kind of lean into Boone and sob while he wraps his arms around me.

"Waylon, I'm Mindy Potter with Celeb Gossip Magazine." She's trying to come around the truck and she's wiggling a card in the air. "I'd like to talk—"

"Please, ma'am." Boone holds her off with a hand in the air. "Another time."

"Take my card. I'll leave."

I feel Boone's shoulder shift so I know he took it to get her to leave. She does after taking a couple pictures, the clacking of her heels echoing behind us not long after. I didn't really care. I'd expected he was going to scream at me, lay into me about attacking somebody like a crazy woman while his kid stood watching. He doesn't. He just pats my back and tells me over and over that it's going to be fine, going to be okay.

Later, I found out Chase took my guitar on stage and bashed it one more time against the floor in front of the audience. They cheered him on while he talked about how I'd left him and how he wrote a song about it. My song. I wrote it. I had the verses on my guitar.

Chapter 24

Buddy mooney - A Piece of Mama's Dark Puzzle

"It seemed like such a good idea at the time." We're sitting in a booth at a roadside restaurant off the highway just outside Nashville. I'm sipping hot chocolate through a straw with melting whipped cream on top. Chey is doing the same. She is watching me pour hot fudge on top of the whip cream and then doing the same across the table from me. "I mean, in retrospect, it seems really stupid. I think God really screwed up when he didn't put a stupid button on all of us so when we're about to do something like drive a car off a cliff, this button goes off bright red with a warning."

Boone grins and shakes his head. "Yeah, I need one of those every Friday night about seven when I head downtown." He shrugs. "I guess I should have foreseen something. I don't know what I was thinking."

I reach into my backpack and tug out the envelope. Then I push it over to Boone. "Do I need a stupid button?"

"What is it?" He takes it in his hands and opens the envelope. "Oh, the checks from your mama's jewelry box."

"Yeah. We're here in Nashville. I wanted to stop at the address and see if anybody knew her or me. What do you guys think? I need your honest opinions." I look at Boone, then to Chey. "It's eating me up inside. I need to know where she went, why she left me."

"Maybe you should wait a week or so and recover from this first. You know, keep it to one traumatic event per week." Boone is drinking a coffee across from me in the booth. He has a piece of strawberry pie in front of him and he keeps poking it with his fork. "We can come back."

"Um, I think maybe we could drive past the address

and see what it is," Chey says softly next to me. I turn my attention to her. "I mean, if it was me, I'd be dying to know and maybe you'd lose more sleep not knowing. I only have a picture of my mom. Nobody ever talks about her."

I reach into my backpack and wriggle out my mama's picture. Then I hand it over to Chey. "I get it. Everybody treated my mama like she was dead. I had a million questions. I was scared to ask because I didn't want to get that look—" I widen my eyes, then look away. I can see the realization on her face. That's what she gets.

"Yeah, that," she says with hardly a whisper. "Is your mama dead too?" She gazes at the picture.

"I don't know. As far as my daddy was concerned, she was. But I knew he still loved her, you know? He couldn't remarry in the Amish community because there's no such thing as divorce. She just—disappeared. Sometimes when I walked into a room where the adults were talking, they'd shut up quickly and I know they were talking about her. I know she was bad for leaving. I didn't care about that. I didn't see her mistakes. I just wanted to know things about her—you know, like did she like to paint or sing or— did she giggle when somebody burped at the table. Did she dress like me when she was my age? Was her hair soft and brown? Stupid stuff I couldn't quite remember. I just wanted to hear it from somebody. I wanted to know where I came from, I suppose."

Chey is quiet when she passes the picture back to me. "What was your mama like?" I ask her. She just shrugs noncommittedly.

"I don't know much about her."

"She had dark hair like you, babe," Boone says. He reaches out and ruffles her hair. "And blue eyes like—I don't know, like the color of that goofy saddle pad you've got for your horse. And she had the same chippy-sounding laugh you've got."

"I bet she didn't laugh at your dumbass jokes," I mutter to Boone before I turn to his daughter. "You know, Chey, the day we met, your daddy asked me—*what did the pirate say on his eightieth birthday?*"

"Oh, no, really? The aye, matey one?" she groans. "You know it's like his go-to joke whenever he doesn't know what to say, right?"

"I know, right?" I roll my eyes. "I'm getting ready to have a baby and I can't hold it back any longer and he tells a stupid joke."

"She laughed at my jokes, girls, I'll have you know," Boone grunts like he's mad. He's not. "All of them."

"Yeah, right. Tell me ten more things about Chey's mom that I won't believe," I challenge him with a smirk.

Twenty minutes later, he's told Chey twenty things about her mama straight down to revealing the picture he still kept of her tucked secretly into his wallet. She's somehow worked her way under the table and over next to him and they are laughing about some silly prank Chey's mama played on the principal in high school.

I realize I've forgotten all about the guitar and Chase and Brooke. When the waitress brings the check and after Boone pays, he comes back with a funny smile playing on his lips.

"I'm supposed to tell my beautiful wife how pretty our family is," he tells me adjusting his hat on his head.

"What'd you tell her? That—" We weren't a family, I was starting to say.

"I told her thanks." He gives me a wink. I shake my head at him.

"You're nuts."

"I am. Chey thinks we should take you to the house here in Nashville. What's the address?"

It's 1010 Copperfield Drive. It is in the rolling hillsides outside the city where farms still thrive. I know because thirty minutes later, I'm staring at the front door of the house. "I'm looking for a Bud Mooney?" I stand at the front door of a 1980s ranch house. It is picture-perfect enveloped in some old maples. The shade is nice against the warm summer sun. I've got the envelope in my right hand. The woman who answers the door just stares at me. She has short, gray hair tied up in a bun on her head. She's tall and lanky, dressed in the light spandex kind of summer clothing older, rich people wear. She just stares at me, her face paling. "Maybe I have the wrong house. I—I just—I'm just looking for people who might have known my mama—"

"Ray, you better come here," she stutters and her voice is shaky. She doesn't take her eyes off me. "Ray!"

I feel my heart start to pump because her eyes get wide and her hand comes out like it's going to latch on to me. I take a step back, look for safety in my truck in the long driveway. It is only seventeen footsteps away. Four of those were concrete stairs I know this because I counted them when I walked up to the floor of the front porch and knocked three times with my knuckle on the door.

"Please, please—don't leave. Don't be scared—" She's telling me not to leave even as I take a step back. She paces forward and begs me with her eyes not to go. "Please, please don't go anywhere. We won't call the police. We just want to talk to you."

"No, I should go." Why would they call the cops? I'm getting a panicky flutter to my chest. I start to turn and just as I do, I hear the sound of a voice, see my shadow swallowed up by a larger shadow behind me. "I think I've got the wrong person."

"Nicky?"

Nicky. The name bounces off the back of my head, slips into my ears. Nicky. The deep, booming voice, I remember. But when? I turn slightly and swing my head around to see the owner of the deep voice.

Chocolate brown eyes and a round face. He's got gray splotches mixed into his brown hair. I vaguely remember him. "You're Bud Mooney?" I ask him. He's pushing himself through the door and the woman beside him is plucking the sleeve of his shirt like she's trying to slow him down.

"No, Bud's my son. Do you remember me?" he asks. "Are you Nicky? Do you know where he is? My grandson?" He's coming down the four steps and looking down at me.

"No." I'm shaking my head at him, back and forth quickly. "I think I've got the wrong house," I lie. He's scaring me.

"You're Nicky, Terry's little girl, right? She was Buddy and Beth's nanny. Do you remember that?"

"No, I'm not Nicky."

"But you left with her. Terry McDaniel, right? Where did she go? Where did she take my little grandson?" The lady at the door had barreled out. She stopped at the top of the stairway and was clutching the bannister. "You remember him, right? My little grandson. You played with him—"

"I don't know anything about your grandson," I mutter. "I don't understand. I thought maybe my mama had lived here once."

The man just stops there. He grabs his temples between forefinger and thumb and pinches them while I turn to run down the steps. "Nicky!" I can hear him calling me. "Please, if you know anything—" That's all I hear. I've got my hands on my ears.

CHAPTER 25

GETTING COURTED BY DALLAS DUNNE

I don't hear from Boone for four days. But I know that amount of time passed because that's when the strange phone calls started. The first night, there were eight. Then after that, two or three. They were all like: *You don't remember me. But I know you. I need to meet with you. I want to talk to you.* There were probably twelve on the phone. I erase them, think maybe they are for Dallas. I finally block them out on the fourth day. But I find myself peering at them in the folder just to see how many are sent. At least twenty a day.

I wasn't surprised Boone didn't come around. It was a strangely quiet ride home except for his occasional *tap, tap-tap, tapping*. I pulled off at a rest stop and asked him to drive. I ended up fiddling with my old guitar in the back seat with a song that came into my head, jotting down the notes on pieces of receipts and a napkin while I had Chey pluck the notes over and over again.

Boone kept looking in the rearview mirror at me while he drove. His expression was blank. He heard the conversation on the porch. I tell him, I don't know what they were talking about. But as secrets go, I do know something. Because mama left that house in the dark of night just like the others. Maybe he can read the lies in my eyes. Because at the rest stop, I take Dallas's phone and I go into a stall and look up Buddy Mooney. I find out they have a boy who was kidnapped twenty-three years ago. Buddy Mooney looked a lot like my little brother, Caleb.

Boone may not show up, but Chey does. I think she's sneaking off, cutting across the fields between Dutch's farm and her grandpa's farm. She shows up the next early afternoon about twenty minutes before Dallas Dunne pulls into Dutch's driveway in his big loaded truck. I'm cleaning stalls because I missed doing them in the morning and Chey is petting one of the horses. I hear the truck. I drag the shovel out with me to the front of the barn and lean hard into it just as he stops three feet away.

"Hey, I'm looking for Waylon Ryder," he says with a sassy roll of his eyes. "You ain't seen her, have you? Little girl with a bad attitude and a funky, dark twist to her look." Then he stops, blinks his eyes and widens them like he's surprised. "Oh, no, that ain't you, is it? Cleaning stalls?"

"Eat shit," I tell him. "There's a whole barn full of it I have to clean. Have at it."

"Looks like you're shoveling it so I don't have to." He thinks his retort is funny and he laughs out loud. There's a guy sitting next to him in the seat and he gives me a nervous smile. "Hey, this is Tyler Cooper." Dallas nods toward his buddy in the truck. "He plays drums."

"Well, good for him." I tear off my work glove and reach out, shove my hand across the driver's side and shake the guy's hand. "I'm Waylon Ryder. I scream music." I waggle my head out of spite. "At least that's what my life coach here tells everybody." Tyler laughs and looks at Dallas, then back to me. "And this week with all the trouble I got into, my Dutch says he's going to have to start offering men horses to take me."

"Yeah, I know who you are." He's short cut, brown hair and stubbled cheeks. He's got on thick glasses and pushes them up like he's nervous when he does.

"Here, look." Dallas pokes his phone, then hands it to me. He's got a video on there and I take it in my hands. I watch it. It's Dallas singing a song. The song we wrote at the motel– *Closest Thing to a Cowgirl You Got Tonight.*

"We put the finishing touches on the music. You think you'd sing it with me?"

"Well, I did write it while you were watching the ballgame on TV and dozing. I did put the pieces together while you talking silly to your wife on the phone and eating cold pizza." I push my elbows on the truck window. They are slanted upward because the truck is taller than me. I can see Chey peering out of the barn. She's got those wide eyes again like she did when she saw me the first time. "That's just Chey. She's paying for her guitar lessons by helping me clean. She's not cleaning much, just mostly kissing the horses on their noses and telling me all about the mean eighth grade girls at Bel-Air Middle School." I grin up at Dallas. "I thought you were going to sing it with that bleach blonde chick."

"I don't wanna sing it with the bleach blonde *chick*—" He stops and makes a point of rolling his eyes while he makes quotation marks with his fingers. "—whose name is Anise Wells, just so you know. She's sweet, so don't put her down. She just doesn't fit the image of the song. You do. I think the words the girl sings are: *Well, I'm tennis shoes, not cowboy boots. You're t-shirt and jeans, no tattoos. Don't think you're what I'm looking for. You're not. But— I'll lie and tell you I drive an old truck, I'll put on a Stetson, just to hang on tight for one night to somebody else's cowboy dream boy. I'll be your cowgirl just one night.*"

"Yeah, well, I'll tell you what," I jab a thumb behind me. "You help me clean the stalls and I'll think about it."

"I already know the answer."

"Huh?"

"You've got goosepimples." He points at my arm, turns off the truck. "I can see through you like I can read that stupid dollar store guitar you got your songs scrawled on in four year-old handwriting."

"Oh, my gosh, why do you have to be such a weinie and point those things out, Dunne?"

Dallas jumps out of the truck, unbuttons his shirt and wiggles out of it. He waves a hand at the man in the passenger seat. "Come on, Skeeter says we got to clean stalls."

"Screw off, Dunne. My guitar might be from a dollar store, but it is the only one I own considering Brooke Canter took my other guitar and broke it into a million pieces on the street. That's my only offer. Get your city boy buddy and grab a shovel and I'll show you how to muck out a barn."

I wait for Tyler to hesitate. He doesn't. Instead, he climbs out and follows Dallas and me into the barns. I watch Chey's eyes do that wide thing again while she looks at Tyler from the first line of stalls. She has slunk back and is hiding in the shadows. She can't even work her way down the stalls, just stands there staring like a child bride seeing her husband for the first time. I hand each a pair of Dutch's old gloves and a shovel.

"Brooke Canter broke your guitar?" Tyler asks me while he's tugging on his gloves. He has to bring the gloves close to his eyes to see which one, right or left, to pull on.

"Yes." I narrow my eyes at him, waiting to hear how cute or sweet she is from him. He doesn't show any expression. "I went to get it back at a street festival in Nashville and she broke it right in front of me. And really, I would rather see it die than be used by her hands anymore. It was sacrilege."

"What do you mean?"

"She was using my guitar to sing my songs. Chase gave it to her like he gave her all my songs."

"Baby, he can't do that," Dallas interrupts. "He's

making a million on your songs and that new album. Christ," Dallas rubs his hands over his face. "You aren't getting anything from the sales, are you?"

"I've never gotten anything, Dallas," I tell him. "Chase handles all the money. His uncle and his cousin manage whatever we do. I ask him for a few bucks here and there for clothes and most of the time, he tells me he'll think about it. Dallas, you know where I came from. You know being in charge doesn't come easy to me."

"Well, you're going to learn. You can't let people run all over you." He bangs his shovel on the floor. "You ever heard of Mindy Potter? She's with Celeb Gossip Magazine."

"I don't know." I shrug. "Yeah, I think she was at the concert where Brooke broke my guitar."

"Well, she's been sniffing around, asking questions about you. I got a call from a couple of your old band members from way back. They asked me what was going on. You keep yourself on guard, you hear me? If those old roadies have a beef with you, they might talk about you. I don't know this one. I don't trust her."

"Yeah, I will. But I liked all the roadies. They kept me company when Chase went out partying."

"What the hell is going on in here?"

We'd shoveled six stalls before I mumbled something about taking a break. I climb up on the wall to talk to Tyler and Dallas while they muck out the rest, toss shovels full of manure into two wheelbarrows. I was always good at doing this to my brothers. Easy peasy. And Jack and Boone and whoever comes out to help me.

"We're cleaning the stalls, Dutch," I answer from my little seat at the top of the stalls. I smile down at Chey who followed us in. She's got her little phone out and is laughing.

She's been taking little videos of us cleaning the manure. Dallas made up a song and we did a little dance in Old Blue's stall for her.

"*We* aren't cleaning the stalls. *You* aren't cleaning the stalls. *The guests*, however, are cleaning the stalls. Skeeter, I talked to you about manipulating all the men who come out here into cleaning for you."

"I'm just taking a break. I'm little like a fairy. I just use my fairy magic and they keep going," I whine while I slide down and take the shovel he is handing me. He's holding Lexie in his arms and she is looking around, trying to move her head a little. I know she's looking for Boone. "She's getting fussy for you, Skeeter," he tells me. "You need to finish up and get us some breakfast."

I reach out and touch her head, those soft white-blonde curls tickle my fingers. She smiles at me. I smile at her. It makes me miss Boone and I really don't know why. Maybe I know my daughter feels the same way I do. It's like something's missing when he's not around us. I turn for just a moment and see Dallas staring at Dutch and then at me. I don't know what he's thinking. It's almost protective like he doesn't approve of Dutch.

"Three more stalls and we're done, Dutch," I say softly. "Can you hold her that long? I'll be right there."

CHAPTER 26
DALLAS TELLS ME HE NEEDS ME

Skeeter's Bar. That's what is says in black marker on a little handmade wooden sign on my front porch. I put up little twinkle lights on the paint-chipped, brown wooden railing and the roof of the porch. There's three little plastic tables with three old lawn chairs on each. All of them have a little plastic cup with a couple dandelions on top. I've got a fire ring with cut wood burning out front.

"What's all this?" Dallas asks. He hasn't said anything about my accommodations, just sits down on a rickety lawn chair around a small campfire I just started. It is nine at night. He has been making up excuses to leave for most of the day, never does. Chey held out until four and then slipped away. I don't think she wanted to go. She was as quiet as a mouse but kept giggling and told me at one point that the guy Dallas brought was in some band called Scenic View. I just know Tyler hasn't complained or muttered more than a few words while Dallas and I drive up to the little cabin and play our guitars. He kind of joins along banging his hands on the chair for drums. Then all of a sudden, it's getting dark and I realize we've been doing this for the entire afternoon and evening.

"I've got a friend that gets into trouble at the bars. I was trying to offer him another option than going to the Crazy Filly on Friday nights," I mutter. "I just haven't been able to find a used pool table and I've also not gotten the nerve up to tell him. He's got a girlfriend." I stand up and make my way through the screen door. I notice Dallas is right behind me, catches it before it slams. I'm getting ready to tuck Lexie into her little bed by mine. She's sleeping soundly in the cleft of my arm, her head sweaty against my skin. We're alone. I turn to Dallas.

"Dallas, why are you hanging out here? You got a million places to go, a million people to be with—" I mutter. "Why are you hanging out at this crappy cabin with me?"

He waits until the door closes. I see him leaning against the bedroom doorframe. He looks back behind him to the closed door. I'm sure he's checking to make sure nobody's within hearing range. "The boy out there is mostly blind, but his hearing, it's twice what ours is—" he lowers his voice. "Waylon, I need a hit," he says, his hands shoved in his pockets. "It's been a while. I'm thinking maybe I need you and you need me right now. You write the songs. They are like gold from your pen to the paper. You're what I got. I'm what you got. I'm dead sure that song you wrote at the motel is great."

I lay Lexie down gently in her bed, pat her rear while she sighs. It is soft and sweet and I catch the scent of baby powder-smelling diapers and find it strangely amusing, it is now one of my favorite scents. "I got more songs, Dallas. They all aren't my usual." I pat her bottom for a minute to make sure she is asleep. "You can have at it if you want."

"Rumor in Nashville is that you're courting new guitar players, starting a new band," he says. "I saw some videos of you playing with a guy named Harley Mason."

"Don't believe everything you see. You know that. And you know me. I'm happy with this—" I look around the room. "I don't know. I really like Boone. That's Chey's daddy. He's sweet, kind and gentle. And he likes Lexie—"

"And he has a girlfriend."

"Yeah. Probably a fiancé by now."

"Baby, that's the sad ending for three of the songs I made that got in the top ten hits."

"I know." I smile sadly. "Can I confide in you?"

"Of course."

"I've got a secret. It's about my mama. I think she did some bad things."

"You aren't your mama, Waylon Ryder," he says sweetly. Then he steps across the room. He pushes an arm around my shoulder, jerks me into him. "Baby, you're a lot of things. But you are sweet and kind and gentle. And you're nothing bad if that's what you're worried about. But you're like this little train that is running out of control. You've got to put on the brakes once in a while. You've got to think things out." He kisses the top of my head. "You feel safe with this Dutch that took you in? He's not hurting you?"

"He protects me."

"Okay, because you don't got to clean up after him and do other stuff, you understand that, right?"

"Yeah, I kind of do. He thinks it is teaching me responsibility, accountability. I like taking care of him and I like him taking care of me."

"I guess it's better than a strip joint," Dallas laughs softly. "You're the poster child for all those girls with daddy issues, you know that, right?"

"I have no clue what you mean."

"I know. And that's good." He chuckles softly.

"Dallas, you've been getting some strange calls on your phone. It sounds like a stalker or something. Just giving you a heads up."

He snickers. "Guy or gal?"

"Guy."

"Um, well, just be careful. Maybe they're for you."

"Who would stalk me?" I laugh. Dallas doesn't. Instead, he shakes his head, gives me an eye roll. "You mind if I get a couple lawyers to look at your case with Chase?"

I sigh, give him a sisterly push away. "I don't know.

I'd just rather forget the whole thing and start over from scratch."

"Tell me yes or I'm sending in Jenna to convince you."

"What do you want from me, Dallas?" I grunt.

"I want you to sing with me. One song. We'll see where it goes. Maybe we can add you to our record label, huh? Late Night Outlaw's looking for new folks. One step at a time. It's an hour and twenty minutes to my sound studio. Come and we'll do the song—"

CHAPTER 27
NOT ANOTHER HEARTBREAK SONG

If you think this is another heartbreak song
You're dead wrong.
'Cause here's the news.
Baby ain't singing the blues.
It's an I hate you boy, glad you're gone, what took you
so long kind of song.
Yeah, what took you so long. Long. Long.

The Daylight Lounge was a restaurant six miles from Huntsville, Alabama. From the old postcard I found online, it was a single floor brick building that served buffet-style suppers. While people ate, they got to listen to a man playing piano. That's all I know except for right now, it is nothing but a big, abandoned building. What windows not once boarded up with plywood are broken with glass splattered on the ground. The roof is sinking inward and the gutters have peeled from their supports and are bouncing up and down with the breeze, banging against the brick walls. The scent of old burned wood slips into my nostrils and the parking lot has turned to nothing more than broken asphalt with grass growing up from the cracks.

"Well, this was a waste of time." I am standing between my truck and the old building and I turn my attention to the napkin where someone had carefully written *Stevie C.* in black pen years ago. I'm talking to myself. I can hear somebody shift in my truck behind me.

"Well, I mean what were you expecting to find, goofball?" Boone says from the passenger window of the truck. "Even if the restaurant was still here, who would be working that would remember somebody like twenty years back?"

Yeah, I'm *goofball.* I'll explain the reason for this nickname. After driving past the Martinez home six times this morning to see if Boone would be my adult passenger, one of their gardeners tells me *they* went to town. I assumed *they* were Boone and Chey. So after driving around town for forty-five minutes, I finally see Boone's truck parked at Berkman's Grocery Store. When I walk up to the window, guess who is inside? Yeah, Adriana and her weird twin friends—Tara and Tessa Callahan and, to my dismay, Olivia DiFranco. I want to backpedal. I'm standing there with my mouth wide open and can't think of a thing. Such, I just say: "Dutch isn't around. Can you ride with me to a place outside Huntsville? It's only about an hour away."

In retrospect, there were fifty things I could have said to Boone's deadpan gaze that wouldn't have led to half of the twenty-somethings in Bel-Air, Tennessee piling into my truck while I awkwardly drive my excruciatingly slow fifty-two miles an hour down the highway toward Huntsville, Alabama. But no witty remarks came to my tongue. So here they are staring at me from the windows. Now, they are also a part of solving my mama's disappearance because Adriana came up with the remark in the grocery parking lot: *Well, yes we'd love to go.* As if I meant them all. Then I had to listen to them chatter about everybody in town, complain about how hot the truck was inside, and how their hair was going to get tangled from driving with the windows down because there's no air conditioner.

So now I'm goofball because *asshole's* girlfriend is sitting in the backseat of the truck leaning hard into asshole and tickling his arms and his hands and playing some silly game trying to get him to laugh.

"I don't know," I bounce my shoulders up and down. "I guess for all I know, Stevie C. was some dude she met in the bar. I just figured if she kept the napkin, it had some meaning."

"Why would you think it had meaning? The woman abandoned you." That's Adriana in her usually limp tone. "It was probably just a one night stand."

"Screw off, Adriana," I mutter. I think it surprises her because she doesn't even bother to do the neck wiggle thing when she sighs a retort. I'm sick of her bitching and staring at me like they all stared dull-eyed at the dead possum bloated on the road four miles back. I'm standing there in ripped new blue jean shorts and a cute cami top and slouch boots. Dutch finally broke down and let me order some clothes online as long as I bought something that he said would look like the normal people in Bel-Air. Still, I'm wearing an old red bandana I found in the barn on my neck.

"Can we go? It is hotter than a Georgia sunset in here." That's one of the two twins. I can't tell the difference between them. I suppose one of them is chubbier than the other. I can't figure out which one. Then Lexie squeals while she plays with a green hangy toy Dutch got her at the store. "There ain't a bit of air conditioning. I've got back sweat."

"You know how gross that sounds, right?" I tell her bluntly. "From one to ten, it is an eleven. Shut up. I think it's disgusting and I grew up with nothing but brothers. So I've seen some pretty gross things." Again, I don't think these girls are used to anyone doing anything more than catering to their every need. They have bitched and whined about everything down to the underwear their boyfriends wear until I finally told them to shut the hell up halfway here. They don't listen regardless.

"Is that why you dress like a skank?" the other twin says low on her breath. I ignore her, turn, and look around. There isn't anything but a deserted gas station and forestland. The bugs are hovering around my face while I wave my hand to swat them away. My phone tings and I dig it out of the back pocket of my shorts.

"What?" I ask because it is Dallas on the other end. "I'm so glad you gave me this phone—" I say while I walk to the right of the building and see a thick, wooden door partially open. He's been bugging me every day. I drove to his house last week and he's got this home sound studio all set up with a couple sound techs ready when I get there and Jenna to babysit Lexie. He tells me we're just going to record one song, but we end up doing two he wants to add to his album. It took three days and me nail-biting every inch of Highway 65 back and forth all by myself. "Now if you aren't driving up my road, you can call me every day."

"Hey, Skeeter, I miss you too." He pauses while I lift up my boot and give the door two hard jabs of my foot. It sways to the right, then careens backward with a hard bang. "What the hell was that?"

"I'm breaking into a building. Why?"

"I'm not going to ask. Please don't make me bail you out of jail," he sighs.

"You didn't care if I went to jail because I was driving without a licensed driver in rush hour traffic in Nashville, Dallas," I whine. I peer into the building. Dust is riding the air and light is spewing through the broken windows. The reek of burnt wood leaves a thick and foul tang in the air. It is old, wet carpet and wallpaper falling down to the floor. The wall between kitchen and dining area is burnt down, the wood is hanging there charred. I can see the kitchen with freezers and cooking areas still intact. Eerily, the dining area is the same as an old postcard I found online and like people were eating at the restaurant tables and just got up to leave. There are tables still in place with cloths donning them. Some have plates and silverware.

"This is creepy,"Adriana's voice slips up behind me

while she slinks up and crams into my back. She is followed by her posse who have linked arms like a scaredy-cat chain. I duck to the right to finish my conversation with Dallas and peer over a couple overturned tables. I'm half expecting to find a dead body. Or a ghost.

"Dude, what do you need?" I ask him impatiently. My eyes veer to the back corner of the room. I think I see a busted baby grand piano laying sideways back there. "Can this wait until later?" I peer over my shoulder, see Boone standing at the doorframe and looking around. He's holding Lexie in his arms. She is reaching for his hat. Olivia is standing with him.

"Skeeter, how fast can you get to Memphis?" he asks me. I can hear someone playing drums around him and the sound of people talking while someone behind me peels back a layer of wallpaper and giggles.

"You're kidding me, right? See, I've got Boone and his friends stuffed inside my truck and we're past capacity and definitely weight load—" I narrow my eyes at the chubby twin.

"You're mean," she retorts.

"You called me a skank." I wiggle my head at her and her sister giggles at me.

"I didn't call you a skank," Dallas snaps back at me.

"I wasn't talking to you. I was talking to one of the twins. Good God, I'm missing Dutch right now. At least at his house, it's quiet. Me and Boone and his friends are somewhere outside Huntsville, Alabama."

"Who is Boone?"

"Just some guy. You know, *the* guy."

"Oh, Boone," Dallas draws it out like he's figured it out. "The boy you like that's got a girlfriend. So bring them. It's only like three and a half hours from where you're at."

I lean in, try to drop my voice. "Well, Dallas, here is the thing. He brought his girlfriend." I can hear him laughing on the other end.

"How'd you do that, Skeet? Or should I ask: how's that working for you?"

"I didn't ask her to come along," I whisper, turn enough to peer through my bangs at the two. They've got their heads together and Olivia is laughing while Boone tickles Lexie and makes her do her deep-belly giggle. "Oh, my God. And right as I speak, the two are having a moment with my daughter. As if this situation isn't really awkward enough without—"

"Listen, figure something out. I've got the stage in four hours. I want us to sing those two songs you wrote."

"What—stage? Two songs? Me too?"

"Yeah," he answers. "*Closest Thing to a Cowboy You Got Tonight* and *Baby Ain't Singing the Blues.*"

"You're kidding me, right? You think we're ready?" I mean, it's one thing singing at his studio where we can dub out the stupid mistakes. It's another when we're live. I scratch my head, cringe as I come upon the piano. Sure enough, it's an old baby grand laying there, broken and lifeless with old papers and pieces of a cash register laying underneath.

"Well, let me put it this way, sweetie," he tells me. "Do a search with my name. Do one with yours or our bands. You know what's coming up this week? It ain't America's Sweethearts, Brooke Canter and Chase Martin. It's Dallas Dunne, Tyler Cooper, and Waylon Ryder cleaning out stalls in an old barn, doing some kind of weird line dance and singing it up like a bunch of clowns."

"Huh?" I don't understand what he's saying until he reminds me that Cheyenne was taking videos of us on her phone. She'd posted it on every social venue possible. It got picked up quicker than free hotdogs at a baseball game.

"Oh, no. I'm so sorry, Dallas, I'll talk to her," I mutter. I'm hardly listening to him while I see a yellowish thick paper pinned up with a tack on the wall behind the piano. It looks like a miniature poster, the kind they tape to business windows to show an upcoming event. I turn my gaze to it, tip my head to see the picture of a thin man in a suit with a piano. "I didn't think anything of it, just thought she was having fun."

"She was having fun. And we were having fun. Now there's this new thing going on about where did Waylon Ryder disappear to and what the hell is she doing mucking out a stall with a country music singer. My marketing staff thinks I bailed on them because it's doing a better job than they are getting me out there again." Dallas chuckles softly. "At first, I was freaking out. I thought, everybody's going to see me like I'm an idiot. Hell, I had my shirt off and I was making fun of you and singing high pitch some of the time. But then you turned around and did the same about me. I guess I'd gotten kind of a big head because all of a sudden, I'm back in the spotlight because folks see me as a guy that'd get his feet dirty cleaning stalls with a rocker chick."

"A rocker chick, really Dallas?" I huff. "You don't clean stalls." I am hardly listening. I'm tugging the poster off the wall, then holding it up to my face. The man is sitting at the piano playing. Beneath it, there is pretty print saying: ALWAYS ON SATURDAYS AT THE DAYLIGHT LOUNGE, THE MUSIC OF STEVEN CALLISTO! Stevie C? I feel my heart jump.

"I cleaned stalls for you," he says with a sly swagger to his tone. "Now please do something for me. Drive that old truck to Memphis and sing with me at this little show in a few hours."

CHAPTER 28
SINGING TO A GUY WITH I LOVE U WAYLON ON A PIZZA BOX

I can see it in your eyes, that faraway stare.
I'm not the one you're looking for,
still I'm the only one here.
It's like they've all paired off in this ol' bar
And I'm not trying to be impolite,
But I'm the closest thing to heavy metal that'll pass your way tonight
What you talkin' about, boy?
I'll lie and tell you I've got a sweet ride, I'll put on a ball cap just to hang on tight for one night to be somebody else's dream girl.
When the morning sun comes up, I'll already be gone
Riding off into the sunset in my old truck with the city in my rearview mirror and the corn fields in my sight.
But I got you. For tonight. Just hang on tight, baby hang on tight.

Skeeter. I got that nickname ten years ago. It was Dallas that gave it to me. But he didn't really even know me back then. I was a scrawny just-turned-fifteen-year-old that could pass as twelve, fresh off Abram Miller's farm and playing at an open band competition outside Memphis.

I was one of one-hundred and forty-two wannabe-superstar artists playing every fifteen minutes on a makeshift stage behind an old high school that was having early season football scrimmage matches. After paying my last ten dollars to enter the competition and camping out for a day and a half on the grass so I could play, I set up at ten-fifteen at night to fourteen tired audience people more interested in eating their corndogs than listening to me. They could hardly hear me over the grind of the high school band celebrating the home team's win on the other side of the school grounds. I didn't even get applause. It was just the sound of mosquitos buzzing around my ears. And some old guy panhandling the few people left in the crowd. He asked me for a dollar to buy a hamburger.

"Dude, all's I got is this guitar and twenty-three cents to my name," I laughed at him. "Oh, and all these skeeters I'd been singing to and now biting at me which I'd love to have a penny for each one leaving me with these stupid welts." But I dug out two dimes and three pennies and handed it to him. "Have at it."

"Singin' for the skeeters." About the same time, someone laughed while they walked with a small pack of people coming out of the high school football stadium and to the parking lot. "But I'm gonna be a rock star someday." I almost ran into the woman. She made a quick retreat to her right. I saw her roll her eyes to the man next to her. I'm sure I didn't smell like daffodils and roses. I hadn't been able to shower in a week. But I slung my guitar over my shoulder and headed out to the highway. I'd never felt so scared and alone at that moment I realized I was—all alone.

"Baby, we can't let her go off by herself."

"That was Jenna Dunne who said that," I tell Adriana who is sitting in the passenger side of the truck when I pull into the fairgrounds. "She was like frigging beautiful. They picked me up and I stuttered every time I talked to her and I like boys. I'm sure she thought I was an idiot."

Adriana actually slips out of her smirk and laughs at this. "So you've known him for ten years?"

"Well, kind of. We really didn't see each other much back then. We're different music and have different record labels. He actually even owns his own company. But I went to stay at her mom's house for a few weeks. Then I met Red Benson, that's the drummer in Chase's old band. But it was before Chase. For a couple years, we went from town to town. I worked restaurants and he bussed tables. Jenna sent me fifty bucks every two weeks and we stopped in at his mom's once a month to keep from starving." I groan, look at the giant stage and crowd. "Crap, he told me the venue was small. This is huge." It's crowded and there are men in yellow vests parking cars. "So, back to what I was trying to make a point about is, I owe him and Jenna my right kidney. I got to sing some good stages because they picked me up that night instead of driving past like the seventy other cars did."

The phone tings and I pick it up while I'm trying to pull the truck in straight in the grass. The yellow vested man is getting impatient with me so I just stop halfway out in spite. While he screams, I answer the phone and flip him off.

"You're peppery today," I hear Boone say. He gets my middle finger, too, and a dirty glare. I'm mad. He's acting like nothing even happened between us. I'm not sure if I'm angry or feeling a little bit of comfort in the fact the girl in the back seat holding hands with him isn't going to punch me out because she knows something went on between us. However, I can't even look at the two. It makes me sick to my tummy thinking they are doing it.

"Hey, this is Graham. We're setting up for Dallas. He's wondering where you are. He's warming up. Who's that yelling?"

"I'm trying to get parked out here in the middle of nowhere," I tell him matter-of-factly. "Tell Dallas I've got twenty bucks to my name and I had to use ten of it for parking and I have to still get diapers for my baby girl. If she gets a big red rash on her pale pink bottom because her mama can't afford the good diapers with the extra absorbing channels or any at all, I'm blaming him."

"Yes, ma'am," Graham mumbles like a kicked puppy. "Just hand the phone to the dude that's yelling at you. Tell him I'm with Dallas Dunne and he'll let you up here."

He's already started singing by the time we get through the final of three security checkpoints. The stage is large and covered above by pretty white tarps that are blowing in the wind. There's men in polo shirts with radios and one comes up to me, points toward the stage. "In three minutes." He holds up three fingers. I see Dallas nod in mid -song, look relieved.

"I really need like five. I don't have a guitar—" Nobody's listening while I'm latched on to Lexie. On either side, two huge screens show the fans in the crowd and Dallas and his band. I'm burping Lexie and at the exact moment I feel the warmth of her throwing up all over my bare shoulder, I hear Dallas say: "We've got a special guest tonight because folks have been asking me online what I'm doing hanging out with Waylon Ryder—" I don't hear the rest. The guy in the polo is holding up two fingers. Two minutes. Crap. I'm not expecting to be herded on stage so fast and I almost toss Lexie at Boone while he takes off his button up shirt he has over a t-shirt so he can fumble with swiping the white river of throw up dribbling down my arm and cami. Then he snatches her from my hands.

"So I gave Waylon a call and she offered to come up here and give me a hand singing a couple songs she wrote for me—" I have to run up on stage to hit my cue. Dallas has a woman hand me a guitar while another hooks me up to a mic and I flip it over the guitar over my shoulder, hope it's ready to go. And Dallas, he looks like he is just going to shoot straight into the song. However, I raise my hand.

"Okay, to get things straight," I say before he can go on. "Dallas called me three hours and fifteen minutes ago while I was in Huntsville, Alabama—" the crowd breaks into applause when they hear the city name and I hold up my fist to cheer them on. "Which is four hours and ten minutes away. But I'm with my friends and I say, how would you like to party in Memphis, Tennessee tonight? And you know what they said—?" I see Dallas hold up his finger to the crowd's delight because he knows what I'm going to say. And this is a family event.

"Waylon Ryder, I know where you're going with this, girl. But, you do this family country style, now."

"I will. They said—oh, H E, double toothpicks, yes!"

We banter back and forth for a minute and then Dallas just lets loose with the song. We've done it so many times by now, I fall right in with my part and we roll into the verse together in perfect harmony. I'm blown away because he's so much more in tune with me than Chase. Because he's watching me and listening to me instead of the other way around. I look up a couple times, play into his smile and grin right back.

Then he goes for the second song and suddenly, the mood changes and he sits down on a stool and wiggles his finger for me to come in closer and sit on the stool next to him. "Now it's your turn to kick it up a bit," he tells me. "Go ahead. They're gonna like it." Then he turns to the crowd. "This is Waylon Ryder and she's gonna let you know what it feels like to—you tell them, sweetie—"

"—to have a guy dump you cold in the middle of the night in the middle of nowhere and drive off. But it isn't about the burn. It's about the coming out of the ashes and starting over again," I say softly. "And knowing folks like Dallas and a whole lot of other good country folk will take in a stranger without blinking an eye and give them—hope."

So we sing the song. And for the count of ten right after, it is silent. I'm thinking, oh-my-God, it's a bust. I'm not used to the softness of it all. Then it is like the crowd is going to blow us away with the applause. It's a good five minutes before I can slip my way off the stage and sit in the back and listen to Dallas do his usual performance.

I can see Boone and his sister and their friends watching from some seating they set up at the last minute for them. They are right up front and the twins look like ten year-olds dancing and screaming at the stage.

"Well, Dallas said he'd think we'd get off without a hitch as long as you didn't start cussing and taking off your clothes."

Tyler Cooper had sneaked up behind me. I didn't hear him over the music. I turn, smile. "He told you to say that, didn't he?"

"Yeah, Waylon. Man, you're great. Is there any kind of music you can't do?" He pushes one hand in a pocket, bobs his head up and down. The other, it taps out the beat of the song Dallas is singing. Then he leans in hard to me because the music's loud. We're like four inches from each other and it's still hard to make out his words.

"That's what happens when a little Amish girl gets an old boombox, a guitar and the dream her mama that left her behind would come back if she got good enough to be a star. She sits in the back field and practices songs over and over for hours and hours."

"Is that so," he says it and it isn't a question.

"I'm surprised he didn't tell you my life story."

"Well, your name did come up a few times." Tyler keeps up the beat on his pant leg. "He also told me not to push so quickly on this because you just got burned a couple months ago. But I want to play drums with you. Harley Mason wants to play guitar with you since you two played at the restaurant last month. He's been bugging the crap out of me and Dallas because, well, he thinks you're going to start a new band. I just don't want to miss the opportunity because you drift off another direction."

I'm floored. I guess I should have seen it coming, Dallas showing up at Dutch's with him like he's trying to fix me up with a little brother. "Well, I sing at a little bar called the Crazy Filly on Friday and Saturday nights. Maybe if you show up there, we can give it a try."

He bites his lip, leans in hard again. "I'm legally blind. I should tell you that."

"Is that a band?" I ask him just when I realize what he meant. He laughs, thinks it's funny. He doesn't get to answer, though. I feel a tug on my shirt and turn.

"Hey, Skeeter."

"Hey, Boone." I lean away from Tyler, take Lexie from Boone's hands. Tyler takes a couple steps away and listens to the music. Lexie's got on a pair of protective ear muffs so the loud music doesn't hurt her ears. They are too big for her head and she looks like a beetle.

"One of the guys gave me these for her to wear. She looks like a mouse." He pokes at the ear muffs. She is making her pucker-lipped face until she sees me. Then she looks relieved. When I look at her smile, it's like the world goes away and the crowd goes away. It's just the two of us because it's what we got, each other.

"Mama's here," I mouth to her, smell her sweet scent. "Everything's okay."

"You're amazing." Boone leans in and says that. I look up and he's just staring at me like he's seeing me in a whole new light. "Thanks for letting us come."

"I didn't have a choice."

"Yeah, you did." He tips his head like he's not sure if I'm kidding or not. "I'm so sorry it worked out this way. You know, with Livie along. She's nice, right? You like her?"

I don't know what that means. It's an odd thing to say to someone you tricked into sleeping with because the other person thought you were single.

"Um, I don't know. Yeah, sure. Barring she called me trailer trash at the bar when I went out with Bobby Moretti."

"She didn't know you." Boone peers over my shoulder. Then he nods. I turn my head to see five or six younger men waving at me. They're asking me to come over, making a big deal I'm looking at them. One's even got a quickly-made, makeshift sign made from a cardboard pizza box that says: I LOVE U WAYLON.

"Can you hold her for five more minutes?" I ask Boone. "Please. I miss this."

"I could make you one of those signs, sit outside your cabin," he says that when I walk toward the little group of fans. I turn and roll my eyes, then I snatch a pen from one of the guy's hands. "You know how I do things, right?" I ask the chubby man with the sign. He's all goofy smiling at me and I reach out and poke him with my finger. "Baby, you got to take off your shirt for me. Show me some skin. You know that's what I like. I like boys. And I like their skin. Then I'll write something sexy on you to think about tonight, right?"

"Yeah," he says with a shy smile and he reminds me of one of Dutch's old geldings he calls Willy while he wriggles off his shirt. He's tame and sweet and he'll do anything I ask for a sweet treat.

"What's your name, baby?" I ask him softly.

"Reynolds." It's usually something like: *Sweet, wet*

dreams I write on their shoulders or their biceps. Sometimes, I put little ditties like: *B My baby tonight* or *love u.* It's my thing and Chase promoted it in the same way he had me sign our little demo CDs with two hearts and *love, Waylon.* But on Reynold's shoulder, I make a big heart and put our initials on it. I can feel his heart beating hard before I go to the next guy who's swiping off sweat while I smile at him. I flirt and sign chubby boys and skinny boys, some between, and a few girls for about twenty minutes and the security comes and plays the bad guys, shooing them away.

I don't even notice Boone watching me until I turn to get Lexie. He's got this funny twist to his lips, sad and like he's a bit sick to his stomach.

"You could have any guy you want," he tells me while he hands me Lexie. I think it's funny. I don't laugh. Because I know I'm staring at him hard with a curious expression.

"Yeah, as long as they don't know the real me," I tell him. Doesn't he see it? Because, no, I can't. It's him I want and he's out of my reach.

CHAPTER 29
LEAVING DALLAS. AND I DON'T MEAN TEXAS

Dallas and I don't fight much. But tonight, he invites all of us to come out to his big traveling bus while he waits for his crew to pack up. It's the size of a house inside.

"Look," I show him the miniature poster with the name Steve Cooper I found at the Daylight Lounge while he swipes down his guitar at a little table in the bus. "This guy's name was on a napkin in my mama's jewelry box. We found it at an abandoned restaurant." He absently looks at the picture. I can tell he's got his mind on other things. "You know it's important for me to find my mama, right? This could be a clue."

"Yeah, I get that, Skeeter." He forces a smile at me and looks like a growling raccoon.

"I found another clue in the jewelry box. It was on some checks with Bud Mooney on it. They knew Mama too. But they didn't know where she went after she worked for them as a nanny." I sigh. "I've got one more envelope with checks from a Wayne Pelosi in Louisville on them. I'm thinking about saving that one for when I get my driver's license. Did I tell you my friend Bobby Moretti, he's a cop, looked up a couple things for me. He couldn't find anything, but he says I'm just about ready for my driving test."

"No, that's good, hon." I see him looking over my shoulder at Boone and Adriana. "You still getting those weird phone calls?"

"Yeah, sometimes."

"You need a bodyguard, baby."

"You're funny," I chuckle at him. I follow his gaze toward Boone. He and his sister are playing cards with one of his band members and laughing loud. Olivia is leaning hard into Boone and once in a while, they peck a couple kisses. The twins are watching TV and eating the pizza Dallas ordered.

"Okay, Skeeter, you may not see this, but the boy's using you. Cripes, I see it. I can't stand to see him doing that crap to you. You need to stop whatever is going on and move on."

"I don't know what you're talking about."

"I think you do." He's shaking his head back and forth, rubbing his chin. "You let everybody walk all over you. I mean, it's got to stop! That old man you're staying with—what the hell? You're cleaning shit out of his stalls and cooking for him. You're like the sixth wife of some polygamy cult. He's got you hidden away in the middle of nowhere in a cabin he couldn't even rent to a pig."

"What brought this on?" I spit at him. "I take care of Dutch. He takes care of me."

"So how well are you taking care of him, sweetheart?" Dallas leans forward stretches his arms over his head. Then he reaches out and snatches up the beer he's got on the table. "You playing wife with him too?"

"No. Stop it, Dallas," I say. My voice is hoarse because he's making me want to cry. I know they can hear every word he says and I feel my cheeks getting red. "You're drunk and you're saying things you'll regret later."

"How would you even know I'm drunk?"

"You want me to remind you in front of everybody, Dallas? Because I will," I mutter. "You're making me mad." Then I narrow my eyes and lower my voice to imitate him. It's low enough nobody else can hear. "Skeeter. Skeeter, I love you. Baby, don't throw no more cold water on me." I bring my voice back up. "Ring a bell from nine years ago outside my hotel room?" Oh, he was really drunk after a fight with Jenna then and so drunk, he was drunk-in-love with me.

"No, girl, I don't. But if it takes throwing that out on the table between all of us to get you to listen to me, I'm all in. I'm tired of watching people run all over you, take everything you got, and it's a lot."

"You use me. You used me tonight singing on that stage. What's the difference, Dallas?" I ask him. "Just like you used me that night to pretend-love me so Jenna would get jealous and come back to you after your fight. I was the only one you could count on to *not* sleep with you. You knew I'd call her and make her come get you before the cops did."

He stares at me long and hard. It is almost silent behind me. His eyes are angry. I'm angry. "You know what? Maybe you're right. It's the other way around. You're using me. You're using him and them. Everything's fake for you so you don't have to deal with the truth." He says it loud and my eyes get wide. I don't turn to see their faces.

"What truth?" I ask him. Then I don't want him to answer. "I'm not discussing this any more with you." I stand up, snatch my keys off the table and they make a scratching scream across the tabletop. "I'm going home. I'm going to take my truck and my fake friends home, then go to my pigsty because I've got to get up in four hours and clean stalls and cook breakfast because that's what is expected of me. And actually, I'm good at it."

"You don't have to go. Because what you're good at is singing and playing guitar, Skeeter. You're going for the easy and not the hard. Your talent is going to waste in that hovel you're staying in. I understand you've come from humble means. I know how your daddy treated you—"

"Abram Miller's a good man," I warn him. "Don't say anything bad about him. He took me in, gave me a home."

"He may very well be a good man, sweetheart, but his way of thinking is to treat his boys like farmhands and his girl like she's nothing but a baby-maker." Dallas breathes in. I know he's waiting for me to give him some snarky retort so he's quick to go on. "You can give that boy your truck keys and stay with us. You won't have to cook or clean or— sing at some old, crappy bar. You can turn and walk away and never look back."

"How'd you know I'm working at the bar?"

"I know everything about everybody my people are thinking about signing on contract," Dallas sighs. "I know you've been singing new songs. I know you work Friday and Saturday nights and you get seventy-five bucks plus tips—"

"Well here's something you don't know," I growl at him. "I don't like you anymore. I don't like you creeping into my business and snooping around when I don't ask you to look around. And I wouldn't sign on with your company even if you begged me. So go to hell, Dallas."

"You have no clue what you're saying and who you're talking to, Skeeter. I've got hundreds of artists begging me to take a look at their work every week. They'd sell their soul to the devil to sign on with me. I can make people. I can break people. So you better watch what you're saying—"

"Okay, I'm watching what I'm saying right now, Dallas. I'd rather rot in some dive bar in Bel-Air than tailor my life to suit your needs in hell. I'm not kissing your ass like everybody else does. Screw off."

I'm in a foul mood driving home. Lexie cries most of the way and everybody else is happy and high off the unexpected road trip and meeting a bunch of bands after the performance. Only Boone looks up once in a while with an angry glare. What the hell did I do to piss him off now? I turn up the radio, and sing along and try hard to forget about the fight with Dallas Dunne.

CHAPTER 30
LAWYERS, STALKERS, AND ANGRY DADDIES, OH MY

Three weeks after I started singing at the Crazy Filly, Oaky put up some posts on a social network about having a live band singing there on the weekends. There's nothing to do from fifty miles south of Nashville and all the way to the Alabama state line on the weekends barring going to fast food restaurants, so now everybody in at least that radius is showing up at the Crazy Filly on Friday and Saturday nights. Well, everybody but Dallas Dunne who seems to have cooled on courting me for Late Night Outlaw Records.

It doesn't stop him, however, from pushing the two songs we sang together on the radio. I hear them every time I get in the truck and I can get in the radio station. One of them has supposedly gotten some kind of a record for the most downloads ever in a two week period.

Oaky set me up in a little recording studio he rented for three days. Last week, I made a CD with six songs on it there. "What label do you want on it?" the guy at the front asks. He was grubby and smelled like B.O. I blinked at him and told him to put: Dead Broke Hearts. What the hell? Why not make my own company?

Actually one of the songs Dallas and I sang is playing softly on the boombox I've got running for Lexie who is laying on a blanket on the floor and trying hard to show off that she can just about push her little chest off the floor with her pudgy arms. I don't know if she recognizes my voice on it, but she grins at me with loving eyes.

"Are you sure you're alright babysitting by yourself until eleven-thirty?"

Chey's been walking over the fields and watching

Lexie for me since the first Friday I started working. Two months in and she hasn't missed a night. She is slipping through the front door and smiling at me. "I mean, that's three hours and she might cry the entire time. Your daddy doesn't mind?"

"She doesn't cry much," she tells me quietly. "I've been telling my dad I'm spending the night somewhere. Then I sneak in the back door. They just figure I decided not to stay or maybe they don't even notice. No biggie. I'll just stay here if it bothers you and leave in the morning. He doesn't need to know."

"He doesn't—know?"

"Nuh uh," she tells me. She seems unconcerned about it. I'm awful at lying. I can't even look Dutch in the eye when he asks me how my job at the restaurant is doing. I'm looking at the clock. I've got twenty minutes before I go on stage.

"Oh, Chey, I've seen movies where that same scenario plays out like a horror movie," I tell her. "Let me call your daddy. Maybe he'll just let—"

"He won't let me stay here, Waylon." She acts far too grown up for her age. I would assume it is from hanging around with Boone's mom and dad so much. Chey's got on a beanie hat and designer glasses. I know she doesn't usually wear glasses at all so I'm assuming she's going for a look. She's always dressed up like a doll in the latest fashion, too, like the really expensive stuff grandparents buy their grandkids. "He promised Papaw we'd stay away from you. Papaw's old fashioned. He still worries about what other people think about our family. And he thinks you're doing drugs and stuff and it would look like we were—you know, bad. Just, please don't call Daddy. It's alright. He's busy and I'm telling you he doesn't care who I'm staying with as long as I'm out of the way."

"Except me."

"Well, yeah, I suppose. But I want to earn my guitar lessons from you and I can't ask them for money to pay you, for obvious reasons. Besides, Daddy and Livie get the house to themselves tonight. I do this all the time."

I feel like she unintentionally shoves a dull butter knife in my heart right then. If Boone and Livie have the house to themselves, they aren't going to be watching TV. I have to let it pass. I mean, I don't know what normal teenagers do. I wasn't one. So maybe she's right. She's safer here than out doing what I've seen other girls her age doing.

I don't know why I would assume free-sailing on my own would be easy. Tyler Cooper and Harley Mason never show up. Oaky's got some old guys playing guitar and drums with me. They aren't that great so I'm assuming they do it for free beer. Their ineptness leaves me cutting corners. Even if nobody seems to notice, I do.

There's a man in a suit waiting for me by the stage. Already tonight, all the tables are full and it is tough for me to get to him without somebody stopping me to say hello. Oaky points him out to me, says he's a lawyer. I reluctantly walk over to the man. My heart's racing. He's carrying a briefcase. I'm hoping he isn't one of the suits like the ones looking for me with the picture of the girl in a dress.

"You are Waylon Ryder?"

"I am."

"I'm Dave Walters with Terrace, Walters and Bean, Attorneys at Law. I've been sent by the Tyrone Canter Enterprises and Tyrone Canter, himself. It appears you've been singing songs signed on for contract with Chase Martin and Brooke Canter. They own the songs."

"What?" I'm staring at him. I know for a few seconds, I'm more interested in a goofy man in a t-shirt jumping up and down waving at me. He's sitting with his buddies and I blink him away and turn to Dave Walters.

"He's going to sue you if you continue to sing the songs."

"They're *my* songs." I hold up a hand and shake my head. "I wrote all the songs Chase and I sang." I feel my heart drop stone cold to my tummy. How dare he tell them he had anything more to do with those songs other than playing the guitar and singing once in a while? "Listen, I came up with the music sheets and the words and—all's that idiot did was sing backup after I taught him the tunes."

"That's not what Chase Martin says. He's willing to fight this out in court. He says he wrote them. Red Benson, the drummer for the band and a couple of the crew, they say Chase Martin wrote them too. I would suppose it is your word against theirs. If you're such a good song writer, then write some more. If you're not, then the proof is in the inability to do that. You're not going to win. Tyrone Canter's got paperwork to prove it."

"What—paperwork?" I ask.

"Have your lawyers contact us. We'll discuss this with them. For now, just know you're advised. If you sing the songs, you'll be in court."

I have two-hundred and twenty-two dollars stuffed in a blue plastic coffee container under my bed. What I don't spend on diapers and food, I'm saving to pay Dutch back for the missing money from beneath his sink. And I don't think that would even give me the gas money to get to the closest lawyer's office, much less the money to hire one. But I have a baby to feed and an angry itch to my back right now over Chase trying to steal my songs.

"I guess I'll take my chances, asshole," I grunt to him. It's a huge crowd. I'm sure Oaky couldn't fit another person in that bar. It is standing room only and people are crushed to the stage. I'm sure if there are fire codes, he is exceeding them. And when I get up on stage, I make sure I cover all the songs I can think of I'd sung with Chase mixed in with those old classics Oaky wanted me to sing. I can see the attorney standing there with pickle lips taking a video with his phone before he leaves. I flip him the finger and the crowd bursts into a cheer. He leaves quite quickly.

It isn't until eleven o'clock and I'm packing up my guitar that Tiffany comes up behind me. "Hey, I couldn't get your attention earlier. But somebody called here and said there's trouble up at your place. There's cops and lights—" I shudder and freeze. My baby. Chey.

There's a fire truck, an ambulance and two Bel-Air police cars parked along the dirt road when I jam on my brakes in front of Dutch's old cabin. My heart is beating like I set off firecrackers inside and I don't even care about Bobby Moretti's glare when I get out of the driver's seat of the car. I'm freaking out. My face is numb.

"Where's Lexi? Where's Chey? Are they okay?" I'm dizzy with fear.

"Stop, stop, stop." That's Bobby and he's waving his hands at me. I suppose I am thinking there is a murder scene he doesn't want me to see because I try to bolt past him and he snatches me up by the arm.

"It's okay. The girls are okay." I hear him. I also hear Lexie crying from the front porch. "There were a couple men trespassing on the property. Under the circumstances, we treated it like a break in and found a couple young men lurking around."

"Cripes, girl, what were you thinking?" It is Dutch that swoops off the steps and I turn to him. He's got Lexie in his arms and she's wailing and he's already laying into me about leaving them all alone especially if I've got someone stalking me. I can see his silhouette and three others against the yellow bug light on the porch roof and the little twinkle lights around the porch railing. There's two men in handcuffs by the police car.

"What the hell were you doing?" Then before I can even open my mouth, it is Boone screaming at me all the way across the yard while he stomps toward me. "What were you thinking? You let my daughter sneak out of the house and come over here without my permission? I trusted you and you—pull a stupid stunt like this? And she's been doing it for a month of weekends, telling me she's at a friend's house and she's not? Have you ever made an adult decision in your entire life? Are you stupid? I think there's something wrong with you, I do. I think all those drugs you took made you stupid. You just don't think things out like normal people do. You do know I could get you arrested for this, Skeeter. You stay away from her. You stay away from us. Don't even smile at her, don't even look in her direction or my direction ever again or by God, I'll call the cops. You're a frigging drug-addict and I don't want you anywhere near us. She could have gotten killed! She—"

I had to listen to Boone tell me how bad of a person I was for eight minutes. Nobody stops him. I guess a couple college boys I inked with my pen at the concert followed me home the other night. They were sneaking around, trying to figure out if I actually lived in such a crummy place. About ten-thirty, Chey peeked out the window and saw them peeking back at her and she screamed holy hell and called her dad who called the cops and the fire department and I'm not surprised if the Navy Seals aren't on their way while his father finally tells him to relax and makes him walk to their trucks in the drive. Dutch just shakes his head at me.

CHAPTER 31
ANOTHER PIECE OF MAMA'S PUZZLE AT SUNNYDALE ASSISTED LIVING CENTER IN ALABAMA

I got my driver's license today. I pass on the first try. Of course, I'd been driving for almost four months. I should be good at it. I hold the hot little plastic card in my fingers and give Dutch a big hug. "That's enough," he mutters and gave me a quick pat of his hand on my back. Still, he lets me drive him to the diner and he buys me lunch. The entire ride, he has his hands on the dashboard and window and his foot slamming to the floor.

I didn't want the celebration to end. So I went for a road trip.

"Hi, are you Steve Cooper?" I am staring steadily at an elderly man at the Sunnydale Assisted Living Center twenty miles west of Decatur, Alabama. It's an economy retirement center with 1970s linoleum floors and it smells like pee and the meatloaf they were serving in the dining room. He's sitting on a faux leather couch with cracked seats and watching an old western movie on the TV. He's smoking a cigarette even though the nurse keeps telling him to put it out.

"Who wants to know?" he grumbles at me.

"Well, that's a good question, I suppose." I sit down next to him and unfold the little poster I found at the lounge.

"You can't pin that baby on me," He wiggles wrinkled knuckles at Lexie's neck and she turns, gives him a sour gaze. "I'm too old and I don't have a cent to my name for child support if that's what you're looking for. This place is stealing my last dollar."

"No." I smile at him. "Me. I'm trying to find out stuff on me, well, my mama. When I was Terry McDaniel's little girl, my name was Nicky. When I was Hannah Schwartz's daughter, I was Gracie. So they say. Everybody calls me Skeeter now. Is this you?"

He snatches the old poster out of my hand and gives a loud coughing laugh, tossing his head back. "Well, lookey there! Twenty years ago, I was a star!" A couple gray heads turn toward him, then look away with bored detachment. "Where'd you get this, girlie girl?"

"At the Daylight Lounge outside Huntsville, Alabama."

"Oh, boy. I thought that place burned down."

"It did. I'm looking for my mama, Mister Cooper," I sigh. "Your name was on a napkin in her jewelry box."

"How'd you find me?"

"I looked up your name and found it under registered voters in Alabama," I tell him. "And a city directory. You used to sell shoes when you weren't singing at the restaurant. Let's see, it said: Steven P. Cooper, 514 Broadway Avenue. Salesman, Roundabout Products. However, you were one of fourteen I rummaged through the phone books and online. I spent two days calling folks."

"I sold a lot of stuff for Roundabout, little girl, but I wasn't as good being a salesman as a pianist. But who hires somebody who is good at that?" he asks me quietly. He looks at me up and down. "You can't make a living off it, I guess. But I had dreams of living in Pensacola, Florida in a little house by the beach. And I'd saved up a good bit of dream money so I could." He sighs. "Then along comes Gwen and her two kids. Gwen Stockholm was her name." He pokes his head with his gnarled forefinger. "See, I've still got my memory. And I remember her like yesterday. She had a little girl named Teenie. At least, that's what I called you. I see your eyes. You had those huge things when you were her age—" He points at Lexie. "Um, maybe a little older. You looked like that baby of yours there." Lexie is getting chubbier by the day. She sinks herself into me, sucks her fist. "Maybe you don't want to hear all this stuff."

"Gwen Stockholm," I whisper. "What did she do? How did you know her?"

He pauses there, looks up to the ceiling. Then he rubs his chin. "Well, dear, when did you see her last?"

"When I was five or six." I tip my head. "What do you mean, I wouldn't want to hear?"

"Oh." He situates himself on the couch, rocks back and forth. Then he looks at the nurse, back to the sun coming through the windows. "What'd you say your name is now?"

"Skeeter."

"Skeeter, your mama was what we used to call a con artist," he says softly. His eyes are kind and gentle, but I feel he is angry at me for what my mama has done to him. "She was a pretty little thing. She came into town and got a room at a local hotel. When she found the right man, she got to know him really well. Then she came up with a sad story and latched on to him and sucked him dry of money."

"You were—one of those men?"

"I was. Thought I loved that woman. Loved you and that little boy, too."

"Will."

"William was his name."

"William," I repeat. I don't know what else to say. I suppose I'm kind of numb. She was my mama. I'd rather hear she went to church every Sunday and worked down at the local homeless shelter passing out food, but she was my mama. I was having a hard time swallowing this pill. "And she left?"

"It's been twenty-some years ago," he tells me. "She stayed with me for six or seven months. I guess I should have known she wasn't gonna stick around, playing wifey and all. I was gone a lot. I guess she was too. The neighbor said she'd hightail it out of the house as soon as I left for work. I wish I could tell you where she went, where she came from—I can't. One night, she had supper on the table just like we always did. It was chicken and mashed potatoes and beans. I left to go play piano about five and when I got back, you all were just gone. She just got up and left. I tried to find her. There wasn't much in the way of internet back then. I called the police. They didn't know anything about her. I guess I'd never known she was a con artist until I saw her picture on the news one night. I was working in West Virginia. It was by chance, I suppose. I was laying in a seedy hotel and watching the nightly news. Up pops a picture of your mama on the screen. She had red hair then. But the nose, the eyes, they were all the same. I guess she'd taken two or three other men for all their money. I didn't have much, but she got it all. And this is the closest thing to my little retirement cottage in Pensacola I'll ever get. It's the hell she left me, nothing but a shithole in the middle of a grocery store parking lot and the knowing that my dream is only five hours away and a straight shot down I-65. And I couldn't even afford the gas for the car to get me there."

I stand up, feeling tired. At least I had some kind of time frame of the path my mama followed. She must have known Steve Cooper first when I was newborn and Will was my only brother. After that, was when she met Bud Mooney. I felt like I was moving backward more than forward. Bobby was wrong. I'm not finding anything going that direction. I suppose I would have just given up then if Steve hadn't stopped me before I went out the door. He'd gone back to his room and returned with a picture that looked like he'd ripped it out of an old photo album.

"Here. It's all I got of your mama," he says to me and hands the picture to me while I balance Lexie on my shoulder. "I wished I could tell you she was an angel, took in stray kittens, and went to church. I can't do that. But I can give you her smile." I blink at him, lower my head to the picture. I see my mama and I see her holding a baby. Then, there's a boy next to her. It is Will. Mama is smiling with pretty white teeth.

"Thanks," I tell him. Later and when I stop in a gas station, I turned the picture over. I see where somebody scratched out something on the back with a pencil. I look at it closer, scrutinize the blue pen beneath. I figure, at first, it is probably something Steve did when he found out mama had left him.

"Holy hell," I whisper instead. Because I can see names printed there. I make a mad dash for the glove compartment and stab around inside until I find an old pencil at the bottom. I take it out, use the nubby eraser end and wipe away the scribbles. Janice Lynn Singleton. Willie –Age 2. Arie, age 9 months, 2 days.

"Janice Singleton," I whisper the name aloud. After, the truck is silent save for the sound of a car pulling into the gas station. Then, my phone tings.

"Skeeter?" Dallas's voice booms over the other end. Part of me wishes I hadn't picked it up. The other feels relieved.

"Yeah, Dallas, it's me."

It's silent for three or four breaths. I look out my windshield and realize there's another crack in the glass I'd never noticed that's probably been there the whole time.

"Sweetie, I just wanted to hear your voice. Now I know you're okay, I'll hang up."

"Don't hang up." I say it so quickly, it sounds like I'm out of breath. Silence again. I suppose we're both waiting for the other one to apologize. We're both stubborn as hell.

"I got my driver's license," I blurt out. I know it sounds stupid like a two year-old proudly announcing she just pooped in the potty for the first time.

"Aw, nice," he tells me. "I'm proud of you. I also hear you got a CD out," he says. "Congratulations."

"I hear you got a song on the top ten."

"Two songs. Our songs. So who's this new label you're going with, Skeeter, Dead Broke Hearts?"

"I did a CD in some back alley sound room, Dallas. I didn't want it to look like I'd sunk so low I was back to doing CDs on my own again. I made the publisher up."

"Dead Broke Hearts. I like that. Maybe I can give you some pointers on—"

"Dallas, I feel so lost right now. I'm at that point I'm free of Chase and I'm not used to doing it alone. I feel like I was walking through a dark woods with him and suddenly he let go. And I turn to follow him and realize he's way ahead of me and so I'm standing there and knowing I'm a big girl. I got to walk this dark place alone. And everybody's a monster trying to get me." I lower my voice. "I'm scared."

"There's nothing wrong with asking for help, Skeeter, that doesn't make you weak. Everything's a learning curve. What happened to that boy you liked?"

"You were right—it's just Dutch and me. And he doesn't trust me because he thinks I stole money from him."

"You?" Dallas laughs softly on the other end. "I remember the night we first met, you were giving some homeless guy your last dime. And you were fifteen and on the streets all by yourself. Why don't you just pay him back?"

"With what? I've got two-hundred and forty dollars to my name and it's all going to a babysitter if I can find one so I can work Fridays and Saturdays at the bar."

"My assistant didn't call you?"

"No."

"Baby, I've got publishing royalties for the songwriting and royalties from singing the song sitting on hold in a bank account in Nashville for you." He laughs out loud like it's funny. "We made it to the top two last week on both songs you wrote. You got money coming out your ass."

CHAPTER 32
|CH LIEBE DICH

There might be money coming out my ass, but I didn't know what to do with it. Dallas sent me a check for four-thousand dollars to get me through until I set up a bank account to have the money deposited. I drove to the bank and Amanda Wells, who shared the hospital room with me the day Lexie was born, helped me open a checking account. She also told me our little girls needed to have a play date because they were born on the same day. "It's like they are twins with different mamas, Waylon," she tells me. Then she confides in me she just hated leaving her at home while she worked, but she had to work. "It's so hard, isn't it?" she tells me. She doesn't look at my high heel boots and my jean shorts and compare them to her conservative polyester suit and pants. "Working and having kids?"

It is and I tell her that and she smiles. I wanted to go to the store and spend some money just for the heck of it. But I didn't even know how to write a check or use the little debit card they gave me at the bank. So I used it as an excuse to walk across the field to the Martinez's.

"Hey, Boone."

Boone is sitting in a section of the Martinez home that is separated from the rest of the house, but is built into it like an enormous A-frame cabin. He's tapping something into the computer before he leans back in the chair slightly and looks at me. He's got a blue pen in his hand and he chews on the round end. It is the offices he's working in. I know this because there's a big sign out to the right of the house and in front of a connected log building that says; MORE SOLAR ENERGY-*BECAUSE YOU CAN NEVER HAVE ENOUGH*—HARLAN MARTINEZ. BOONE MARTINEZ.

It is the kind of space that smells new and looks new and has expensive, wooden furniture. The room Boone is in has a huge glass window and it overlooks the hills toward Dutch's land. I can see the trails where I ride the horses and the field where I've been working with some of the mares with racing barrels. There's a meeting room enclosed in glass on either side with huge TVs.

"Hey, I bet if you get to work early enough, you can look out that window and see me working the horses, huh?" I tease him, point toward the window.

"Seven-fifteen," he answers. "Pretty much by the book every day. Six horses bareback, two with saddle and one gelding that kicks you off and runs to the barn more often than not." He looks at me deadpan. "What can I do for you?"

I'm stunned. He's right. But, God, he's so cold. I almost turn to leave. I feel like a bad waitress who is serving a haughty, rich man's table. I'm doing a nervous twist of my fingers. I see him look down, follow my hands. He's got this knowing gaze like a male lion looking for the weakness in another pack member. I wish I'd never come here.

"More Solar Energy. I thought you just did cattle."

"I started this company. My dad funds it."

"I bet that put a thorn in Bo Littleton's ass," I say softly. "You're kind of the opposite of fracking right?"

"Yeah, I guess. What do you need?"

"Um, I just wanted to tell you I got my license." I hold up the little card they gave me at the license bureau. "I'm kind of legal now."

"Well, good for you," he tells me flatly. "Is that all?" I try to toss it aside and I feel kind of stupid. Everybody else gets their license at sixteen.

"I guess I just came for some advice." I hold up the

little debit card and the check book with a blue faux leather case. "I—"

"Legally, I can't give you advice, Waylon. It would be unethical since I work for my dad and he's with the attorneys that are collecting information on Chase Martin's lawsuit against you."

"Your dad's—an attorney?" I ask him. Oh. That's why he's acting so strange and why he won't come around me. Is there not anyone in this whole world that isn't in the long line waiting to pummel me in the belly right now?

"Yes. I am."

I twist around, see the open door to my right. I didn't even notice the office there. Now I see Harlon Martinez in a button up shirt and khaki pants. He's using a letter opener, slipping the sharp end along the edge of the envelope.

"I didn't know that or I wouldn't have come," I say hoarsely.

"So now you know. You need to stay away from Boone and Cheyenne. I don't want anyone believing that our family would associate with someone—like you. You're lucky we didn't file charges against you for making Chey lie to us."

"Making her lie?" I spat back. "You're kidding me, right?"

"You need to leave, young lady," he says firmly and dismisses me with his hand. "Boone has a lovely fiancé and it is inappropriate for you to come around—"

I can't get to the entranceway quick enough. I want to cry. I don't. I wait for the door to slam behind me and it doesn't. I don't realize the reason until I'm four steps along the walkway.

"You know, I could say screw it to all the other things." Boone is standing at the door, half in and half out.

"Videos don't lie. But I get it, you're exposed to so much crap with your lifestyle."

"Exposed to what? And what videos?" I ask him. "Drugs? Because I've never touched them."

"Well, I don't know," Boone looks off and away. "I can't say. But I'm assuming you didn't see the videos that Red Benson and some of your other band members posted about you online?"

I feel my face flush. Videos? I mean, I shared my life with Red and Chase and half a dozen others for the last ten years. I'm sure there are videos with me being goofy or whatever.

"No."

"Maybe you better look. But it all comes down to one thing. You're not over him."

I turn, see Boone standing halfway in and halfway out of the doorway.

"Why—why would you say that?" I ask.

"I don't know, Skeeter. I could just tell by the things you said, stuff you did. I was kind of always in the mode that you were going to leave. I was going to come over to Dutch's and you'd be gone."

"Like your wife left you."

"I guess, yeah. Is that all?"

"So what part of me says I'm leaving? What did I do to make you distance yourself from me?" I stop. I'm beating a dead dog. I'd danced this dance with Chase. Do I really care if he likes me or not? Not if he's running for the door every time I do something to embarrass him. "Never mind, Boone. I don't want to know. I'm me. I can't change that."

"Alright. Because you say his name, Skeeter, when we're together, you know, when you get to that point—"

"No, I don't."

"Yeah, well, you do. *Come on, Chase.* You say it every time. Maybe you didn't even realize it. It doesn't matter."

"I'm sorry." I don't remember saying it. Ever. I'm embarrassed. "Boone, I—"

"Don't sweat it," he says and waves me away.

"Ich liebe dich."

"Yeah, that's what you say."

I laugh with a snarky shake of my head. Then, I reach into my purse, grab a pen and part of a receipt. I write down the word. "Here. I wrote it down for you, asshole. Look it up."

CHAPTER 33
DUMPING DALLAS (AGAIN) HALFWAY BETWEEN NASHVILLE AND BEL-AIR

On the second week of July, I meet with Dallas halfway between Nashville and Bel-Air.

"How come I had to drive forty miles and you only drove thirty-two," I gripe to him. He just shakes his head and chuckles.

"Because I make more money than you."

"Not for long," I tell him. I push a couple sheets of music over to him and he rolls his eyes, takes them in his hands. He's got a man sitting next to him who looks like a giant.

"Waylon, this is my security guy, Wade." Dallas nods at the man. He's staring hard at me. I mean, the guy is seven feet tall and probably three-hundred pounds. Not one inch of it is fat. "Jenna says I got to quit running around without one. I made the mistake of telling her about the messages on the phone you got. People can be weird. You should think about getting one too." He looks at the music I handed him. "What's this?"

"More songs for you. It's been raining and the train has been running every night. I put the two together and made a couple songs about it and love and all that stuff."

"Keep 'em coming, Skeeter," he tells me. "But sweetie, we need to talk."

"About what?"

"A few things. I heard you're taking on Brooke Canter and Chase Martin in the lawsuit."

"Well, that's true." The day I saw the picture Red Benson posted of me online, I decided it was time to fight back. Red, who I thought was my best buddy forever, posted videos of me from behind and running mostly naked down a hotel hallway. He was having a water balloon fight with some of the crew and I was changing out of a bathing suit. He came into the bathroom and I hightailed it out for safety. Nobody knows the story, only uses their imagination for the picture. Then there's me fake-sniffing sugar off a counter. But it didn't look like sugar. And nobody got to see the first part where I was sitting at a little restaurant doing sugar shots with the little white packets from the table while I waited for a burger. That part was cut out as was the part where I dumped it on the table and picked up a straw and pretended to suck it in. The only part you see is me running the straw up the little white line.

How quickly he turned on me when something better came along. Dutch said it wasn't very gentlemanly of the man to do it. It was probably for the bigger picture and that was to make me look bad to my fans. He said if he was Jesus, he'd tell me to turn my back and love my enemies.

"But I ain't Jesus," Dutch says softly. "And I know'd the little girl inside here. She's got a heart of gold." He pokes my flat chest with his finger. "I'm going downtown and hire a lawyer today to come up and talk to you."

"Dutch, we can't afford a lawyer."

"Well, we'll just take one step at a time."

I tell Dallas that and he is shaking his head. "We've been to three lawyers and they've all said the same. I need proof or it is just their word against mine. Chase's lawyers keep bothering Dutch over the phone, threatening me and him and saying they're gonna take all we got."

"They probably will," Dallas says. He doesn't think I'll ever win and it isn't just because Tyrone Canter can afford the best lawyers in the United States. It's also because I've got no proof I wrote the songs and Chase didn't.

"Skeeter, it's just hearsay, but Chase has every band member signed on that he wrote those songs. He's talking to every gossip magazine he can find and giving them dirt on you. He's got—"

"It's not true. And it isn't fair." I feel so little then like Dallas is against me too.

"Sweetie, it's the belly of the beast. You come off as a wild rocker with attitude. I guess it's going to bite you in the butt sometimes."

"Well, maybe they can sit us down in a courtroom and have us each try to write a song," I tell him. "Chase can't even recite a nursery rhyme, much less write a verse."

"But you got to understand. His lawyers will lie. They'll do anything to smear your name to make you look bad because it is all they have." Dallas sighs. "Chase has been calling me too. He told me to tell you to just stop. When you do your singing at the Crazy Filly, you're telling folks he dropped you in the middle of nowhere and ran."

"He did."

"It's his word against yours again. And his lawyers want you to shut your mouth before you smear his name."

"He's smearing my name. You just said it. His name should be smeared."

"Okay, here's what I'm getting at, here's the point. I can't sing with you, don't you get it? His lawyers have talked to my lawyers. They are saying if you say one thing on stage to badmouth that boy, he's going to sue me. He's going to win. Just duck and cover and run. Start over again."

"Dallas, they are my songs," I say softly. "They are like my babies. It is like a dagger in my heart knowing

Brooke Canter is stealing my babies." I watch him joggle the music sheets against the table as if he is trying to align the edges. I know it is a nervous gesture while he lifts them and runs his finger along the bottom to make sure it's even. "I know it might get messy. I just want you to know once the dust settles, I'll be there for you. But until then, I've got to step away. My attorneys say I've got to keep a bit of a distance from it all so my label doesn't get bashed in the process."

"So are you in with the Martinez family? Because that's the same story I heard from Boone."

"No. I don't know what you're talking about."

"Is that all you needed?" I'm suddenly digesting what he's telling me. "Do you want your phone back? You can have it and the stalker too."

"Of course not—"

But I stand up, tug the phone from my purse and drop it gently on the table. Then I pluck the song sheets from his fingers. "Because that's what friends are for, right? To have your back whether they are on the winning side or not? Or is it only being there when everything smells like roses?"

"Waylon, wait," Dallas rises too. The man sitting next to him looks unsure, rises.

"No."

CHAPTER 34
SALVATION GUARANTEED AT HOLY UNITY CHURCH (BUT MAYBE NOT SO MUCH FOR THOSE WHO SIT IN BACK)

"Get out from under the sink, Skeeter. There's no money down there."

"Ouch." I bang my head on the old wood with a startled reaction when I hear his voice. I'm rubbing my head with one hand and I've got the coffee can in my hand, a sure sign Dutch thinks I'm up to no good.

"I'm not taking out, I'm putting in," I tell him.

"We're going to church this morning," Dutch acts like he doesn't even hear me. "Put on something—that don't look heathen-like."

"What's that mean?" I ask, tossing the can back under the sink. "And church? I don't want to go to church. Everybody stares at me—are you trying to fix me up with a church man because not even the cop wants me?"

"People stare at you whether you're in church or not, baby girl," Dutch tells me while I close the cabinet. "You're like a daisy in a rose garden. You stick out."

"A daisy? Why can't I be a rose in a daisy garden?" I huff. "Daisy's stink and nobody likes them."

"Naw, she's like a dandelion growing on Harlan Martinez's front lawn." Jack is coming through the kitchen door and he snuffles a laugh. "One little speck of yellow out there and he's calling in that expensive lawn care company from Denton to spray the place down."

I suppose he's right. I still ignore him. "Dutch, the only dress I have is the one I wore on that date with Bobby Moretti. It's thigh-high and sticks to my skin like paper sticks to a stick of butter." He just stares at me, so I throw my head back and groan. "I thought we went to breakfast on Sundays with all the heathens? What's so different about today that we can't just skip church and go sit with the sinner cowboys?"

"Baby, this was the day my little girl died. She liked church. So I feel closer to her today if I go to church. So I'll put on a suit and tie. Then we'll go in and shake things up a bit."

"Okay." I feel a bit humbled he had to tell me the truth. So I drive back up to the cabin and put on my dress and stiletto heels. Then I put Lexie in a frilly pink dress and laugh because her hair's so short she looks like a little boy in a pink baby prom dress.

The church is in downtown Bel-Air. It's an old white church with a steeple, fresh paint, and a sign out front stating the time of the services. It has a little saying underneath: SALVATION GUARANTEED, OR YOUR SINS REFUNDED. Inside it is like tepid ice tea left out on a porch in mid-July. And stuffy. On the walls, there are pretty pictures of Jesus and then right before they stop, there is a picture of Bo Littleton and his family. I walk up and stare at it. THE LITTLETON FAMILY. MAYOR BEAUREGARD LITTLETON. LARGEST DONATION TO BISHOP'S FUND.

"Watch who you worship," there's a whisper behind me. "I'd stick with the ones on the right. But don't tell anybody I said that."

I turn. It is Boone Martinez. He's dressed in a suit and tie. "B—B—B—" I almost drop Lexie while she squirms toward him. I just blink at him. Dutch swoops in and scurries me off to the sanctuary. We sit down in the third row from the last on hard wooden pews.

Preacher Irving is fifty-something and big smiles. He's got a wife and four kids and a fifteen year-old boy who looks like he'd rather be shopping for underwear with his mom than squirming awkwardly in the front row between his little brothers and sisters. I remember him. He's the one Chey's kind of admitted having a crush on when her daddy dropped off the curtains at the church. There's a choir, I think, of two women and three men singing acapella. They are ear-achingly off-key because there's no music backup.

The preacher's telling the story about the widow's mite from the bible. He's at the part where Jesus and his disciples are sitting near a temple and watching the rich old men toss loads of money into the temple cash boxes. Then along comes a poor widow who gives her last two coins. I'm halfway listening and worrying my tummy's going to grumble loud enough they can hear it two rows back. I yawn, stifle it with my fist and push Lexie to my shoulder.

"B—B—B—" Lexie is starting to get fussy. I realize why when I peer slightly to my left. The Martinez's are sitting on the opposite side one row back. I can see Harlan Martinez's tight-lipped stare toward the front of the sanctuary. I see a prim-looking woman with long dark hair sitting next to him looking at Boone, then following his gaze to Lexie. Then Boone giving me a funny stifled grin. He knows what I know and it's that Lexie would rather be with him than me right this moment. I shift her sideways and for the moment, she finds solace in Dutch's truck keys he wiggles at me for her.

"Now, Jesus tells us that her contribution is so much greater than that of the rich who gave just gave a small percentage of their huge wealth," the preacher is saying while I juggle Lexie in the curve of my arm. Dutch keeps checking his watch. I see him do it for the fortieth time.

I realize that I just don't get what the preacher's saying. I chew on his words for a moment, think about how twenty minutes earlier, Bo Littleton stood up as one of the chairpersons for making money for a new kitchen. He was asking everybody to give five or ten bucks for a new floor in the church kitchen. Those who gave a hundred dollars or more get their pictures put up in frames around that room.

"Hey, can I ask a question?" I raise my hand and I see Dutch blanch, slide a bit down in his pew. He slowly turns his head and I look toward the preacher who has stopped and looks just as caught off guard as Dutch. The seats are creaking while people turn to look at me. "Um," I stutter, rising. "So what you're telling me is that although the widow in the bible got to be the hero for giving her last change, in real life and nowadays, it's different. It's whoever gives the most who gets the honors."

"Well, no sweetie, it is all the same."

"Well, no it isn't. Because what you say and what is happening in the church, it's conflicting. Mister Littleton—" I throw out my hand to the family sitting at the front of the room. "—he just told us earlier that whoever contributes the most for the kitchen fund gets their picture on the wall like his big picture sitting next to Jesus in the foyer. You know, the wall out front that has a picture of each of the disciples, then Jesus and then the Littleton family. Like since they gave money, they're like saints or something. Shouldn't it be based on how much each person makes and how much they are giving up? I mean, somebody who makes three-hundred dollars a week could give ten percent and that's thirty bucks. Mister Littleton makes about a million a week on his oil, and he could give a hundred thousand. That'd be more what Jesus was saying, right?"

"I don't think Mister Littleton meant that at all," the preacher stutters.

"Yes, sir. Well, it's because he's rich and he doesn't have to think things out. I do I mean, you can look at it as this widow being a hero, giving every last dime while some rich dudes just give enough of their money to make them look good. But if you look a little deeper, I think it's about the stupid way we've got things set up in our society. That poor woman felt like she had to give her all to have a seat in heaven and compete with the rich kind of like how all the rich folks here are sitting in the front while the poor or people who maybe don't rate are sitting in the back, right? What about her kids now? How's she going to feed them? That's just stupid to look at it that way. It's kind of like all us people sitting in the back like we've got the chicken pox. I bet you could look at these pews and figure out how much money each person makes and where they came from by how close to the preacher they're sitting, how close to God and the pulpit they are. But that aside, I'm thinking that sermon was so good, I want to sit up front. I'll buy the linoleum for the floor and carpet for the foyer if anybody who wants to gets to sit in the front too."

Everybody's looking over at me. Even the preacher's son has scooted up in his seat and is craning his neck back to the last row where I'm sitting.

"You don't have enough money to even buy a proper dress for the church, young lady, or a door for that shanty you live in." Bo Littleton doesn't even bother to turn. I see the back of his chubby, bald head.

"Well, it is the only dress I have. But I don't think God cares as much about what I'm wearing or where I live as much as he might be a bit offended about you watching that baseball game and texting the entire twenty minutes while Preacher Irving was giving his sermon so you didn't get the message he was trying to teach. And yes, I do have the money. So I want to get my picture up on that wall so every day you people who think they are better than the rest of us have to stare at it and be reminded that, well, you're not. How much did you donate to sit by Jesus? I'll beat it by fifty-thousand bucks."

When the service is over, Dutch just gives me little jabs while he hurries me out the door. The choir and the preacher have already walked down the center aisle and we have to follow them. I think Dutch is trying to get me to pass the preacher so we don't have to shake his hand before we leave and get dirty looks. Or maybe he's just trying to avoid Bo Littleton who looks like a bull getting ready to attack with a face beet red.

"Stop, stop, I need to ask you something."

Preacher Irving snatches at my elbow just as Dutch's right foot breaks past the threshold of the door. I know he's thinking we're home free. We're not. Dutch outwardly winces and I can hear his teeth grinding while he turns back and forces a funny cat-grin at Preacher Irving.

"I'm sorry, Preacher Irving, we need to get back. Skeeter, here, left the oven on."

"It's nice to see you here, Dutch," the preacher says, ignoring Dutch's pretext to escape. Then he turns to me. I cringe and try to swipe the sweat off my brow that's trying to dribble down. It's hot right now and Lexie is fussing. "And you—you're Waylon, right? There's hearsay you grew up in the Amish communities in Ohio. I was thinking, we don't have a person to play the piano and I was wondering if maybe you'd learned to play at your church back home? Maybe you could play the piano—?"

"No, the Amish don't have musical instruments," I tell him. "At least not where I grew up."

"Oh, how'd you learn to play the guitar and sing?"

"She learned from a Mennonite lady down the road. She gave her piano lessons."

I turn, see the preacher's son standing stiffly beside his dad. He's smiling at me though.

"At least, that's what I heard you tell Boone that day

you dropped off the curtains," he goes on. "Mom sent me over to help Boone. I overheard. Waylon sneaked over to her house every day. I'm Zach. I thought that was you. Nobody believed me at first."

"Oh," Preacher Irving twists his head to look at his son curiously. Then he turns back to me. "So you can play the piano?"

"She can. She heard the music while she was playing in a creek behind her home and followed it to the house. She had eight years of lessons. She started when she was six. Then she got an internship for gifted musicians because her piano teacher put in an application." He turns to me. "I found that online. She was the youngest musician to attend. She had to run away from home to do it." Zach goes on.

"I bet she knows all the hymns," Preacher Irving asks me. "You do, don't you?"

"Do you?" Dutch asks me.

"Ask him." I point to Zach. "He knows more than me, I'm thinking."

"Yeah, she does. I heard her playing that old stupid stuff like you listen to, Dad. She usually plays the stuff Mom likes."

"It isn't stupid," I correct him with a sigh. "It is Beethoven and he was pretty radical for his time. He reinvented classical music. He was the first composer to add voices to his music. And the girl who sang as part of the first one, Symphony No. 9, wasn't much older than you are now. So back then, it was pretty wicked." I jab a thumb to Preacher Irving. "Or in his case, groovy."

"I'm not that old."

"Not saying you are old—looking, just thinking," I tease him. I poke a finger at Zach's mom who has just scooted between the two. She's nice blue dress and lipstick and short blonde hair. "She likes my music, so she's Gucci."

I can see the impatient stares of the line behind us. I give a quick shake of the preacher's hand and Dutch scoots me off toward the porch and grumbling.

"Dangit, girl, we almost got herded into going to church every Sunday because of your silly antics," he berates me in his grumpy way in the parking lot.

"Silly *antics*?" I roll my eyes. "What does that mean?"

"It means you just need to fly a little lower under the clouds and keep your mouth shut sometimes. I think I liked it better when you was quiet like a mouse instead squawking like an old buzzard."

"I'm offended," I tell him getting into the truck. "I am not an old buzzard. And I don't squawk."

"You're squawking now."

"I wouldn't squawk if I didn't have to squawk. You're an old buzzard—"

I hear snickers from a couple trucks down in the parking lot. Both Dutch and I look up and to my horror, the entire Martinez family is stopped in mid-opening of their truck doors and laughing at us.

"Good God." That's Dutch grumbling when he gets in the truck. "Now look what you've done. Made us a laughingstock. I thought I almost had that town cop interested in you. Now, I'm gonna have to fill my barn with horses to get someone to take you."

"You shouldn't say the Lord's name in vain," I taunt him shoving Lexie into her car seat. He just glares at me. "And it wasn't me. It was you. You always have to get the last word in."

"Do not."

"Do too."

CHAPTER 35
ACTING GIRLY GIRL SO I CAN GO FISHING WITH BOONE ON SUNDAY

"I need some advice. I haven't been fishing before. Can you show me how to put a worm on a hook?" I'm gazing at Boone, dangling a fishing pole and a big, fat night crawler six inches from his face. In the other hand, I'm dragging Lexie's car carrier. He's sitting in his truck at the little pond between his dad's house and Dutch's. He's listening to music and it's loud. That's how I knew he was here. I heard it from the barn. I also know that he got in a fight with his sister and his dad who said he shouldn't be alone today.

Their voices carried across the fields. They don't want him shooting beer bottles off Charlene's grave again. He left in a spew of gravel and yells. Twenty minutes later, I hear the music. But I know he spends a lot of time up here alone so it isn't that much out of the ordinary. However, it's usually when it rains. He parks and turns his radio on and listens to the music. It's his place to be alone. I usually leave him alone. Today, though, I agree with his sister and his dad. He needs somebody around.

"Damn, Skeeter, get and go," he tells me. "Go ask Dutch. I want to be alone. Don't get worm guts in my truck."

"Dutch told me I was being annoying and went somewhere with his old-guy friends." He pushes my hand away with the worm. "Please. Five minutes of your time and I'll leave you alone. Just show me how."

He pushes open the door of his truck and almost hits me. "I find it hard to believe you've never been fishing."

His sarcastic allegation is correct. I used to fish all the time. I wiggle the pole at him, show I've got two fishing poles slipped in my fist. "Hey, if you want, I got another pole—"

"I don't want to fish." He struts down the little path and I follow a bit slower with all the weight of a chubby baby. There's two white buckets Dutch uses to sit on when he fishes. I sit down on one and play with the worm. Boone evil-eye stares me for three seconds right in the face, then snatches the worm and pole from me. He deftly impales the worm while I make girly-girl remarks that I would never lower myself to say in front of my brothers like *ewww* and *yucky*.

"Good to go?" He thrusts it back at me. He smells good. I know because the wind is blowing my direction and he's got on some kind of sports cologne scent.

"Yeah, sure." I bring up the reel and roll it the wrong way. I look down at Lexie. She's sound asleep. "Crap, maybe not. Now, how do I toss this without losing the pole?" I jiggle the pole, tap the end. He snatches it out of my hand and winds up the spool. Then Boone leans back and casts it out into the water. "Like this."

"That looks hard."

He gives me five, terse minutes of step by step instructions while I give him stupid girl stares. Boone holds out his hands. "There. You're good to go." Three steps away, I give him a *hey*.

"So when I catch a fish, how do I get the fish off?"

"I don't know. Figure it out."

"Okay."

I see him hesitate. I know why. I'm really good at making my eyes kind of tear up, look misty like I'm going to cry, but I'm holding it off. It was always my last defense with my brothers. There was threatening them I would tattle, first. Next, was pitting them against each other. Third was running. And fourth, when nothing else worked, I'd nibble on my bottom lip and work up a few tears in my eyes.

"Skeeter, really?" he asks me. "I'm not an idiot. Quit doing that."

"What?"

"Looking like you're going to cry."

"I just miss my brothers. They used to yell at me too."

"I didn't—shit." He turns around and plops down on a bucket. "Go. Fish. I'll sit with you ten minutes. I'm timing it." He gets out his phone from his back pocket and stares at it. Then I listen to him text while I feign learning how to cast the pole. After three or four minutes, I get a bite. Two minutes later, I'm reeling in a twelve inch bass.

"You're lucky as shit," Boone tells me with a curiously competitive glint to his eyes.

"Beginner's luck. That's it." I dangle it in his face. "Now what do I do with it?"

So he takes the hook out of the mouth, turns over a bucket and fills it with water. Then he plops the fish inside.

"Oh, what a smart idea," I say like I've never seen this done before. "Your mom must be so proud of you."

He rolls his eyes. I see him eyeing the second pole like he might want to fish. I eye it too. "Hey, if I caught one fish with one pole. I can catch two with two poles—" I start to snatch the second one up and Boone pushes his foot on it.

"If I'm going to put bait on a pole again, it's going to be mine."

"Fine, be a spoil sport," I mutter. We fight over the only other bucket and he wins so I steal one of Lexie's little blankets and set it down. We sit there fishing for a half hour or so in silence except for the wind blowing the two trees above us. Then I pull out a little brown paper bag and turn it upside-down.

"Sandwich?" I ask Boone. "I just happen to have two. And funny thing, two bags of potato chips. And two sodas and two cookies."

"You know how to fish, too, don't you?"

"What?" I ask and let it roll across my tongue.

"You cast better than the pros on Sunday morning sports shows."

"You shouldn't be alone today. And I hate being alone on cloudy gray days, Friday nights, and right before I sing on stage—"

"It's none of those, Skeeter."

"And Sundays," I hold up my hand. "You wouldn't let me finish. Dutch didn't want me around today. I think he putters around her room when I'm gone. I think he deserves that. So it is Sunday and I'm alone."

"You don't think I deserve my time to be alone?"

"This isn't about you, dumbass, it's all about me. I just told you I didn't want to be alone. I miss my brothers. It was always noisy on Sundays around our house." I shrug. "So tell me, Boone, what kind of knife do you want to cut with?"

"Huh?"

"What kind of knife do you want to clean these fish when we're done? Because I'm going to bet you a fish dinner right here on the banks that I'm going to catch more fish than you. And if I do, you're gutting the fish. You're scaling the fish. And you're cooking supper—"

CHAPTER 36
COVERING FOR HORSE THIEVES

My truck is sideways on the muddy road and hanging partially over the incline. I'm soaking wet and covered in muck and a Bel-Air policeman is standing beside me scratching his head.

"You know, I wouldn't have seen you here if I wasn't on the tail of a horse trailer with stolen horses in it. You're lucky, Miss Ryder, that I came along. I'll call Dutch down the hill and have him bring his tractor up here."

I'm praying that he doesn't see the marks of the hooves on the ground or the second set of tire prints next to mine. My heart is beating hard. "That's for sure," I mumble. "You're a real hero."

"I'd be a real hero if I'd caught those folks stealing Bo Littleton's horses down at his slaughterhouse. We just need one break. I thought I had it." He shakes his head. "How'd you do this so close to your house?"

"I, um, was backing up. I was getting my truck straightened out in case it rained hard. It floods up here." What a stupid thing to say.

"It floods—up here?" he asks me.

"I mean, it gets big puddles. I'm afraid of puddles. It's an old truck and I'm a new driver."

He narrows his eyes. "Have you been drinking?"

"No, sir. I was half asleep when I remembered I needed to turn the truck around. I'm not good at backing. You can ask Bobby Moretti. He took me out driving. I just got my license." I hear the low yell of a horse far away and toward Dutch's old buildings.

"Was that—was that a horse I just heard?"

"Maybe it's my baby crying. She's inside." I freeze, watch his eyes walk over toward the house. I wonder how the heck I got into the middle of this.

It was just a stupid, normal night less than an hour ago. It had been quiet at the cabin. I was listening to the rain hit the aluminum roof and then, sometimes the ting-ting when it bounced off the bottoms of the little pots and pans sitting on the counter, and the table, and the floor when the water leaks through the roof.

Lexie was asleep in her hand-me-down crib across the room. She's safe and I felt safe. I checked on her, patted her warm back and tugged the sheet over top of her. The sound of a truck and horse trailer made a grinding dash up the old road in front of the cabin. Nobody's supposed to cut through the old township road that is now nothing more than an extension of Dutch's driveway eventually ending in a raggedy, dirt and grass service road that cuts up to the Martinez farm. It really is almost impassable. The two, short bridges between the two farms are dilapidated and nothing more than old railroad ties laid down on top of steel beams. Dutch's got a yellow DEAD END road sign at the end of his drive to keep folks from cutting through.

Once in a while, though, I see a truck with a horse trailer drive through. I figure it is one of the Martinez's employees taking a shortcut from town along Dutch's gravel driveway passing his house and up along this old service road. They have to make a jagged veer to the right and pass some of Dutch's old barns far back in the woods. Such, the trucks have to come to almost a complete halt a stone's throw from the cabin because of the sharp curve in the road and the first of two bridges. Then they slide and shoot gravel all over the place to get speed back again.

This time, however, I could hear the engine gunning, but the truck wasn't moving. I peered out the window through the curtains. I could see the lights of the truck and part of the trailer that appeared to be slightly slanted.

I don't have a phone so I figure I'll wait it out, see if they can get the trailer unstuck from where it appears to have gone slightly off the little bridge. After ten minutes, I peered at Lexie. She was still asleep. Then I grabbed a plastic garbage bag and held it over my head and walked out to the truck.

"We're stuck."

I'm kind of struck dumb that it is Adriana Martinez with one of their million dollar trailers. I can tell she's been crying. They appear, however, the kind of tears that come with frustration. She's holding a tire iron in her hand and her hair is plastered to her head. She's sopping wet from head to boot. I can hear someone in the truck hitting the gas again to no advantage. The stench of rubber tire burns my nostrils and I fan away the smoke from my face.

"I'll go down and get Dutch. He can get the tractor and—"

"No." Adriana's eyes are wide, she's shaking her head fast. "Oh, Skeeter, we need your help. The cops are coming. They are probably at Dutch's by now. We need out before they get here or we're dead. We got to get the horses out. There's too much weight."

"Okay, so let's get the horses out and I'll tow you out with my truck."

I don't ask questions while Adriana and I open the back of the trailer. Because nothing in this town would surprise me. I have to assume the cops coming means that they either stole the horses or the truck or they tried to outrun the cops because they were going too fast.

The horses are panicking and it takes a few minutes of calming them down to even get into the trailer and back them out. Even then, they are wild-eyed and dancing and I don't even notice Boone until he snatches one up and takes the rope from my hand. He leans in and flashes me an evil smile. "Still whining over having to clean those fish?" he asks me. I roll my eyes. It was so close. We fished until nine that night and Dutch came out with pans to cook the fish in and some bread and cheese and sodas. I caught ten fish. Boone caught nine. Mine were little so he decided they didn't count as high. He said two looked more like minnows.

"Ha ha. I still think I won. You cheated." I nod toward the side of the hill. "Dutch has an old lean-to up the hill," I tell them. "We can take them there for tonight. There's hay up there because he keeps the extra in the far barn." I take one and Adriana takes the other two. It is a slip-sliding, horse-traipsing walk up the gravel road while Boone gets my truck keys and works the trailer tires from between the railroad ties of the bridge.

"Dutch just texted me," Boone announces. He is standing in the rain. He's just parked my truck back in front of the cabin. He pulled out his truck and he's got the trailer freed. I can see him patting his leg nervously. "They are on their way up the hill. We got to go home and spray the mud off the trailer."

"Okay, get and go," I say to them. "Now." They just blink at me while I turn around and run toward my house. I just hear the sound of their tires running on the mud and gravel, peeling around the curb before I snatch up my keys and peek at Lexie. She is still sound asleep.

I know there's truck ruts and hoof marks and clods of mud kicked up from the trailer where it dug hard into the furrowed muck to its wheel wells. It looks like a crime scene with two of the railroad ties laying sideways along the old bridge. So I see the flash of lights slowly easing up the gravel road about a quarter mile away and I make a mad dash to my truck and send it careening toward the little bridge. I don't stop on a dime and almost wind up on the hillside.

So that's why the cop is standing there in the rain with the plastic cap over his Smoky Bear hat and blinking at me through the raindrops. I'm buying time because I'm hoping the downpour is obliterating the tracks.

"Or it could have been Dutch's horses. They come up on the hill when it rains. There's horses everywhere up here." I push the rain from my face. "You ever ride? I've got a couple Dutch loaned me. I'm always looking for people to ride with."

"You're the one that's got the hit song, aren't you?" he asks and suddenly he's got this dopy look on his face.

"I am."

"You think you can get me a CD with your autograph on it?"

"Well, sure. I've got my new CD and I can get you one of Dallas Dunne's when his album comes out with the songs on it."

He asked me out on a date. I told him I'd think about it, but he knew I just broke up with Chase. Thirty-five minutes later, the cop is sitting in my little cabin drinking some hot cocoa and telling me he'd better get back out on the road again before they noticed he was taking a break. He stayed for a good hour and I sang him a song on my guitar while he patted out a beat on his knee. When he left, I'm sure I saw Dutch slipping along the tree line trying to see the outcome of whatever event occurred that I had unintentionally been led into.

Chapter 37
My Stalker finds me in the dark crazy filly parking lot

"Hey, Waylon?"

The parking lot is dark behind the Crazy Filly. I've got my guitar slung around my shoulder and my keys in my hand. I'm hunkered down with eyes peering left to right. Because for the second night in a row, I've seen Rod Elkhart in the crowd listening to me sing. He's still sore about me kicking him in the crotch and unloading that Toxic Twelve Bear Deterrent in his face. I can tell. He sits out there in a chair in the back and stares unsmiling like a cat that's biding its time to catch the little mouse when it accidently creeps out of the light and into the darkness.

The darkness. I look up and the parking lot light flickers. I hear the voice and turn, see a huge man. Holy hell, he's seven feet tall and makes Rod Elkhart look like a baby Sasquatch. He's got beefy arms, a thick red beard and a ball cap. He looks like every serial killer I've watched on late night crime shows. My heart jumps.

"Hey," I mutter. My voice is scratchy while I try not look like I'm scrambling for my bear repellent in my purse that isn't there anymore. I used the entire bottle on Rod Elkhart about fifty feet from where I'm standing right now the night I picked up drunk Boone and brought him back to Dutch's.

"I've been following you for weeks. I called a million times and left notes at the bar for you. You didn't answer."

"Following me?" I repeat. I feel sick to my tummy.

"Yeah, okay. Well, I've got to get home—" He's coming up closer, like three feet from me and I'm staring up at him, enveloped in his shadow.

"You really shouldn't come out here in the dark by yourself."

Yeah, dude, I'm thinking that too. I see his hand come out. I know he's going to grab me. He'll probably hit me over the head with the hammer he's got tucked into his belt. Then, he'll shove me in the trunk of his car. We'll drive off and while I'm—

"There's some dude back there following you."

"Huh?" I say, craning my neck around and thinking it was another stupid move. He is just trying to get my attention away so he can crack me over the head. But, oh-shit, he's right. I can see Rod standing in the shadows looking like he's just leaning against a car and smoking a cigarette. "Oh, no. That's Rod Elkhart. He doesn't like me."

"I'll take care of him."

So just like that, I get to watch this dude slide a tire iron out of Rod Elkhart's fingers like a daddy wiggling a toy out of the fingers of a two-year old. With one hand, he escorts him to the back door and when the bouncers and a security guard from the bar come tearing out because of Rod's yelling, he's holding Rod up by his collar and just hands him to them.

"You should have a police officer walk you to your truck at night, Waylon." He reprimands me when he returns. I'm still standing exactly where I was when he walked away. I'm kicking myself for not scrambling to my truck. "It's not safe. Jessie. My name's Jessie Adams. You probably don't remember me. I knew you way back when you just got started."

"Jessie," I whisper the name to myself. Yes, I do remember him. He was shorter then, chubby and not as buff. He was shy and quiet, didn't say much to me but always smiled. When Chase partied, I used to go hang out and watch TV with some of the roadies at the hotels. Jessie was one of them.

"Okay, wait a minute," I say. "Jessie. You had a little sister named Emma. She was like six or seven when you worked with us. She had a ballet recital and you wanted to go to it. Chase wouldn't let you. We sneaked you out in the middle of the show, right? That was you. You also were the only one that stayed up late enough to watch the stupid women's channel romance movies that made me cry, but always ended happy."

"I still watch them."

"Me too."

"Can we talk somewhere?"

"I got your number from Tyler Cooper," Jess tells me over a cup of coffee at the Bel-Air All-Nighter Motel and Diner. It's dark where we're sitting. "He's wanting to play guitar for you. He had Dallas's number. You have Dallas's phone."

"I *had* Dallas's phone. I gave it back."

"Oh, that would be the reason you didn't text me back." Jess takes off his ball cap and scrubs a hand across his hair. He's got a tattoo on his neck and it runs all the way to his temple. "I worked for Tyler for a while until his lead singer flew the coop. Now I'm doing what all roadies do who get laid off."

"Yeah, what's that?"

"I'm a warehouse worker. I'm hauling frozen boxes of food from truck to warehouse over and over and over. Then I go home and babysit my sister's kids while she works third shift at the hospital because I don't have enough money to rent a place myself."

"How's that working for you?" I ask him.

"Not well."

"Maybe I need to hire you as a bodyguard," I tease him.

He almost looks at me like I'm not kidding. Then he just stops and pokes the sugar. "I was there when you wrote those songs."

I look up at him. "What are you saying?"

"*Heartbreak Song, Before You, Bitch Don't Got Nothing on Me*— I can name twenty songs you wrote that I personally saw you write and compose. Chase Martin is a liar. I read in a magazine that he said he wrote them. I sat in the hotel rooms with you while you wrote the songs. There was me and Kenny and Dalton and that weird girl that ate cold soup out of the can. They watched movies. I watched you do it. They saw you do it," he tells me. "He treated us like shit. All of us. He'd make us go out for candy bars in the middle of the night, then lock us out of the hotel. He thought it was funny. He'd just all of a sudden tell us we were fired or just didn't pay us. I've been texting back and forth with them over the years. They are wanting like crazy to stick it to Chase. We'll tell the world the truth about that jackass." He holds up his phone and I see a video of me sitting on one of those faux leather couches that pull out to couches. I'm strumming my guitar in my pajamas and making faces at him.

"Proof." Then he wiggles a thick finger at the guitar I'm playing. "And there's proof in your guitar, too. You've got your songs written down there even before they were big."

I stare at him. It's almost too good to be true. "So— what's in it for you?"

CHAPTER 38
STOLEN HORSES & TELLING BOONE TO BUGGER OFF

"I don't want to know." That's what I'm telling Boone Martinez while I stand inside a stall in Dutch's back lean-to. I'm pasting a little homemade salve on the girth of the white and brown Paint Horse that had been on the trailer that jackknifed on the bridge. He bangs his back hoof nervously and I pet him, give Boone a quick gaze over the horse's back.

"Is he alright?"

"He needs a hundred bucks worth of hay stuffed into him. He's got girth sores. Somebody rode him too hard and used old, cruddy tack," I tell him. "And he must have gotten the crap kicked out of him at the sale barn. Otherwise, he's fine. Maybe you ought to get your fiancé out here to look at him. I'm just guessing. I'm not a real cowgirl."

Boone doesn't answer. It's been two days since he left the horses here. Dutch said to feed and water them and add them to my stall cleaning list. Such, I'm stuck with another three horses to care for while Dutch is sipping coffee at the kitchen table and pretending not to watch some silly 1980s soap opera.

"I think I need to explain what was going on." He's patting his hands on the stall door while he lays his arms over the side. He's been up here fiddling with the horses every day, grooming them and feeding. I wait until he leaves, then come out and clean the stalls. I'm mad so I make a point of looking down. He stops, shoves his hands in his pockets.

"No, actually, you don't." I lean over rub the horse's sides, check it for other abrasions. I don't see any. It's just skinny and malnourished, nothing a few months of Dutch's good hay won't mend. "It is none of my business. Because if it becomes my business, I am a part of whatever you are doing, legal or not. I'm already in too deep with my own legal problems. I don't want to be a part of it."

"I don't just mean the horses. But, okay, that's fair." Boone pats the stall door, turns like he's getting support from the young woman sitting in the truck and staring out at us. I pat the horse on the neck with my hand. Then, I scoot out the stall door, giving it a little push so Boone steps back.

"So, are you taking them or do I need to come up here and feed them another day?"

"Dutch said we could keep them here. He might keep one for his barn." He makes the tap-tap-tapping on the door, then drops his head. "Ich liebe dich."

I sniff a laugh. "You love me?" I hardly look up. "Why, because it is convenient? Because you think I'll tell Bobby you stole horses from Bo?" I ask flatly. "Because the other day, it was *get out* and your dad saying—" I raise my voice. "*Livie is his fiancé and an angel sent down from heaven.*"

"He didn't say that last part."

"I improvised, but you get the gist of it." I am grabbing a flake of hay from the bale sitting next to the stall and tossing it into the wire hay rack. "I know I'm not anything close to an angel and I'm never going to be the perfect ten. I'm barely a high school degree and tattoos and screaming a song into the microphone when I'm pissed off at the guy at the fast food drive-thru for forgetting my fries. She's the pedigreed Christmas pup all wrapped up in a pretty little package with a bow, I'm—"

"—the snarling little Chihuahua somebody dumped

on the road?" He smiles and I don't think he realizes what he said until I actually look up with a glare. "Oh, I didn't mean it that way—because of what Chase did to you."

"Listen, you told me from the start, your heart was dead broke. I didn't listen. I should have. My bad. Now I get it," I tell him leaning against the second stall door. "I just figured you were like this old boy behind me—" I nod my head to the raggedy gelding whose head is dropped and his eyes are sagging. "You got beaten, dragged down, and overdone. But after a couple months of love, you'd be kicking up those wild stallion feet again, all sassy and spirited. I didn't realize you actually meant you were dead inside—"

"You okay?" That's Jessie's deep voice. It's followed by a coo from Lexie who he's cradling in his arms. She likes him. He likes her. I see Boone look toward the far side of the barn and to the two coming toward us. He had started to say something, stopped. Then he gets a funny twist to his lips when Jessie comes around the corner holding her. And he starts tap-tap-tapping on his leg.

"Yeah, I'm fine," I tell Jessie. Then I wave a hand at him. "Boone Martinez, this is Jessie Adams. He's my bodyguard—and my first band roadie I've hired on my own."

"And nanny," he adds with a roll of his eyes.

"I can't help if she likes you," I smile at Jessie. "You're like a big live teddy bear." Cupped in his huge arm, Lexie looks like a tiny pickle in the middle of a giant subway bun. "And Boone here," I say, wagging a hand at Boone. "His daddy is one of the attorneys who is getting the lawsuit together against me. So I really shouldn't be talking to him. I mean, isn't that what your daddy told me, Boone? So bugger off."

CHAPTER 39

I've been spending my whole life
Figuring out who I am
Then here you come.
And I start all over again.
Maybe I'm crazy
But are you feeling it too?
I'm thinking I might be someone
Other than the one I was before you.

"You sure you're okay for the rest of the night?"

"Yeah, of course." I flip off the TV and sit back on the couch. Jessie always hesitates before he leaves. "I got my new phone and your number on speed dial." I raise up the cell phone Jessie made me buy. I feel like he's me and Lexie's babysitter more than anything. And although he doesn't imply it, he makes me feel like I have to buy friends to watch TV with and go for walks. But he says if I'm paying him for a forty hour week, he's working forty hours. So he hangs with me when I'm not singing at the Crazy Filly, then at night, he drives back to a little town outside Nashville where he lives with his sister.

"I got the next two days off, remember?"

"I do."

"You're okay with that?"

"Yeah. You got your check?"

"I did. I think you should look up Harley Mason," he tells me right before he goes. "And Tyler Cooper. Both of them. I know they want to play with you. You just got to ask."

"I'll think about it." The only thing I can think about is Preacher Irving calling me and asking me if I'd play piano for the church. He said I could just try it out. I said maybe.

Maybe not.

"You think I let my fans down by singing those two country songs with Dallas?"

He hesitates, shrugs. "I just think they're a little confused, Waylon. There are so many rumors flying, they don't know what to think. I think you did what you had to do. Songs are songs. I like the songs whether you scream them or sing them like a lullaby. I would assume you got heavy metal folks listening to country now. Maybe you can do country music a favor and give them a taste of heavy metal, huh? I mean, the whole world needs to hear your voice, not just one genre."

"Thanks, Jessie."

I tug out Mama's jewelry box. It takes my mind off things when I get lonely. Oaky asked me a couple months ago if I'd want to do a big outdoor concert with some old bands. I told him yes then. It was before all the crap with Chase and his lawyers started. It is coming up in two weekends and now, I'm not so sure I want to do it.

Wayne Pelosi. I'm staring at the envelope when the knock comes on the door. I didn't hear a car drive up and it had only been a few minutes since Jessie left.

"Hey, thanks for covering for me," Chey says. She's wearing a dress that's way too short and heels too high for a thirteen year-old. "My grandpa would have killed me if he knew I was sneaking out." I am staring at her while she pushes her way inside and plops down on the couch. "God, you are so cool. I mean, it's so cool to have somebody close to my age that's not all in my face and stuff. You mind if I wait here until my ride comes? How's Lexie? Is she asleep?"

"You have—like a parent picking you up?" I ask her. She thinks I'm joking and giggles. I look at the clock. It is ten.

"No."

"Okay."

I wait until she flips on the TV. Then I text Boone Martinez. *Your daughter is at my house.*

"That's my ride," Chey gets up to the sound of a vehicle outside four minutes later. I'm still staring at Wayne Pelosi's envelope, but I'm not actually thinking about whoever it might be. I know the sound of the truck and it is familiar. I watch Chey get to the door, open it wide and stare out. Then she pales from temple to neck and snaps her head around to me.

"What's my daddy doing here?"

"It's your ride," I tell her.

"You bitch!" She screams that at me and slams the door shut right in Boone's face who must have jogged right up to the porch. I know she's caught between the two of us.

"Why did you do this? Why? I liked you—I babysat for you, you witch!" She starts screaming more cusswords than I've heard at a rock concert and is only stopped by Boone coming through the door and telling her to shut her mouth. Now.

I can hear Lexie crying from her crib in the little cubby of a room we share.

"What's going on here?" Boone is standing there in jeans and a t-shirt. He looks like he jumped straight out of bed to get here. "I don't understand. Why is she here? Is this a thing, Waylon?" Then I see him eye his daughter up and down from the thick eyeliner to the stiletto heels.

"Are you—wearing Aunt Adriana's clothes?"

"It's not my fault. You never let me do anything! I hate you! I hate everybody!" And that's when the screaming starts between the two. I push past Chey to get to Lexie and snatch her up from her bed.

"Stop!" I have to yell it. "Both of you screaming is scaring Lexie," I tell them. "Just stop." And for the moment, they are quiet while Chey makes a big deal of sobbing.

"You had no right to call my daddy," Chey huffs at me, wagging a finger. "I hate you. I hate you so bad. You are going to hell."

"I may be going to hell, but it isn't because I called your dad, Chey."

So this is the point Boone starts yelling at her to get into the truck. Chey refuses and locks herself in my bathroom yelling that we are ruining her life and she wants to die. I can hear a car pull up the drive. It stops. Then, as if the driver sees Boone's truck, it spits out gravel and tears back down the road. And Lexie is bawling out her *B-b-bs* so Boone will take her. Her little fists are clenched.

"Shit." Boone is standing in the middle of my tiny living room. He's got his hands on his head and he's looking at the ceiling. "When did she stop being my little girl?" he mutters. "She was so easy back then. God, Waylon, I don't know what to do with her. I can't take her back to the house dressed like that and screaming like that. If my mom and dad know she sneaked out—they'll take her away from me. I can't do this."

I'm staring at Mama's jewelry box and thinking about Abram Miller. We never talked things out. He just shook his head until the day he told me I had to make a choice to either join the church or leave.

"Okay, so you're going to sit down and talk right here."

"Is that what your dad did? How did that work for him, Waylon? Should I just assume she's going to run away?" He stops, shakes his head. "I'm sorry. I shouldn't have said that."

"To answer your question, no, he didn't. He was a quiet man. My big brother talked to me. But Chey is not me. And your home is not—closed in its ideas like my Amish family's was."

"I'd rather just leave her in the bathroom."

"Well, that's easier. This is the messy part. Love is messy and I know you got a thing about things not being messy by avoiding them. But you can't."

"What makes you think that?"

I think he's being snarky. He's not. I see a sad smile creep up on his lips.

"She's not okay. You're not okay. Your family's way of dealing with this is to ignore it, sit in different rooms and wait for it to go away. It's not going away, Boone."

"Here, give me Lexie." He holds out his hands. Lexie is at the point where she is just huffing and arching her back. When she sees Boone is going to take her, she nearly throws herself toward him.

"Yeah, it's Boo, baby. I missed you." He grins up at me. "Wanna trade?"

"Lexie would like that. I don't know if Chey would right now."

She's like coaxing a wild kitten out of a pipe. Chey doesn't want to come out. When she does, she's angry quiet and refuses to look at Boone.

"Listen, Chey, you need to talk to your dad." She deadpan stares at me like she is wishing I would just explode and disappear when she shoves past me.

"Why don't you leave us alone?" she spats at me. "We were doing just fine before you came along."

"Okay, well, I'm not the one who came over here an hour ago and tried to use me to sneak out. So maybe we should start this conversation differently with like: Okay, Waylon, I'm sorry I lied to you and told you my daddy said it was okay if I babysat while you went to work. Then I lied to him and told him you asked me not to tell him."

"What?" Boone is standing three feet from me. He's patting Lexie's back and suddenly seems to actually hear what I had said. "You what, Chey? You told me she told you not to tell me—"

"She's lying!" she twists her head around and points at me. "YOU BITCH! I don't have to tell him because he's not my real dad. He doesn't want me and I don't care!"

I see her reach out. I don't quite assess the situation quickly enough to note her hands are reaching for my mama's jewelry box. It is like it happens so fast. One second the jewelry box is sitting on the little table and the next, it is flying headlong on to the floor with a crash.

We're all just standing there. It's not registering, at first, the shards of wood and little pieces of copper locking mechanism splattering across the room. I know my hand has come to my face. I see both Chey and Boone turn to me as if in slow motion. I'm stunned, I suppose. I don't move. The only piece of my mama that I have is laying shattered on the worn deerskin and the dark wooden floor.

"Oh, my God, what have I done?" Chey says softly. She's staring at the floor. I'm staring at the floor. The only one moving is Boone who is rolling his hand through his hair.

"Oh, Waylon." Boone is tap-tap-tapping his leg. "I'm so sorry. I can fix it. I can—"

My eyes wander over to his. I know the truth. It is shattered. The rings and the envelopes, the necklaces and little coins in there. They are laying on the floor as much a part of the broken box as the ripped red silk cover on the inside of the lid. I honestly think at this very moment while the only sound in the room is Chey sniffling and her daddy's fingers tapping on his jeans, he thinks this is the last shred of his heart pummeling down to the ground.

"No, you know what," I say with a throaty whisper while I watch Chey fall to her knees and try to sweep up the mess with her fingers. She's crying softly, telling me sorry over and over. "Baby, stop," I tell her, my fingers on her arm. She looks up, her eyes red and wet with tears. "Stop right now. My mama left me. She's not coming back. I was five. Why the hell would you leave a five year-old? Because she had temper tantrums? Because she asked for too many cookies or had too many questions? No, it wasn't my fault. I could spend the rest of my life trying to figure out what the hell I did wrong to make her leave. And you know what? I'm sitting here with a perfectly good daddy down the hill that likes me even when I'm on my period and in a crappy mood. I'm wasting my time looking for acceptance from a man who won't even talk to me when I try to go back to Ohio and a mama who didn't even care to send me a letter in twenty years. I don't need them. I don't need the box."

"I'm sorry, Waylon," she says with a whisper. "Daddy, I'm sorry. I lied. She's right. She didn't know I sneaked out."

"What makes you think I'm not your daddy, Cheyenne?"

"I heard Livie and Tessa Callahan whispering about it when they came to get Aunt Adriana a couple years ago," she whispered. "Am I?"

"You know, people are going to talk, Chey," Boone says softly. "They always are. But you're my little girl. I held you like I'm holding Lexie now. I gave you your first bottle, I stayed up with you when you got colic. I changed more diapers than I can count and lost more dates because you cried when I tried to leave. I looked in your eyes and I saw your mama in them. I saw me in them. Let me tell you this. Even if I got you out of a cereal box, I put in all the work up to this point on you. I get to claim you one way or another."

"A cereal box, really?" I ask him while I make myself busy and Chey sniffs a half-sob laugh. They need to talk. And they do. I pitter around and clean Lexie's room. Then, I walk over and grab a grocery sack from under the sink and pick up the little pieces of the jewelry box and toss them in. I try not to linger on the rings too long when I pick them up and plop them in.

After a while, Chey goes to the bathroom. I can hear the sink running. Boone squats down next to me while I'm digging more pieces under the couch. I look up and he's got this half-smile on his face. He reaches out, pushes back a tendril of hair that has slipped in front of my eyes. He just stares at me. I stare at him.

"You're killing me, Skeeter," he says softly. "When I'm alone, I can only think of the taste of your skin, the scent of your body. It's like—like the smell of horses fed on molasses sweet feed. I'm like drowning in you and I can't get to the surface. I don't want to get to the surface. I go to the Crazy Filly every Friday night and every Saturday night, sit in the back where you don't see me—"

"You don't have to go to the Crazy Filly. I set up Skeeter's Bar so you didn't have to go there. You'd come here instead."

"No shit?" Boone chews hard on this, looks toward the front door. "I wondered what those signs were."

"Just trying to keep from having to drag my baby down there and fighting off creeps in the parking lot." I stare at him hard. Surely, he knows the truth. I can't stand to be without him.

"Yeah, well, it's harder now to go there," he mutters. "I see the other guys looking at you like I'm looking at you and I—I think why would she even look my way? Me with this stupid blind eye and the scar and I sometimes think I've got this borderline compulsive disorder with my patting. And I'm saying things I'd never say to anyone—" He laughs nervously, sees the wood slivers I'm holding in my palm. "I'm sorry my daughter broke the only thing you've got of your mom."

"Naw, it's not really the only thing. I've got her picture. You want to see it?"

"Yeah, sure."

I go to my purse, tug open the little pocket on the side. I pull out the old, smudged picture with tatty edges and worn sides. I point out each of us— "That's Mama. She's holding me." I poke the tiny figure of a boy by her side. "And that's my big brother Will."

Boone looks hard at the picture and nods. Then he leans a little closer. "I—I've seen this woman before."

CHAPTER 40
A SECRET NOTE HIDDEN IN MAMA'S JEWELRY BOX

I kind of smile, thinking he's joking. "Don't play with my head, Boone, not funny."

"I'm not," he says. "Skeeter, she was sitting right next to me last Friday." He takes the picture from my fingers, walks over and holds it under the little lamp on the table by the couch.

"I know you think I'm crazy," he tells me looking up. "Maybe I am. But I know that was her at your performance at the Crazy Filly. She was older and a little chubbier, but it was her. Her face looked the same."

I rise, come up beside Boone. I've got my hands full of broken jewelry box. I set it down on the couch. "Please don't play a joke on me. Chase used to think it was funny to tell me the same thing."

"I wouldn't do that," Boone says with a shake of his head. "And I wasn't drunk, before you ask me. She just sat there with a drink staring at you. I mean, everybody was watching you on stage. But something about her staring at you without laughing or smiling was—different. Everybody was laughing or singing along. They were kind of dancing in their chairs or where they stood. She was—rigid."

I know I get stupid when I focus on Boone's eyes. I just can't help it. I swear if I look out while I'm singing and see him in the crowd, I'm worried I'll just stop right there ogle him like an idiot. I'm doing that right now before I shake my head like I'm shaking out hay and shrug. "I guess I said it doesn't matter, all this stuff—" Even if it did, Chey was coming out of the bathroom then. I'd been waiting for Mama for twenty years to return. But, at the moment I saw her look at the box she'd broken again, it just didn't matter.

I think she's going to burst into tears. I just make a quick pick up of it and shove it in the plastic bag. I toss it toward the kitchen table.

"Hey, I was working on a song for Dallas before I got mad at him. You guys want to hear it?" I look at the two standing there. "I know it's almost—" I look up at the clock. "—eleven-thirty on a Wednesday. But it's summer and not a school night. And," I add, "you can show your daddy what you learned in those guitar lessons he didn't know you were getting by babysitting, right?"

"Really, Chey?" Boone teases her, reaches out and chucks her on the arm.

"Yeah, daddy, she couldn't afford to pay me and I couldn't afford lessons from somebody like Waylon Ryder. So we improvised."

"Improvised." Boone shakes his head. "You hang around your aunt too much. That's the kind of words she'd use. But it's cool you earned your lessons so your grounding might be two weeks instead of three."

"Really?" Chey rolls her eyes and Boone nods. I reach around and hand her the guitar I borrowed from Oaky to use on stage and show her the notes to pick. We both sit down on the couch.

"It's called *Before You*." I grab up my own guitar and start in while Chey strums her notes. When I start singing, Boone comes over and sits down right next to me. I look up and do my stupid grin. Chey starts giggling because I think she knows I'm stupid-crazy over her daddy.

"Shush, now," I tell her and reach over and give her a gentle shove. She laughs out loud. Then I see the tears come again. I know that it's the confused kind that come after you're happy again, but still stuck in the crying mode.

"I'm so sorry about all this, Waylon," she says. "Promise me you don't hate me."

"Like you think I'll leave like your mama did kind of hate you?" I ask her softly. "Nuh uh. I'm not the leaving kind of person. Ask your daddy how many times I tried to get to the end of the driveway a few nights after Lexie was born. It's just not me." I turn and look at Boone holding Lexie who is staring stupid at him just like I do, trying hard to touch the stubble on his cheeks. "You can spend your entire life wondering what if and why. I always thought the worst thing that'd ever happen was to lose it all. And look at me—" I stop because Chey is staring at her fingers twiddling on the guitar. "No, baby, look at me. That day you and I were sitting in the truck with Lexie and we were playing guitar and singing while your daddy drove, I think it was the happiest I've ever been. I mean it. It always sits there in my head like a cup of hot chocolate with cool whip cream on a cold winter night. This is what I like doing, coming up with the songs and being with you guys. I didn't realize it riding around with Chase and bouncing stuff off him. It was always push, push, push for me to write him songs and honestly, I wasn't feeling it. But this—like I'm doing now with you. This is life and happiness. And I wouldn't have known it if I didn't hit that rock bottom, lose it all."

"Well, I don't think you lost it all. I think Chase Martin took it from you," Boone says.

"Let's not talk Chase Martin," I grunt, push my guitar to the table. "Considering—" *Your dad's part of the lawsuit.* I suspend my words because Boone's shaking his head back and forth like he's telling me to stop.

"What?" Chey asks. "I can tell you don't want her to say something because I'm here."

"It's nothing, sweetie," Boone says.

"And this is why I get so mad at you, daddy," Chey huffs. "Because you keep stuff from me like I'm a baby."

"She's right," I shrug. "She isn't a baby."

"Alright," Boone shifts Lexie on his arm. She's fast asleep and he gets up, takes her to the room and lays her down. When he comes back, he looks at Chey, then at me.

"Your grandpa is part of the law team working for Tyrone Canter. He's doing background research. Tyrone Canter is Brooke Canter's dad. She is the one who sings with Chase now. They are suing Waylon for singing the songs at the Crazy Filly. Chase said he wrote them all."

"Did he?" Chey turns to me. "I mean, I always thought you wrote them."

"I wrote them all. I put Chase's name on some of them—I don't know why. I guess I was thinking we were a team singing them. I was fifteen and sixteen and in stupid-love."

"How do you prove he's lying?"

"She can't," Boone says. "There's no way that's—"

"Um, yes, there is," I correct him. I turn and poke my finger on my guitar. "My guitar has all the songs on it. I started doing it when I was around thirteen."

I suppose the moment I saw Boone's face go blank, I should have known my mistake. But like Chase used to say, I was so dumb I probably couldn't find my way out of a plastic bucket.

"Oh, so you'll get your songs back?" Chey asks.

"I'm hoping."

"Hey, I've got a new joke," Boone is suddenly happy as hell. It's like the whole mood has changed between us all. He reaches out, tickles his daughter in the ribs.

"Oh, no, no—" Chey giggles. "No stupid jokes."

"What kind of eggs does an evil chicken lay?" he asks and then holds up his hands before we can answer. "Deviled Eggs. Get it?"

We shake our heads back and forth. Unfortunately, we do understand.

Chey falls asleep at twelve-thirty and halfway through a sappy western romance. Boone asks me why I am mad at Dallas again. I tell him it wasn't me. It was him. He has to keep his distance because of the bad publicity the lawsuit will bring. It is one thing singing together. It is another working together writing songs, being on his label.

"I just want to sing," I tell him. "Why does there have to be all this shit?" I push myself up from the couch, take a bag of popcorn we'd been eating and dump it in the trash. Boone follows me.

"You were the one saying life was messy," he tosses at me. He grins sleepily, reaches out like he's going to touch my face. I hold up my hand.

"Please don't, Boone. It was not my intention to have you come over here tonight. I like being with you, but—"

"But I'm not good enough for you."

"No, I didn't say that," I sniff a laugh. "You've got a girlfriend or a fiancé, I'm not sure where you are at this point of your relationship. But I'm not going to waste my time on a relationship that isn't going anywhere. I like to be held at night. I like to have conversations that have more depth than how many times we can have coitus in an hour. I could have sex with lots of guys. I choose not to do that."

"You were the one who walked in on my relationship," Boone throws back at me. "I can't just walk out on her like Chase did to you, right? I've got family obligations, they've made plans. I guess, I'm afraid to bet all my money on a horse that might buck."

"You're kidding me, right?" I laugh sarcastically. "I don't know, Boone, what to say to that. I'm not a horse to bet on. Again, not my problem. I'm just not that girl. Honestly, I couldn't trust you wouldn't do this to me if we were together, you get it? Maybe as soon as something prettier comes along, you're out that door."

"And if I didn't have a girlfriend, it would be different?"

"Well, yeah. Isn't it a little too late for that?" I ask him. He nods.

"I didn't plan this, Waylon. I was blindsided." He acts like he wants to say more. He doesn't. He just walks into the living room and gently awakens Chey. After they leave, I drowsily clean up the rest of the jewelry box from the floor and under the couch. Part of the lid is settled between the leg of the couch and the little table pushed up next to it. I wiggle it out and sigh while the thin, red material rips from the wood.

That is when I see it. It is a wadded up piece of paper secretly stuffed between the red material and the wood of the lid. I tug it out. It has been there so long, it is sticking to the material meticulously pulled from the lid, then re-glued to hide the note within.

Carefully, I unfold it. It is a newspaper article. I squint in the light, find myself sitting down on the couch while I do.

WHATEVER HAPPENED TO LITTLE DANA? Some stories never fade away. Those with mysteries attached will, most likely, be talked about for years and years. Will they be solved? Who knows? It may be just a mystery to those who sit back and once in a while pick up a newspaper and see the story. But it is an excruciating journey into hell for those who loved the missing. Most questions will never be answered. Most mysteries will never be solved. The answers will go to the grave with those who made them. It is the three year anniversary of the disappearance of newborn Dana Delano. In our award winning series on those who have vanished over the years across the U.S., we are bringing you a special report on this child who would have turned three this year.

"That's the hard part, not knowing. The nanny had both Dana and her own son in the car when they disappeared. No trace of any of them could be found. With Dana, the police found the car our nanny had been driving in Lake Borgne six days after she came up missing. This was four years ago. The car was empty. Dana's car seat was empty as was our nanny's son's seat." Says Miriam Delano of Gulfport, Louisiana whose newborn daughter vanished with a nanny after a typical drive to pick up Dana's older sibling from preschool. "Were they sucked into the water? Who knows? We had no pictures of the nanny. We had hired her through a newspaper clipping. Paige Long was her name. It was a fictitious name. Police found no footprints on the shoreline. They found no traces of Dana."

The search for the missing nanny and the two children were taken out of the spotlight because of Hurricane Andrew rolling through Florida and Louisiana three years ago in August of 1992. The car was found two days after the hurricane in a marshy area of a lake off the Gulf of Mexico, Lake Borgne. "I suppose it is unfortunate that at the time, news of the hurricane and its path of destruction through Louisiana was more important," Miriam Delano says. "However, we may never know what happened to Dana because it wasn't as high profile as it could have been at the time it needed to be prominent— Was it planned around the hurricane? We don't know—"

"Shit on a stick," I whisper. I push back the creases of the newspaper. I stare at the face of the woman who was being interviewed in the newspaper dated August of 1995. "She looks just like me."

CHAPTER 41
DUMPED ON A BACKROAD IN A SPRAY OF GRAVEL

The next morning, I'm riding to town with Dutch to get feed.

"What are you wearing?"

"It's a dress." It is a dress. It is black and has a lacy edge. It is stretchy and soft and sexy.

"A dress." Dutch blinks at me. "You look like you're ready to go to a dance. We're going to get feed."

"I'm trying something new," I say. I am. I just don't want to be myself today so I'm wearing one of the dresses I ordered to wear to church to play piano. It feels awkward and takes my mind off Mama. It is probably a little risqué for Holy Unity. But it's black and tight and suits my mood.

"Well, that'll get me two horses, I think," he tries to tease me. I just stare at him. "You alright, Skeeter?" Dutch has asked me the same question five times already. "You're pale and quiet. You worried about the lawyer junk? Because you let them do their job. That's what we pay them for. Don't worry until they tell you if Chase is gonna sue you or not."

"No, I'm not worried about Chase. I'm fine. I was fine when we left. I was fine five minutes ago. I'm fine now."

No, actually, I'm not. I didn't sleep. I couldn't eat this morning. I just got on my phone and poked in the name *Miriam Delano* twenty times. I found the missing persons posters—a picture of a newborn plastered on poster board along with a sketch artist's rendition of a dark haired woman, the newspaper articles, the police reports. I found the newborn hospital pictures of a little stranger that wasn't a stranger because she kind of looks like Lexie. I can't quite wrap myself around it. Maybe it isn't me. Maybe those two babies and that nanny died in that Louisiana lake. Or maybe everything Mama told me about being the daughter of an evangelical preacher in Texas was a lie, a big fat frigging lie. It's like all I've ever known about me is—just a weird dream and I'm waking up realizing none of it is real. My world feels like it is crumbling down around me.

"Talk to me then. You're usually annoying me with chatter."

"Huh? Oh. Okay, so where's Jack?" I try to let it fall off me. *Mama's a liar, Mama's a liar.* The sing-song voice keeps slipping into my head. "I thought he was your usual sidekick getting feed and supplies."

"Jack ain't working for me no more."

"What?" I draw it out, snap my neck to the left. "Who's going to work on the horses?"

"Not Jack." Dutch gets his little plastic soda bottle from the door panel, opens it up, and spits tobacco juice into it. "Honey, I didn't know you'd put a whole wad of money in the can under the sink until I caught him getting into it the other day. You didn't steal that money, did you?"

"No."

"Then why'd you pay me it back?"

"Because I love you and I didn't think you'd believe me."

"Well, I love you too. And it ain't just because you paid me back. I miss you being at the house. I miss peeking in at you and that baby at night after you've gone to bed and knowing I made you safe and sound."

"I did feel safe and sound," I whisper. That's why he was looking at us and not because he was trying to decide if he should filet me or stuff me upstairs in the attic. He loves me. I feel like crying and I know the tears are coming. I sniff. My own words had just popped out of my mouth. Then I felt stupid, didn't expect him to return it. "So we're like a family, kind of, right? You'd love me no matter what?" I ask him. He knows I'm working up to something. I can see him peering at me out of the corner of his eyes.

"I suppose you've growed on me. Quit your cryin'. You ain't in no trouble are you?"

"No more than usual. Okay, so how long have you all been stealing horses?" I ask Dutch. He is quiet a moment, turns his head toward me.

"Who says we're stealing horses? Is that what's bothering you?"

"Oh, come on, Dutch," I mutter, shove away the tears with my fist. "Two or three times a month, somebody drives up the old back road from your place. It isn't always Boone and his sister. It's you, too."

"It's a game, you know," he says.

"A game?"

"Yeah, old Bo Littleton gets a bunch of horses for auction from all over the United States." He sighs, pulls the truck to a slow halt off the side of the road. Then he turns to me. "Hundreds of horses a month that stick in his barn until sale time. They got buyers from slaughterhouses coming in and once in a while, they buy these poor old dead broke horses as part of a lot that are good as gold. About ten years ago, his boy started sneaking one or two out. He got them. My little girl and Harlon's girl, Adriana, hid them up on top of my hill."

"Bo Littleton's a crap," I mutter. But Dutch shakes his head.

"You're quick to judge, baby girl," he tells me softly. "Some people with a hard edge, have a soft side too. After Charlene and Marcus were killed, he called me one night.

He said he had four good horses up there. If I came to get them, nobody'd know the better. He'd give three-hundred dollars to the slaughterhouse buyers for each to make it legal. Just like he used to do for the kids. Now, he calls the cops. They come out, pretend to try to find them. They could, I suppose, but they don't."

"So they are *kind of* stolen," I say.

"No, they are stolen," he laughs. He's got a twinkle in his eyes. "So don't go around telling nobody. We protect our own here."

"Am I included in that, Dutch, *your own*?" I ask him. I'm afraid of his answer.

"I wouldn't have told you about them horses if you weren't, baby girl."

"You know I've been singing at the Crazy Filly."

"I heard tell."

"You still include me in your own?"

"I do." He just stares at the windshield. "Maybe we could go to church on Sunday mornings to wash away the sins of that bar. What do you say about that?"

"Preacher Irving called and asked me if I'd play the piano for the songs. If I do, will you come with me and sit up front?" I ask. "Because everybody was really quiet after I said that stuff about Bo Littleton's picture being beside Jesus. I don't want everybody staring at me."

"You set aside the money for the new kitchen floor and I think everybody will be happy," Dutch tells me. "He called the other day to tell me you didn't have to do it. I told him, you had the money and it would be a fair price for interrupting him in the middle of the sermon. And he invited us back and said Bo Littleton's picture was moved to the hallway by the Sunday school classrooms. Is that fair?"

"Yes, sir."

I chew on his words for the ride to town. Up one gravel road to the next, then along the buckled asphalt of the main roads. He stops at the feed store. Then Dutch eases into the parking lot of the Whip and Dip Ice Cream Stop to get me an ice cream cone.

"One more thing, baby girl," Dutch says softly while he jams the truck out of gear in the parking lot. He waves at another old man and gives a flirty smile to a woman getting out of her car. "There's a little sandy-haired woman named Mindy Potter snooping around town. She's with some magazine in New York. She's a cute thing, kind of bubbly. She's been asking questions about you just like those suits did until they disappeared. Folks like her. They been chittering and chattering about you to her. I just want you to know because I just don't know what those people do. I got a bad feeling about her. She's just got a way about her that makes people talk and talk and talk—"

"Did you talk?" I ask him softly.

"Sweetie, I did just a little," Dutch sighs. "She came up beside me at the grocery store last Tuesday. I was getting some of that diaper rash stuff for Lex and she started telling me which worked better. Then she was like *oh, I know you, you're Skeeter's pop*— And I kind of told her what happened that night you came knocking on the barn door with a belly full of baby. I thought she was Charley Wright's little girl."

"That's okay, Dutch," I tell him. "It's happened to me before. They're good at what they do. Dallas used to tell me that those gossip magazine people, they can talk a flea off an old dog without a leg to scratch them."

We're starting to get out. I see Dutch look over my head just as Adriana Martinez pulls up beside us. "Waylon, we need to talk. I'll give you a ride back to Dutch's."

It isn't a question. I stare at her. She looks just like a

girl-Boone without the stubble on her face. "I don't have time now. We're getting ice cream." I jab a thumb to Dutch who is getting out of the driver's side of the truck to get our ice creams. "Lexie is asleep, so I'm staying here until he brings me back an ice cream cone."

"Well, maybe I can get you both an ice cream," Dutch offers and you two can eat them while you head back to the house. I'll keep the baby with me, meet you there."

"No, that's okay—" I try to get out of riding alone in a vehicle with Adriana, but Dutch is so dang smitten with her, I swear he'd ballet dance naked down Main Street if she asked him to do it. He waves me away with his hand, then goes to the window and brings us both back twist cones with sprinkles.

"Oh, my God, are you wearing—a dress?" she asks, looking at me up and down.

"Yeah."

"Hmm." That's all she says about it. It makes me fidgety. Then Adriana tells me if I drop one sprinkle on the leather seats of her sports car, she'll clean it off with my face when I get into her car.

"You're not that much bigger than me," I mumble. "I'd get a good kick in, at least."

"What'd you say?" she asks. I was thankful she didn't hear and wished Jessie was with me.

"Nothing." I look through the driver's side window to Dutch getting into his truck. He's ignoring my pleading gaze to save me.

"Buckle up and spread napkins all over you," Adriana tells me. I'm looking at my lap at the two napkins I have wondering if that will take care of the blood when she shoots me dead on some backroad.

She doesn't say anything while we're pulling out of

the ice cream shop parking lot. I tell her she's going the wrong direction when she goes right and she just rolls her eyes at me like I'm an idiot.

"Okay, so let's talk about my little brother."

"I'm staying away from him. Is that what you're getting at? I mean, I can stop this whole bloodbath right now. You don't have to fire a single shot, ruin the interior of your car with my guts and entrails." I take a long lick of my ice cream and Adriana looks at me like it makes her squeamish. "He's made it clear he's got a girlfriend and family obligations. Your daddy has told me—"

"My daddy's an idiot sometimes." She rolls her eyes. It's awkward and silent while we drive out of town. Then about ten miles out, she puts on the brakes and pulls over to a crossroad. She taps something in her phone, looks at the road signs three or four times. Then she sighs, looks at me.

"I don't like your kind of music," she tells me. "I don't know how anybody could. It's like—" She shakes her head and puckers her lips. "It's like acid to my ears, like slicing the first layer of skin from ankle to knee when I use a new razor on my shins." She shivers, then turns. "But to each their own. You've got a few fans, I suppose."

"What's your point, Adriana?" I stare at her without expression. "You didn't have to drive all the way out here to ridicule me. You could have done that in the parking lot of the ice cream shop. And if I'm in crappy mood and feel like having my confidence sabotaged, I can just open any shopping network that sells my CDs and dig up a few bad customer reviews to send me over the edge."

She settles back in her seat, rests her hands on the steering wheel, and looks out the windshield. There's nothing but trees, a field of tall green cornstalks, and roadway in front of us.

"Do you like my brother?"

I answer blandly: "Yeah, he's a good guy."

"You're missing my point." She turns her head. "Do you love him?"

"Well, you didn't ask that," I return. "It doesn't matter. He's got a girlfriend."

"Yeah, well, she isn't much of one," Adriana divulges. I'm surprised and narrow my eyes at her. "She's what dad calls an easy keeper. You know, the kind of horses that you can toss a bit of feed and hay into their stalls and they stay fat and healthy regardless of how much work you're putting into them. She comes. She goes. She doesn't—care."

"Easy keepers are a lot less work, Adriana. You don't have to worry about them. You don't have to monitor their feed or check on them a thousand times in the field or when it's snowing," I tell her. "What's your point?"

"Boone likes to check the horses. He likes to hang around them. He's always fiddling with them in the barn. He like gets high when we get one of those old horses that is skinny and rode hard and he feeds it up and gets it fat and full of spirit again."

"Oh, my God," I hiss. "You're comparing me and Olivia to horses. I'm the old dead broke horse. Am I right?"

"You're perceptive," Adriana tells me. "So do you get what I'm saying? You came into Bel-Air looking like one of those slaughterhouse horses we get from Bo. Now look at you, all pink cheeks and full of sunshine." She stops, tips her head. "Okay, maybe not full of sunshine. But my brother, he's like dancing on daisies since you came here. He's been pushing his hat up a bit, not hiding his scar. He's happy. I haven't seen him happy since—" she stop. "You know, the wreck. And Chey's been happy."

"It doesn't change the fact that he is choosing Olivia over me. And it doesn't change that your daddy is trying to take me to the cleaners."

"That's just silly stuff." Adriana waves a hand in the air. She's got dark eyes, almost black. I think she might be a demon. "I can't tell you what to do. I personally believe Olivia would be better for Boone even if she is superficial. There wouldn't be that many bumps in the road. They'd have a nice bland life, two easy keepers in the barn."

"What's your point? You dragged me out here in the middle of nowhere to—"

"To tell you that Boone couldn't stop talking that day about being at the cemetery and you almost backing into that grave. He laughed until he cried, Waylon. Then you bear-spraying down that creep in the parking lot of the Crazy Filly. He thinks you're his stupid hero." She's pointing her finger at the door and I'm turning, following her finger. There's nothing there but trees and field. "Get out. Bumps in the road. That's what he needs. He needs somebody to sit with him like you did the other night fishing. He'll die inside if he has to sit in the stall with another fat horse and stare out at the little filly with a spirit bounding around the pasture. You being the filly. By the way, I hate dealing with fillies. They're moody and mean."

"Are—are you kicking me out of the car? Because that would imply I'm a pup you're dropping off on the side of the road and not a horse," I say slowly. "You're confusing me. Are you—?"

"Get out!" She yells it. I jump, startled. Then I sigh and push my way out of the door.

"You know, this is vaguely familiar to my last boyfriend leaving me in the motel parking lot."

"Well, this time you've got pants on and Boone will be here in about twenty minutes or so to pick you up." She hardly lets me close the door before she takes off in a spray of gravel.

CHAPTER 42
TAKING THE LONG WAY 'ROUND TOWN

"See, I'm confused. My sister called and said she was broken down on West Elkton and the main county road going out of town." Boone just stopped his truck. He is rolling down the passenger side window and leaning a little to the right while I push up from the curb.

"Ha ha," I grunt, jerking open the passenger side truck door and sliding inside. "You're hilarious. No, she picked me up at Whip and Dip Ice Cream Stop and dumped me out here like a dog that peed on the carpet too much. What took you so long?" I see him eyeing me with a hard gaze and this stupid grin crossing his face that he's trying to wipe away with his hand. It's like he's going to tell a joke but he can't quite make it to the punch line before he starts laughing himself. "And before you say anything, Boone Martinez, yes, this is a dress—"

"Okay, but barring the fact that I'm never in a hurry for my sister, I was out trying to find a cow that was supposed to be having her calf this week. I was three pastures over and on the other side of the hill from the cell phone tower so I didn't get it for a half hour."

"Did you find her?"

"My sister?"

"No, dumbass, the cow." He's like stupid-staring at me when I sit down in his truck. I wave it away with my hand. "Never mind. Can you give me a ride home?"

"Why'd she dump you out here?"

"Guess." I tell him while I pull my seatbelt around my chest. "But before you answer, here's a hint. She compared me to a wild filly."

"Yeah, she doesn't like fillies. She got kicked once longeing one on a short rope."

"I would have liked to have witnessed that," I muse. "However, here's another hint. She said you do—like wild fillies, though."

"I'm partial to geldings."

"Really, you don't see the parallel here? I got it." I roll my eyes. "You've got a college degree. I've got my GED and you're not getting it. Because you don't act like you are interested in *boy* horses, either stallions or geldings—"

"Oh, I get it."

"So tell me, Boone," I sigh. I watch him make a U-turn and start back toward town. "There's Olivia and there's me. If you had a choice, who would you choose? I mean, because I know it would appear obvious, at this point, because you're with her and not with me. Your sister believes that you may not know what's good or bad for you. Be truthful. Because if I have to drag you kicking and screaming into a relationship, I've got to be honest, my little heart can't take being left on a dark, wet parking lot again." I rub my temples between forefinger and thumb. "By the way, does everybody know I was in a t-shirt and panties that night in the parking lot watching him leave?"

"Well, I did. I was there. The story came up—"

"That was you by the trucks?"

"Yeah, early breakfast."

I sit back in the seat, get quiet.

"What's the matter? I figured you knew it was me." He huffs a deep sigh, turns left on an old backroad. I kind of get the feeling he's putting off going into town.

"I didn't. It's humiliating. Do you just feel sorry for me?" I roll a finger along the lace of my dress right at the thigh.

"No, not really." He looks over at me, drops his eyes to my finger before he snaps his gaze away. "But I guess we need to lay it out on the table."

"Can you find a place to pull off the road?" I ask him. I want to see his face. I hate that he's just staring at the windshield. "Because I know guys like to talk things out." I joke with him, reach across and tickle his side.

"Yeah, yeah okay." He fake-groans. "I can do that."

We don't really talk a whole lot when he finds an old lumber road and drives in a bit. When he stops, we just sit there a few minutes and stare at the dashboard and the windshield and the huge pine trees. "Hey, I've got a joke for you," I suddenly say and turn to Boone. "Why can't you hear a pterodactyl use the restroom?"

"Because the *p* is silent," Boone answers.

"Crud. I suppose you know all the bad jokes. I even looked that one up."

He laughs. "I used to have a joke book when I was a kid. I'd go around messing up jokes with everybody. I did know them all, I think."

I take off my seatbelt. Then I slide along the seat until I'm next to him. "Okay, so maybe this is a game breaker." I slip up between the steering wheel and Boone's chest. The buttons slide along my belly. I'm skinny. I fit, but it's tight. My boobs are right in his face and he grins, looking up at me. His breath is warm against my chest. I know my nipples are rock hard against him. He has to feel them straight through my bra.

"Got to say, Waylon, this is my favorite way to sit in a truck." Boone's holding my shoulders when I lean down and kiss him on the lips. I take out one hair tie, then the other. My hair is dripping down on him, touching his shoulders.

My eyes are open and I see his close. He looks like an angel right then. His lips are cool to my warm. They are soft and sweet and taste like cherry candy. I wonder if mine taste like ice cream. I kiss him again and take his hat from his head, slip it on mine. His right hand slips up along my side. I think he wants to slide it up my dress.

"I do love you, you know that right?" he says. I'm not sure how to take his words. It's almost like an apology. It's almost like he has to put a *but* on the end. His fingers are dancing along my ribs. I try to push them upward, but he stops them with his hand. "No, listen to me. I want to be with you. I do. But it's not easy—it won't be easy. If you want easy, we need to stop."

"Do you want easy?"

"I want you. Right now, I want you." He slides his palm along my side until he's cupping my breast. He's rock hard when I slide down to his lap. I'm wet.

"Do you need to take your underpants off?"

"I'm not wearing any." I'm not. They were all dirty and Dutch was out of laundry detergent.

"Oh, shit—okay." I reach down, unlatch his pants and slide down on top of him. He's rocking slowly back and forth and my back is riding the steering wheel and his hat keeps sliding across my head. But I'm not feeling that part, not at all. I'm just feeling Boone and feeling whole and happy and listening to our moans.

Five minutes later, we're back to sixteen miles of car seat between us while he pulls off. I feel strangely used even though I initiated the sex. I'm just not one of those girls that likes to have sex in trucks. It makes me feel sleazy. I think Boone must recognize the pinched expression on my face. He leans over and pats the leather seat next to him.

"You want to come over and sit next to me and let me

feel what it'd be like to ride with you like you're my girlfriend? Maybe I can give it a spin and see."

I unlatch the seatbelt and slide across the expanse, eyeing Boone warily.

"You're going to either kick me or buck on me, aren't you?" He laughs at me. "Because you do look like a new four year-old mare we just got in. She's got that same mischievous glint to her eyes." I smoosh up next to him. He slings an arm around me. I feel my tummy make a jerk right to left, followed by a bunch of butterflies tickling inside.

He gets to the stoplight just outside the city center of Bel-Air. I know he is either going to stay on Main Street or turn left to go the long way around town where nobody sees us sitting together like a couple. It's like the deal breaker for me. This very moment all of a sudden and Boone's choice of whether he's willing to let people know he might be dating a girl like me. I suppose until that moment, I didn't think about the choices we'd have to make, the things we might have to give up. Maybe we should have just gone for a walk and held hands or talked about stupid stuff like what our favorite colors are this week. We didn't. And for that, I feel strangely motivated to put it all on the line right then because we'd gone all the way.

He just sits there a second. I don't know if he's thinking what I'm thinking. Then he flicks on his left turn signal and I feel my heart drop. It just sinks. I know I'm being critical. I try to smile up at him while he takes the backroads to Dutch's.

"Hey, just drop me off at my place. Don't stop at Dutch's. I'll walk down in a few minutes and get Lexie," I say. He hesitates, then makes another right to the road that climbs the couple of steep hills between the two properties.

"You want to hang out?"

"Naw, not right now." Maybe not ever.

CHAPTER 43
SETTING ME UP SO THEY CAN STEAL MY GUITAR

My guitar's gone. The door is closed when Boone drops me off. It is unlocked. I step inside and everything's the same. Like I always do, I look over to where my guitar is always settled on an old chest. And it is gone. Gone.

"Gone." I tell Dutch who promptly takes the truck up the road and helps me look for it like I would have misplaced the bulky case and the thing that has been with me through thick and thin. My lifeblood.

"You sure you didn't put it somewhere?" he asks me while we're waiting for Bobby Moretti who is working this shift at the Bel-Air Police Department.

"Other than you and Lexie, it is the one thing that is irreplaceable to me, the one thing that gets me up in the morning. Dutch, I wouldn't have put it anywhere else," I groan, toss my hands on my head. "It is, quite possibly, the one object I can hold up that is going to prove I wrote those songs."

"Who would have known you were gone?" he asks me. "Your truck was parked right here. And of all the things that could have been stolen—" He waves his hand to the little curios I have on the fireplace mantle, a twenty dollar bill sitting on the table. "Why that?"

"Because it is evidence in the lawsuit." That's Bobby coming through the screen door. He must have had lights and sirens going because he gets to Dutch's in twenty minutes flat. "Waylon, you should have locked that guitar up."

"Shoulda. Woulda. Coulda." Dutch tosses out one of his sayings. "But she didn't. So what do we do?"

"Who knew you were gone?"

I cringe, look at Dutch. "Well, Adriana, who showed up at the ice cream shop and made me go for a ride with her. And Boone. How could I be so stupid?"

"What do you mean, sweetie?" Dutch is tipping his head to the side. I can't say. I just plop down on the couch, throw my hands to my head again and groan loudly. "They had to have been setting me up, right? Their daddy is one of the lawyers taking care of Chase's lawsuit against me. If they have the guitar, I've got absolutely no physical proof."

"You're pointing a finger that could hurt a lot of people if it isn't them, Waylon," Bobby says softly. "I know it's my job to look into this. But I've known that family a long time and I don't think they've ever broken the law."

Well, they steal horses, I think to myself. And they had just enough time to get somebody to steal the guitar. "I'm not pointing a finger. I'm just making a point. Who else would have taken it? And why?"

"I don't know. A fan? But let's sit back and take the report without accusations, alright?" Bobby suggests. "I'll informally question a few people that might have been up here—maybe off the record so nobody's hurt, okay?"

"I just fired Jack. He was stealing money from me," Dutch offers. "But he's dumb, that boy. I don't think he'd have the brains to put two and two together to take a guitar and sell it or something."

I fell into a funk then. I just sat on the couch while Dutch and Bobby talked back and forth. Forty-five minutes later, Jessie comes in and grumbling that if he hadn't hit rush hour traffic in Nashville, which he says is twenty-four hours a day, he would have been here and it wouldn't have happened.

"You got something to play with this weekend?" Dutch asks me softly before he goes.

"She uses an electric guitar and an acoustic on stage. I can get her one to match the sound," Jessie pauses, pushes a hand on my arm. "Replaceable in sound and quality, not in your heart, okay? I get it." I nod. Maybe it's Jessie who stole it. Maybe he was here all along. Maybe he needs to feel irreplaceable too. No. I push the thought aside.

"We'll run to Nashville. I know a guy who has great guitars," Jessie tells me. "He'll get you fixed up."

"Yeah, that takes care of the performance Friday and Saturday," I nod. "But what about the Bel-Air City Limits Festival Oaky's having? And the lawsuit?"

"I'll figure out where that guitar disappeared," Bobby tells me. "We'll figure it out, Waylon. We'll figure it out."

That night, I can't sleep. I slip off the bed and jiggle my phone in one hand and the envelope with Wayne Pelosi written on the top in the other. I should have done this a long time ago. I suppose I didn't really want to know the truth. It's hard to stare into a picture of a woman you've conjured up as being an angel in your eyes for twenty years and think she might be the devil. Even if she left me.

I poke the name into the search engine browser. A string of pictures comes up and a long line of results with the same story. In 1989, Wayne Pelosi, an evangelical minister in Louisville, and his wife, Dianna, had gone shopping for baby diapers at a large retail store. One second, their little boy was in his car seat in the shopping cart. The next, he was gone. A ransom note was sent. Wayne Pelosi left blank checks throughout the city at different locations for the abductor that were never cashed. Three month old, William Gerald Pelosi, vanished and was never found.

CHAPTER 44
NO BAND AND ONE SECURITY GUARD/ROADIE/NANNY

"So you want to tell your side of the story or do you want Chase Martin and Brooke Canter to get in the last word?" Mindy Potter with Celeb Gossip Magazine confronts me at the back door of the Crazy Filly Friday night. She looks exactly the same as I remember her in the parking garage at Chase's concert—sandy hair and local six o-clock news gorgeous. "Because what I got from the townspeople of Bel-Air is quite different from the story he's been screaming to every chop shop, horror-gossip tabloid out there. I'm thinking there may be some question as to the accuracy of his statements. But if I can get the story straight from your mouth, maybe we can let the world know the truth." I didn't see it coming. She had sneaked into the bar dressed in t-shirt and jeans like the drink servers. It's packed. She blended right in. "Because I think the main cover for their side said: WAYLON RYDER RIDES AWAY INTO THE SUNSET. But from what I saw tonight, you were heading for the stars."

"Please leave me alone," I am saying. The stars, really? I'm thinking I'm one flush away from heading down the nearest septic tank. I am looking around wildly for Jessie who has slipped away to help load band instruments. I am realizing I need six of him. "I'm just not the kind of person who wants vengeance, you understand?"

"Because of your Amish background?" she asks me.

"Well, maybe, but I don't want my words misconstrued. No offence, Mindy, I have felt the pain of the tabloids before. I won't remind you of the hospital incident when I had the flu and fell off the stage. I did not, I stress this point, do drugs."

She ignores my statement. "It wasn't mean that Chase left you in the parking lot of—?" she pulls up her tablet to look up the name of the hotel. She is taking a step forward, cornering me against the refrigerator in the kitchen. I have to say I'm more terrified of her than meeting six Rod Elkharts in a dark parking lot.

"It's the Bel-Air All-Nighter Motel and Diner. He left me at the motel."

"And nobody would help you? One of my contacts said the owner of the motel kicked you out knowing you were in labor and hocked your guitar—"

"She didn't know I was getting ready to have the baby. They fed me a free meal at the diner. And it was Chase who hocked my guitar. She had no clue it was my guitar."

"And the local mayor coerced the police to take you to the outskirts of town and drop you—"

"No, that's not what happened at all." I shake my head. "None of it. Please go away." Okay, I'm not a fan of Bo Littleton, but he helps save slaughterhouse horses for the sake of his dead son. If she writes that he drops pregnant girls off in the middle of nowhere, his name is trashed in this small town. And every small town mayor in America will get a black eye over it whether they are kind or not. "Please just don't write the story. I just—think it's mean, trying to take revenge. Every time you guys write something in an interview, it isn't what I said."

"Um, I don't think I need to do that, Waylon." She stops, looks me in the eye. "I believe Chase Martin took advantage of you. Off the record, I really, really want to tell your side of the story. The truth sells too. And it is going to be written whether it is by me with the information I have, or somebody else. I want it to be me. I'm willing to tell your side. I've been a fan of yours for years. I lived your songs through every shitty relationship I had and every bad day or good day. I just don't think the songs you two sang were something a guy would write. I'd be damn disappointed to find out they were. I want to hear what you have to say. I want to write it. I'll do the damn thing word for word for the truth straight from your lips and you can check it if you want. I want your story. Lots of people want your story."

"I told you no. I don't—"

"So you want him to win? Because the buzz at Countdown Celebrity Magazine is that he's filing a lawsuit and you're losing fast. He's got all the money. You got nothing but a job on Friday and Saturday nights at a podunk town bar." She shakes her head, steps back. "Tell me no and I'll walk out that door and print what I have. Tell me yes and tell me the truth and I swear to you I'll let you check my accuracy. Because I think the truth is far more attention-grabbing and will sell far more magazines than if I made something up. I mean, what is the worst that can happen? I misconstrue your words. Then you just deny you had anything to do with it onstage and in front of the world." She looks like she is going to say more. I hear a deep voice in the background coming through the doors. "If I convinced you, call me tomorrow before ten. I will tell you I tried to interview Chase two days ago. The rumor was circulating that he was going to have you arrested at the outdoor performance at the Crazy Filly. He refused comment. However, he laughed and told me his lawyers have everything they need to prove he wrote those songs. Just saying—"

I didn't see him standing in the darkness of the kitchen until Mindy Potter left through the back door. Arms crossed, I make out Boone's figure when he steps into a bit of light from the stoves.

"Well, the cops came to my house last night. It was two in the morning," he tells me. "They dragged me and my dad and mom and sister out of bed. So you thought it was some kind of a trick to get you out of the house, Adriana taking you for a drive? Then, I suppose you thought the sex was just giving her more time to steal your guitar."

"What am I supposed to think, Boone?" I ask him.

"You think that maybe my sister was trying to fix us up. That I'm as surprised as you are that she did it."

"Yeah, that's why you make the long drive around town so nobody sees us," I spit back.

"You know why I did that."

"Tell me."

He doesn't get to do it. Jessie comes through the doorway. He's looking from me to Boone.

"I need to talk to you," he tells me. "We've got some problems."

"You're kidding me," I laugh sarcastically. "Really?"

"We can't afford to get arrested." Ted James has been playing guitar for me since I've been performing at the Crazy Filly. He's sitting in Oaky's office with Nick Palmer, the drummer, to his left and Oaky is facing him at his desk. I don't know these two well. We practiced a couple times together, then they just followed my cues. It isn't the best setup, but it's an old bar. Our gigs became practices in themselves. So I don't know them well.

Ted turns in his seat when Jessie and I push through the wooden door. Oaky wags a hand at me. He's scrubbing his hand across his gray beard.

"Hey, shut the door." He waves a hand toward us and Jessie can just barely fit between chairs and door. It is standing room only. "We got a problem. And I'm trying to talk these boys out of quitting on the spot here. If they quit, you got no band. If you got no band, I'm going out of business. I've invested a shitload of money into this event this upcoming weekend—"

"I'm not getting arrested, Oaky," Ted interrupts. "No way." He turns to me. "Bo Littleton shows up at my house last night. I'm eating supper with my three little boys and my wife. He says if you sing any of your old songs, he'll cart us off to jail." He's forty-something and gray-haired. He's lackluster, but what Oaky had to offer. I wasn't surprised to hear those words while Nick, a pudgier version of Ted and the drummer, nods. They are holding up a Nashville newspaper. I take it in my hands. BATTLE CONTINUES OVER SONGS AND COPYRIGHT INFRINGMENT. RYDER BUSTED is the title. I scan it. "They haven't proven anything yet. Can they arrest us for using the songs? I mean, it's just rumor, right?"

"Mayor Littleton said he'd figure out a way," Ted tells me. "If he had to, it would be for inciting a riot."

"I had a DUI in '99," Nick says. "I can't take the chance. We're stepping down, Waylon."

"I'll talk to my attorneys—" I try to convince them. Because without them, I've got no band. I've got me and one security guard/roadie/nanny. But they shake their heads, apologize profusely and leave me standing there staring at Oaky who has thrown up his hands.

CHAPTER 45

THE DIRTY LITTLE SECRET MY FAKE MAMA PASSED ON TO ME

I receive a message from Mindy Potter on Tuesday. She leaves it in Dutch's mailbox in a generic white envelope. It says: *Meet me for coffee at the Bel-Air All-Nighter Motel and Diner at noon. I have a surprise for you.*

I'm intrigued. My life is at a standstill. I'm four days from an event. I've got no band. I obviously don't have any friends, nobody I can trust. It's just me and Lexie and a new guitar that looks oddly like my old one, but feels like a stranger in my arms. However, after searching through sixteen music stores, Jessie looked worn yesterday. Lexie was out of diapers. We went back to the third one in line and bought the one I'm holding and trying to adapt to. I feel like I spurned an old lover for another who looks slightly the same, but feels different in my embrace.

"I wouldn't do it," Jessie is growing some scrub on his chin. He rubs his hand across it. He's sitting on my couch holding Lexie and I'm sitting on the armrest plucking the guitar. "It's a trap."

"What could she possibly trap me with?" I ask him. I'm plucking the guitar and wincing at the same time.

"I don't know. It's just weird." Then he points his finger at the guitar. "Listen, quit making faces. If you don't like it, boss, we'll hop in the truck and get you another."

"It's fine. It's just new to me."

"Did you take my other advice and call Harley Mason and Tyler Cooper?" he asks me. "Maybe you should call Dallas. You know he'd help you out. You need people to run this, not just some bar owner that's signing you on for a gig for a couple thousand bucks.”

“Is he paying me that much?”

“Oh, hell girl, I don’t know,” Jessie throws back his head. “You don’t know?”

“No, Chase’s uncle did all that. And I don’t know if he even did that much. I just went and did whatever Chase told me to do.”

“You need a producer and makeup artists. You need a studio. Hell, you need an accountant.” He jabs a thumb at the six coffee cans on the table. “You need everything. You’re still shoving money in a can instead of having somebody take it to the bank for you. You’re a business. You can’t run a business like this.” Jessie shakes his head, narrows his eyes to tiny slits. “I’ve got to be honest, I don’t even know if that Oaky dude has hired security and people to set up and run equipment.”

“I thought you did that.”

Jessie goes blank. I think for a moment I must have said the stupidest thing I’ve ever said. He just laughs and laughs. “Baby, you need a friggin’ entourage. At night, I pick up your guitar and stick it in the box. Then I take you home. I drive an hour and ten minutes home, sleep for three hours, then turn around and come back here at six in the morning. I spend six hours cleaning up the stage, uncurling wires, good God, doing the job of ten. What do you think I do while I’m not here?”

“I guess I just didn’t think it out.”

I didn’t think it out that morning when I headed to the diner either. Jessie had snatched up my phone, poked in a text and handed it to me. “This is to Harley and Tyler. It says you need a band. If they want to play a big gig next weekend, rehearsal starts tomorrow afternoon at four. I’ve kept in contact with your old roadies. I'll text them, see what they are doing this week and next. Hit send. I'm begging you. Hit send."

I did take Jessie's advice and hit the button and sent the message to the two men. I didn't take his advice about meeting with Mindy Potter. I don't know if it would have made a difference in my life. It was spiraling out of control the moment Chase left me at the motel.

"So where does it begin, Waylon?" she asks me while we sit across from each other in a booth by the window. She's got a photographer, a tall man that is continuously taking photos of both of us. "Just start where there's a starting point."

"Well, I'd say it started when I was six and my mama bought me the guitar. It was too big for me and I didn't quite know what to do with it—" I told her everything. Well, almost everything. I told her about Mama leaving me and learning to play the guitar and the piano. I told her about all the things that made me Waylon Ryder. I didn't, however, tell her anything about me and Mama before we got to Abram Miller's farm. I just didn't think it needed to be noted. Three hours, five cups of coffee and two trips to the bathroom later, I've told her about Chase leaving me and Dutch taking me into his home and the town embracing me even though they thought I was homeless. I'm just about finishing up on talking about playing at the Crazy Filly when Mindy Potter taps something in her phone. She turns, waves a hand in the air by the doors. And I see someone outside.

"So, here's your surprise," she says. And she is beaming like she's bringing me a Christmas puppy in a pretty ribboned box. "It's your mother."

It didn't register at first. I tip my head at her. "My—

mother?"

"Yes." She beams at me. "You were searching for her. We found her. Hannah Schwartz. She actually contacted us after we left advertisements in newspapers throughout the Midwest. She had some pictures of you. And here she is—"

The photographer is going nuts with camera shots and video. I feel my heart make a wiggle-waggle in my chest when I look up to where Mindy is staring. She has risen and the six or seven guests in the diner are turning curiously to where there is a sudden burst of doors opening.

I see her. I feel the blood rush from my face. It is her, I suppose. I'm trying not to feel something. I do, however. I try to remember the scent of her skin, the kisses on my head. All's I can remember is Abram Miller rocking me in the chair when she left. I remember my brothers keeping me busy, taking turns letting me ride on their shoulders. I remember bits and pieces of the other daddies she'd chosen to take care of us before Abram. But I can't quite put my finger on anything other than the constant fear I felt when I was with her that we were going to run again, the woman with so many names. *She stole me.* She's bleach blonde now and a little wrinkled. *Maybe I'm wrong. Maybe she didn't. Maybe she was really running from the man in San Antonio.* She's chubby and smiling and looking around the restaurant like she's a princess in a ball looking for her prince. I feel myself rising. I wonder if she knows I know the truth about her. She doesn't seem to know or care. She's wearing a too-short skirt clinging to her chubby body. She's got on a tight green camisole that looks like it's going to burst buttons at her boobs.

"Baby!" she calls out. I blink, look at Mindy who is acting like she has just won a million dollars for us.

"Well?" she asks me. And all's I can do is fumble my

way out of the booth and take two steps backward.

"That's—that's not my mama," I say hoarsely to Mindy, shaking my head. "Mindy. It's not. Tell her to stop. She isn't—my mother." But she's trundling forward and there's more cameras coming through the door like this is some sort of grand finale to the tale.

She stops one step from me, arms wide. My back's to the table. I am breathing hard. I feel nothing for her but anger when I shake my head. "You're not my mother," I say. "Get away from me. I know the truth. One more step and I'm going to say something you wish I hadn't."

Her face just drops. She knows I know. I see it in her eyes, crazy eyes. "How much did you offer her to come here, Mindy?" I hiss. I don't look at the journalist, I stare at the woman who I called Mama. Mindy doesn't answer. "Was it more than you got for those men you sucked dry of their retirement? Or maybe the welfare checks you got for having kids? Kids that you stole—Fake kids. Fake mama."

Mama starts screaming then, "Liar! Liar!" It's like she goes completely nuts while she snaps her head to the doors and makes a quick exit toward them. It was Gin who called the cops. It was only moments before I had stood up when I saw Mama. I must have gasped because it freaked her out. She called the police department, asked for Bobby because she knew I was friends with him. I don't know the first officer who responded. I only know four minutes after, Bobby was there.

"She's not my mother," I tell him in a daze. "She stole me as a baby. She stole my brothers. I should have told you sooner. I didn't." And now, while the cameras roll, the whole world will know the dirty little secret my fake mama passed on to me.

CHAPTER 46
TRUTHS AND LIES ABOUT MAMA

"Hey, Skeeter."

I'm sitting in the back of the Bel-Air Police Department cruiser. I must be in shock because I feel numb and dazed. I'm playing with a raggedy string on my ripped jean shorts that stop just above my knee. I'm focusing on that until the door opens and Boone sticks his head inside.

"Hey, Boone."

He slips inside and pushes me over with his butt. Then he closes the door. He just sits there a minute while I listen to the sirens, hear the people talking outside. Then he reaches out and pushes a hand on my shoulder just like I did to him at the cemetery four months ago. I push him away like he pushed me away. He keeps trying until I give up.

After a minute or so, he says: "Bobby called me on my cell phone. He said you might need some company. They are trying to question everybody. They caught your— the lady that—your mama."

"I told him to call you. She's not my mama, Boone," I say softly. In my fingers, I'm holding the old photograph I keep in my purse of the woman I thought was my mama. I stare at her. She stares back at me. Nothing. I feel nothing now. "I mean, she was my mama for a couple years. But she's a frigging crazy woman that's too irrational to grasp she would get caught if she did an interview. She was just looking for money again; I guess willing to risk it all. I figured out she kidnapped me and my brother, Caleb. Maybe Will, too. I don't know. It's just a mess. I figured I could just let it go when I found out and it'd go away. It didn't. I've carried this stupid picture with me everywhere I go. I get it out; it comforts me. Now, all that feeling safe seems like a lie."

"I want to say something profound that will make it alright, Skeeter," he tells me softly. "All's I can do is be here with you, maybe make you feel safe, alright?"

"I don't want Caleb to hear it from the newspapers."

"Okay." Boone looks out the window. Bobby and another officer are pushing someone into the back seat of the second police cruiser. I think it is Mama. "As soon as this clears, we'll get in my truck. I'll take you to him." He sighs deeply, moves over and smooshes up next to me. "I'm here forever. Or as long as you need me." He tells me what I told him the day at the cemetery. I look up, smile at Boone.

"I think you said I was annoying, then," I say. "When we were at the cemetery."

"I did. You were."

He's warm against me. It feels safe. I feel like all the worries could just go away even though my world is spiraling out of control.

"I—I didn't take the guitar. Adriana didn't either—"

"It doesn't matter. I can't win. I just want to sing. It's just little me against the world. Well, me and Dutch and Jessie and Lexi and—"

"I'm on your side," Boone says. "I am. It's just hard letting go. You know that, right? I see it in your eyes too."

"Look at me, Boone," I tell him and turn. I look up at him, look in those blue eyes. I feel my heart lurch with that same kind of excitement I get right after I crest a hill a little too fast in the old truck Dutch bought me. "The only thing I had when Chase dropped me in Bel-Air almost four months ago were the clothes on my back, the baby in my belly, and this darkness that I just didn't know how to escape. Then I'm lying in that barn and in comes this dumbass cowboy telling me jokes and looking me in the eyes and telling me he'll make everything alright. My mama left me when things got tough. Chase hightailed it out of town when I got pregnant. And here you are sitting in the backseat of a cop car when I know your dad is going to shit a thousand golden bricks when he finds out."

We sit there in a comfortable silence. Me, I'm still staring at the picture until Boone slides his hand down and gently takes it from me. He leans forward, pulls out his wallet and flips through the little plastic picture inserts. I watch him wiggle his finger into one and tug out a picture.

"Here, try this one for a while. I'll hold on to the other."

I take the picture from his fingers. I squint, see me and Chey and Boone holding Lexie and we're all making a funny face at whoever is taking the picture. "It's from the rest stop in Kentucky, remember? When we went to see your family. Chey made one for me, one for her, and one for my mom."

"Your mom?" I ask him. He shrugs.

"She likes your song. The one you sing with Dallas. She says it reminds her of the first time she danced with Dad at their wedding. He can't dance. Did I tell you that?"

Boone makes small talk for twenty minutes while I hold on to the picture and bob my head up and down so he knows I'm listening. Then Bobby gets into the car, asks me what information I have on Mama.

"Can you take me back to Dutch's?" I ask him. He nods. "Because I'll give you what I got."

"My real name's Dana Delano," I tell Bobby. He's sitting next to me on the couch in full Bel-Air Police Department uniform. Boone is on the rocking chair flirting with Lexie who is giggling at him. "My birth mother and father were from Gulfport, Louisiana. The hired a nanny from the newspaper, a woman by the name of Paige Long. One day the nanny went to pick up their oldest daughter from preschool along with their newborn daughter, Dana, and a son named Will she had before she worked for them. She never made it there and they found the car in a nearby lake. They didn't find the three bodies." I turn to Boone. "Can you give him the picture I had of me, Mama and Will?"

Boone stands and opens his wallet with one hand, flips it open and walks over so I can pick up the picture sitting on top. I look at him and he smiles.

"You realize he might have to keep it," Boone mutters. "For evidence."

"I've got a replacement," I tell him, forcing a smile back. I give the picture to Bobby. "She had a little boy who was about two when she came to work for the Delanos. I always called him Will. He was a couple years older than me." I sigh, lean over and dig a plastic bag from under the sink I tossed the broken jewelry box in. I set it in front of Bobby and tug out the envelopes. I hand him the envelope with Wayne Pelosi on the front. "This is probably Will's real dad. The Pelosi's had a child kidnapped about two and a half years before I was born. William, that's what they called their newborn, disappeared from a Taggart's Retail Store while his parents were shopping. There are blank checks they might recognize that were never cashed. They said ransom notes were sent. I'm assuming Mama recognized if she cashed checks, she'd get caught." Bobby looks at the blank checks, takes some notes on some paper in front of him.

"So, there's a third child, too, she abducted," I say. "It's my little brother, Caleb," I tell Bobby and hold up the picture with the names on the back. I rub my forehead, look at Bobby who is studying me more than the paper he is writing on. "What?"

"She's kidnapped three kids. This is pretty big stuff. So you got anything on Caleb?"

"Yeah. Bud Mooney's his dad." I bring out the envelope with Bud Mooney written on the top. "I stopped in at the Mooney's home one day and they nearly chased me down the street. They recognized me, my eyes. I'm assuming Bud Mooney's son is my little brother, Caleb, who lives on an Amish farm in Ohio. He's—he's lived there almost his entire life. We went to live there when I was five and Mama called herself Hannah Schwartz then. I grew up thinking my name was Gracie. She left not long after we moved there and abandoned me and Caleb. She took Will with her." I shrug. "That's all. It will all check out. I've looked it up online."

"Have you had any contact with Will?"

"No. I don't remember him much at all. I just grew up with Caleb. We were pretty close as kids."

"Does this brother in Ohio—Caleb—know this?" Bobby asks me.

"No."

"You know the report will become public information as soon as it gets written," he tells me. "We've already gotten calls from that Mindy Potter. She's going to know. Then the world is going to know."

"I'm just asking, Bobby, that you can write it slow and give me enough time to drive to Ohio and let Caleb know before somebody else tells him, before the reporters start showing up at his front door."

"I can try," Bobby relays to me. "That, I can do."

CHAPTER 47
LITTLE CREEK STONE

After an explosion, everybody always waits for the dust to settle. I figure it's that way in life when big things happen like they did today. It's just that in my case, it is like there is a huge bomb sitting next to a bunch of fireworks. There's one big boom. Then, it sets off a series of smaller, more colorful blasts.

I sit on the back of Boone's truck for forty-five minutes at the end of the drive to Abram Miller's house. I see faces peering out the windows. It is always Caleb that comes. And so he walks slowly down the little drive alone and meets me on the main roadway.

"What do you need, Gracie?"

"I found Mama," I say after I hand Lexie to Boone. Caleb looks away from me toward the house or the sky. I'm not sure which one. He's so big and tall, I can't tell if he is ever going to look back at me so I reach out and poke at his belly. "Look at me." Then he turns back, looks over my shoulder to Boone who is leaning against the truck.

"Look at you." He huffs a sarcastic laugh. "Is that your husband?"

"No."

"Is that your baby?"

"Yes, her name is Lexie," I say.

"You should have stayed with us."

"I couldn't. Talk to me about Mama."

"I don't care. She didn't raise me. Why are you telling me this? Abram Miller is my father whether we are of the same blood or not. He was yours—"

"She's not our real mother," I tell him. "She took us

from our parents. I'm not even your birth sister." He looks away again. I don't know what he's thinking. "Your parents have never stopped looking for you. They are going to find out and I'm afraid they will come here."

"I don't care. Again, I belong here. I'm happy. I have a wife and two sons. I've got a home and land and a family that loves me. I don't want anything else." Caleb is looking down the roadway. I know he is checking to see if the Bishop or some other church person is watching us. "You were always the one that wanted to make little dolls out of the eggs, Gracie. You'd put little faces on them with a pencil. You always knocked over the basket full of your little babies because you wouldn't stop playing with them. You haven't changed. You mess with things and they break. I wish you would not have upset the basket again. Why could you not just be happy here?"

"Because I always had the music in my head, Caleb," I tell him softly. "I'll leave. Tell Daed and the boys I love them."

"Here." He reaches into his pocket, pulls out a small, creek-worn stone and hands it to me. "In case you need it." I stare at my hand. "It's from God's hands and Daed's creek. Look at it and make good decisions where you go. Like Daed."

"Like you," I add. "I will." I realize my brother is grown up. His words sound like Abram's, profound. He turns and trudges back toward the house. Boone settles Lexie into her car seat, comes around, and walks me to the passenger side of the truck. He opens the door for me. Just as he starts to close it, he stops. I'm staring at the stone.

"What's that?"

"Caleb used to bring me stones when we were little, like gifts. I liked to draw faces on them and make them into baby dolls."

"That's a pretty one." Boone whispers. I know I must have that ready-to-cry look, because he blurts out: "What did one ocean say to the other ocean?"

"I don't know, Boone, what?" I say flatly.

"Nothing, it just waved." He closes the door, walks around the hood of the truck. Then, he opens his, slides in. He wiggles his fingers above Lexie's car seat carrier and pats the seat next to him. "Do you want to trade her places, try this again so I can do it right?"

"You don't have to do it, Boone." I listen to him pat his knee and I take up the beat with my fingers on my legs.

"I'm going to write a song with that beat," I tell him. He just stares at me until I work my way over, unbuckle the car carrier and scoot her to the passenger side. Then I plop down next to him. "Alright, let's roll."

I think I slept most of the way back to Dutch's. Boone stopped twice for gas and to talk to somebody on his cell phone. I roll the stone around and around in my hand. I think it is too late for it. I should have started making good decisions a long time ago. Boone's quiet, has the music on low and his arm around me when we swing through town around four in the morning.

"You got off easy," I tell him while he pulls off the main road. I don't. I see three trucks in front of Dutch's house and the lights are off inside. "Oh, no, now what?" I wheeze. "That's Dallas's truck."

The house is dark when I drop my purse on the little table by the front door. The floorboards creak while I try to tiptoe through the foyer and into the living room. Boone's steps are louder behind me. He's lugging Lexie's car seat.

"Baby?" I hear Jenna Dunne's voice. "Skeeter, is that you?" It is scratchy like she's been sleeping. She has been.

Hell, she's even beautiful when she wakes up. I can see two bright brown eyes blinking at me underneath the spray of kitchen light slipping across the floor. She's laying on the couch with one of Dutch's quilts and sits up. "Come here." I can see Dallas pushing up from Dutch's recliner. He has on a blanket too. He's yawning, rubbing his chin with his hand. He's not quite awake and definitely not as pretty as Jenna.

"Yeah," I say softly. I can see three kids sprawled on the floor sound asleep and flopped together like a basket of puppies. "What are you and the kids doing here?"

She's tugging the blanket over her shoulders. Her dark hair is slipping over the edges while she reaches out for me and tucks me into her arms. "I knew you needed us. We heard what happened."

"You—heard about Mama?" I start to lean down and give her a hug. She tugs me forward instead and pulls me almost on top of her and cuddles me in like one of her kids between herself and the couch.

"Oh, baby, yes." She's holding me tight and I swear she is crying. "You poor thing. You poor, poor baby."

"Are we still mad at each other?" Dallas sits down by our feet and pats my legs with his hands. I'm so spooned into Jenna I can hardly see him.

"You're worried about her being mad at you, Dallas Matthew Dunne?" Jenna scolds him. "Shame on you."

"No, Dallas Matthew," I repeat and he groans. I stick my tongue out at Dallas and he rolls his eyes. "I'm not mad."

"You're just stubborn, right?" he asks me.

"I'm stubborn?"

"Quit fighting, you two!" Jenna says. "How do you write such beautiful love songs together? You sing of love and you write of love and you fight like two mean little pit bull pups." She pauses and tickles my tummy. "I guess I shouldn't complain. You could be getting along *too* well."

"Ew-oh!" Dallas and I say that at the same time. We both have the same cringe-yucky expression. I look up, see Boone smiling politely while he sets Lexie down near the far edge of the couch. She's fussing a bit while he kneels down, unbuckles her and tugs her out.

"Aw, man, she pooped," he announces softly with a twist of lips. He brings her up, holds her out from him and makes a funny face.

"Well, whoever's holding her, changes her," Jenna mutters over my shoulder. "So that's the little mini-size Skeeter, huh?"

"Yes and you act like that's a threat for him," I mutter. Jenna smells like cherry cough drops. "He likes changing diapers, I think. He changed two on the way home. Didn't even gag once."

"Oh," Jenna looks up, takes Boone in. "Where were you when I was trying to dig gold and find a rich man to marry? I get stuck with him." She drags a hand up, points to Dallas. "He gagged when the kids ate because he was thinking eventually they were going to poop."

I see Boone tip his chin shyly. Hell, he's never done that to me. "I—I don't mind so much," Boone stutters. He makes a quick getaway to retrieve a diaper upstairs.

Jenna squeezes my arm. "Well, darn, where did you find that hot cowboy?"

"He's the one that thought he was coming to the barn to deliver a calf and found me."

Jenna thinks this is funny and laughs. I feel loved right then. She pats me on the back. "You let him take care of that little bugger and I'm going to take care of you. You need to sleep, Skeeter. Sleep. Everything's better in the morning."

"Yeah, well I should be rehearsing, Skeeter, rehearsing," I gripe. "I don't even know if Oaky's got a microphone that'll work outside. The one inside smells like beer from a hundred years ago."

"You know, I can take care of that," Dallas says softly. He looks over at Jenna like they've got a secret.

"What happened to," I lower my voice to imitate Dallas's, *"his lawyers have talked to my lawyers and they'll sue me if you're naughty?"*

"I can set you up with a crew and the right equipment. We can test it out on Saturday. I've had a few folks that used to work with you contact me to see if they can work for you."

"Seriously?"

"Yeah, the same ones that talked to the attorneys and gave police statements saying they saw you write the songs," he sighs. "I just can't sing with you. Do you understand?"

"You're being a dick again, Dallas," Jenna says in a soft tone. Dallas rolls his eyes. "Just let it roll. Sometimes you've got to just be a friend."

"Says the woman who buys four-hundred dollar boots by the dozen," Dallas snaps back with a smile and pinches her foot. "I could lose it all and you'd have to go to the dollar store for clothes."

"That's where we started, sweetheart. Just tell Skeeter you want to help her with her label, add it to your own." I think about what Jenna says. I think she's right. I'm too stubborn and I probably should let Dallas help me out. I hear them banter back and forth until I fall asleep and their voices fade away.

CHAPTER 48
THE TRUTH ABOUT CHARLENE

"I'm back," I whisper that at the frame of Dutch's door. I know he's awake. I could hear him coming out to the kitchen to feign getting a drink of water. Lexie was fussing and I know she's hungry. I slipped out of Jenna's arms, snatched up the baby, and worked my way to his room. I can hear the shuffle of bed sheets.

"Are you okay, Skeeter?" he asks me.

"Yeah, I think I am."

"I hope you don't mind they stayed for the night. The kids were tired and grumpy. I put on a movie for them and they fell to sleep."

"It's your house, Dutch. You can have them even if I didn't like them."

"It's your house, too, baby girl. But old men got to sleep or they're grouchy in the morning." He is quiet a moment, then I hear him move around again. "I was thinkin' about cleaning up those rooms upstairs, getting rid of the junk and making room for folks that come to visit like those friends you got downstairs."

"I love you. You're gonna to be my family, right?"

"Do I got a choice?" He says in a surly voice.

"Yeah. You can still trade me for a donkey."

"No, I don't got no choice. I don't like donkeys. But if I did, I'd still keep you. A donkey don't clean barns good and it'd burn the bacon too bad."

I have to wipe the tears away. I trudge upstairs to the bathroom to feed Lexie; Boone took the room I'd been using. I just keep wondering if old Dutch is going to finally figure out what I'm really like and kick me out of the house.

I fall asleep twice feeding Lexie, then start out the door, turn to shut off the light.

"Goodnight." It's Boone. Does nobody sleep at night? I pass the door and stop. Lexie is asleep but I pull up her little limp hand and wave it at Boone. "Night, night."

"I'm scared. I think there's a ghost under the bed," he says in a soft, high-pitched voice. "Come lay down with me until I fall asleep."

"Okay."

"You're kidding me, right?" he asks, his voice back to normal again. "That easy?"

"Holy hell," I whisper, slipping into the room and stopping at the bed. I hand him Lexie. She coos in her sleep while he scoots over and lets her lay on his bare chest. "There's no way I want to wake up next to Jenna. She's like the most frigging beautiful woman in the world, am I right? I'd feel like a toad next to the princess. Her hair wasn't even messed up when she got up earlier."

"Yeah, hardly," Boone yawns while I scoot in next to him. "You like blow her away ten times." I turn to my side and let my head rest on his arm.

"You're hot when you say that," I tell him. "I can do this for about an hour. Then I got to beat Dutch up or he'll have—" I pause. "What was the word he used when he was waving his hands over his head the other day because Bo Littleton wanted to raise the city water fees?"

"A conniption."

"Yeah, that's it," I say and tickle him. He jerks and pushes my hand away gently.

"You're going to make me drop Lexie."

"You know, that's not fair to me. You're using my baby as an excuse to not—get close."

He looks at me long and hard. It's quiet. I think I said something wrong. Then he kisses Lexie softly on the head, gets up, and lays her in the tiny playpen in the corner of the room.

I think he's going to leave. I'm cussing myself until he lays back down. "This isn't enough?" He tugs my arm, pulls me so I'm lying on top of him belly to belly, my elbows pressed to his chest. I see his hat next to his shoulder and hanging on the headboard. I stretch my arm out and snatch it up. I shove it on my head and it sinks to my eyes.

"Emotionally, no." I sigh. "Maybe if I'm dressed like a cowgirl you might like me more?" I'm looking down into his eyes. They are sleepy, happy.

"You're more cowgirl than anybody I know." He pushes a hand on my chest and my t-shirt tickles my belly. His fingers are cool and chills slip along my shoulders, make my nipples hard. "In here. And I like you enough."

"Enough?" I don't say it. I should have asked him if he'd like me more than *her*. I don't want to ruin the mood. I need somebody tonight. I need Boone to just be there for me. "You just wanted to feel me up. That's the only reason you are saying that."

"Maybe." He smells so good, sweet and musky. We're locking eyes. I reach out and touch his cheek with my fingers, let them dribble down to his chin. I think we're having a moment. "Boone, you're the most beautiful man I've ever met." His face turns red. I can see it even in the fading light of the hallway slipping through the door.

"Did you just blush?"

"I've never had anybody tell me that."

"Oh."

"Are you trying to charm me into getting into bed with you? Because we're already here."

I laugh. "No, I'm trying to make good choices like Caleb told me to do." I just say it. Because I know what he's thinking. It isn't hard when I'm resting on top of him to know that he's getting horny as hell.

"It's too late for that," he tells me teasing.

"Obviously," I banter back. "But, no, I just can't get things out of my mind. I've got nobody to bounce them off." I sigh. "I just need a friend tonight."

"Okay." He smiles softly, shifts me to the side. "Then we got to lay like this. Because the other is killing me." He kisses me on the forehead. "Bounce them off me."

"There's rumors that if I sing any of my songs I wrote when I was with Chase, I'm going to be arrested."

"They can't do that, can they?"

"Well, legally, probably not. I don't know." I shrug. "I wouldn't be in jail long, but it would become a part of the court case. It might show I'm not good at following rules or I'm just plain bad. I do know that is one idea the lawyers threw out at Dutch last week. But Chase gets to sing my songs without those repercussions, right? I say, screw it. I'm going to sing them. And it seemed so easy to sing them then. Now, while I get closer, I'm nervous."

"Who is going to arrest you?"

"Who do you think? Tyrone Canter has enough money he can pay off people to say I was doing other things. One is inciting a riot for singing them. Or I could be taken to jail for disorderly conduct."

"Well, there was some rumors flying at the Bel-Air All-Nighter Motel and Diner that Bo Littleton was talking to that reporter who's doing the article on you." Boone looks up at the ceiling. "Crap on a stick. This is why I shouldn't be hanging with you right now. Because I friggin' look at you and I'll tell you everything—"

"Yeah, that's it. Let Chase come between us here, too."

"It wouldn't matter. You're so damn gorgeous. I'm like an idiot around you." He scrubs a hand on his head. "Bo's been talking to dad. He said he'd do what he can to get you out of this town—"

"Well, *I'm* not the one he needs to worry about. People said some pretty bad things about him," I interrupt. "Mindy Potter quoted them for me. She said people were more interested in getting rid of him and crowing like early morning roosters about stuff they'd heard him do than saying anything about me. He's a jerk. I, personally, can tell you twelve things he's done to people including kicking them off their property to frack—"

"He doesn't really do that. Every one of those people sell."

"Because they have to—" Lexie grunts an angry cry. I can hear her kicking in the crib. My voice must have awakened her. "I'm not fighting with you. We need to keep stuff separate." I sit up. "It's just this. Mindy interviewed him. He said that if I was going to say bad things about him, he'd be happy to tell stuff about me. And he would do whatever it took to get me out of town even if it was arresting me."

"Like what could he say?"

"I don't know, Boone," I whisper. I push off the bed, walk over and take Lexie from the playpen. "The stuff people said about him, it was just cruel stuff and I don't think half of it was true. He's just a guy. He's a jerk. But he's got family and kids and slaughterhouse horses he saves." Boone is wiggling his fingers at me.

"Come and lay down with her, with me."

I nod. I'm a bit surprised. I figured we were done for

the night if we weren't having sex. I lay down with Lexie between us. She is smiling at Boone, snatching at his fingers he is dribbling above her. "Go on," he tells me.

"I asked her to take that part about him out. It wasn't needed for what she was writing. She told me she would if I could give her something more scandalous to write—"

"Maybe she's bluffing."

"Maybe. Who knows? Could I take the chance? No. He is a jerk. But he doesn't deserve to have millions of people hating him for it. So she's not going to write it."

"Really?" Boone is staring me hard in the eyes. "What did you tell her?"

"I told her all about how Mama abandoned me. And I texted her this afternoon while we were driving. I told her about the police report. And I told her if she showed up today, I'd tell her everything straight down to me being kidnapped. She'd be the only reporter I would use to tell my story. She just couldn't put anything damaging about folks in Bel-Air."

"Oh, my God," Boone whispers. "Skeeter, why'd you do that? Nobody needs to know that. Why—?" He stops and tips his head. Realization seems to flow through his eyes, rivers of comprehension flooding over the banks. "It isn't just Bo, is it? You didn't just throw yourself under the train for him. You know something more, don't you?"

I snuggle in close, reach out my hand and Boone tangles his fingers in mine while we hold them up between us. We twine them, touch our fingers together. "It doesn't matter. It won't be told by Mindy Potter in her Celeb Gossip Magazine."

"It does matter. What do you know?"

I breathe in, breathe out. "I found a box in Charlene's old room. I found a police report that was exchanged for another. It wasn't you chasing Charlene and Marcus Littleton down in your car the night they died. I'm assuming you didn't know those two were seeing each other on the sly. Because you were in the car with them, not driving your own truck. Dutch found a note about her leaving. He called Bo and your dad, said Charlene was going to break the news to you that night. They were trying to stop you from doing something stupid. Only, they were the ones that screwed up. They found you guys halfway to Denton, started chasing you three down yelling and screaming. Marcus stopped for a flashing train light and for some reason, you got out."

"It was getting crazy. I didn't know why my dad and his dad were chasing us down. I thought it was cool that one of the high school teachers wanted to hang out with us. *Us.*" he laughs sarcastically. "Well, Charlene. I was in the back seat. But they started trying to get us to pull over and Marcus was freaking out. I told Charlene we had a baby to take care of and I didn't want to get killed. We needed to just see what they wanted. I just wanted out of the car. I started to open the door while he was going sixty miles and hour. He stopped and started screaming for me to get out. I tried to get Charlene to get out too. That's when she told me that she didn't want to have anything to do with Cheyenne and that she and Marcus were leaving town together. It was so weird. He was our English teacher. He'd been seeing her for almost a year. I don't know, the whole thing was like getting hit with a flyswatter in the face right then."

"Then, I guess, Marcus saw his dad's truck and hit the gas, tried to outrun a train. He didn't make it."

"Yeah, the train hit the passenger side. The coroner said they were both killed instantly on impact. Me," Boone points to his eye. "Part of the bumper flew back and nearly killed me."

I reach out, lay my fingers on his scar. It is soft against my skin. I feel Boone clasp my hand in his.

"So why'd they cover it up?" I ask him softly.

"My dad didn't. Bo was worried about his political career. He changed the paperwork. Dad didn't know it until it was three years down the road. Then he knew it was going to be a huge scandal and too many people would have been hurt, including him for not disclosing the truth that he knew Bo changed it. It was enough, he thought, that we lost two people we loved. But I gained two, right?" He slides his fingers down my arm, then Boone tickles Lexie's fat belly. "You're sticking around, right?"

I remember him saying that just as my eyes closed. I didn't answer. I didn't know. I'm wondering if I'm not like my fake mama, not the sticking around kind.

CHAPTER 49
I CAN'T COMES BACK TO HAUNT CHASE

I didn't see it coming. You caught me off guard.
You stole my songs. You hocked my guitar.
I can't. I won't. I didn't. I don't.
That's what you wrote.
When you left that night, me standing in the rain.
Barefoot and begging you to stay.
Babe, hindsight's a funny thing.
You'll be with her
You'll wish it was me.
But all's you'll have are old memories.

"—I didn't want to put up with your stupid shit anymore! God, Waylon, you're like dragging around a four year-old that can't make a decision to save her life. And apparently, your shoes aren't that difficult to fill because Brooke Canter pretty much stole the last three shows we've played. I don't think folks can tell the difference. Now instead of bouncing around from hotel to hotel on my bike, we take the RV, live in style—"

This is what I come face to face with on Friday morning in the Bel-Air All-Nighter Motel and Diner. Chase Martin slams through the door with his lawyers in hot pursuit. He's jabbing his finger at my face so hard, I'm leaning back on the little red barstool seat at the counter. Jessie jumps up from his seat. I watch Chase make a narrowed eye comprehension, although I don't think he understands the capacity of Jessie's job position with me.

"Back off, Martin," Jessie says, pushes out a hand and holds him at bay.

"Go to hell, meathead," Chase spits at him. Then he ignores him altogether. "You think nobody can write a song but you? Is that what I heard? Because Brooke and I just wrote one. And I wish I'd called it *I'll See You Rot in Jail.* Because if you sing that song or any song that I wrote Saturday, I'm going to—"

The song he's talking about is what I called *I Can't* on the CD I showed Dallas I'd made. Before Dallas and Jenna left, he made an offhand remark that he sent it to some radio stations and I'm assuming they are playing it. I don't know. I've been doing nothing but rehearsals with Harley Mason and Tyler Cooper since I got back from Ohio. This is the first break I've had and only because Dutch made me sleep in until eight this morning and threatened my life if I didn't come to the diner and eat lunch with him.

"Everybody knows that song is about me. You've ruined my name."

"I'm fair warning you, Martin," Jessie is saying. "I provide security for Waylon Ryder. If I think she is in danger, I will do what it takes to protect her."

"Easy, Mister Martin." A double-breasted suitcoat is getting the message even if Chase is not. He is gently towing Chase back by his shoulder even while Chase waggles his neck to push him off.

"Now, you leave her alone, young man. " Dutch turns, stands up from his chair.

"I didn't write anything that wasn't true." I sit up straight, look to Dutch who is standing right now from his seat. We're both in that surprised-blinking stage.

"Bullshit." Chase is livid. I've seen this look before on him. He's a little guy that can't be wrong even when he is. Chase gets this pinched-lip, bull-snorting face when he's beyond mad, his shoulders back and his head thrust forward. "Nobody'll believe you," he growls at me. "You lie. I didn't leave you. You left me. You slutted around." His finger is poking toward me. His eyes are at Lexie in my arm. Jessie is coming between us and then all of a sudden, Gin steps up.

"Yeah," Gin is standing behind the counter. "I saw it. You left her. It was right outside this diner. It was raining. You took off on your bike. And you hocked her guitar. Everybody knows that." She waves a hand around the diner. It's pretty full. Eyes are on Chase, angry eyes. Heads are wagging up and down at Gin's words. I see him grasping that for the first time, he's not the center of attention, not the golden boy. I got folks who've got my back.

He shivers, pushes the guy in the suit away and takes a step back. "It isn't happening," he mutters. Then he does something that is even out of line for Chase. Not that he wouldn't do it. It is just that he's never done it when people are around to see. When everyone relaxes as he starts to pivot to leave, he wheels around quickly and thrusts a hand at me.

I think he was just going to scare me with a fake slap. He's done it before when nobody was around. I don't think he meant to actually go through with it. It was just a warning, I suppose. But he shoves out his hand and it is hard enough Jessie nearly misses catching the blow with his fist. Dutch jumps up, comes between me and him. In a blink of the eye, Chase's hand is an inch from my face right before Jessie snatches his wrist.

"Get him out of here or I'm calling the police," Dutch says while I press myself against his back and Jessie does this dance walk backwards with Chase. "Get him out now!"

But the police are already on their way. It is for a different reason, however.

"So they've officially arrested the woman who kidnapped you." Bobby tells me. He catches me at my truck a half hour later and just outside the diner. "I wanted to tell you in person. I don't know how these things work with celebrities, but I'm sure there's somebody digging it up as we speak."

"I'm not a celebrity," I tell him. He laughs.

"Okay. But the family is asking for a blood sample to check to see if their DNA matches your own. They've had two people claim to be Dana. They've had hundreds of bones and clothing they've had to look at over the years from dead bodies found. They are a bit unsure. They called this afternoon and—"

"I don't care. I don't really want to meet them or anything," I say. "I don't know them. They didn't raise me. If I am their kid or not, does not bother me."

"Waylon," Bobby pats my arm with his hand like he's trying to get my attention. "Maybe you don't care, but they need closure. You might have been their baby, their blood. They have a right to know. And if you don't want to have anything to do with them after, then it is your choice. But it will also help build a case against the woman who took you from your real parents, if she did." Bobby chews on his lip a moment, pushes out a hand and places it on mine. "You told me your mama kept telling you she lived in a big mansion with a fence and gates in San Antonio."

"Yeah."

"Well, it wasn't a mansion. It was a women's detention center, a jail," Bobby tells me gently. "Before she allegedly kidnapped your brothers and you, she was a bad person, had an affair with one of the guards and escaped. It will help us keep her behind bars a lot longer if we have solid evidence you were kidnapped. Your brother, Caleb, doesn't want to do it. It will take the pressure off him."

"Then, I will get a blood test," I tell him. He smiles.

"You should know that Mayor Littleton is concerned about the safety of the police who are providing security for the event," he tells me, then. "There's been no ruling, but he's afraid your fans will turn on us in the event we have to make an arrest."

"It could really happen?" I ask him.

"Yeah, I suppose. Off the record, there's probably six or seven laws that can be manipulated to our advantage pertaining to the performance. I want you to know that none of us want that to happen. But it's our job. We have to do as we're told."

"I get that." I nod. "Can you wait until after the performance is over to make the arrest?"

"Yes. That was suggested, although Martin wants it done during the event to make a point." Bobby leans in. "You know. I'm on the law's side. Always."

"Yeah, I hear you pull people over for going two miles over the speed limit," I snicker.

"For what it's worth, I believe you when you say you wrote those songs," he says. "But I will do what I am told. However, I am recommending that the police all wear ear plugs to protect their ears, for safety reasons."

"Okay," I say. I think I caught his gist.

"So don't speed through town, get it?"

"Uh yeah," I tell him. "Can I give you some advice?"

"Yeah," Bobby's head is tipped toward me curiously. "I suppose."

"Ask the girl out." He just looks at me and smiles. "You aren't ever going to know if you don't ask."

CHAPTER 50
A THIEF CONFESSES

It's Friday night, ten o'clock. It's just me and Harley Mason and Tyler Cooper finishing up one last song for a crowd at the Crazy Filly. It's a tired, drunk crowd who'd rather have straight country. But we had to run through all the songs and it didn't leave much time for my usual fare I give them. It is kind of a practice run and it goes as well as expected.

We're well off stage and walking back along the thin hallway toward the office.

"Just follow the smoke, you'll find Oaky," I mutter. Oaky's got another band at ten o'clock and they are setting up their equipment, warming up. Between, the sound of the jukebox plays and bangs heavy on the old wooden walls. I'm almost to the storage closet that's my changing room.

"Hey, we'll do the same thing as we practiced tonight on the big outdoor stage they've got up tomorrow." I see both the men nod while they follow me in succession. "Then, you'll need to watch me. If I turn and nod, know that will be your cue to get off the stage."

"So you're going to do it?" Harley's got these lips that are always set like he's getting ready to grin. He is kind of the joker of the three of us. He's always doing something quiet-silly and trying to get me to laugh.

"I don't know," I say softly. "I'm walking a fine line. Dallas says I need to be careful and I'm trying to listen to him now, take his advice." I crane my neck to take him in. "He said he'd pick up Dead Broke Hearts as a sublabel if we agreed."

"We?"

"Yeah, you and Tyler. We're working on being a band, right?"

"Hell, yes."

"And I don't want the cops to get hurt. I don't want my fans to get hurt if the cops arrest me. I don't want to let my fans down because—singing those old songs is exactly what they expect I'll do. They know they came from my heart. They know they are mine. If I step down, don't sing them, it makes it look like Chase is right. It takes away my image as a rebel who doesn't give a shit."

Right now, he bangs a hand on Tyler who is the quietest man I know and who is adjusting his glasses. "You listening?" Tyler's got on a beanie hat and it smooshes down the hair to his eyes. "We're a band."

"Yeah, damn," Tyler answers gruffly. "Yay." He stops and Harley almost runs his guitar into him. "I'm almost blind, not deaf."

"Well, you looked like you were going to fall asleep. You almost ran into the wall."

"Again, I'm almost blind. You could have helped me out, steered me in the right direction."

"Ha ha, that wouldn't be as funny," Harley laughs. Tyler rolls his eyes. Then he laughs along with Harley. They have this new, strange relationship—two brothers always competing against each other. When there isn't anything to compete against, they poke, jab and terrorize each other. They had a water fight in the kitchen last night with hoses in the sink. I felt almost like I was back at Abram's house with my brothers. It was strangely—soothing.

"Hey, Skeeter." Gin's soft voice slides from Oaky's office. She comes around the corner with a box. "My grandma got done with your wardrobe alterations. You want to try on your outfit for tomorrow?"

I nod to her, head into the old closet and she follows giving shy eyes to Tyler and Harley.

"They're so cute," she tells me when I close the door behind us. The room isn't much bigger than Dutch's bathroom. It's got big cardboard boxes shoved to three walls and cleaning supplies slapped on a metal shelf on the fourth.

"I know somebody who's cute and likes you," I say. "You been out with anybody since Jack left town?"

"No." She opens the box and pulls out the little outfit I had special made for tomorrow. It is red, white, and blue and has little fireworks on them for the Bel-Air City Limits Festival. It's a tiny wraparound bra and a teeny-weeny pair of shorts that look more like a bathing suit.

"Who is it?" She asks me while I tug off my shirt and jeans and slide into the outfit. Then she blinks her eyes at me. "Oh."

"Oh? Is there something wrong? What does that mean?"

"It means—I don't know. It doesn't leave much for the imagination. And how the hell do you look that skinny after having a baby four months ago?"

"Well, that's kind of my thing and I've been so stressed out, I can't eat."

"Oh, okay. So who is it that likes me?"

"I told him I wouldn't tell you." But her pleading eyes won't let me keep the secret. "Okay, it is Bobby Moretti."

"Bobby, the cop?" She laughs softly to herself. "The stuck up one that sits out on the highway and gives everybody a ticket for going two miles over the speed limit?"

"Has he ever given you a ticket?"

"No."

She chews on the thought for a minute while she

adjusts the shoulders, then she gets this little smile on her face. "You're kidding me, right?" she asks me. "I mean, he's a cop. He makes good money. He can have any girl—"

"He doesn't make good money. He works for the city," I tell her. "But it's alright. He likes kids and wants a big family. He coaches soccer, for God's sakes. He's a good kisser. And he likes you. He told me he's had a crush on you since tenth grade and he saw you at a basketball game at Bel -Air High School."

"I thought you were dating him?"

"We went out once. He talked about you the entire time. I didn't see the relationship going anywhere considering—"

There's a knock on the door. "I'll get it." Gin turns and opens it slightly, peers out. Then she turns.

"It's Boone Martinez. He wants to know if you can talk a minute." She's standing in the opening between door and frame, her eyes questioning. "He says he brought you a coffee and something from the diner because Dutch said you didn't eat supper."

"Before you say no, it's your favorite," Boone makes a muffled reply on the other side. "It's a side order of mashed potatoes and two sides of grits with cheddar cheese."

"I'm not turning down food," I tell her and wave a hand to let him in. I watch him come around the corner. He's smiling at me, then does the same blinking thing Gin just did right before he gets a goofy-ass grin on his face and smacks into the metal cabinet holding the cleaning supplies. Bang! About six rolls of toilet paper come flying down on his head while Boone dances around them. Then he tries to recover by thrusting a Styrofoam food container at me and hits me in the boob. It bends slightly and a glob of mashed potatoes careens downward to the floor toward his cowboy boots.

"Ow." I mutter while he catches the mashed potatoes in his right hand and stands there staring at it like he can't believe he reached out to catch it.

"I'm sorry," Boone mumbles about ten times. "You still have the grits." His face is turning redder and redder.

"That's what I was trying to explain to you," Gin is giggling. "That's what *oh* means."

"Well, that's what I wanted to know," I click my tongue, feign shooting her with my forefinger before I take the container oozing gravy to the floor. "The boys will like it, right?"

"Like what?" Boone is still holding the mashed potatoes. "That?"

"Yeah, that's what I'm wearing for the performance. Well, the last few songs. For the first part, I'm in jeans."

"Stripper jeans so she can rip them off," Gin adds.

"Okay. Yeah, the boys will like that." He's doing that goofy grin again, then he takes in a breath. "I need to talk to you alone. Can you come to the back door?"

"Back door?"

I dress. Gin hurries back to serving beer and I wave at Jess who is lugging Tyler's drums to a back room. He's got help, three of the old roadies that used to run with Chase and me.

"You good, boss?" he asks me while I'm digging my plastic fork into the little bowl of grits with shredded cheddar on top. I give him a nerdy thumbs up before I cut behind the guy flipping burgers they call Decker and tug on his shirt to say hello. He smiles a toothless grin back at me. "Busy night. You need to tell Oaky I want a raise," he says in his thick Alabama accent. "I burned myself twice tonight. On my way past, I tickle Paul in the sides who washes dishes and he drops a plate into the sink full of water and it splashes me.

"Dammit, Skeeter," he cusses me, annoyed.

Then I stop dead at the open doorway. It is Harlan Martinez and Chey and Boone is leaning with his back to the door keeping it open. It isn't the three I'm staring at, it is the big, ratty-tatty guitar case. My guitar case. My heart makes a funny flutter.

"Is—is that my guitar?" I look to Boone, then his dad. His dad has this pinched expression, lips nearly white. He looks so much like his son, I work my eyes back and forth between the two like I'm trying to identify what they most have in common. I see Harlan looking over my shoulder. Decker is waggle-eyeing us and I snatch up the door, take a step outside into the back lot and pull it closed. It is oozy dark. Only the headlights from Boone's truck are illuminating the back lot.

"Everybody talks," I mumble. "I can't have a private conversation. Five minutes after I say something, it's viral online. If it's something really stupid, it's less than thirty seconds."

Harlan actually chuckles. It kind of clears the air. "I don't know what you want me to say." I take the guitar.

"Chey has something to say to you," Boone starts. His dad holds up a hand.

"No, son, I'll do the talking." He takes a step forward and I watch as Boone shakes his head and holds up his own hand.

"No, Dad, she needs to be accountable, know there are consequences to her actions. Period." Before his dad can challenge him, Boone wiggles a finger at Chey. "Tell her, hon."

She starts with this little head-waggle like she doesn't

want to follow through. Boone steps forward, pushes an arm around her. "Come on. Confess."

"You do realize the ramifications of this, don't you son?"

Boone turns, eyes his dad. "Yeah, I do."

"I took your guitar." Chey thrusts it at me with both hands. "I stole it. I don't want to go to jail. They said whoever stole it would go to jail—it was in the newspaper today. I saw it. They had a big story on it in the Bel-Air newspaper and the big newspaper Papaw gets from Nashville."

I'm still looking back and forth between Boone and Chey. I blink, focus on Chey. "Why did you steal it?"

"Because I heard you say it had all your songs on it," she sobs into her hands. "Papaw said you were going to jail. He called you a liar. I wanted to show him you weren't. I didn't think, I guess. I knew you wouldn't let me take it. I thought I'd get it back before you noticed."

"She told us this morning. She'd been hiding it—"

"—under my bed. I got scared. I heard everybody talking about it being a felony and even worse because it was part of a court case and—I'm scared you hate me now."

"We're just asking you don't press charges." Harlan reaches into his breast pocket and pulls out a thin leather wallet. He takes a paper from it and thrusts it at me. "I'm willing to make an offer and pay you whatever compensation for your suffering. This is what I suggest."

I look at Boone before I wiggle the paper in front of my eyes. He's a bit green in the face. "Oh, that's cool," I exclaim. "Like this is a lot of money. I could put a pool behind Dutch's cabin."

"You could."

"Can I talk to you two alone, please?"

Silence. Harlan Martinez narrows his eyes. I know he wants to look at his son. He doesn't. Boone steps up, tells Chey to go and sit in the truck. Her face turns even whiter than it was a few moments ago. She heaves another sob and walks with her fists to her sides to the truck and gets inside.

I can see Harlan thinks I'm the cat right now, he's the mouse. He's uncomfortable, tugging at his collar.

"How much more money will it take."

"I don't want your money." I thrust the check back at him. Then I look at Boone. "When I was eleven, I went to Missus Becker's house every day. She taught me piano without charging my daddy a dime. Every day I went there, I would stare at this pretty little blue butterfly pendant she kept on the top of the piano. For three years, I watched it vibrate like it was alive while I played. It was mesmerizing. Then one day, I took it home with me when she went into the kitchen to make us hot chocolate." I take in a breath. They are both staring at me intently. "I couldn't eat. I couldn't sleep. For a week, I had that little blue butterfly pendant. Then Missus Becker came to me and asked me if I had taken her blue butterfly pendant. I burst into tears and told her I had taken it. She told me if I returned the blue butterfly pendant and made some sort of penance, she would forgive me. But I had to do it on my own so I learned a lesson from it." I sigh. "I cleaned my daddy's stalls for two weeks and washed Missus Becker's dishes. I made my brothers' beds and I collected night crawlers for fishing." I turn to Harlan. "You're paying for her mistake, do you get that?" I ask him and turn to Boone. "She's not learning a lesson. She's going to keep doing stupid stuff unless you have her make amends herself."

"And that is supposed to convince me of what?" Harlan asks. "That she'll turn out worse than you?"

"Okay, we're going there," I say, close my eyes for a

second. "You can judge me on my appearance and what others say, Harlan Martinez. Judge me. I don't care. Yes, I have tattoos. I have piercings. My hairstyle's offbeat, my clothes different than yours. My best friend is my guitar and I play it loud and I cuss like crazy on stage. But you don't know me. You've not walked in my shoes or even walked behind my shoes. You only know what a liar has told you. And fine, Chase Martin pays you to believe his lies. But I don't do drugs. I never stole again. I've done stupid stuff, who hasn't? I'm a good person, an honest person. You can take it or leave it. I don't want your damn money. I just don't want to see Cheyenne turn out like Chase Martin. And if it's any inspiration, he grew up just like she did, rich and spoiled and somebody always paying off his bad deeds. I didn't have that luxury." I shrug. I turn away from Harlan and look at Boone. "So here's my counter offer. Chey comes over and helps me clean Dutch's barns for two weeks at seven in the morning. She babysits three hours on Thursday nights for a month so I can take a bubble bath without my stupid baby monitor sitting two inches from my head and the ting-ting-ting of the baby swing rocking back and forth." I whip around and poke a finger at Harlan. "And she has to come up with another penance on her own to make it up to you for having to sit here and humiliate yourself in front of someone you think is a liar and a cheat and a thief."

"Okay, are you going to be there tomorrow at seven or will it be starting on Sunday?" Boone asks me, his hand held up toward his dad to stop whatever he thought he might respond. "She'll be there."

"I clean Dutch's stalls rain or shine," I tell him. "Now that Jack's gone, I'm cleaning hooves and feeding too."

I don't get to leave the Crazy Filly until eleven-thirty. I want to make sure Jessie and the crew are settled into their hotel rooms. Then it is twelve-thirty before I make my way up the old gravel road and pick up Lexie from Dutch's. He's already asleep and she's sound asleep in her little playpen. I whisper that I'm back through his door and he grunts a goodnight. Then I head toward the cabin.

The light is on in the cabin. Boone's truck is outside. I hesitate getting out of my truck. I am thinking he is going to berate me for ranting to his dad. I finally grab up my guitar and work my way to the door. I can hear water running when I open the door.

"Hey." Boone jumps up from the couch and smiles.

"You're not mad?" I ask him, lugging Lexie's car seat into the door.

"Why would I be mad at you?"

"Because I yelled at your dad."

"He's an attorney. He's used to that. I think that's how he communicates," Boone tells me. He's got a half-smile. "I got a bath running. I figured maybe you could use one. Not that you stink," he says quickly. "But because you need to relax. Like you said. It's not Thursday, but it's the least I can do for not turning Chey into the police."

"Well, if they carted her off to jail, she'd have my company tomorrow night."

"You're singing the songs?"

"I don't know. I'm like standing on the edge of the cliff and trying to figure out if I should jump or not."

He takes my guitar, lays it on the couch. I appreciate the gentle way he handles it. Then he reaches for Lexie's car seat and with the same care sets it on the floor before he kneels down to slip her out of the seat.

"I met Chase today," he whispers. Lexie is sleeping soundly.

I snap my head up. "You met him?"

"Yeah." Boone is standing across from me. "Dad had me drive to Nashville for a meeting with him. He wanted me to see what he was like."

"I don't understand. Why would he do that?"

"He wanted me to know what I would be dealing with being with you."

I just stare at Boone. "Was he trying to threaten you—?"

"Skeeter, no, he wasn't," Boone answers, waves a hand. "But there's a kid involved here. Between you and Chase and at some point, he might decide he wants to see her. He might use it as a tactic to hurt you." He nods to the bathroom. "Hold that thought. I've got to turn the water off in the bath or it's going to overflow." I follow him into the bathroom, watch him lean over, turn off the faucet. "Olivia and I were never really together-together, you know what I mean? We went to different colleges and after I graduated, she kept going for another three years. It's just not there. She realized it. I realized it. It's just hard when you're friends, breaking it off."

I sit on the side of the tub while Boone goes into the bedroom and lays Lexie down. I wait for him to come back.

"So, when did she start rolling over?"

I blink. Not yet. She's been pushing herself up and shifting, but not rolling. He must read my expression.

"Oh, no, not again." He cringes when I drop a glower at him. "She's just showing off the stuff you've taught her."

"I guess it only makes sense," I wiggle my brows at him. "I got your daughter's first felony. You get to see my baby roll over for the first time."

"Well, I'll thank you again for not flipping out so she would be in jail tonight instead of tucked safely into her room and softly crying with two months grounding." He chucks me on the chin. "Are you over Chase?" he asks me right out of the blue.

"Yes."

"You understand he abused you, right? He emotionally tried to own you." Boone's voice is quiet. He's ready for me to get angry. I don't get angry. He's right.

"Yeah, I get it."

"I'm not like that. I know it's your background. I understand how you were raised to some extent. You're taught to do as you're told. Period. My dad has always taken the initiative with raising Cheyenne. I kind of stepped back because I was so young. I was always scared I'd make some big mistake and he'd get custody of her. I realized tonight, that was never his objective. He just wanted us to be happy." Boone reaches down wiggles his fingers in the water. "You should get in before it gets cold. But he looks up again. "You and me, we've been in this strange place since you came here, right? We've been tiptoeing around old relationships that weren't working, trying not to hurt everybody around us and hurting each other. I don't want to do that anymore. I probably don't need my dad's approval for who I date or who I love. But I have to face him every day at work and at least for a few weeks, at the breakfast table."

"I can't change who I am," I tell Boone. "That's why I left Abram Miller's."

"Nobody wants you to change, Skeeter." Boone smiles. "Not at all." He chuckles. "I think that's where we kind of go wrong. We're two different types of people." He taps his head. "You'll have to understand that while you're a free spirit and you're not afraid to express yourself, I am an accountant with the opposite mentality. I need some semblance of order. So, right now, I'm trying to establish a foundation for our relationship because I like to have some—sort of order."

"So, are you saying you need a binding contract?" I ask him, hiding my smile.

"Oh, no—no." He shakes his head hard, then stops, sees my half-grin. "You're kidding me."

"Yeah, I am." I look at him hard. "So all those words you've been saying. It's as simple as you're trying to tell me you love me. You're ready for a relationship and although your dad might not be there yet—"

"He's almost there. We talked about building me a place down the road so I can—raise Chey on my own and be with you—if you want to be with us."

"Almost—" I think almost is like a million miles. "I do—want to be with you, but—"

"But," Boone says that word, looks at his boots. They are pointy-toed boots and black leather. "That's not good."

"It's just that Dallas asked me—I mean, me and Tyler and Harley, to jump on board with him, sign on as a sublabel. I mean, I could be my own little label, Boone. I could make something big, help other people like me sing. He's talking about opening a bar to do it and—"

"Yeah, and you can't do this with us here?"

I see it in his eyes. It's like he's fake-smiling and his eyes just get that old glaze to them. Dead broke. Crap—

"It's a good drive to Nashville—fifty miles. And you might want to hold that thought about me sticking around until after tomorrow and you see me sing," I tell him, holding up a finger. "I'm not as laid back as I am usually at the Crazy Filly—"

Chapter 51
Paying Penance

Holy Hell. The day starts at four when Oaky calls to make sure it's alright if Dallas is setting up an outdoor concert stage. I tell him I'll be there in an hour and run down to the stalls to clean and feed. I'm a half hour late. I come through the doors and Dutch is standing there with his hands on his hips.

"Well, I'll be darned," he says to me while I stop right behind him. "Little girl, I don't know how you did it." He cranes his neck backward to snap a quick glare. "And it ain't that fairy magic." Harlan Martinez is donning Dutch's old work gloves. He gives us a quick nod. He's wearing coveralls and lugging out a wheelbarrow full of manure. Chey is leading out a horse. Boone is filling another wheelbarrow.

"We got this covered." Boone stops long enough to swipe an arm over his forehead. He smiles. "Go do your thing. I'll see you later, right? I figured Chey and I will take care of Lexie today, bring her out when it's time to eat."

"What's it mean he's paying penance?" Dutch asks me when he walks me to my truck.

"Chey's paying penance for taking my guitar," I tell him. "Please don't tell anyone. We are keeping it secret. I am just going to say it showed up on my front porch."

"No, Harlan was clear." Dutch shakes his head. "He said he was paying penance for something."

I stop, reach out and snatch at Dutch's arm. "*He's* paying penance?"

"Yeah."

I didn't question. I hoped it was a sign that he saw through Chase's deception.

CHAPTER 52
WALKING THE LINE, GETTING READY TO JUMP

Bo Littleton corners me just inside the Crazy Filly door. I've never been face to face with him. Dutch has always seemed to feign his blows at me. He folds his bulky arms across his chest, nods to the two cops who came in with him. They turn and scoot the three drunks out that have snuck into the bar area. I'm alone, uncomfortable. I'm not scared. However, my heart is thumping wildly.

"My boys have orders to close this place down if you sing those songs," Bo tells me, watching the cops escort the men out. "I've got every cop in a three county radius ready to drag you off that stage, toss tear gas at your fans if they fight back."

"There's been no ruling yet," I tell him. "You've got no right—"

"I can do anything I want in this town," he says. "I don't like the riff-raff you bring into the county. You give us a bad name, your kind—"

"Well, my *kind*—" I say softly, "—are bringing in lots of tax money. My kind are saving your ass. So I would suggest, Mister Littleton, that you watch what you say and what you do."

"What do you mean by that, saving my ass?" He gruff-snickers, rolls his eyes to the ceiling.

"I know what you did to save your political career." I fold my own arms against my chest, make a cocky tip of my chin. "I know about your son and the wreck and how you hid the fact you were chasing him down in your truck. I know you made sure your name wasn't on the police report. That, in itself, is probably a felony. I mean, I'm not a lawyer, but I do know with this information, I could have let the entire world know how corrupt you are. I didn't." I pull out the magazine Dutch had run to the store early morning to get for me. I hold it up and slap it down on the counter of the bar. Then, with two fingers, I slide it over toward him. "I didn't divulge any of your stupid secrets to the magazine. I didn't think it was good and fair to do so. You might get hurt. However, you're threatening me and you're threatening my fans. And we can play this war game one of two ways." I clear my throat, make mean eyes at the man who is staring sharp-knives at me. "You can stop having your cops follow around Harlan and Boone Martinez. You can stop threatening everybody in this town and especially Dutch Cates that you're going to frack their land if they don't do as you say. Then, I won't sing like a spring bluebird the next time the magazines do an interview or the newspaper wants to run an article on my life. I won't sing about you like you're the bigot and the asshole you are in a song or do what I'm going to do to Chase Martin in about an hour and a half and let the whole world, or at least a small audience, hear the story straight from my mouth. Because, Mister Littleton, I will. So it is your choice. Arrest me if you want. Continue being the town dick if you want. But take a look at that magazine. Read it. Then imagine what life would be like if I start singing about Bo Littleton, corrupt and prejudiced mayor and how he treats his own kind."

"What's this?"

Dallas plops something on the table in front of me. It's a makeshift makeup counter in my closet-dressing room at the Crazy Filly. Jenna is doing my makeup.

"What was the very first thing you said when Jenna and I picked you up in the truck that night coming out of the football game? You were singing at that teeny weeny competition outside Memphis."

"I said I was singing for the skeeters."

"After that."

"Oh, I told the homeless guy I was going to be a rock star someday." I grin. It sounds stupid saying it now. But I was fifteen and fresh off the farm.

"Yeah." Dallas takes his finger and bangs the knuckle on the magazine sitting there. "Well, according to Mindy Potter with Celeb Gossip Magazine, that's what you are. You're a rock star."

"Yeah, I know. Dutch ran down to get me a copy of it right when the grocery store opened." I lean forward. "I scanned it. I didn't read the whole thing. I got enough out of it to use as a battle plan. I couldn't tell if she was she being serious or making fun of me. How'd they get it out so quickly?"

Jenna scolds me. "Dallas, if it's that important read the article to her."

"They get it out fast with stories like yours before another magazine gets it, that's how. They've got it all ready to go, then they print the hell out of it. I got a copy last night delivered to me. I had it yesterday, asked her for it so I knew how to prepare for the event."

"Are you courting me?" I ask him. "Because I feel like you're professionally sending me flowers and flirting."

"He's trying to show you that his label wants you and can handle somebody big."

"I'm tiny." I roll my eyes at Jenna. "Did you read it? Am I going to have people shooting at me during the performance? A guy threw a beer bottle at me two Friday's ago because he said my singing sucked."

"So here's the title: *Waylon Ryder. The Story You Don't Know,*" Dallas tells me while he sits down on an old metal chair next to me. "Let me read the first paragraph, then I'll let you know about the rest. Here goes: *I sat down and drank a cup of coffee with Waylon Ryder this week. It wasn't in Craig Hill Luxury Rehab as former partner and boyfriend would have everyone believe. In fact, it was in a tiny farming community fifty miles from Nashville and about as far away from rock and roll as you can get. Or so I believed. But what I did find from a series of interviews around the country, were all the stories Chase Martin has been saying aren't true. So the big question is, did he lie about the songs being written by him?"* Dallas slaps the magazine on his leg. "I'll condense the five full pages for you."

"Oh, no," I groan. My heart falls.

"No, baby, whatever you did, this woman had your back. It is pretty much a professional lynching of Chase Martin. You come out smelling like roses for once. I just want you to know that she also put in the part about the kidnapping."

"I know. I told her it was okay."

"Okay, so we're ready to roll. All the cards are on the table. I got everything running. But I've got to stand back, you understand that?"

"I do."

"I'm just kidding. I got your back, Skeeter. I'm here for you. You just let me know if you want to sing our songs. People are expecting it."

"I'm still singing for the skeeters." I laugh. "I think the Crazy Filly only holds a couple hundred on a good night. I started out singing for mosquitoes and now I'm—"

"Baby, have you looked outside?"

"No."

"You ain't singing for the skeeters anymore—"

Dallas is right. When I walk out on stage at eight that night as the main performer, there's a good three-thousand people out there. Families, adults, kids, cowboy hats and tattoos. Every kind of music character I can make out. It doesn't throw me off. It's what I like doing. I sing the new songs and some old ones Chase didn't claim. Then about nine o'clock, I hear them chanting for a song called *Darkness in Decay*. And I know this is the point that I either stay on the safe side of the fence I'm walking or jump off the other side. And so, I choose to jump to the unknown.

"Alright, so here's where the theme changes. We're going from Rated G to Rated R. I'm going to sing a song with Dallas Dunne—" I have to stop for the roar of the crowd. "And that'll give time for anybody that doesn't want to hear that old music, to leave or hold their hands over their ears for the rest of the show." I wipe the sweat from my forehead, take a quick swig of a water bottle Jessie's handing me. "For those of you who may have noticed I've been missing for a few months, I want to let you know I wasn't in rehab. Far from it. Chase Martin and I were coming back from a California tour and we stopped in a little town called Bel-Air. Four o'clock in the morning, I hear his motorcycle taking off from the motel parking lot. Gone. He left me there with a belly full of baby and not a dime to my name." There's something just short of silence while faces stare up at me. I look down at my guitar. "He hocked my guitar for gas money. I had nothing but the clothes on my back, and all this. And I'm staring down cowboy hats and camo clothes trying to figure out how I'm going to feed me and a baby on the two dollars and twenty-five cents I got left in my pocket. If you're thinking this story is going to turn out bad. You don't know country folk. Folks like Dallas Dunne who helped me get back on my feet and Trisha Leonard who gave me her son's old crib and

Paula Johnson who brought me bags and bags of baby clothes. I got somebody to take me in, gave me a home even though he says I dress like a heathen. And I've got a horse named Old Blue a guy named Dutch gave me. I could go on. But there's one last person I'd like to thank and it's Bobby Moretti with the Bel-Air Police Department who taught me how to drive without taking out every guardrail from here to Nashville. So it's like this. I'm going to sing my songs, the ones Chase Martin says I stole. And it just might get me arrested. So if I do, let's just remember the Bel-Air cops are just doing their job, following the rules. And if you want to know my story, get a copy of Celeb Gossip Magazine —" I hold the one I got up in my hand and wave it around. "You'll be *f-in* blown away!"

Dallas jumps up and starts playing then. Two songs and you can hardly hear us above the crowd singing along. Then it's time and I start blasting out my old tunes. I turn to Tyler and Harley and wiggle out of my Rated G outfit and it's time to let loose. I nod my head so they know to leave.

"We're sticking around." That's what quiet Tyler says and he lets loose on the drums better than old Red used to play, maybe ten times better. And I look down, see Bo Littleton standing there with his arms crossed, and the old dude is singing along. Who the hell would have known?

CHAPTER 53
FINDING HOME

It's drizzling and dark, like ten o'clock at night. I'm standing in the parking lot of the Bel-Air All-Nighter Motel and Diner leaning against my truck. It's quiet except for a few trucks coming and going. It's been four days since the concert. Dallas wanted me to come to the city to tie things up with a contract.

"Hey, you alright?" It's Boone and he's parked his truck next to mine and getting out. I can see the shadow of Chey inside, her head bobbing like she's watching us. "Dutch said you wanted to meet me here."

"Yeah, I'm kind of putting off going back there for a few more minutes. He said he was going to sit me down. He wanted to give me a *good talking to* about what I wore at the performance." I smile, roll my eyes. "He thought it was a bit risqué."

"It was. I liked it," Boone smiles back, then he starts patting at his leg. Uh oh. "I didn't get to see you after the performance. You didn't call today. I, um, wasn't sure if you were—coming back." He stops. "Is that wrong to say?"

"I guess we've never really talked about it more than chitchat. I never expected Dallas would go through with offering me a business deal. So, no, it's a valid question considering my life is suddenly taking a new path—again. Still, why wouldn't I come back, Boone?" I ask him softly. I know why. Because she left him. I get it. Boy, do I get it. "You don't have to answer that. What can I possibly do to let you know I'm sticking around?"

"Okay, what if you get to know me six months down the line and realize—"

"You don't think I know you?" I laugh gently. "I know that when it rains, you like to listen to country music low and by yourself in your truck behind the old barn on the hill. I know you like the smell of bacon cooking on the stove. You stop and sniff when you come in the door and you get a little smile on your face like you've just had your first kiss. I know you kind of like me, but you don't know why because we're like fire and ice. I'm the fire because I'm so hot," I tease him. "But, I catch you looking at me, trying to figure out why you like me. I'm not your style, your type. I kind of hit you like sparrow hitting a glass window. So maybe I'm a bit scared too. So the question is, do you know me enough to keep me around?" I hold out my hand, let it settle on his arm. "Ask me what there is to know."

"What is there to know?"

"Maybe more than you think." I look up, catch his eyes. God, they are beautiful in the light. "It was raining tonight on my way home. I couldn't see the lines on the road and some idiot just outside Nashville was on my ass for twenty minutes. But I could hear the rain hitting the roof of my truck driving home. It reminded me of you sitting on the hill and it made me feel safe. I turned on some country music and let it slide around my truck and I thought about you riding that old horse with me." I see him smiling a little so I go on. "I like seeing the look on your face when you come in the door for breakfast. It makes my heart beat fast knowing you like something I can do as simple as not getting your eggs too dry and knowing that you like them over-easy. You got caught off guard? What about me? I meet this man who is surly and growls he's got a heart as almost-dead as Dutch's old dead broke horses he saves from the slaughterhouse. But I see this light in his eyes and I can't help but follow that light. It's like it leads me home."

"Damn, girl."

"No, damn boy. You got me tied to you like a lead rope to a fence. I'm not going anywhere." I puff out my cheeks, blow a big breath. "I met my parents, the people from Louisiana," I reveal to him. "I went there today to meet them in Nashville after my meeting with Dallas. It was strange. The red-haired man and the men in suits were private detectives they hired to find me. Mama called him the Bogeyman. He was actually just the opposite, I suppose. But everything the lady I thought was my mama told me was a lie." I stop. The meeting was strange and awkward. My birth mother looks like me and so does my sister, Emory. She's two inches taller and is girly-girl. But we both have heart tattoos on our left legs. "I was sitting there and thinking, well, wishing you were there to hold my hand."

"Why didn't you ask?" He stops, then gives his head one of those shakes like *oh, yeah, I know why. You didn't want to ask me.* "You could have asked regardless."

"Regardless of what?" I ask him. "I wasn't going to do it. Then Bobby calls me on the phone and tells me the DNA came back and we were a match. They were willing to drive up from somewhere outside Nashville just to see me. I couldn't say no. I wish I could have called you."

"I'm assuming you're leaving to be closer to Nashville since the case was settled." There never was an arrest at the concert. The attorneys called me yesterday and told me Chase *and* Red wanted to settle out of court if they could. Both begged me not to sue them and I pretty much closed their checking accounts out.

"Yeah, it is settled." I nod toward Chey in the truck. "I guess I have to thank your dad for stepping down and turning coat on his team. And Chey. She showed him each of the songs and helped them correspond them to the dates on the videos Jess took." Chey must have seen me note she was in the truck. I can see her scooting out, making her way toward us around the truck. "So maybe you'll be there with me when I meet with Will, my older brother?" I ask him quickly. "He sent a message through Bobby. He wants to meet. I want to meet. I'm scared. I see it coming, you know after today? That feeling I need you there. I'm kind of scared."

"I'm here—"

"Are you leaving?" Chey makes it there before Boone can do anything more than say those two words. We both turn and follow her shadow dripping along the parking lot light toward us. I went back to Dutch's for a few days of quiet, then Dallas called me said he had an offer for me to join his Late Night Outlaw label. He said he'd come up with a plan for us.

"Naw, I told Dallas I wasn't moving," I say, but I'm looking at Boone. "I'm home here, you know?"

"You still like me?" Chey asks. I just notice she's in pajamas. She must have awakened when I called.

"I like you still. And I love you, sweetie." I reach out, wiggle my fingers like Jenna does to me. Then I give her a little bear hug.

"You're not kidding me, right? You're not moving?" Boone asks. He takes a reluctant step forward.

"Yeah," I tell him. "And Dallas said we could work it out so I could be home here with you and Dutch and everybody. He says folks like my music." I laugh, reach out a hand and wiggle my fingers. "It helped that I gave him two songs I'd been working on."

"You're staying."

"I'm staying. I'm commuting. Yuck and halleluiah both at once, I guess." I roll my eyes. "Boone, I've written more love crap since I met you and your little girl than I've ever written. Dallas says I've got to stay here. You're like my muse, he thinks. I love you."

"I love you." He reaches out, takes my hand. "I suppose I'm going to have to buy a donkey."

"Huh?" I ask him, feel myself taking another step and leaning into Boone and dragging Chey with me. Holy hell, I've never felt so great even if my tummy is twisting and turning and doing flip-flops right now.

"A donkey," he sighs, shakes his head, then kisses me on my forehead. "Isn't that what Dutch always kids you about? He'll trade you for a donkey."

"Um, yeah," I answer.

I should have thought that out. Later that night while I'm lying in bed back down at Dutch's house with Lexie cooing softly in her sleep in the little playpen, I am only thinking that this is the first time I've felt like I'm home. I'd walked through the door that night and Dutch was watching TV by himself with one of the microwave meals he used to keep in his freezer.

"What the heck, Dutch?" I'd asked him while Lexie tried to reach for him out of my arms. "You like this crap and not my cooking. I left you three homemade frozen meals in the freezer to last until I got home."

"I—I guess I thought you wasn't coming back.

"You're kidding me, right?" I'd plopped down next to him, handed him Lexie. "I know a good thing when I see it."

"So you're home."

"I'm home," I sigh. "I got a favor to ask you, though."

"What's that, hon?"

"One of Mama's—" I hesitate to call her that, but I don't know her name. "One of her boyfriends used to play piano in an old restaurant outside Huntsville, Alabama. I called the folks who own the land and they said I could get the piano from the old building. They said I can take it. I just need a couple of your buddies and your truck. I want to have it fixed up and take it to the nursing home he's in so he can play. She left him with nothing. I want to make it up to him."

"You're a good girl, Skeeter." He pats my leg. "I'm proud of you even if I can't approve of those clothes you wore on stage." Ug. I roll my eyes.

And so I fell into a deep sleep later, my mind still racing from all the new stuff going on. Then I was awakened just at dawn by Dutch yowling out the front door.

I sit up in bed, scrub my hand over my eyes. "What— what's going on?" I grunt softly, trying not to wake up Lexie. But I hear a grumpy Dutch yelling up the stairs to me. Lexie starts her grouchy cry and I snatch her out of the playpen and trundle downstairs to the bottom of the steps.

I can hear Dutch grunting and growling, yelling out the front door. And I can hear the loud clop of hooves bouncing off the hard summer lawn and the front porch and the gravel road.

"What the hell, boy? What are you doing? You're going to be the death of me!"

Something sounds like it's breaking, a window maybe and then comes the whinnies of what sounds like fifty horses arguing at each other. I come to the front porch with Lexie screaming holy hell and Dutch yelling and me scrubbing at my eyes in the almost-light of dawn. I look outside and there are horses everywhere. There's six trying to figure out how to get off the porch and probably twenty milling around and kicking up in driveway. There's dust flinging around another ten or so and I think I saw two of Harlan Martinez's farm hands herding horses away from the road. And one that breaks away and comes pell-mell toward the front porch.

"Boone?" I almost have to yell over the stampede and the farm hands driving the horses away from the garden out front. I hear Dutch cursing and waving a boot at the horses jumping on the porch.

"Yeah." He whoas his horse five feet from the bottom step.

"What happened? Did your barn burn down?" I ask because this must be every one of his family's horses running amuck in Dutch's front yard.

"Did I ever tell you you're a hundred horse keeper?" Boone is just leaning over on his horse as calm as a millpond.

"A hundred horse keeper?" I yell back. "What's that mean?"

"Aw, dammit!" Dutch is slapping the boot on a horse's rear and it almost runs him over. "It means he wants to marry you. Are you stupid, girl? He's being an idiot and making a point of bringing down a hundred horses to trade for you. Boy, could you have just brought one as a case in point?" Dutch is shaking his head, growling. "You two belong together—Stupid and Idiot."

But Boone is just giving me this dumbass grin. "Yeah, kind of what he said. So if you're sticking around and you don't mind a cowboy hat hanging on your headboard—"

"Yeah, I can do that. And you don't mind—all this." I wave a hand at me.

"Yeah, I like all that. I did the second I saw it. I just couldn't figure out *why* I liked it."

"Marry me, then." I tell him. I'm giggling and Lexie is sniffling at him, reaching out her little arms while Boone hops down from his horse and barely misses getting kicked by a mare bucking off the porch.

"Yes, ma'am," Boone says, leaning down. And we peck out a kiss. "Now hop on my horse. The three of us. We're riding off into the sunset like they do in all those goofy romance westerns you like." He holds out a hand, then stops. "Oh, yeah, why did the horse cross the road?"

"Really, Boone?" I ask him. He wiggles his eyebrows at me. "Okay, why did the horse cross the road?"

"Because somebody on the other side yelled, Hay!"

And so as sappy as Dutch thought it was when he groaned and waved us away, we do ride off—into the sunrise.

www.ingramcontent.com/pod-product-compliance
Lightning Source LLC
Chambersburg PA
CBHW020515260626
47156CB00006B/2017